GOLDEN LION

Wilbur Smith was born in Central Africa in 1933. He became a full-time writer in 1964 after the successful publication of *When the Lion Feeds*, and has since written over thirty novels, all meticulously researched on his numerous expeditions worldwide. His books are now translated into twenty-six languages.

For all the latest information on Wilbur visit his author website, www.wilbursmithbooks.com. To learn about the work of the Wilbur and Niso Smith Foundation visit www.wilbur-niso-smithfoundation.org

f WilburSmith

🐦 @thewilbursmith

Giles Kristian is the author of the bestselling Raven series of Viking novels, *God of Vengeance*, and two novels of the English Civil War, *The Bleeding Land* and *Brothers' Fury*. He lives in Leicestershire. For more information about Giles and his books, please visit his website, www.gileskristian.com

Also by Wilbur Smith

The Egyptian Series

River God
The Seventh Scroll
Warlock
The Quest
Desert God

The Courtney Series

When the Lion Feeds
The Sound of Thunder
A Sparrow Falls
The Burning Shore
Power of the Sword
Rage
A Time to Die
Golden Fox
Birds of Prey
Monsoon
Blue Horizon
The Triumph of the Sun
Assegai

The Ballantyne Series

A Falcon Flies
Men of Men
The Angels Weep
The Leopard Hunts in Darkness

Thrillers

The Dark of the Sun
Shout at the Devil
Gold Mine
The Diamond Hunters
The Sunbird
Eagle in the Sky
The Eye of the Tiger
Cry Wolf
Hungry as the Sea
Wild Justice (UK); The Delta Decision (US)
Elephant Song
Those in Peril
Vicious Circle
Predator

GOLDEN LION

WILBUR SMITH

HARPER

For all the latest information on Wilbur visit his author website,
www.wilbursmithbooks.com. To learn about the work of the Wilbur and
Niso Smith Foundation visit www.wilbur-niso-smithfoundation.org

Harper
An imprint of HarperCollins*Publishers*
1 London Bridge Street
London SE1 9GF

www.harpercollins.co.uk

This paperback edition 2016
1

First published in Great Britain by
HarperCollins*Publishers* 2016

A catalogue record for this book is
available from the British Library

ISBN: 978-0-00-813280-4

This novel is entirely a work of fiction. The names, characters
and incidents portrayed in it are the work of the author's
imagination. Any resemblance to actual persons, living or
dead, events or localities is entirely coincidental.

Set in Minion by Palimpsest Book Production Limited,
Falkirk, Stirlingshire

Printed and bound in Great Britain by
Clays Ltd, St Ives plc

MIX
Paper from
responsible sources
FSC C007454

FSC™ is a non-profit international organisation established to promote
the responsible management of the world's forests. Products carrying the
FSC label are independently certified to assure consumers that they come
from forests that are managed to meet the social, economic and ecological
needs of present and future generations, and other controlled sources.

Find out more about HarperCollins and the environment at
www.harpercollins.co.uk/green

I dedicate this book to my wife, Niso.

From the day we first met she has been a constant and powerful inspiration to me, urging me on when I falter and cheering me when I succeed. I truly do not know what I would do if she were not by my side. I hope and pray that day never comes.

I love and adore you, my best girl, words cannot express how much.

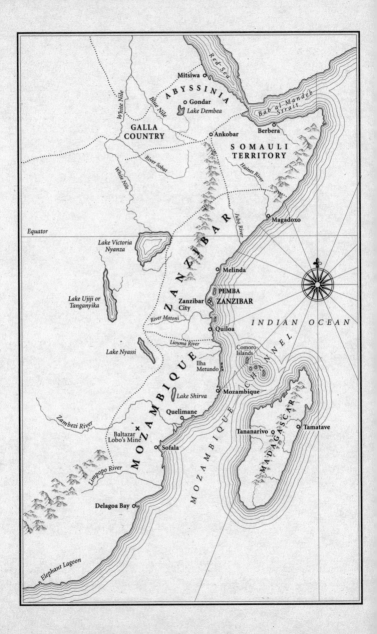

They were no longer men. They were the detritus of war cast up by the Indian Ocean upon the red sands of the African continent. Most of their bodies were torn by grape shot or hacked by the keen-edged weapons of their adversaries. Others had drowned and the gas in their swollen bellies as they rotted had lifted them to the surface again like cork bungs. There the carrion-eating seabirds and the sharks had feasted upon them. Finally a very few of them had been washed through the breaking surf onto the beaches, where the human predators waited to pick them over once again.

Two small boys ran ahead of their mother and grandmother along the water's edge, squealing with excitement every time they discovered anything deposited upon it by the sea, no matter how trifling and insignificant.

'There is another one,' cried the eldest in Somali. He pointed ahead to where a ship's wooden spar was washed ashore, trailing a long sheet of torn canvas. It was attached to the body of a white man who had lashed himself to the spar with a twist of hempen rope whilst he still lived. Now the two boys stood over his carcass laughing.

'The birds have pecked out one of his eyes,' shouted the eldest boy.

'And the fish have bitten off one of his arms,' his little brother gloated, not to be outdone. A shred of torn sail canvas, obviously applied by the man while still alive, was knotted around the stump of his amputated arm as a tourniquet, and his clothing had been scorched by fire. It hung off his gaunt frame in tatters.

'Look!' screeched the elder boy. 'Look at the buckle on his sword-belt. It must be made of gold or silver. We will be rich.' He knelt beside the body and tugged at the metal buckle. At which the dead man groaned hollowly and rolled his head to glare at the boys with his one good eye. Both children screamed with horror, and the elder released his grip on the sword-belt and sprang to his feet. They rushed back to their mother and clung to her skirts whimpering and whining with terror.

The mother ran to examine the booty, dragging the children along with her on her skirts. The grandmother hobbled along behind them. Her daughter dropped to her knees beside the body and she slapped the man's face hard. He groaned again.

'Zinky is right. The Ferengi is still alive.' She reached into the pocket of her skirt and pulled out the sickle with which she cut the grass to feed her chickens.

'What are you going to do?' Her mother panted from her run.

'I am going to cut his throat, of course.' The woman took hold of a handful of the man's sodden hair and pulled his head

2

back to expose his throat. 'We don't want to have to argue with him about who owns the belt and buckle.' She laid the curved blade against the side of his neck, and the man coughed weakly but did not resist.

'Wait!' ordered the grandmother sharply. 'I have seen that buckle before when I was in Djibouti with your father. This man is a great Ferengi Lord. He owns his own ship. He has great wealth. If we save his life he will be grateful and he might give us a gold coin, or even two!'

Her daughter looked dubious, and considered the proposition for a while, still holding the sickle blade to his throat. 'What about his beautiful metal buckle of great value?'

'We will keep it, naturally.' Her mother was exasperated with her daughter's lack of acuity. 'If he ever asks for it we will tell him we have never seen it.' Her daughter removed the sickle blade from the man's throat.

'So what do we do with him now?'

'We take him to the doctor in the village.'

'How?'

'We lay him on his back on this strip of lembu.' She indicated the canvas strip wrapped around the spar. 'And you and I pull him.' She turned to regard her grandchildren sternly. 'The boys will help us, of course.'

In his head the man was screaming. But his vocal cords were so parched and cracked and ravaged by smoke and flame that the only sound that emerged was a reedy, tremulous wheezing, as pitiful as the air escaping from a pair of broken bellows.

There had been a time, barely a month or two ago, when he had set his face to the storm and grinned with savage glee as the wind and sea-spray hurled themselves against his weather-beaten countenance. Yet now the warm, jasmine-scented breeze that barely wafted into the room through the open windows felt to him like thorns being dragged across the pitiful tatters of his skin. He was consumed by pain, scourged by it, and though the doctor lifting the bandages from his face was doing his best to work with the most consummate delicacy, each additional inch of exposure stabbed him with another needle-sharp stiletto of pure, concentrated agony. And with every infliction came a new, unwanted memory of battle: the searing heat and brightness of the flame; the deafening roar of gunfire and burning wood; the crushing impact of timber against his bones.

'I am sorry, but there is nothing else to be done,' the doctor murmured, though the man to whom he spoke did not understand much Arabic. The doctor's beard was thin and silvery and there were deeply lined, sallow pouches beneath his eyes. He had practised his craft for the best part of fifty years and acquired an air of wisdom and venerability that calmed and reassured most of the patients in his care. But this man was different. His injuries were so severe that he should not be alive at all, let alone sitting virtually upright in bed. His one arm had been amputated, only Allah the merciful knew how. His ribcage on that same side of his body resembled the side of a barrel that had been stove in by a battleaxe. Much of his skin was still scorched and blistered and the scent of the flowers that grew in such profusion beneath the open window was lost in the roast-pork odour of burned flesh and the sickening stench of pus and putrefaction that his body now exuded.

The fire had claimed his extremities. Two of the fingers on

his remaining hand had been reduced to stumps of blackened bone that the doctor had also sawn off, along with six of the man's ten toes. He had lost his left eye, pecked out by sea vultures. The lid of the other eye had all but burnt away so that he now stared out at the world with a cold, unblinking intensity. But vision was not the worst of his losses; the patient's manhood had been reduced to little more than a charred stump of shiny, livid scar tissue. When – or more likely if – he ever rose from his sickbed, he would have to squat like a woman to urinate. If he wished to satisfy a lover, the only means available to him would be his mouth, but the chances of anyone being willing to let this particular maw anywhere near her body, even if being paid to do so, were very remote indeed.

It could only be by the will of God that the man had survived. The doctor sighed to himself and shook his head as he regarded the devastation revealed when the bandages were unwound. No, such an atrocity could not possibly be the work of Allah, the almighty and most merciful. This must be the handiwork of Shaitan, the devil himself, and the monster before him was surely no better than a fiend in human form.

It would be the matter of a moment for the doctor to snuff out this satanic being that had once been a man, and by so doing prevent the horrors that it would surely inflict if left free to roam the world. His medicine contained a sweet, syrupy tincture that would dull the pain by which the man was plainly wracked before sending him to sleep and then, with the softness of a woman's touch, stopping his heart for ever. But the Maharajah Sadiq Khan Jahan himself had sent word from Ethiopia commanding that this man of all men should be taken to the maharajah's personal residence in Zanzibar and there be treated with particular care.

It was surely, Jahan had observed, an act of divine providence

5

that anyone had survived a burning by fire, the amputation of one arm, the loss of one eye, drowning in water and a roasting by the sun in the hours or days before he had been found by local children, cast up on the beach.

His patient's survival, the doctor was therefore informed, would be rewarded with unbounded generosity, but his death would be punished with correspondingly great severity. There had been many times in his long career when the doctor had discreetly put suffering patients out of their misery, but this was most assuredly not one of them. The man would live. The doctor would make absolutely certain of that.

The man could not so much see as sense a glimmer of light, and with every orbit of the doctor's hand around his head, and every layer of bandage that was removed, the light grew less dim. Now he became aware that the glow seemed to be reaching him through his right eye only. The left one was blind but he could still feel its presence as it fell prey to the most damnable itching sensation. He tried to blink, but only his right eyelid responded. He raised his left hand to rub his eye, but his hand was not there. He had, for a second, forgotten that his left arm was long gone. Reminded of it, he was conscious that the stump was also itching. He raised his right arm, but his hand was caught in a strong, dry, bony grip and he heard the doctor's voice again. He could not understand a word of what was said, but the general meaning was clear enough: don't even think about it.

He felt a cool compress being held to his eyes, soothing the itching somewhat. As it was removed, slowly, slowly his vision returned to him. He saw a window and beyond it the blue of the sky. An elderly Arab in white robes and a turban was bending

6

over him, unwinding the bandage with one hand and gathering it with the other. Two hands, ten fingers: how strange to look upon them with such envy.

There was someone else in the room, a much younger man standing beyond the doctor. He had the look of the East Indies in the delicacy of his face and the tint of his skin, but his white cotton shirt was cut in a European style and tucked into breeches and hose. There was white blood in there somewhere, too, for the man in the bed could see that the Asiatic brown of the young man's complexion was diluted by a pale pinkish tinge.

Now he looked at him and tried to say, 'Do you speak English?'

His words were not heard. His voice was barely a whisper. The man gestured with his broken claw of a right hand for the young half-caste to come closer. He did so, very clearly having to fight to keep a look of utter revulsion from breaking out across his face as the sight before him grew ever closer and clearer.

'Do you speak English?' the man in the bed repeated.

'Yes, sir, I do.'

'Then tell that mangy Arab . . .' He stopped to drag some air into his chest, grimacing as it rasped his smoke- and flame-ravaged lungs. '. . . Tae stop being so bloody lily-livered wi' my bandages.' Another breath was followed by a short, sharp gasp of pain. '. . . And just pull the buggers off.'

The words were translated and the pace of removal was greatly increased. The doctor's touch was rougher now as he ceased to bother with any niceties. Evidently the translation had been a literal one.

The pain merely increased, but now the man on the bed was starting to take a perverse pleasure in his own agony. He had determined that this was a force – no different from the wind or the sea – that he could take on and master. He would not

7

be beaten by it. He waited until the last scrap of rank, fetid fabric, sticky with blood and raw skin, had been torn from his head and then said, 'Tell him to fetch me a mirror.'

The young man's eyes widened. He spoke to the doctor who shook his head and started jabbering at a much faster pace and higher pitch. The young man was clearly doing his best to reason with him. Eventually, he shrugged his shoulders, waved his hands in a gesture of exasperated defeat and turned back to the bed. 'He says he will not do it, sir.'

'What's your name, boy?' the wounded man asked.

'Althuda, sir.'

'Well, Althuda, tell that stubborn bastard that I am the personal acquaintance, no, the brother-in-arms of Ahmed El Grang, the King of the Omanis, and also of the Maharajah Sadiq Khan Jahan, younger brother of the Great Mogul himself. Tell him that both men value the service I have done them and would be mightily offended if they knew that some scraggy old sawbones was refusing tae do as I asked. Then tell him, for the second time, tae fetch me a damn mirror.'

The man slumped back on his cushions, exhausted by his diatribe and watched as his words were conveyed to the doctor, whose attitude was now magically transformed. He bowed, he scraped, he grovelled and then he raced across the room with remarkable speed for one so apparently ancient and returned, rather more slowly, with a large oval looking glass in a brightly coloured mosaic frame. It was a heavy piece and the doctor required Althuda's assistance to hold it over the bed at such an angle that the patient could examine his own appearance.

For a moment the man in the bed was shocked by what he saw. The iris of his sightless eye was a dead lifeless blue, surrounded by a ball of raw, bloodshot white. The cheek beneath it had been burned so badly that a hole the size of a

8

woman's fist had been burned in it and his jaw and teeth were clearly visible in a gross display of the skull beneath the skin. His hair had all been scorched off save for one small ginger tuft that sprouted just above his right ear, and the skin of his scalp was barely visible beneath all the scabs and sores that marred it. He looked like a corpse that had been a good week or two in the ground. But that, he thought to himself, was exactly how he should look, for he wasn't really alive any more. He had once possessed an enormous gusto for life. He plunged into his pleasures, be they drinking, fucking, gambling, fighting or grasping whatever he could get his hands on. All that had been taken from him now. His body was a ruin and his heart was as cold as the grave. Yet all was not lost. There was a force within him that he could feel rising up to replace all his old lusts and impulses. It was as powerful as a mighty river in full spate but it ran with bile rather than water. For this was a flood of anger, bitterness, hatred and, above all, an overwhelming desire for revenge against the man who had reduced him to this ruinous state.

The man fixed Althuda with his one good eye and said, 'I asked you your name, but do you know mine?'

'No, sir.'

A skeletal grimace spread across the man's face in a ghastly parody of a smile. 'Then I will tell you. I am Angus Cochran. I'm a proud Scotsman and my title is Earl of Cumbrae.'

Althuda's eyes widened in horrified recognition. 'You're . . . You're the one men call the Buzzard,' he gasped.

'Aye, that I am. And if you know that, perhaps you've also heard of the man who did this tae me, a cocky English laddie by the name of Hal Courtney. Oh, yes, I can see that rings a bell all right, doesn't it, boy?'

'Yes, sir.'

9

'Well let me tell you this, then. I'm going tae find Courtney, no matter how long it takes me, or how far I have tae go. I'm going to bring him down. And I am going tae wet my beak with his blood.'

The battle had swept back and forth across the Kebassa Plateau of north-east Ethiopia, from soon after dawn until the dying light of day. Now its clamour had died down, replaced with the triumphant whoops of the victors, the desperate pleas for mercy from their defeated enemies and the piteous cries of the wounded begging for water or, if their ends were close at hand, their mothers. An army of Christian Ethiopians had inflicted a third overwhelming defeat on the Muslim host that had been raised at the behest of the Great Mogul himself to invade their land. The first two had proved to be false dawns and any sense of security they had engendered had swiftly proven to be unwarranted. But this victory was so complete as to put the matter beyond dispute. The enemy's forces were routed on land and any ships bearing reinforcements and supplies that had dared to attempt the

11

crossing of the Red Sea from Aden to the Eritrean coast had swiftly been sunk by the vessel that commanded those waters single-handed, an English frigate named the *Golden Bough*. The vessel had been commissioned to sail in pursuit of financial gain. Now her captain led her in the service of freedom and the preservation of the most important religious relic in Ethiopia and indeed all Christendom: the Tabernacle itself, in which the Jews had carried the tablets of stone, brought down by Moses from Mount Zion and where the Holy Grail itself was now said to reside.

A large tent had been erected behind the Ethiopian lines. A company of warriors clad in steel helmets and breastplates stood guard at its entrance. Inside it was hung with precious tapestries illustrating scenes from the life of Christ. They were woven from silks whose colours shone like jewels in the flickering light of a dozen burning torches and a myriad candles, while the halos around the Saviour's head gleamed with threads of pure gold.

In the middle of the tent stood a large table on which a model of the battlefield and the surrounding countryside had been built. Hills were shown in exact topographical detail; streams, rivers, lakes were picked out in blue, as was one edge of the model, for that represented the sea itself. Exquisitely carved ivory figurines of foot soldiers, horsemen and cannons represented the units of infantry, cavalry and artillery that had been arrayed on either side. At the start of the day they had been arranged in a perfect copy of the two armies' orders of battle, but now most of the figures representing the Arab forces had been knocked over or removed entirely from the table.

The atmosphere in the tent was subdued. A tall, imposing figure in ecclesiastical robes was deep in conversation with a knot of senior officers. His grey beard flowed down almost to his knees, and his chest was as bedecked with golden crosses and chains of rosary beads as it was with medals and insignias of rank. The low murmur of the men's voices was in stark contrast to the high-pitched squeals of excitement and delight coming from the vicinity of the table. 'Bang! Bang! Take that!' a small boy was shouting. In his hand he held a model of an Ethiopian cavalry man, mounted on a mighty stallion, and he was sweeping it back and forth across one corner of the table, knocking down any Arab figures that had somehow been left standing after the battle.

Then a guard opened the flap at the tent's entrance and in walked a soldier whose white linen tunic worn over a shirt of chain mail seemed designed more to emphasize the wearer's slim, willowy physique than to offer any serious protection.

'General Nazet!' shouted the little boy, dropping his toy soldier and racing across the carpeted floor to hurl himself at the soldier's steel-clad legs, on which wet, scarlet splashes of enemy blood still glinted. He then hugged them as tightly as if he were snuggling against his mother's soft, yielding bosom.

The general removed a plumed helmet to reveal a bushy head of tightly packed black curls. With a quick shake of the head they sprung to life, forming a circle whose unlikely resemblance to one of the halos on the nearby tapestries was only enhanced by the golden glow of the candles. There was no sign of the sweat and filth of battle on the general's smooth, amber skin, narrow, almost delicate nose and fine-boned, hairless jawline; no hint of stress or exhaustion in the soft, low voice that said, 'Your Majesty, I have the honour of informing you that your army's victory is complete. The enemy is vanquished and his forces are in retreat.'

His Most Christian Majesty, Iyasu, King of Kings, Ruler of Galla and Amhara, Defender of the Faith of Christ Crucified, let go of the general's legs, took a step backwards and then began jumping up and down, clapping his hands and whooping with glee. The military men approached and congratulated their comrade in a more sober fashion, with shakes of the hand and pats on the shoulder while the priest offered a blessing and a prayer of gratitude.

General Nazet accepted their thanks with calm good grace and then said, 'And now, Your Majesty, I have a favour to ask you. Once before I resigned my commission as the commander of your forces, but circumstances changed. My emperor and my country needed me and my conscience would never have allowed me to turn my back on my duty. So I put on my armour and I took up my sword once more. I was a soldier general and yours to command. But I am also a woman, Your Majesty, and as a woman I belong to another man. He let me go once to return to your service and now, with your permission, I wish to return to him.'

The boy looked at her. He frowned thoughtfully. 'Is the man Captain Courtney?' he asked.

'Yes, Your Majesty,' Judith Nazet replied.

'The Englishman with the funny eyes that are coloured green, like leaves on a tree?'

'Yes, Your Majesty. Do you remember, you welcomed him into the Order of the Golden Lion of Ethiopia as a reward for his bravery and service to our nation?'

'Yes, I remember,' said Iyasu, in an unexpectedly sad little voice. Then he asked, 'Are you going to be a mummy and daddy?' The boy emperor pursed his lips and twisted his mouth from side to side, trying to understand why he suddenly felt very unhappy and then said, 'I wish I had a mummy and daddy. Maybe you and Captain Courtney can come and live in the palace and be like a mummy and daddy to me.'

14

'Well now, Your Majesty, I really don't think that . . .' the cleric began. But the boy wasn't listening. His full attention was directed at Judith Nazet who had crouched down on her haunches and was holding out her arms to him.

Iyasu went to her once again, and this time it was like a child to its mother as he laid his head on Judith's shoulder and fell into her embrace. 'There-there,' she said. 'Don't you worry. Would you like to come and see Captain Courtney's ship?'

The little boy nodded, wordlessly.

'Maybe you can fire one of the cannons. That would be fun, wouldn't it?'

There was another nod against Judith's shoulder and then Iyasu lifted his face from the folds of her tunic, looked up at her and said, in a small voice, 'You're going to sail away with Captain Courtney, aren't you?'

'Yes, I am.'

'Please don't go,' Iyasu asked and then, with desperate determination, cried out, 'I command you not to go! You must obey me! You said you had to!'

Then the dam broke and, sobbing, he collapsed back onto her shoulder. The cleric took a step towards his young master, but Judith held up her hand. 'One moment, Bishop. Let me deal with this.'

She let Iyasu cry a little longer until he was calmer and then dried his eyes and wiped his nose with her tunic. 'Now,' she said, 'you know that I like you very much, don't you, Your Majesty.'

'Yes.'

'And even if I go away, no matter how far, I will always like you and remember you. And just think, if I go to faraway countries like England or France I will be able to write and tell you all about the wonderful extraordinary things I see there.'

15

'Do you promise to write to me?'

'You have my word, as a soldier, Your Majesty.'

'And if I go on Captain Courtney's ship, will he let me fire a cannon?'

'I will order him to do so. And since I'm a general and he's only a captain he will have to obey me.'

The Emperor Iyasu pondered a moment, gave a thoughtful sigh and then turned away from Judith and said, 'Bishop Fasilides, please be good enough to tell General Nazet that she has my permission to leave.'

The armed East Indiaman *Earl of Cumberland*, named after the first governor of the Company of Merchants of London trading with the East Indies, was forty days out of Bombay with a hundred tons of saltpetre on board. She was bound for the Port of London where the saltpetre would be unloaded and taken to the royal armoury at Greenwich Palace, there to be mixed with sulphur and charcoal to provide gunpowder for His Majesty King Charles II of England's army and navy. At the stern of the vessel, where the captain had his quarters, there were a number of other cabins for the ship's senior officers and any important passengers that might be aboard. In one of these cabins a man was on his knees, his hands clasped together in prayer and his eyes closed as he sought permission to kill.

His name was William Pett. He had come aboard with official

papers identifying him as a senior official of the East India Company and requiring any person engaged in Company business to provide him with whatever assistance he might require in the furtherance of his duties. Pett had approached Captain Rupert Goddings, master of the *Earl of Cumberland*, at a dinner hosted by Gerald Aungier, the first Governor of Bombay. He explained that his business in India was completed, hinting that it had been a delicate matter, involving negotiations with various Portuguese and Indian notables that he was not at liberty to discuss in any detail.

'You understand the need for discretion, I'm sure,' Pett said, in the tone of one man of the world to another.

Goddings was a large, ebullient, cocksure man with a splendidly upturned black moustache, whose years as a merchant captain had made him a considerable fortune. He was a perfectly competent seaman, and, if only because he lacked the imagination to be scared, possessed a degree of bravery. But not even his closest friends would have called him a great intellect. Now he adopted a suitably thoughtful expression and replied, 'Quite so, quite so . . . Very easily offended, some of these Indians, and the Portuguese aren't much better. It's all that spicy food, in my view. Heats up the blood.'

'I have, of course, sent regular reports home, summarizing the progress of our talks,' Pett continued. 'But now that they're done it's essential that I return home as soon as possible so as to discuss them in detail with my directors.'

'Of course, quite understand. Vital to keep John Company fully informed. You'll be wanting a berth on the Sausage, then, I dare say.'

For a moment, Pett had been caught unawares. 'I'm sorry, Captain, the sausage? I don't quite follow.'

Goddings had laughed. 'By God, sir, I dare say you don't! It's

18

Cumberland, don't you see? They make sausages up there, so I'm told. I'm a Devonshire man myself. Anyway that's why the *Earl of Cumberland* has always been known as the Sausage. Surprised you don't know that, come to think of it, being a Company man.'

'Well, I've always been more involved with financial and administrative functions than with nautical affairs. But to return to your kind invitation, yes, I would be very grateful of a berth. Of course, I have funds with which to pay for my passage. Would sixty guineas be sufficient?'

'It certainly would,' said Goddings, thinking to himself that the Company must really value Mr Pett if they were prepared to let him spend that kind of money. 'Come aboard!'

Pett smiled, thinking to himself how easy it was going to be to earn the five hundred guineas he was being paid to kill Goddings. It was apparent, even on this brief encounter, that Goddings was prey to a trait that Pett had observed in many stupid people: a total unawareness of his own stupidity. This blissful ignorance led to a fatal excess of self-confidence. Goddings had, for example, believed that he could cuckold an elderly director of the Company by the brazenly public seduction of the old man's much younger wife, and that he would get away with it. He was about to discover, a very short time before he departed this world, just how wrong he had been.

Upon boarding the *Earl of Cumberland* Pett had taken his time before making his move against the captain. He needed to find his sea legs and to learn as much as he could about the ship's company and the various friendships, alliances, enmities and tensions that existed within it, all of which he intended to exploit in the execution of his plan. More than that, however, he was waiting for the signal without which he could not kill, the voice in his head, a messenger from heaven whom Pett knew

19

only as the Saint, who came to assure him that his victim deserved to die and that he, William Pett, would be rewarded in heaven for his efforts to purify the earth of sin.

Pett slept each night in a wooden cot that was suspended from hooks in the timbers that spanned the cabin, so as to keep it stable when the ship rolled. Now he knelt by the cot as the presence of the Saint filled his mind and soul – indeed, his entire being – with the knowledge that he was blessed and that the whole company of angels and archangels was watching over him and protecting him. For as long as the vision lasted, Pett experienced a blissful ecstasy greater than any he had ever known with a woman, and when he rose it was with joy in his heart, for he would be doing God's work tonight.

His chosen weapon was a perfectly ordinary table knife that he had taken from the captain's table, where he ate every night with Goddings and his senior officers. Pett had honed its blade with a whetstone he had discreetly purloined from the ship's stores until it was as sharp as any dagger. Once he had used it to kill Goddings, he planned to take advantage of the confusion that the discovery of the captain's body was bound to cause and leave it amongst the personal effects of a sulky, unpopular young midshipman, whose incompetence and bad character had made him the target of the captain's wrath on a number of occasions. No one would doubt that the lad had reason to want revenge and he would have no friends to speak in his defence, though Pett was minded to volunteer to act on his behalf as summary justice was meted out. That was for later. Now, however, he placed the knife in the right-hand pocket of his breeches, left his cabin and knocked on the door of the captain's quarters.

'Come in!' Goddings called out, suspecting nothing for it had become the two men's custom to share a glass of brandy every evening, while discussing the day's events aboard ship, ruminating on the ever-growing might and wealth of the East India Company (with particular reference to how a man might get his hands on a larger share of it), and generally setting the world to rights.

The two men talked and drank in their usual companionable fashion, but all the while Pett was waiting for the moment to strike. And then the Saint, as he always did, provided the perfect opportunity. Goddings, by now somewhat befuddled by drink, having consumed much more than Pett who had discreetly kept his consumption to a minimum, got up from his chair to fetch more brandy from a wooden chest whose interior had been divided into six compartments, each of which contained a crystal glass decanter that was filled with a variety of spirits and cordials.

Goddings turned his back as he rummaged through the decanters to find one containing more brandy, quite oblivious to Pett, who had risen silently from his seat, taken the knife from his pocket and was crossing the cabin towards him. At the very last moment, just as Pett was about to stab the blade into Goddings's right kidney, the captain turned around.

For Pett, moments such as these seemed to stretch out forever. He was aware of every movement his victim made, no matter how tiny; every breath he took; every flicker of expression on his face. Goddings's eyes widened in a look of utter bewilderment, the total surprise of a man who simply could not understand what was happening to him or why. Pett delivered three quick stabs, as sharp and fast as a prizefighter's jabs, into Goddings's fleshy gut. The captain was too shocked to shout out in alarm, or even to scream in pain. Instead he mewled like an infant as he looked down helplessly at the crimson outpour of blood that was drenching his white waistcoat and, for he had wet himself with fear and shock, the stain of urine spreading across his breeches.

With his last iota of strength, Goddings attempted to defend himself. He hurled the decanter, missing Pett who easily swayed out of its way, instead striking the lantern which hung from a low beam above his desk, knocking it off its peg onto the escritoire on which lay his open logbook and a nautical chart. The oil from the lantern and the brandy from the decanter were both highly inflammable, as were the paper documents. The lantern's flame was the final ingredient and soon fire was flickering across the varnished wood of the escritoire and running in streams of burning liquid across the cabin floor.

Pett did not move. He was still glorying in what he had done. He remained in the cabin, even as the flames crackled and the air filled with smoke, with his pulse racing and his breath coming in ever shorter gasps, as Goddings suffered through the final seconds of his life. Finally there came the moment of death for Goddings and ecstatic release for his killer and now, as if awoken from a trance, the latter began to move.

Pett knew full well that fire was the deadliest of all perils at sea, and a ship whose cargo was saltpetre and whose cannons were fired by gunpowder was little more than a floating bomb. Now the fuse had been lit, he had to escape the *Earl of Cumberland* as fast as he could. Like him, Goddings slept in a cot. It was made of wood and would serve as an impromptu life raft. Moving swiftly, but without the slightest panic, Pett unhooked the captain's cot from the hooks to which it was attached. Then he carried it across to the windows that ran across the stern end of the cabin, pounded at the glass until it shattered and then hurled the cot out of the opening he had made. A moment later, Pett climbed up onto the window ledge and, heedless of the glass shards scraping against his skin, threw himself out into the warm night air.

As he fell through space, towards the glittering blackness of the sea, Pett had little idea of where he was, other than somewhere between India and the Cape of Good Hope. He was not sure that he could find the cot, or even if it was still floating on the surface of the waves. He had no idea what manner of sea-creatures might be lurking in the depths beneath him, ready to attack him, kill him and eat him. And quite apart from all of that, he did not know how to swim.

None of that mattered, not in the slightest. William Pett had answered the voice of the Saint. He was doing God's will. And thus no harm could befall him. He was absolutely sure of it.

As the first rays of the dawn sun cast a soft orange glow across the harbour at Mitsiwa, the pride of the Ethiopian fleet sat at anchor, joyfully flying the Union Flag of her native British Isles. The *Golden Bough* had been built on the orders of George, Viscount Winterton, at the stupendous price of almost two thousand pounds. Winterton already possessed a substantial private fleet of merchantmen and privateers. His intentions for the *Bough* were to provide his beloved son Vincent with an agreeable vessel on which to follow the family's seafaring traditions, while providing himself with further additions to what was already one of the largest fortunes in England.

The Honourable 'Vinny' Winterton now lay buried on the shore of Elephant Lagoon, beside the waters of the Indian Ocean a short way north of the Cape of Good Hope, killed in a duel that was, in truth, little more than an act of murder. Yet his father's money had been well spent, even if the *Golden Bough*'s recent incarnation, as the flagship and sole fighting vessel of an African navy, was no more part of the viscount's plans than his boy's demise. She was as slim and pleasing on the eye as a thoroughbred racehorse and could cut through the water with rare speed and grace. On a broad reach, with her sails full and a good breeze blowing, she could escape any warships that outmatched her and catch any that did not. And like a horse with a winning jockey, the *Bough* rewarded a captain who was strong in skill and nerve, for she could be sailed tight into the wind when other vessels would be left floundering or forced to change their bearing.

In all his months of commanding the *Bough* in peace and in combat, on windless millponds and storm-tossed maelstroms, Hal Courtney had come to know his ship from bilge and ballast to bowsprit and rudder. He knew precisely how to squeeze every last knot out of her and how best to arm her for the perils she was sure to encounter. Hal knew that every captain had to balance the firepower gained from additional cannons with the weight they added to his ship's displacement. Some chose fewer guns for a faster, more nimble ship, whilst others preferred to rely on firepower. With the *Golden Bough* Hal had both speed and armament. The pick of the guns with which she had originally been provided had been combined with the finest pieces captured in countless engagements. Now he could call on a deadly assortment of cannons and small arms, from mighty culverins, whose twelve-foot barrels fired cannon balls that weighed almost twenty pounds apiece and could snap a mast in two, to much smaller (but equally deadly) falconets and murderers, which could be loaded with grapeshot and turned at point-blank range on enemies trying to board the ship.

So the *Bough*'s teeth were as sharp as her limbs were swift. And that was why her captain adored her so.

Naturally he wanted one of the great loves of his life to look her best when she was reintroduced to the other. Four months earlier, Judith Nazet had been aboard the *Golden Bough* when the leisurely voyage she and Hal were making down the east coast of Africa, bound for England, via the bay where his family fortune was hidden, was interrupted by a dhow bringing a desperate plea from her emperor. During the few days Judith had spent on the *Bough*, however, the crew had come to admire her almost as much as Hal did. They were awestruck by her achievements on the battlefield and lovestruck by the beautiful, utterly feminine woman she became when she laid down her sword and armour. So when Hal had ordered that the ship should be readied for her return, adding that he wanted her looking even more perfect than on the day she had first been launched, his men set to work with a will.

For a full week they had hung over the sides on ropes, scrubbing and tarring the hull and hammering new nails into the planks so that no sign remained of the months of naval service – all the broadsides fired, boarders repelled, timbers burned and blood shed – that the *Bough* and her crew had given. Every piece of accessible timber received attention, repairing, replacing, scraping, caulking, tarring, greasing and painting. The mastheads were blacked and the fore and aft staysails along with the mainsail were unbent for repair. They tarred the lines and polished the culverins and put up more awnings on deck to provide shade for their honoured guests. They scraped every scrap of rust or blood off the ship's cutlasses, lances and boarding axes and polished the muskets and swivel-guns until they gleamed fit to dazzle in the burning tropical sun.

One particular bloodstain had been caused by an unfortunate

Arab warrior who had been shot at close range in the thigh by a musket ball that had ruptured an artery and sent a crimson fountain spurting across the oak planks from which the deck was made. The blood had soaked deep into the wood, leaving an unsightly discolouration on the quarterdeck, just aft of the mainmast. He had his men sluice down the deck and scrub it until its second washing was with their own sweat, but even when they had finished there were still shadows on the boards where the blood had soaked deep into the grain. Mitsiwa harbour was ringed by a sandy beach, so Hal sent a party ashore to gather up buckets filled with the coarse, rasping sand and then bring it back to scrub into the planks so that their surfaces would be scraped away, and the stain with them.

Hal had stood over the men as they worked deep into the night and had even got down on his hands and knees and started scrubbing alongside them when they flagged, for he believed that no man should ever order another to do something he was unwilling to do himself. Finally he had been forced to admit that the deck, which was shining a silvery-white in the moonlight, was as flawless as it was ever going to be and such blemishes as did remain would be lost in the shade thrown by the awning with which the whole area would be covered for the day and night that lay ahead.

Hal had decreed that his beloved's return would be marked by a feast befitting such a joyous occasion. The men of the *Golden Bough* had sailed hard, fought hard and seen a dozen of their mates die in battle before being wrapped in shrouds and committed to the sea. They had earned the chance to eat, drink and generally let their hair down and Hal was going to make sure that they did it in style. Yet for all that this was a happy day, it was also a momentous one. He knew that whether they were married or not – and Hal was determined that when

27

he wed his bride it would be in an English church with a Protestant vicar – he and Judith were committing their lives to one another. He had loved before, and known both the bitterness of being deceived and the pain of great loss, but there was a sense of certainty and permanence to his love for Judith that he had never known before. She was his woman. She would be the mother of his children. That was a lot for a young man to take in, no matter how sure he felt.

Dawn found him leaning against the poop rail, from which he could survey every mast, every spar and every scrap of sail of the ship under his command. Now, though, the sails were all furled and the ship was at rest. Off in the distance Hal could see the activity on the shoreline as local merchants prepared to fill their boats with the carcasses of goat, mutton and chicken; the baskets of vegetables and fruit; the huge earthenware pots filled with several varieties of *wat*, the thick, spicy stew of meat or vegetables that was Ethiopia's national dish, and the piled loaves of *injera*, the sourdough on which *wat* was customarily served; sacks of green coffee beans (to be roasted, ground, brewed and then served with sugar or salt), barrels of strong, red wine from the vineyards of the Lebanon and flagons of *tej*, or honey wine, as potent as it was sweet; and finally great garlands of flowers with which to bedeck the ship and provide a suitably beautiful and fragrant setting for the bride.

Hal watched the distant bustle for a few minutes. Though he was barely twenty years old, he had acquired a grown man's strength and an air of absolute command, earned by his seamanship and courage in battle that made men twice his age happy to follow his orders without question. There was not yet the faintest trace of grey in the thick, black hair that Hal tied with a thong behind his head, and the green eyes that had so amazed the Emperor Iyasu were as clear and sharp as ever. Yet the almost

28

feminine beauty that he had possessed just a few years earlier had entirely disappeared. Just as his back still bore the scars of the whippings he had been forced to endure as a prisoner – little more than a slave – of the Dutch, so his experiences had made his face leaner, harder and more weather-beaten. His jaw was more firmly set, his mouth more stern, his gaze more piercing.

Now, though, his eyes dropped to the water lapping against the *Bough*'s hull and he said, 'I wish my parents could be here to meet Judith, though I don't even remember my mother, I was so young when she died. But my father . . .' Hal sighed. 'I hope he'd think I was doing the right thing . . . I hope he wouldn't think badly of me.'

'Of course not! He was always so proud of you, Gundwane. Think of the very last words he said to you. Say them now.'

Hal was unable to speak. In his mind's eye, all he could see was his father's rotting, dismembered body hanging from a gibbet in the Cape Colony for all its inhabitants to see and for all the gulls to feast upon. Having falsely accused Sir Francis Courtney of piracy, the Dutch had tortured him to the edge of death, hoping to discover the location of his treasure. Yet Sir Francis had not broken. His enemies had been none the wiser as they hanged him from the gibbet while Hal looked on help-less and heartbroken from the high wall where he was serving a sentence of hard labour.

'Say them, for him.' The voice was gentle, but insistent.

Hal breathed deeply, in and out, before he spoke. 'He said that I was his blood and his promise of eternal life. And then . . . Then he looked at me and said, "Goodbye, my life."'

'Then there is your answer. Your father sees you now. I who took him to his final resting place can tell you that his eyes face towards the sun and he sees you always, wherever you are.'

'Thank you, Aboli,' said Hal.

Now for the first time he looked at the man who had been his father's closest companion and was now the closest thing he had to a father figure. Aboli was a member of the Amadoda tribe who lived deep in the forests, many days' journey from the coast of East Africa. Every hair had been ceremonially plucked from the polished ebony skin of his scalp, and his face was marked with ridged whorls of scar tissue, caused by cuts inflicted in his early boyhood and intended to awe and terrify his enemies. They were a mark of royalty for he and his twin brother were sons of the Monomatapa, the chosen of heaven, the all-powerful ruler of their tribe. When both boys were still very young, slavers had attacked their village. Aboli's brother had been carried to a place of safety, but Aboli had not been so lucky. Many years had passed before Sir Francis Courtney had freed him and, in so doing, created a bond that had endured beyond the grave, from one generation to another.

The nickname Gundwane by which Aboli referred to Hal meant 'Bush Rat'. Aboli had bestowed it when Hal was just a boy of four and it had stuck ever since. No other man on board the *Golden Bough* would have dared be so familiar with their skipper, but then, everything about Aboli was exceptional. He stood half a head taller even than Hal, and his lean, muscular body moved with a cobra's menacing, sinuous grace and deadly purpose. Everything that Hal knew about swordfighting – not just the technique or the footwork, but the understanding of an opponent and the warrior spirit needed to defeat him – he had learned from Aboli. It had been a tough education, with many a bruise inflicted and a quantity of blood spilled along the way. But if Aboli had been tough on his young pupil, it had only been because Sir Francis demanded it.

Thinking of those days, Hal gave a wry chuckle, 'You know, I may be master of this ship, but every time I stand here on

30

the quarterdeck I think of being back on the *Lady Edwina*, getting a roasting from my father for whatever it was I'd done wrong. There was always something. Do you remember how long it took me to learn how to use the backstaff and the sun to calculate the ship's position? The first times I tried, the backstaff was bigger than I was. I'd stand out on the deck at midday, not a scrap of shade, sweating like a little pig and every time the ship rolled or pitched the damn staff almost knocked me over!'

Aboli gave a deep laugh like the rumble of distant thunder as Hal went on, 'And making me speak to him in Latin, because it was the language of gentlemen! You have no idea how lucky you are never to have had to learn about gerunds and ablative absolutes. Or cuffing me round the ears because I couldn't remember the name of every single sail the ship carried. Even when I got one answer right he would tell me a hundred things I was doing wrong. And it was always right here on the quarterdeck, where every single crewman could see me.' Hal's expression suddenly turned serious. 'You know, there were times when I really, truly hated him for that.'

'Yes, and the fact that he did what he did, knowing that you would not understand and would hate him for it, was the proof of his love,' Aboli replied. 'Your father prepared you well. He was hard on you, but only because he knew you would be tested time and again.' The African smiled. 'Maybe, if your god wills it, you will have a little Courtney of your own to be hard on soon.'

Hal smiled. He was having a tough enough time imagining himself as a husband, let alone a father. 'I'm not sure that I'm ready to be a father, yet. I sometimes even wonder if I'm ready to be a captain.'

'Ha!' Aboli exclaimed, laying a huge hand on Hal's shoulder.

'You have slain your mortal enemies. You have saved the Tabernacle and the Holy Grail. You have won the heart of a woman who has defeated mighty armies.' Aboli inclined his head slowly. 'Yes I think you are ready to rock a baby to sleep in your arms.'

Hal laughed. 'Well, in that case I think we'd better get ready to meet its mother.'

The captain was the master of a ship crewed by living skeletons. Having spent almost all his money on the cargo stashed in barely a score of wooden cases that took up just a fraction of his ship's hold, he had bought the cheapest provisions he could, and thus been sold biscuit that was riddled with weevils and fungus before he had even left harbour, vegetables that were rotten and dried meats that were so tough as to make for better shoe leather than food. He and his crew were fugitives. They could not put in to any civilized port to buy, work or beg for more supplies without risking immediate imprisonment, always assuming that they would not be blown out of the water by any of the ships pursuing them long before they sighted land. He was, in short, a man in no need of any further troubles. And yet another was headed his way.

He knew that a bad situation was about to get worse the moment he heard the voice from the crow's nest: 'Captain! There's something floating in the sea, just off the starboard bow! It looks like a piece of wood, or an upturned boat.'

The captain shook his head and muttered to himself, 'Why do I need to be told this?'

His question was immediately answered as the lookout shouted, 'There's something moving! It's a man! He's seen us . . . And now he's waving!'

The captain was aware of fifty pairs or more of hungry eyes, staring in his direction, willing him to give the order to sail on and leave the man to his fate. The last thing the ship needed was another mouth to feed. And yet the captain could hardly claim to be a man of honour, but he wasn't wicked. A scoundrel, perhaps, but not a villain. And so he ordered the ship to be hove to. Then he had a boat lowered to fetch this man who had appeared out of nowhere, hundreds of leagues from the nearest shore. 'Never mind, lads,' he called out. 'If we don't like the bastard we can always eat him!'

A short while later a bedraggled, sunburned figure of above average height, but almost as thin as the crewmen who surrounded him, was dragged up the side of the hull and deposited on the deck of the ship. The captain had come down from the poop deck to greet him. He spoke in his native tongue and asked, 'Good day, sir. Whom do I have the pleasure of addressing?'

The man gave a little nod of the head and replied, in the same tongue, 'Good day to you too, Captain. My name is William Pett.'

Judith had given considerable thought to what she should wear on the day that she and Hal were reunited. She had been tempted to commission a steel breastplate, moulded perfectly to her figure, around which she would drape a silk sash in the national colours of red, yellow and green, upon which her decorations would be pinned in all their golden and bejewelled splendour. The emperor had given her a rapier of fine Damascus steel, a weapon that was both deadly and perfectly designed to suit a woman's size and strength. These martial adornments would look well hanging from her hip as she stepped onto the deck of the *Golden Bough* and would serve to remind the men aboard that she was not a helpless, delicate creature with nothing to contribute to the life and work of the ship, but a warrior as battle-hardened as any of them.

And yet, as much as she wanted the men to respect her, she also wanted her man to love and desire her, and, yes, though she hated to admit it, she wanted to look pretty for him. They had managed to snatch a single precious hour together a month earlier, when both had been called to a council of war. But even though they put every second they had together to the best possible use, and her longing for him was slaked at least for a short while, the reminder of the ecstasy that he could induce in her served only to make their subsequent parting even harder to bear. She never wanted anything whatever to come between them again. So although her sword and armour and military decorations were all stowed in her luggage that she would be bringing aboard, Judith herself wore a traditional Ethiopian dress of pure white cotton that fell to her ankles. The hem, sleeves and the neck were all decorated with bands of brightly coloured embroidery, bearing a pattern of golden crosses. There were necklaces of gold and amber beads around her neck and she wore circular golden earrings, with pearls at their centre.

Her hair had been woven into braids that lay close to her scalp and over them she placed a headpiece formed of two finely worked strands of pearls and gold beads. One ran horizontally around her head and was linked to the other that ran from back to front, over the top of her head. A small gold and pearl brooch that matched her earrings lay at the centre of her forehead, just below her hairline, attached to both strands and holding them both in place. Finally Judith draped a shawl of white linen gauze over her head and across her shoulders as a mark of modesty. In private, she was willing to play the concubine, but in public, at least, her reputation would remain unsullied.

She rode in a carriage to the port of Mitsiwa, escorted by a troop of the emperor's mounted guard, all dressed in their finest ceremonial uniforms, with pennants bearing the lion of Ethiopia fluttering from their lances. The carriage halted by the dockside and the guard was immediately called upon to form a perimeter around it as a flock of locals rushed to cast eyes on their nation's heroine, scarcely able to believe that the great Judith Nazet, who had become a figure of almost mythical glory in their eyes, could possibly be here, in person amongst them. One of the guardsmen dismounted and walked to the carriage door. He opened it and pulled down a set of steps. Then he stood back, so that all could see Judith as she emerged from within.

At the very last moment, partly because she had anticipated that her arrival might draw a crowd, and partly because she wanted to give her people a reminder of the glorious victory in which they could all take pride – for many of the men had been in the army she commanded – Judith had decided to wear the sash bearing her many honours. As she stepped out into the open, the dazzling, mid-morning sunlight shone down upon her, and upon the gold, pearls, jewels and brightly enamelled and beribboned medals and awards with which she was adorned so that she seemed to sparkle and glow more like a goddess than a mortal woman. A sound rose from the crowd, less a cheer than an awed gasp. But though she smiled and waved to the people, Judith's eyes and her heart were given to one man only.

Hal Courtney stood waiting for her at the foot of the steps. Though he was the captain of a fighting ship, he wore no badge of rank. Though he, too, was entitled to call himself a member of the Order of the Golden Lion of Ethiopia, and held the rank of a Nautonnier Knight of the Temple of the Order of St George and the Holy Grail – the band of navigators whose origins lay in the medieval Knights Templar, to which he, like his father before him, belonged – he bore no medals nor badges of honour.

Instead he stood there before her, with his hair tied back with a plain black ribbon, wearing a freshly laundered white shirt, loosely tucked into his black breeches and open at the neck. The gleaming fabric billowed a little in the gentle breeze, giving occasional hints of the lean, strongly muscled torso beneath it. At Hal's hip hung his sword, a blade of Toledo steel, below a hilt of gold and silver, with a large star sapphire on its pommel that had been given to Hal's great-grandfather by the greatest of all Elizabethan admirals, Sir Francis Drake himself.

As she looked at her man, so filled with strength, and confidence and vigour, his face, which had looked almost stern as she first caught sight of it, broke into a grin filled with boyish glee, enthusiasm and unabashed desire.

Judith had stood firm in the heat of battle. She had held her own in the council chamber against men twice or even three times her age, who towered over her in both physical stature and hard-won reputation. Neither they, nor her enemies, had ever intimidated her. And yet now, in the presence of Hal Courtney, she felt her legs weaken beneath her, her breath quicken and she was suddenly seized by such a feeling of light-headedness that if he had not stepped forward to take her in his arms, she might easily have fallen. She let him hold her for a second, letting herself enjoy the delicious sense of helplessness, barely hearing the cheers of the crowd, or even the words that Hal was saying over the beating of her heart.

She was dimly aware that he was leading her through the mass of delirious townspeople, with guardsmen up ahead of them using their horses to force a path down to the jetty. She heard cheers for '*El Tazar*' – the Barracuda – for that was the name by which Hal had come to be known as he preyed upon their enemy's shipping. Then she held Hal's hand as he guided her down the stone steps and said, 'Be careful now, my darling,' as she stepped onto the *Golden Bough*'s pinnace, an armed launch whose single sail was furled, though there was a man at every one of her eight oars and Big Daniel Fisher, Hal's senior coxswain, was standing at the rudder.

'Welcome aboard, ma'am,' Big Daniel said. 'I hope you won't think me forward or nothing, but you're the prettiest sight any of us have clapped eyes on in a very long time.'

'Thank you, Daniel,' said Judith with a happy little laugh. 'I don't think that's forward at all.' She looked around the boat and then asked Hal, 'Where's Aboli? I can't believe he'd let you out of his sight on an occasion like this.'

Hal gave a huge shrug, throwing his hands up as if to suggest complete bafflement and with an exaggerated look of wide-eyed innocence replied, 'I don't have a clue where he's got to. You seen him, Daniel?'

'No, sir, can't say as I have.'

'Anyone?'

The crewmen shook their heads in a pantomime of ignorance and said no, they didn't know either. It was obvious that they were up to something, but Judith was happy to play along with the game. 'Well, I am sorry not to see him,' she said, and then settled herself on a bench next to Hal as he ordered, 'Cast off and take us back to the ship, please, cox'n.'

'Aye-aye, sir,' said Big Daniel who started barking out orders to the oarsmen to back them away from the jetty, before he swung the pinnace around and set a course to the *Golden Bough* which lay on the water, a couple of hundred yards or so ahead of them.

'She looks beautiful,' said Judith, watching Hal look towards his ship and knowing the pride that he took in her.

'Well, the men and I did a bit of cleaning and tidying up,' said Hal, nonchalantly.

'Had us working our fingers to the bone, night and day for a week, more like, ma'am,' Daniel observed.

'Poor Daniel, I hope he wasn't too much of a hard taskmaster,' said Judith.

'Oh you know what Captain Courtney's like, ma'am. Takes after his father, so he does, likes to run a tight ship.'

The words were almost thrown away, but Judith knew Hal well enough to realize that Daniel could not have paid him a higher compliment and she gave his hand a squeeze to signal that she heard and understood it. As they drew close to the *Golden Bough*, Daniel ordered the men to stop rowing and ship their blades. As one, the oars were raised into a vertical position and the pinnace was brought to rest with just the lightest of touches against the larger ship. Lines were thrown down from the deck above and made fast against the pinnace's cleats. A net was hanging down the *Bough*'s hull to enable those in the pinnace to climb up to the deck. Judith stood and took a pace towards the net, but Hal gently held her arm to stop her and shouted up.

'Lower the swing, lads, nice and gently if you please.'

Judith looked up and saw a boom hanging over the side of the ship.

'We use it to bring supplies aboard,' said Hal. 'But I thought we could put it to a better purpose today.'

The boom was garlanded in a profusion of vividly coloured flowers, like a horizontal, tropical maypole. From it there hung a canvas sling that had been decorated with coloured ribbons, signal flags and anything else the men could find to make it look jolly. The sling was lowered down to the pinnace and Hal helped Judith sit on it, as if on a garden swing.

'Make sure she's safe and sound,' he ordered Daniel, then pecked Judith on the cheek and said, 'I'll see you on deck, my darling.'

Hal leaped onto the net and started clambering up it with what looked to Judith like the speed and agility of a monkey up a tree. She giggled at the thought, then held on tight to the sling as Daniel shouted, 'Haul away!' and she was lifted up into the air. By now all trace of the warrior General Nazet had disappeared and Judith was simply a young woman in love, having the time of her life. She gave a little squeal of alarm and excitement as she rose up through the air, watching Hal come to the top of the net and then spring onto the deck where he stood, surrounded by the ship's company.

'Three cheers for the captain's lady!' shouted the *Bough*'s veteran helmsman Ned Tyler. 'Hip-hip!'

A great cheer rang out as Judith appeared on her swing, several feet above the level of the deck.

'Hooray!' the men cried, waving their hats in the air as the boom swung her over their heads.

As the second cheer rang out she was lowered to a patch of deck that had been cleared to receive her. As Ned Tyler gave the third 'Hip-hip!', Judith let go of the sling and jumped the last few feet to the bare wood, landing with the grace and agility of an acrobat, and as she found herself again in Hal's arms the third cheer echoed around them and grew even longer and louder as he gave her a single, all-too-short kiss whose burning intensity filled her with a thrilling sense of anticipation of what would follow that night, and a terrible frustration that she would have to wait so long.

Hal pulled himself away and said, 'You were asking after Aboli. Perhaps this will enlighten you.'

He shouted a few words in a tongue that Judith knew was African, but could not comprehend. A few seconds later there came the reply, a loud keening cry that she instantly recognized as the start of a chant. It was answered by a mass of deep, masculine voices grunting, 'Huh!', followed immediately by feet stamping the deck as one. The first voice continued with the chant and, as it did, the sailors fell back to either side so that the deck in front of Judith emptied and there before her came a sight that thrilled her heart almost as much as the feel of Hal's arms around her.

Aboli stood on the bare planking. On his head he wore a tall headdress of white crane's feathers that seemed to increase his already magnificent height so that he resembled a giant or a jungle god rather than a mortal man. In his hand he carried a broad-bladed stabbing spear and around his neck there was a kilt of leopard's tails.

Behind him came the Amadoda, men of his tribe who had been recruited to serve on the *Golden Bough* and who had swiftly proven to be as powerful and deadly at sea as they had been in the forests and open savannah that was their native land. They, too, wore crane-feather headdresses, though none was as tall or as splendid as Aboli's, for he was their chief.

Forward they came, their voices joining with his in rich, sonorous harmonies that proclaimed their valour, their comradeship and their willingness to die for their cause. All around, the rest of the crew looked on in slack-jawed amazement, for they had never seen the Amadoda like this, in all their glory. The men came forward until they were just a few paces from Judith and Hal and their song, their foot-stamps, their grunts and their perfectly co-ordinated movements combined in a way that was part dance, part military drill and part sheer celebration of the joy and pride of being a true warrior.

Their song finished and all around burst into applause, none more than Judith, for she, too, was a daughter of Africa and even though the words they sang were not known to her, she

41

understood the spirit in which they were sung completely. Then Aboli stepped towards her. With courtly dignity he removed his headdress and placed it on the deck beside him. Then he got down on one knee, reached out and took Judith's right hand in his, lowered his head and kissed her hand.

It was the tribute of a born aristocrat to his queen. Judith was all but overcome with the magnificence of his gesture and as he rose to his feet again, she kept hold of his hand and said, 'Thank you, Aboli. Thank you with all my heart,' for she knew that he had pledged himself to her and that she could count on him, absolutely, forever.

Hal was next to take Aboli's hand. 'Thank you, old friend. That was magnificent.'

Aboli smiled. 'I am a prince of the Amadoda. What else could it be?'

And so the festivities began. As morning gave way to afternoon, and afternoon to evening, food was eaten, and drink consumed, then the crew's musicians got out their fiddles, pipes and drums and the singing and dancing began. Judith let Hal lead her out to the floor and they improvised a combination of reel and jig that seemed to match the band's seafaring tunes well enough. Some of the native cooks and serving girls also found themselves pressed into service on the dancefloor, though Hal had made it very clear indeed that no liberties were to be taken and that any man found to have forced himself on a woman could expect a taste of the lash. Finally, as the sun went down, Hal stood on the steps leading up to the poop deck, looked out over the revellers and called for silence.

'Right, you drunken scoundrels,' he shouted, sounding less than entirely sober himself, 'I have a few words to say to you all.'

He was greeted by shouts of encouragement and a few

42

good-humoured catcalls. 'Now, my name – my proper, formal name – is Sir Henry Courtney.'

'It's all right, skipper, we know who you are!' a wag called out.

'Good, because there's a reason I said that, which will soon become clear. But first, let me say this: tomorrow we set sail for England!'

A huge roar of approval arose from the Anglo-Saxon contingent of the crew. 'Of course,' Hal went on, 'those members of the ship's company whose homeland lies here in Africa will be free to return to their homes. But not before we have completed one last task.

'As many of you know, my father, Sir Francis Courtney, along with the help of many of you here, captured many ships, sailing under Dutch and other flags—'

'Damn cheese-heads!' someone shouted, to great approval from his mates.

'—and from these prizes he took a very large amount of gold, silver and other valuables. We are going to go and recover that treasure and all of you – every last one – will get his share, fair and square, according to his length of service and seniority. And I can promise . . .' Hal had to raise his voice over the babble of cheers and excited chatter, 'that not a man-jack of you will walk away with less than fifty pounds, at the very least!'

Hal grinned at the cheers his promise provoked, then raised his hand for silence again. 'You all fully deserve your reward. No man could ask better, braver, more loyal crewmates than you have been to me. You've proved your worth as sailors and fighters a hundred times over. You have pledged yourselves to me and now I make this pledge to you. I am going to lead you back home and give you all you need to lead a fine life when

43

you get there. But first, gentlemen, I wish to propose a toast. Would you please raise your glasses to the woman that I will be taking back to my home, there to become my wife, my beloved Judith. Men, I give you: the future Lady Courtney!'

When the toast had been drunk, along with several more proposed from various members of the crew, Hal and Judith were finally free to retire together to his quarters. Being the creation of a wealthy aristocrat, the *Golden Bough* did not lack for creature comforts. There was not a battleship in the Royal Navy that housed its skipper more comfortably than the cabin provided for the *Bough*'s master. An elegantly carved desk provided the perfect place for the captain to keep his logbook up to date, while fine Persian carpets were enough to make guests feel that they were in the drawing room of a gentlemanly country house or London pied-à-terre, rather than the lower deck of an ocean-going sailing ship.

'I have made one significant improvement to our sleeping arrangements since you last sailed on the *Bough*,' said Hal as he paused outside the door to his cabin. 'It kept the ship's carpenter busy for a good week. Now, close your eyes . . .'

Judith did as she was told as Hal opened the cabin door then took her hand and led her into his personal domain. She took a few more blind steps until he said, 'Stop!' and a moment later, 'You can open your eyes now.'

Before her hung a sleeping cot, but this was twice the width of a normal berth and hung from four hooks instead of the usual two. Diaphanous white gauze curtains were gathered round the ropes on each corner, and a coverlet of silk damask whose pale grey and silver pattern glimmered in the light from the stern windows lay over sheets and pillows of finest Egyptian cotton.

'Hal, it's so beautiful,' Judith gasped.

'I found the linen aboard a dhow we captured,' Hal said with a grin. 'The captain said it was bound for a sheikh's harem. I told him I had a better use for it.'

'Oh, really?' said Judith, teasingly. 'And what use in particular did you have in—'

She never had the chance to finish her question, for Hal simply picked her up and deposited her on the silken bedcover, thinking how wise he had been to make the carpenter test the hooks from which the cot was suspended to make sure they could handle any conceivable strain.

When the Buzzard had first sailed north to seek his fortune in the service of the Arab invasion of Ethiopia, caring not a jot for the religious or political issues at stake but choosing the side he believed most likely to pay him best, he barely spoke a word of Arabic. He considered it an ugly tongue, one beneath his dignity. He soon realized, however, that his ignorance was a great disadvantage since men around him could converse without him having the first idea what they were saying. So he began to study the language. His endeavours had continued during his convalescence so that it was now no difficulty for him to comprehend the Maharajah Sadiq Khan Jahan when the latter said, 'I must congratulate you, your lordship, on your remarkable recovery. I confess, I had not believed you would ever rise from your bed. But now just look at you.'

46

In his pomp, the Buzzard had been a master of sly condescension and insincere compliments and he was not inclined to believe that the haughty figure before him meant a single one of his honeyed words. The contrast between the Indian prince in his silk and gold-threaded finery, dripping with more jewels than a king's mistress, and the Buzzard, a decrepit, one-armed Caliban, with his skin like pork crackling and a face uglier than any gargoyle ever sculpted was simply too great to be bridged by words. But the Buzzard was a beggar and could not afford to be a chooser, so he gave a little nod of his head and wheezed, 'You're too kind, your royal highness.'

And, in all truth, his recovery, however partial it might be, was indeed the product of an extraordinary effort of will. The Buzzard had lain in bed and made an inventory of his body, concentrating on those parts of it that still functioned at least moderately well. His legs had not been broken, and though they were covered with burns and scar tissue, the muscles beneath the ravaged skin seemed to be capable of supporting and moving his body. Likewise, though his left arm was no more, his right arm was still whole and his hand could still grasp, so he might yet hold a sword again one day. He had the sight of one eye and hearing in one ear. He could no longer chew properly and his digestion seemed to have become unduly sensitive so that he could only eat food that had already been broken down into a soft, mushy porridge. But it was enough that he could still eat at all, and if his food was nothing more than a bland, tasteless porridge, it hardly mattered, since his tongue seemed unable to distinguish flavour any more, no matter how much salt, sugar or spice was added.

Above all, however, the Buzzard's mind was still sound. He had suffered terrible headaches and the pain in every part of his body – including, strangely, those that no longer existed –

was unrelenting. Still he was able to think, and plan, and calculate, and hate.

It was that hatred above all that drove him on. It had forced him to keep getting up when at first, unused to the imbalance of his body, he kept falling. It drove him through gruelling physical activities, in particular the building up of his surviving arm's strength by the repeated lifting of a sack of millet, procured from Jahan's kitchens, when with every single breath he took the air cut through his throat and lungs like caustic acid.

The black, burning fire in the Buzzard's soul seemed to fascinate Jahan. 'Please, don't let me interrupt you. Pray continue with your exertions,' he said, and stepped right up to his guest, making no effort to disguise the mix of revulsion and fascination he felt in the presence of such a foul and monstrous distortion of a man.

The Buzzard felt Jahan's lordly eye upon him and the urge to defy him drove him on. He lifted the sack, which he held in his hand by the neck, again and again, though his exhausted muscles and scorched chest begged him to stop. He was feeling faint, lathered in a film of pus and bloodstained sweat and on the point of collapse when there was a knock on the door and one of Jahan's functionaries entered. The man was unable to conceal the shock on his face when he set eyes on the Buzzard, who was bent almost double, his one good hand resting on his knee and his back heaving up and down. But he re-gathered his composure and spoke to Jahan. 'There is a man at the gate who insists that you wish to see him, your sublime excellency. He says his name is Ahmed and he is a leather worker. It seems he has finished the task you set for him. When I asked him to explain himself he refused, claiming that you had sworn him to secrecy.'

Jahan smiled. 'That is indeed true. Send him in.' Then he bestowed a particularly condescending smile upon the Buzzard, and said, 'I have brought you a small gift, your lordship. Just a miserable thing, but I believe it may be of interest.'

William Grey, His Majesty's Consul to the Sultanate of Zanzibar, stood in the line of supplicants waiting to plead their case outside Maharajah Sadiq Khan Jahan's palace, cursing the bad luck and even worse judgement that had brought him to this intolerable situation. Through all his years in Zanzibar, Grey had been welcomed as an honoured guest by Jahan, as he was by far the most powerful, wealthy and influential members of Zanzibar society. For Grey was not only the representative of one of Europe's greatest monarchs, he was also a convert to Islam, a change of faith that had brought him much favour and granted him access to places and people beyond the reach of any Christian. Then that conniving Scots rogue Angus Cochran, titled the Earl of Cumbrae, but more aptly nicknamed the Buzzard, had arrived in Zanzibar, closely followed by an arrogant young pup called Henry Courtney, whereupon the life of ease and privilege that Grey had constructed over many years had fallen apart in the matter of a few short months.

It had all begun with the Buzzard pestering Grey to use his influence to obtain him a commission to fight for the Sultan of Oman against the Emperor of Ethiopia. The piratical Scot planned on growing rich in war booty taken from the Christians and was happy to pay the very reasonable fee Grey charged for his services. To give the Buzzard his due, he had kept his word. The moment the Letter of Marque was placed in his hands he set sail for the Horn of Africa and set to work on the task for which he had been commissioned.

Five weeks later, young Courtney arrived, apparently eager to join the struggle against Ethiopia and, like the Buzzard, he also purchased a Letter of Marque. Not surprisingly, Courtney was eager to hear all he could about the war and had been fascinated to discover that the Earl of Cumbrae was also playing his part. Grey had not given Courtney's interest in the earl a second thought. Why should he? The Muslim cause was about to receive a second heavily armed warship, with which it would exert total control over all the waters between Arabia and the coast of Africa. As the man who had helped procure the ships, Grey would be held in greater esteem than ever.

In the event, however, Courtney had weighed anchor and chased after the Scotsman without so much as a by your leave, sneaking away like an ungrateful, deceitful, two-faced traitor and fighting for the Ethiopian emperor and his general Nazet. It transpired that his real intent all along had been the pursuit of vengeance against the Buzzard, whom he held responsible for his own father's death. A short while later news had reached Zanzibar that Courtney had found the Scotsman and engaged him in battle. The story went that the Buzzard, fighting till the last, had been burnt alive and gone down with his ship, the *Gull of Moray*.

In the old days, Grey would have been able to confirm the veracity of this account and uncover a great deal more information to which the common herd were not privy. But this was no longer possible, for Courtney had taken to harassing, capturing and sinking Arab vessels up and down the Red Sea, to the consternation of the men who owned the stricken vessels and could no longer profit from their cargoes. These men now held Grey at least partially responsible for their losses and shunned him accordingly.

Every door in Zanzibar, or at least every door that mattered, had been slammed in his face and Grey now knew no more than the lowliest guttersnipe or coffee-shop gossip. All he could do was keep coming here, to the maharajah's palace, in the hope that one day his serene, magnificent and merciful highness Sadiq Khan Jahan would show compassion for his plight and allow him to plead his case. Grey looked ahead of him in the queue and saw Osman, a procurer of women and small boys with whom he had once done regular business. But he'd not laid hands on one of Osman's pretty little fancies, male or female, in months. Osman – a mere flesh-peddler! – had given him a regretful shrug and said he could no longer be seen to do business with a man of Grey's reputation.

Grey seethed as he watched Osman gossiping with one of the guards at the gate. The press of people, the clamour of their pleading voices and the smell of their unwashed bodies combined to form an unbearable assault on his senses. Grey had long lived in the tropics and affected Arab dress as well as religion, for long flowing robes were more comfortable by far than the heavy coats of thick wool that most Englishmen insisted on wearing, as if entirely indifferent to their geographical and climatic circumstances. Nonetheless, he was perspiring like a pig on a spit and his temperature rose still higher when he saw a leather-peddler he knew, Ahmed by name, given the sign to enter the palace. Ahmed was carrying a large box, similar to the ones ladies used to convey their headgear. Grey paid it no mind.

A few minutes later, another of the palace functionaries appeared at the gate and had a word with one of the guards. At once three men were despatched into the crowd, beating men and women out of the way with long wooden staffs as they forced their way through the mob. With a start Grey realized that they were heading directly for him. He panicked and

51

tried to get away but the sheer press of bodies was so heavy that he could not force his way through and suddenly he was not only sweating like a pig but squealing like one too as he was grabbed by the arms and half-dragged, half-carried up to the gates and then through them before being deposited unceremoniously on the ornately tiled floor.

Grey rose to his feet to find the same official who had summoned Ahmed standing close by. 'If you will come this way, *effendi*, His Excellency, in his great wisdom and mercy, wishes to speak to you.'

As he followed the official along a cool, shaded cloister, through which he could see the waters of a fountain glittering in the noonday sun, Grey realized that the three guards who had been sent to fetch him were following close behind. They no longer carried their staffs, but each bore a wickedly curved scimitar tucked into his scarlet waistband.

It struck Consul Grey that the invitation to an audience with the maharajah might not turn out to be quite the blessing he'd been hoping for.

T he Buzzard might not have many of his senses in full working order, but he was still perfectly capable of smelling a rat when one went by right under his nose. That heathen bastard Jahan was up to something, he was sure of it, but what? And how in heaven's name did an insignificant little man who worked in leather fit into the maharajah's plans?

Before the question could be answered there was a knocking on the door. Jahan called out, 'Enter!' and who should step into the room, looking like a huge jellied pudding, trembling with fear, but His Majesty's Consul in Zanzibar himself. The Buzzard waited while his fellow Briton bowed and scraped to the maharajah and then rasped, 'Good morning, Mr Grey. Hadn't expected to clap an eye on you again.'

The Buzzard was becoming used to the successive expressions

of shock, disgust and barely suppressed nausea (or even expressed nausea in some extreme cases) that his appearance provoked. But Grey's discomfiture was even more absolute than most. His mouth opened and closed wordlessly as he searched in vain for something remotely appropriate to say before he finally gasped, 'But . . . But . . . You're supposed to be dead.'

The Buzzard stretched the remains of his lips into something approximating a smile. 'Evidently I am not. Apparently the Almighty still has plans for me in this world, rather than the next.'

'Truly, Allah is all-knowing and merciful,' said Grey, darting a glance at Jahan to see whether his piety had been appreciated.

It was the maharajah who spoke next. 'Now that you two gentlemen have become reacquainted, let me explain the purpose of this audience. I shall start by saying this: I hold the pair of you personally responsible for the insufferable loss of life and the damage and loss of property caused to our people's shipping by that filthy infidel Henry Courtney. It is my fervent desire, and that of my brother the Grand Mogul himself, to seek vengeance in the fullest measure against Courtney and his men. We find ourselves, however, in a quandary.

'My brother is currently concluding an agreement with the East India Company, concerning trade between our lands in India and the kingdom of England. He believes that such an agreement will deliver enormous rewards and he naturally does not wish to endanger the prospect of great riches by conducting a public campaign against one of His Majesty the King of England's subjects, particularly one who comes from an eminent family.'

'The Courtneys, eminent?' the Buzzard thought to himself. 'That'll come as a shock tae all the lords and ladies who've never even heard of 'em!'

'As a result, we must seek retribution with discretion and

54

subtlety, using proxies who can act as figureheads for our venge- ance. And who could be better suited to that role than two men such as yourselves? You both have very good reason to hate Captain Courtney. You know something of this man and how he thinks and you must, I am sure, be keen to atone for your own recent failings, for which many a ruler less merciful than myself might very well have you both executed.'

'Does your royal highness wish us to kill Captain Courtney ourselves?' Grey asked, in tones of barely disguised alarm.

'Well, perhaps not with your own blades, no,' Jahan reassured him. 'I fear you would prove no match for him, Consul, and as for the earl here, he was unable to best Courtney with two hands, so I hardly give him much chance with one. But I feel certain that you can devise a way to bring him down. You can find him and trap him, even if others must come in for the kill. And you can then take responsibility for his execution, for who would not agree that you had reason to take his life after the deception with which he tricked you, Consul Grey, or the hideous *djinn* into which he transformed you, my poor Earl of Cumbrae.'

'And if we do not agree tae pursue him for you?' the Buzzard asked.

Jahan laughed. 'Come now, of course you will agree! In the first place I am offering you all the resources of men and equip- ment you need for the vengeance you desire above all else. And in the second, both you and Consul Grey will die here, in this building, on this day if you do not agree to my terms. I am a merciful man. But I will not be wronged a second time and let that insult go unpunished.'

Grey threw himself to the floor and abased himself in a grovelling *salaam*. 'Your highness is too kind, too merciful for a wretch like me. I am honoured and grateful beyond all telling for the chance to serve you in this way.'

'Yes, yes, Consul, thank you, but please, stand on your own two feet like a man,' Jahan replied. Then he looked at the Buzzard. 'And you?'

'Aye, I'll do it. I'll even tell you where the conniving sod's bound for too, because there'll only be one place he'll want to go.'

'All in due course,' Jahan said. 'First however, it has struck me, Cumbrae, watching you in recent weeks, that your skin must now be especially sensitive. You will not, I believe, be able to survive exposure either to our burning sun, or the winds and spray that will buffet you should you ever step aboard a ship. I have therefore commissioned a form of headgear that will protect you.'

He clapped his hands and at once Ahmed the leather merchant opened his box and pulled out what looked to the Buzzard like some kind of leather cap, or hood. There was a design upon it, too, but the way that Ahmed was holding it made it impossible for him to work out exactly what it was.

Ahmed now approached the Buzzard, his eyes cast down at the floor as he walked, as if he were too terrified even to glance at the face of the monster before him. When the leather merchant reached the Buzzard a new problem presented itself: he was a good head shorter than the Scotsman. Ahmed looked imploringly at Jahan who nodded and said, 'Be so good as to bow your head, Cumbrae.'

'I'll bow tae no man!' the Buzzard rasped.

'Then you will lose it.' Jahan paused and then went on in a conciliatory tone, 'Please do not force my hand. Bow your head and let this craftsman do his work and I will reward you with everything you need to gain the revenge you so desperately crave. Defy me and you will die. So, what will it be?'

The Buzzard bowed his head. A moment later he winced

and then cried out in pain despite himself as the leather hood was pulled over his raw skin and worked into position. The Buzzard now found himself looking out at the world through a single eye hole, cut into the leather, which was fitted tight, in fact almost moulded to the shape of his face. He could breathe through two more openings beneath his nostrils, but so far as he could tell, the whole of his head was covered except for his mouth. A moment later, even that freedom was curtailed, for Ahmed brought up another flap of leather. Part of it was formed into a cup that fitted around the Buzzard's chin. There was a gap between the flap and the rest of the mask just wide enough to allow him to move his mouth a little. The Buzzard felt a tugging to one side of his face as the flap was tightened and then he heard a click that sounded very much like the closing of a padlock. Yes, he could feel the weight of it now.

The Buzzard felt a sudden surge of alarm, verging on panic. He jerked his head up and with his one good arm lashed out at Ahmed, knocking him to the ground. Before he could make another move, the soldiers raced across the floor and one of them grabbed his right arm and forced it up behind his back, until the Buzzard had no option but to bend his body and head down.

Once more he felt the tradesman's nimble fingers, as a broad leather collar was placed around his throat and, like the mask, padlocked. The Buzzard heard Jahan say, 'Mr Grey, be so good, if you will, as to carry the looking glass that is lying on that table to your right over to your fellow countryman. I'm sure the earl would like to see how he looks now.'

'M-m-must I . . . ?' Grey stammered.

'Please,' Jahan said, with cold-blooded calm, 'do not oblige me to remind you of the alternative should you refuse.'

The Buzzard heard Grey's shuffling footsteps coming towards him and then the soldier let go of his arm and he was able to straighten his body. As he lifted his head, the Buzzard's eyes were directly level with the mirror, barely two paces away from him. He saw what the world would see and now it was his turn to cry out in revulsion at what confronted him.

His head was entirely enclosed in leather the colour of a tarred ship's plank. Crude stitches of leather thread held the various pieces of the mask together and formed the sharply angled eyebrows that gave the impression of eyes set in a furious, piercing stare. To make the effect even more shocking, the blank eye was painted with white and black paint to look as though it was open and all-seeing, while the hole through which the Buzzard now gained his pitifully limited view of the world appeared to be a blank, blind void. The nose was a predatory beak, a hand span long, that thrust from his face in a cruel visual pun on his Buzzard nickname. Further stitches shaped the mask's mouth into a permanently manic grin, made all the more ghastly by the jagged white teeth, with pitch black gaps between them that had been painted around the orifice through which he was expected to speak, eat and drink.

The Buzzard had once seen a mask like this hanging from the wall in a Portuguese slaver's house. He had got it from the witch doctor of some tribe deep in the hinterland of Musa bin Ba'ik. Now this was his face . . . The Buzzard could not bear it.

Crying out in pain and frustration he clawed at the padlocks on the side of his head and neck, as if his few remaining fingers could break through the iron that bound him, and as he did so he encountered one last humiliation: a metal ring, attached to his collar, underneath his chin. He at once knew what it meant. If he displeased Jahan, or tried to escape, he could be chained to a wall, or dragged through the streets like nothing more than the lowliest pack animal or whipped dog.

The Buzzard fell to his knees, a broken man. He had survived burning and near-drowning. He had clung to life when the ocean and the sun had done their best to destroy him. He had endured pain beyond any mortal man's comprehension and the looks of disgust from all who laid eyes on him. But this was the final straw.

Now Jahan came across and crouched down on his haunches beside the Buzzard and held out a metal cup, decorated with exquisite patterns of dark blue, turquoise and white enamel. Speaking as softly as he might to a frightened, angry young horse who had just felt a saddle on his back for the first time, he said, 'Here, this is sweet, fresh sherbet. Drink.'

The Buzzard took the cup and drew it up to his mouth. He tilted it to drink and the cup banged against his leather beak, so that none of the liquid could escape it. He turned his head to one side and tried to pour the sherbet into his mouth but it just spilled across his mask and not a drop fell into his mouth. He nodded and bobbed his beaky mask into every position he could think of, but he could not find a way to drink.

As they watched this performance the other men in the room were first intrigued and then amused. Grey could not help himself. He gave an effeminate titter that set off the guards, and even Jahan, so that the room soon echoed to the sounds of their laughter that quite drowned out the Buzzard's screams of impotent rage. Finally he threw the cup away and the clatter it made as it skimmed across the marble floor silenced the other men. Jahan spoke again, 'Know this, you who used to be a lord and a ship's captain. You have ceased to be a man. Stand, and I will show you how you will be given water to drink.'

Jahan clapped and a black African servant came into the room bearing a copper jug with a long spout of the sort used to water plants. The servant approached the Buzzard with wide-eyed horror on his face and, holding the jug as far away from himself as he possibly could, lifted it and poked the spout into the mask's mouth hole. The Buzzard's lips took the spout between them and he drank the cool water with pathetic eagerness and gratitude until Jahan clapped again and the spout was withdrawn.

'You will be fed and watered by slaves, for whom the duty will be a form of punishment. When you walk through the streets women will turn their heads away from you for fear of what they see. Children who misbehave will be told stories of how you will come in the night to seize them unless they change their ways. Young men who wish to prove their courage will dare one another to throw rotten vegetables at you, until one of them is foolish enough to do so and is executed by my men for his impertinence. And then the people will truly fear and hate you.

'But next to yours their hatred will be as a grain of sand is to a mighty desert. For your whole being will be consumed by hate. And because you hate, and because I alone can offer you the chance to satisfy that hate, you will serve me.

'As for you, Mr Grey . . .' and now Jahan's voice became cold and hard as he looked at the consul, 'you will leave my house and you will not come back, ever again, unless it is with Henry Courtney's head upon a platter, or the means to destroy him in your possession. Bring me either of those things and your previous standing here will be restored and enhanced, so that you will enjoy honour amongst my people once again. Until then, however, you will be counted a pariah. Now begone!'

The Buzzard almost managed a smile to match the one on his mask as he watched the downcast Grey make his exit. Then Jahan turned back to him and said, 'It occurred to me just now that you are a eunuch, and so I will grant you a special favour that I would never bestow on any man who was complete. You may accompany me as I have dinner with my favourite concubines. They are creatures of flawless beauty, plucked from India, from Persia, from the Russian steppes and even one seized from a fishing village on the coast of your own island. They will all be fascinated to meet you. I dare say the braver ones will even wish to handle you, just to see if you are real. Of course, you may not touch them, nor eat my food, nor sup my drink. But you can be present and feast your one true eye on the treats laid out before you. And on the day that Henry Courtney dies, I will give you the choice of any woman in my harem and you may do whatever you wish with her, anything at all. So think on that, why don't you, when they are petting you this evening. Imagine how you will find a way to satisfy your desires. And ask yourself whether any of these women, as lovely as they are, could ever bring you quite as much pleasure as watching Captain Courtney die.'

Three days later, the Buzzard was commanded to make his first expedition into the outside world. Dressed in a hooded black *djellaba* he was walked down to the docks and back, escorted by six of Jahan's men, whose job was both to protect their charge and to ensure that he did not escape. They were specifically instructed to march sufficiently far apart so that all whom the Buzzard passed were afforded a good look at him.

Exactly as Jahan had predicted, the masked man's appearance caused something close to panic among the people thronging the narrow streets of Zanzibar. Women turned away and covered their children's eyes. Men spat on the ground as he passed, or held up blue *nazar* amulets to ward off the evil eye that gazed so balefully from the leather face. Finally, as they were walking through a square ringed by shops and eating houses, one hot-blooded young daredevil reached down into the open sewer that ran down one side of the square and with his left hand – the one he used for wiping his backside – picked up and threw a mass of foul-smelling excrement at the Buzzard. Whether by good aim or good luck the noxious projectile flew between the guards, and hit the Buzzard on the left side of his body, just where his arm should have been. At once two of the guards darted into the crowd and seized the young man before he had a chance to make good his escape. He was dragged, screaming insults and curses to the middle of the street, where the commander of the detachment was standing, his scimitar drawn, waiting to carry out Jahan's orders that anyone who assaulted the Buzzard in any way should be subject to instant, public execution.

When the culprit drew near it became clear that he was no more than fourteen or fifteen years old, a hot-headed lad who'd acted in youthful high spirits without giving the slightest thought to the consequences. The commander hesitated. He was a decent man with a son of his own and he did not want to deprive another man's family of their boy, simply for expressing the disgust that everyone – the commander included – felt in the presence of the masked man.

The Buzzard noted the commander's hesitancy. He could hear the first, nervous cries for mercy coming up from the crowd. Every instinct told him that this was a crucial moment: one that might determine whether he was seen as a monster to be feared or a freak to be pitied, and of the two he knew exactly which he preferred.

'Give me your sword,' he growled at the commander, then reached out with his right hand and ripped it from the man's grasp before he had a chance to argue.

The beak and the glaring eyes turned their predatory gaze on the two soldiers who were holding the boy. 'You two, tie his hands behind his back!' the Buzzard commanded. 'And look sharp or I swear the maharajah will hear of it.'

The men, who looked almost as frightened as their captive, immediately did as they were told. The Buzzard heard one of them apologizing to the boy and begging for his forgiveness. 'Silence!' he rasped.

A heavy weight of bitter resentment settled over the watching throng, but no one said a word as the boy was bound and then forced to his knees. All his adolescent bravado had vanished and he was just a fearful, weeping child as one of the soldiers forced his head down so that the back of his neck was exposed.

The Buzzard looked down at the boy's bare, brown skin, raised the scimitar and swung it down as hard as he could.

He missed the neck.

Instead the blade sliced into the top of the boy's back between his shoulder blades. A terrible, high-pitched wail of pain echoed around the square. The Buzzard tugged on the blade that was stuck between two vertebrae, forced it free and swung again, hitting the neck this time, but failing to sever it.

Three more blows were required and the boy was already dead – a corpse held in place by the two soldiers – before his head finally dropped from his shoulders onto the dusty ground. The Buzzard stepped back, his chest heaving, and looked right around the square, turning through three hundred and sixty degrees as he surveyed the scene and all the people in it, basking in the fear and hostility he saw on every face. Then he ordered the commander of the guards, 'Take me back tae the palace,' and as the soldiers reformed the escort around him he thought to himself, *Aye, that'll do it. I believe I've made my point.*

A ship's captain had to be on duty, or ready to be summoned by those who were, at any hour of day or night. Once Hal had set to sea, he did not allow Judith's presence to distract him from his responsibility to his ship and all who sailed in her. To do so would have been to take undue liberties with the admiration and affection his crew felt for him. Nor would Judith have allowed it. She knew what it was to be a leader and would not have wanted to come between Hal and his duties, nor would she have respected him if he had allowed that to happen.

But if there was one hour of the twenty-four in each day that they could dedicate to one another, rather than anything or anyone else, it was the one that preceded the dawn. This was the time when the ship seemed at its quietest, when the sea and wind were most often at their calmest and when they could take advantage of the peace and the silence to express, whether in words, or actions, or both, their love for one another.

Hal could never sate his desire for Judith. He loved the moment when he thrust into her, plunging so deep that he could hardly tell where his body ended and hers began, fusing as one being and experiencing the same ecstatic moment of release with such intensity that for that one blissful moment there was nothing and no one in the whole universe but them. And yet for all that shared passion, there was no moment more soothing to Hal's heart than waking to see Judith still asleep, her lovely face just visible in the darkness of the cabin, her breathing soft and gentle. There was something so peaceful about her, so trusting. She felt completely safe with him, and the depth of her trust and love for him filled Hal with a desire to keep her and protect her for as long as he lived.

One morning, however, when they were eight days and around a thousand miles out of Mitsiwa, heading almost due south along the east coast of Africa, rarely more than thirty miles or so from land, Hal was awoken by a groaning sound. When he opened his eyes, Judith was not lying peacefully beside him but was curled up, with her back towards him and her knees pulled tight to her chest. From the noises she was making, she was in a great deal of physical distress.

'My darling, are you all right?' Hal asked, unable to keep the alarm from his voice.

'It will pass,' she replied, but then her body shook and she retched convulsively, though nothing but sound came out of her mouth.

'You're sick,' he said, stating the obvious. He put a hand to her forehead. 'You feel hot. Do you have a fever?'

Judith swallowed hard then rolled over so that she was facing him. She propped herself up on one elbow and laid her other

66

hand on Hal. 'Don't be worried, my love. I'm not sick. Far from it. Indeed, I have never in my life been more healthy.'

Hal took the hand she had placed on him and held it tight. 'Please, my darling, do not feel that you have to reassure me. You're so brave, but . . .'

'Shh . . .' she hushed him. 'I promise you, there is no need to be alarmed.' She managed a faint smile. 'Not unless you are troubled by the thought of impending fatherhood.'

'Impending . . . what?' he gasped. 'Do you . . . I mean are you . . . ?'

'Yes, my darling, I am with child. I am going to have a baby, your baby . . . our baby.'

'That's wonderful news!' Hal exulted, and then he seemed stricken by doubt. 'But are you sure? How do you know?'

'Because we were together more than two months ago for the council of war, if you remember . . .'

'Oh, I remember perfectly, believe me!'

'Well, since that time I have not bled and now I feel sick in the mornings. If I were at home, my mother and my aunts and all the women of the family would be telling me what I am telling you.' She gave a contented little laugh. 'Perhaps I will have a son who is as strong, and handsome and kind as you.'

'Or a daughter as beautiful, and loving and as brave as you.'

For a moment they basked in the glow that lovers know when they are young and in love and have just accomplished the miracle that is the most ancient and universal of all human accomplishments and yet for two people is also the newest and most unique. And then Hal started, almost as if he had been shocked or stung, and turned his head away from Judith. He stared out into the darkness beyond the cabin windows, his ears pricked, his nose sniffing the air like a hunting dog that has caught the scent of his prey.

67

'What's the matter, my love?' Judith asked. 'Is something troubling you? Have no fear, I will keep our baby safe inside me. All will be well.'

'No, it's not that,' Hal replied. 'Something else.'

He rose from the bed and dressed hurriedly, pulling on shoes and breeches and leaving his shirt unfastened as he bent down to kiss Judith's forehead. 'I just want to check something. Don't worry, it's probably nothing.' Seeing her anxious face Hal grinned reassuringly. 'It's wonderful news about the baby. I love you with all my heart. And I'll be back here with you in a trice.'

As he headed up to the quarterdeck, Hal's mind snapped free of the bedchamber and concentrated instead on his captain's duty.

Two days earlier, a lookout had spotted a Dutch caravel, several miles off to starboard. For the rest of the day, the Dutchman had come in and out of sight as the wind and visibility changed, so that it had seemed as though the *Golden Bough* were being tracked. At a time of war, this would be an alarming turn of events. The caravel in itself was smaller than the *Bough* and no threat to her safety, but Hal would be bound to wonder what other, more powerful vessels might be lurking out of sight, over the horizon. But England and Holland had been at peace for over a year, so there was no cause to be worried. Furthermore, when dawn had broken the following day, the caravel had disappeared. Yet still a nagging suspicion had played at the back of his mind, a seaman's instinct that told him to be on his guard.

Now that same instinct had tugged at Hal again. Something told him, and for all the world he could not be certain what it might be, that the Dutchman was still out there. He would not be able to rest easy until he was sure of what the captain of that mysterious caravel was up to.

Hal emerged on deck to be greeted by something close to serenity. The wind was little more than the most gentle of breezes, and the silvery light of the moon was reflected in the still, glassy waters. Across the deck lay the scattered, sleeping forms of the Amadoda warriors, who always passed the night in the open air rather than endure the filth and stench below decks. Ned Tyler was at the helm and he nodded a greeting to his captain. 'What brings you up here so early, Cap'n?' he asked. 'Can't believe you're tiring of the company in your cabin.'

Hal chuckled. 'No chance of that. I just had a fancy that the Dutchman was still out there.'

'There's not been a sound out of young Tom, sir. And he's a good lad. Not like him to sleep on duty.'

Tom Marley was a spotty, jug-eared lad, the youngest member of the crew and the subject of much good-natured teasing. But Hal agreed he had the makings of a decent seaman. 'Get him down here, if you will, Mr Tyler.'

'Aye-aye, sir.'

Ned looked up towards the top of the mainmast and gave a short, piercing whistle. Tom Marley immediately waved back, whereupon Ned gestured to him to get down on deck. Marley began descending the rigging with a fearless speed and agility that reminded Hal of the time, not so very long ago, when he was up and down to the crow's nest at his father's behest, several times a day.

The lad reached the deck, ran across to where Hal and Ned were standing and stood straight up, his hands behind his back, looking nervous.

'It's all right, Tom, you've not done anything wrong,' said Hal and the boy's shoulders relaxed as the tension left his body. 'I just want to know if you've spotted anything recently, like that Dutchman that was following us two days ago, for example.'

Tom shook his head decisively. 'No sir, I ain't seen nothing like that Dutchman, nor any other ship neither. And I've kept my eyes open, Captain. I've not been dozing off or nothing.'

'I'm sure you haven't. Now, Cook should be up by now, you run along and get something to eat.'

'But my watch ain't finished yet, sir.'

'Don't worry,' Hal said, suddenly feeling an urge to see for himself for once, rather than rely on others as a captain so often had to do.

'You sure it's a good idea you going back up there, Cap'n?' Ned asked. 'Been a while.'

'Are you suggesting I can't still get up there faster than any man on this ship?'

'No sir, wouldn't dream of it.'

'Well, watch me and I'll show you.'

And with that, Hal ran to the mast, grabbed a rope and started clambering up the rigging, past the limp, windless sails towards the inky sky above.

Pett was hungry. Of course, everyone aboard was hungry. The ship's decks and even the bilges had been scoured for rats to eat. Any gulls that were foolish enough to land on deck or perch in the rigging were greeted with volleys of stones, small pieces of shot, or anything else anyone could grab and throw that might kill or stun a bird. Playful dolphins that swam alongside the boat found themselves attacked by the ship's smaller guns and any shots that managed to hit their targets were swiftly followed by splashes as the crew's best swimmers dived into the water to retrieve the corpses before the sea of nearby sharks could take them.

Pett's hunger, however, was of a different kind. He'd spent the past week locked in a dark, stinking, rat-infested cockpit on the orlop deck. He had assured the ship's captain that he was a senior official of the British East India Company and demanded to be treated as a gentleman, but the man had refused to listen, insisting that this imprisonment was for Pett's own safety.

'You must understand that it is not long since my men were fighting the British, so they have no great love for your people,' the captain had said, with a regretful shrug of the shoulders. 'They are also starving and so desperate for food that they might resort to – how shall I say? – inhuman methods to find it. You should count yourself lucky, sir, that I gave the order to have you rescued. Many of my men were very displeased by that decision. They did not like the idea of adding another mouth to feed. Forgive me; I made a foolish jest: I said that if they did not like you, they could eat you. It is my honest fear that some of them might have taken me at my word.'

Since then, Pett had survived on what amounted to barely starvation rations. His body, already thin, was becoming close to skeletal. But he was never a man who possessed the slightest interest in or appreciation for the pleasures of the dinner table, so a lack of decent meals was no loss to him. No, he suffered from another hunger, that which clawed at his guts when the voices called him, the Saint's voice above all, imploring him to do God's will by scouring the world of sin and the impure souls who perpetrated it. Pett could never be sure when the voices would come. Sometimes, months would pass without a single visit, but there were also times like this when the clamour in his head would barely die down at all from one day or even week to the next: always the voices, shouting at him, imploring him, repeating again and again the same implacable commandment: *thou shalt kill.*

Yet there could be no candidates for his deliverance as long as he was locked away in this solitary confinement. And then the Saint, as he always did, provided the means of Pett's salvation. He was an emaciated, thirst-ravaged member of the crew. His crime, so far as Pett could gather, was that he stole one of the very last crusts of stale bread from the locked chest in the captain's quarters. The man was delirious. He must have been, Pett thought, to have thought he could possibly succeed in his theft when the only way of opening the chest in which the precious crumbs were located was to blow the lock off with a pistol shot that could be heard from one end of the ship to the other.

Or perhaps the man just didn't care. For twelve hours he had sat opposite Pett, occasionally breaking into rambling, slurred, incomprehensible speeches before falling into an uneasy slumber, during which he still cried out in tones of rage and alarm, though he remained asleep all the while. Pett would long since have despatched him into a silent, eternal slumber were not both men chained to iron rings set in the ship's hull with a good ten-foot span of filth-encrusted planks between them.

Pett's chain, attached to another ring round his ankle, was just five feet long, making it almost impossible for him to reach the other man and strike a fatal blow. But he felt entirely confident that the Saint would not have brought him the man without providing the means with which to send him from this world to the next. Sure enough, events were moving in Pett's direction for the ship's company – or at least a goodly portion of it – appeared to be setting off on an expedition. The ship's walls made it hard to work out exactly what was being said, but one message came through above all others: this was a do-or-die attempt to seize more supplies. Orders were barked and passed on. There was much bustle, movement and all the noise that one would associate with a group of men preparing for an important endeavour.

Eventually Pett heard boats being lowered, along with muffled demands for silence. Wherever they were going, clearly they did not wish to alert anyone to their movements. But no sooner had the boats set off from the ship than those who had been left behind settled down to what sounded like heated debates, presumably about the likely outcome of the expedition. No matter: the key point was that they were not paying the slightest attention to William Pett, or his cell companion.

He thus had the perfect opportunity to take action without being interrupted in his labours. That was why he was already on the move. Slowly for the first few inches, silent as a leopard in the dark, ignoring the cramping pain in his limbs from long confinement.

Pett made every effort to remain completely silent as he moved, so it could only have been pure chance that his intended victim chose this precise moment to awaken. He stared at Pett for a second or two, evidently trying to make sense of his sudden appearance in the middle of the floor, realized he was in danger and scrambled away in the gloom, extending his chain as far away from Pett as possible. The man's irons rattled and terror made the whites of his eyes glow against the blackness as he shouted for help, throwing himself back against the damp plank walls, somehow knowing that the other man meant to kill him.

Pett kept moving. He had almost reached his fear-stricken target, but then his leg chain pulled taut. He cursed and threw himself forward, stretched like a striking mamba, and managed to grab hold of the other man's foot. The man kicked and convulsed but Pett clung on, taking blows to the face which he did not feel, and hauled the man towards him, inch by inch. The man tried to seize hold of the deck itself, to dig his fingers into it like grappling hooks, but the boards were slick with rodent faeces and slime and he could get no purchase.

74

The man shrieked again, his voice breaking with terror. He cried out to God, but the Almighty was not interested – He had other plans – and the Saint and all the angels were crying out to Pett to execute them on His behalf. Now Pett's face was level with the man's stinking crotch and still he hauled as though his own life depended on it.

'Keep still and I'll make it quick,' Pett said, knowing he was wasting his breath. Frenzied, slime-fouled fingers clawed at his head and face as the man tried to push him back whence he had come. But there was no going back. Pett thrust his hands up and they found the man's throat, thumbs crushing the bony cartilage of the larynx, fingers binding at the back of his emaciated neck like the lacing on a lady's corset.

For all his lack of nourishment the jailed sailor was surprisingly strong. Years at sea, hauling on the sheets and climbing the shrouds had seen to that, and now he clawed at Pett's hands, trying to tear them away from his own neck. But William Pett was a man of experience. He had done this many, many times before and knew that he only needed to hold on a little longer. Just a little longer.

Pett was also a connoisseur, a collector of other men's deaths. In his mind he ordered them: the peaceful and the violent; the many who met their ends with terror and the very few who were composed and tranquil at the last. A less elevated distinction divided those whose bowels loosened at the moment of passing and those who remained unsullied. Had Pett given the matter the slightest thought in advance, he would have wagered that the lack of any material in a starving man's digestive system would tend to suggest a clean death. But no, though the sailor's defecation was only modest in quantity, it wanted for nothing in stench. At the very same moment, the hands on Pett's hands relaxed. The man beneath him shuddered like a spent lover and went still.

Pett held on still, gasping for breath in that dank, airless place. The dead man convulsed one last time, his heels tapping out a ragged beat against the deck, and then it was over. *You did well*, the Saint whispered in his mind. *But you are on a ship. Next time, thrust a sharp sliver of wood, or a metal pin through the ear canal into the brain. You will achieve a quick kill and no telltale signs left behind to arouse suspicion.*

The Saint was right, Pett thought, as he often was. No matter now. It was time to prepare for the moment of discovery.

He would have preferred to put the dead man up against the side and make it look as though he had died in his sleep, but Pett's chain would not let him push the body up against the far wall of the cockpit. So he rolled the body over and it lay face down in the filth, the dead man's befouled petticoat breeches the first thing anyone would see when they brought a light into the place.

Then Pett scrambled back to his own corner by the cable tier and waited.

Hal ascended the mainmast with lithe assurance. As he dropped into the bucket of the crow's nest just below the top of the mast he looked up at the thin cloud skating across the moon. His breath was a little shorter than it had been when he was a lad and making the climb to the masthead several times a day. But it was still just as much of a pleasure to drink in the cool clean air up where the breeze was an elixir, cut only with the scent of the tarred lines, the musty smell of the sail canvas and, now and then when the wind was right, the sweet, spicy aroma of the soil of Africa itself wafting across the ocean from the coast.

He peered north into the gloom for a sign of the Dutchman that had last been seen three leagues off the *Bough*'s stern. A glimpse of white caught his eye, where the cloud had torn to let the last glimmer of moonlight through. Hal knew his eyes were as good as those of any man aboard – that was one reason he had chosen to look for himself, rather than rely on another to do it – but as he searched the ocean the clouds closed ranks once more, the darkness returned and then there was nothing to be seen.

'Where are you then?' he murmured.

Dawn came, a bloodstain on the hem of night's gown as the last of the northerly played out across the canvas and the *Bough* slowed to a crawl, then drifted without purpose as she lost steerage, eventually refusing to go another yard into the south. As the sea mist settled over the surface, shrouding the ship and the waters around her in a soft blanket that muffled sound as much as it hampered vision, the *Bough* rolled gently in the swells. Hal might have been lulled to sleep like a baby in its cot had he not been startled by Ned Tyler calling up to him. The helmsman was asking permission to let go the anchor, for it was better to stay where they were than risk drifting blindly at the whim of the tides until they found themselves high and dry on a sand bar.

Hal felt a little guilty then, being up there like a young ensign instead of on the quarterdeck or the poop like the captain he was. But he refused to abandon the search just yet, not when every instinct told him it must be the Dutchman out there. She was a small caravel: three-masted and square rather than lateen-rigged. A captured prize most likely, taken from the Spanish or Portuguese Hal guessed, for it was rare to see such a ship flying Dutch colours. She would still be getting enough out of the breeze to keep her moving for she was only half the size of the *Bough*. Hal knew he had nothing to fear from such a ship, and not just because his culverins could blast her out of the water if it came to a fight.

'Damn this truce,' he whispered, narrowing his eyes as if they could somehow penetrate the mist and catch another glimpse of canvas. Peace now prevailed between the English and the Dutch, though Hal wished it did not. It had been a Dutch governor of the Cape Colony who had ordered the torture and murder of his father and Dutchmen who had followed his instructions to the brutal, gory letter. Hal longed for the legitimacy that war provided. For then he would be able to spill Dutch blood by the gallon in retribution for his father's suffering.

Suddenly he fancied he caught the Dutchman's scent in the air, a waft of fresh tar and the stale sweat of her crew, but it was gone again in a heartbeat. Aboli was right to say that Sir Francis had prepared Hal well for the responsibilities of captaining a ship. And yet there was something else too, something that even his father could not have taught him, and that was the warrior's instinct. Hal felt that coursing through him like the blood in his veins. He could, when it was called for, be a killer. That instinct had made him leave his soft bed and the beautiful woman sleeping in it to climb up there to the masthead. It was that same instinct that alerted him to the danger now.

He had not seen the first of the cloth-muffled grappling hooks that clumped onto the *Golden Bough*'s deck, but Hal saw the first dark shapes coming over the side in the mist.

'To arms! To arms!' He gave the alarm, as the first pistols spat flames which cut through the murk, briefly illuminating the faces of the men who had come to kill them. Hal was already out of the crow's nest. Down he came into the chaos that was enveloping them.

He thanked Almighty God for inducing the Amadoda tribesmen to sleep beneath the stars, for now they were leaping to their feet, seizing their weapons and hurling themselves into the fight. Faced by the tribesmen's ferocity, spears and axes, the attackers must be regretting their impertinence. But even from halfway down the mast, Hal could tell that those men clambering over the *Bough*'s gunnels were heavily armed. Each had a pistol in hand and another pair tied with cords around their necks. As Hal glanced down he saw one of the Amadoda thrown back by the force of a pistol ball that blew a hole in his naked chest. The man fell to the deck, with the whites of his eyes rolling up into his skull.

Hal jumped the last five feet to the deck. As his feet hit the planking he suddenly realized that he was unarmed. He had not thought to pick up his flintlock pistol or his sword when he left his cabin.

'Here, Gundwane!' Hal turned and caught the sabre by the hilt, nodding to Aboli who had thrown it. Then he launched himself into the chaos, slashing open a man's face, then spinning away to stab the blade deeply into another's guts.

'*Golden Bough* on me!' he shouted, and the Amadoda cheered, as they surged forward. Others of the *Golden Bough*'s crew were pouring up through the hatches.

Shoulder to shoulder Hal and Aboli hacked their way into the enemy. And yet the Dutchmen still had loaded pistols and these roared, spitting out death and disaster.

One huge Dutchman whose features were masked by a dense growth of dark beard, fired his pistol then reversed it and clubbed down the black man who opposed him. Three Amadoda went down before him but then Big Daniel was there. His sword had lodged in a dead man's shoulder, but his own raw strength was weapon enough. Daniel threw up a brawny arm to block the Dutchman's pistol, then clutched his beard in both hands and pulled its owner's face towards him as he thrust his own head forward, smashing the big man's nose with a splintering crack that Hal heard even above the din of battle.

The Dutchman staggered, blood cascading down his face and beard. Big Daniel glanced to one side, retrieved his sword from the dead man's shoulder and went at the bearded man like a butcher at a side of beef.

Hal shouted with exultation. Any advantage the Dutch may have gained with the surprise of their attack had been nullified by the speed and ferocity with which the *Bough*'s men had responded. Victory was still not entirely his, but even in his young life Hal had fought enough ship-board battles to know when the balance was shifting. One last effort and that shift would be decisive. He was about to utter his rallying cry when he heard Aboli's voice call out, 'Gundwane!'

Hal glanced across the deck and saw that Aboli was pointing with his sword aft towards the mêlée around the foot of the mizzenmast.

'No!' he told himself in despair. 'That cannot be!'

Because she felt sick, Judith climbed out of her bunk, if only to find a bedpan to vomit into. That nausea saved her life. It meant that she saw the shadowy figures emerging out of the mist and clambering up the stern of the *Golden Bough*, climbing past the windows of the captain's cabin. Then one of them braced his feet against the stern, pushed away to make the climbing rope swing out like a pendulum and smashed through the glass and into the cabin.

Judith was already waiting for him, dressed only in her night-gown but with her sword in hand. Her hesitation over what to wear to go aboard the *Bough* had saved her life, for instead of being packed in one of her trunks and stowed away in the hold, her *kaskara* sword had come with her in her travelling baggage and had been placed in her cabin.

The man who was first through the window had barely laid a toe on the cabin deck when he took the point of the *kaskara* through his throat. Judith pulled the blade away. Then as he went down she spun as nimbly as a dancer around the second boarder as he blundered past his wounded comrade. Then she aimed a savage, slashing blow across the small of his back that sliced through one of his kidneys and dropped her arm, with him writhing, screaming and bleeding at her feet.

More men were piling into the cabin now and Judith realized that she was in danger of boxing herself into a corner, for the men she'd downed had formed a barrier, partially blocking the way between her and the cabin door. She moved fast, fighting her way to the door, her sword flashing from side to side as she parried, stabbed and slashed, struggling to defend herself against the increasing number of men who now opposed her. She fended one thrust away above her left shoulder, then swung her curved sword down and across her body, back-handed, slicing deep into another man's arm, almost chopping it in two. But amidst the mayhem Judith's mind remained calm. Hard-fought experience had taught her that the key to survival was maintaining the ability to concentrate and calculate while others around were letting rage, fear or panic cloud their minds. Examine the enemy. Look him in the eyes. Read his mind.

Even as she fought for her life, Judith was doing these things, and what she saw in her enemies was desperation. These men were wild-eyed, haggard and starving. If she exchanged more than three or four clashes of the blade with any one of them she could feel his strength dissipating as the power in his sword-arm ebbed.

She was a child of Africa. She knew all about hunger and she knew a starving man when she saw one. Whoever these raiders were, they attacked with the savage frenzy of men who had nothing to lose. She heard the sound of gunfire and the shouts and screams of men in battle coming from the decks above and knew that Hal and his crew must be fighting for their lives too. They had been taken by surprise. The fate of the *Golden Bough* was hanging by a knife-edge. But if she and they could only hang on long enough for the enemy's strength to fade, they could still triumph.

And they had to win. Judith had to survive – not for herself but for the child she carried inside her. She felt a new, unfamiliar spirit surging through her, the passionate defiance of a lioness defending her cub, and she knew that she would not – could not – give in to the men confronting her. Two more of them lay dying by the time she reached the cabin door. She sprang through it, bought a couple of precious seconds as she slammed it closed behind her, dashed to the steps that would take her up on deck and scrambled up them, waiting at any second for the clamp of a man's hand around her ankle. None came. She ran out onto the quarterdeck, in the shadow of the mizzenmast and looked around to get her bearings and see how the battle stood.

Judith barely paused for a second, but that second was too long. She suddenly felt hands grab her from behind, one around her waist and the other locked around her neck. She was lifted off her feet and though she flailed her arms in a frantic attempt to retaliate against the man who had her in his grasp she could do nothing and her efforts just seemed to amuse her captor who was laughing as he shouted, '*Kapitein! Kijk eens wat ik gevonden!*'

Judith did not speak Dutch, but she could recognize the language well enough and it wasn't hard to work out that he was calling out to his captain. She knew her man well enough to know that Hal would never knowingly risk her life, not even for the *Golden Bough*. So whoever held her held the ship.

Judith's arms fell motionless by her side, she let her sword fall to the deck and her head slumped. The battle was lost and it was entirely due to her.

The battle fever was upon Hal. He had seen a tall, thin scarecrow of a man loom up behind Judith, realized she was unaware of this new threat and roared a warning but it was lost in the battle din. There were Amadoda and Dutchmen between Hal and Judith and he thrust into the press trying to force a way through, parrying sword blows aimed at him, striking back where he could and yelling to Judith in vain. But when he broke through the chaos of seething steel, flesh and pistol flame, he saw that he was too late. The man now had an arm across Judith's breast, a knife to her throat and one pox-scarred cheek pressed against the black crown of her head as though he were inhaling her perfume.

In front of them stood a man whom Hal marked as the Dutchman's captain, for he wore a silk-edged waistcoat and fine breeches rather than the canvas petticoats of most sailors. He confirmed his command by stepping forward and sweeping the broad felt hat off his head and waving it through the pistol smoke that hung over the deck. The sun had by now broken free of the eastern horizon and burned away the early morning mist and it crossed Hal's mind that had the Dutch come any later he would have killed them before they ever stepped foot aboard. Fortune had favoured the enemy, it seemed.

'Englishmen!' The Dutch captain shouted, still waving the hat above his head to catch the men's attention. 'Stop this madness! There is no need for more blood to be spilled.' His accent was thick but his English was good. 'Where is your captain?'

Hal stepped forward, his gore-slick sword still raised before him, but making no attempt to use it against his adversary. Gradually, the realization spread that the battle seemed to have ended, though the reason for it ending was not yet clear to many of the combatants. Men broke off from the fight, gasping for breath, some screaming in pain. One man held his severed left arm in his right hand and was staring at it as though unable to comprehend how it had got there.

'I am Captain Sir Henry Courtney of the *Golden Bough*,' Hal announced, pointing the sword at the Dutch captain, 'and you, sir, are a coward, to seek advantage by threatening a woman.'

The Dutchman frowned at this, then glanced behind him. 'That woman fought like a man. Perhaps we should treat her as one . . . Ach!' The captain shrugged and his face broke into a disarmingly friendly expression. 'What does it matter, eh? Let us all just stop this senseless fighting, and talk a little sense.'

Hal was gripped by indecision. He had seen his last love, Sukeena, killed by a poisoned blade when she too was with child. She and their baby had died in his arms and he would not see Judith suffer the same fate, nor let another child of his be killed before it had ever taken a single breath.

Yet how could he yield his ship and everything he and his crew had fought so hard for? What manner of captain would that make him? Instinctively he glanced up at the quarterdeck half expecting to see his father Sir Francis standing there proud and steadfast and unafraid, his hard eyes boring into him, judging Hal against his own tall measure as he had ever done.

But there was no ghost to tell Hal what to do. The *Golden Bough* was *his* ship. *He* was its captain.

'I am Captain Tromp of the *Delft* and now it seems . . .' the Dutchman said, a smile tugging the corner of his mouth '. . . of this fine ship the *Golden Bough* also.' Tromp's men cheered at this, evoking curses from the *Bough*'s crew who clamoured at their captain to be released once more to the slaughter. For still more men had come from below and now stood blinking in the dawn light, clean blades and primed pistols in their hands. One word from Hal and the *Bough*'s deck would become a slaughter yard again. But one of the corpses could easily be Judith, his love and her infant.

'We outnumber you five to one, Captain Tromp,' Hal called, trying to hide the desperation he felt for Judith, hoping she would not see it either, for it was important for a captain to appear decisive and composed.

'And yet you are not fighting,' Tromp said. 'Which tells me that you would do anything to save this woman from harm. And though I am sure that you are a gentleman, Captain, I suggest that the reason you stay your sword is not a matter of mere chivalry. She has your heart, does she not?'

Hal locked eyes with Judith and even by the early light of the dawn he could see the steel in them. She showed no sign of fear, only a cold resolve, as the pox-marked man with the knife to her throat growled obscenities in her ear.

'I do not think he will kill her, Captain,' Aboli said, breathing deeply at Hal's right shoulder. 'Because if he does then he knows he and all his men will certainly die.'

'Let us carve them up, Captain!' Robert Moone, one of the *Bough*'s boatswains, called.

'Aye, we'll feed their craven livers to the sharks!' boatswain John Lovell yelled, pointing his sword at Captain Tromp.

Hal wracked his brain, trying to find a way out of the choice that confronted him between his boat and crew on one side and his woman and child on the other.

'How can I let them hurt her, Aboli?' Hal hissed and was on the point of lowering his sword when Judith threw back her head, smashing her skull against her captor's nose like a hammer against an eggshell. He howled in pain and let her go, dropping his knife as he instinctively raised his hands to his broken nose and bloody face. In a single, flowing sequence of movements Judith broke free, picked up her sword, slashed the razor edge across the belly of the man who had grabbed her and leapt at Tromp. His attention had all been on Hal. He was slow to react to what was happening behind him. By the time he had turned round Judith had covered the ground between them, and had put the pin-sharp tip of her blade to his throat before he could raise his own sword.

Seeing this, some of the Dutchmen threw themselves at Hal's men, believing they had no choice but to fight or die, but they were cut down where they stood and the rest of Tromp's boarding party dropped to their knees and hoisted their swords and boarding axes above their heads.

'It is over, Captain,' Aboli said, stooping to saw his blade across the throat of Judith's would-be captor who now sat slumped against the *Bough*'s side, his gut ropes lying in a glistening, bloody mess between his legs.

The knowledge that Judith had been in danger, and the guilty awareness of how close he had come to surrendering his boat and with it his honour combined to drive Hal into a state of barely controlled fury. He was striding forward, ready to cut Tromp down, but Aboli gripped his shoulder with a big hand.

'It is over,' he said again. The bloodlust abated and Hal stood for a moment letting the tremble work through his arms and the big muscles in his legs. Then he walked over to Judith and Captain Tromp, who held out his sword hilt first. Judith was still holding the point of the *kaskara* at his throat.

'You have my surrender, Captain Courtney,' the Dutchman

said, looking down his nose at Hal because he dared not move his head.

'Not too soon,' Hal snarled at him, snatching the sword from his hand and passing it to Aboli behind him. 'You were a damned fool to think you could take my ship.'

Hal looked at Judith, who gave him a quick nod of the head to signal that she and her child were unhurt. There would be a time for them to hold one another tightly, to kiss and to celebrate their survival in the act of love, but this was not it.

Tromp was watching the personal dramas being played out before him, noting the connections between the big African and his captain, and between the captain and the woman who appeared so perfectly feminine and yet could fight like the fiercest trained warrior.

'I am an ambitious man, Captain Courtney,' he said, almost casually, as though ambition rather than hunger had driven him to attempt a reckless assault on a larger, better armed vessel with a much more numerous crew.

'Your ambition has cost you dear, sir,' Hal said, trying to keep a rein on his fury. In victory a true warrior must show forbearance, his father had once said. He must not give in to the base instinct for revenge. He must summon that forbearance required to show clemency. Yet even the noblest warrior was not expected to ignore wrongdoing when he saw it. 'You have broken the truce between our two countries, Captain Tromp,' Hal said, making a show of calmly pulling his sword through a handkerchief to clean the blood off it.

'There is a truce?' Tromp said, doing a passable job of seeming surprised, for the truce by now was over a year old.

'You lying cheese-head!' one of Hal's men yelled from the mainmast shrouds up which he had climbed to get a clear view of proceedings.

'Well you are not alone in wishing that there were no truce, Captain Tromp,' Hal admitted. 'I would gladly hunt Dutchmen below the Line, above the Line, and to the very gates of hell, if I only had a damned Letter of Marque. I would be the scourge of the Dutch as my father was. And I would have run you down when I first laid eyes on your ensign two days ago.'

'Then I admit I am relieved that our two countries have put aside their differences,' Tromp said with an easy-going, roguish smile that Hal suspected had put many a pretty girl deeply in his thrall.

Tromp's face was haggard with starvation, yet Hal could see that he was a handsome man, with sand-coloured hair and mariner's eyes the colour of the Indian Ocean itself. Hal was now almost certain that Aboli had been right. Tromp would have never killed Judith. The man had rolled the dice and he had lost, and now he was Hal's prisoner and by the law of the sea his ship, the *Delft*, now belonged to Hal also.

The Dutchmen had come in two pinnaces and when he examined them Hal recalled the brief whiff of tar he had smelt on the air, for they had tarred their sails black to conceal them against the night. It had been a bold move on Tromp's part and Hal almost admired the man for fighting from the front rather than sending another to lead the boarding party. They might have succeeded in capturing the *Golden Bough* by stealth, too, had the Amadoda tribesmen not leapt up from their beds on the deck and fought like panthers in the face of all that pistol fire. And then there had been Judith. If not for her bravery and martial skill Hal would have given Tromp the *Bough*, and now his heart was bursting with pride in her.

That pride only grew when he looked at his crew and saw the way they regarded Judith. They already loved her, and admired her reputation, but now that they had witnessed what she was capable of with their own eyes, she had earned their profound respect and perhaps to an extent their fear. Few of them had seen a woman fight the way she had done and word was coming up from the captain's cabin of the havoc she had wreaked upon her assailants down there, also.

'Go and rest, my love,' Hal told her while Big Daniel and Aboli oversaw the binding of Tromp and his surviving men, and another boatswain, William Stanley, had the *Bough*'s crew gather up the dead from both sides.

'I'd prayed that I would never have to kill again,' Judith said, placing a bloody hand on the swell of her belly as though she feared that their unborn child was now somehow tainted by her own actions.

'You saved the ship, my heart,' Hal said softly.

'I feared that I had lost it,' she replied. Then she looked at the Dutch prisoners, who were now being led away towards the *Bough*'s lowest decks and laid a gentle hand on Hal before she said, 'Do not harm them.'

'There will be no more killing today,' he assured her, looking to the east where the sun was a blazing orb rising above a bank of grey cloud to flood the ocean with molten gold and blood. 'Not if this Captain Tromp gives me his ship.'

'Which he will do, ma'am, don't you worry, unless he wants us to feed slices of his raw bumfiddle to the sharks,' Big Daniel said, shoving Tromp towards the steps that ran down to the bowels of the ship.

Aboli watched the defeated captain's head disappear and then, speaking in his native tongue so that the others would not hear him question their leader, asked Hal, 'What if the crew of his ship put up a fight, Gundwane? We have lost enough men today. Is she worth the loss of any more? And this wind is weaker than a warthog's fart. If she knows we are coming after her and runs it will take us a day or more to overhaul her.'

'Hmm . . .' Hal grunted, noting what Aboli had to say. But he was a predator, born, bred and raised to hunt the seas for maritime prey and he could no more turn down the prize of a ship and its cargo than a hungry lion could resist the chance of fresh meat.

'Mister Moone, strike the colours if you please!' Hal called. Then he turned to Aboli. 'I have an idea,' he said with a wolf's grin, speaking in plain English so that his crew could hear their captain and take strength from his confidence. 'Tell Daniel to bring Tromp back here. I think we'll need him topsides after all.'

Aboli, who was as pleased as anyone else on the ship to know that he had his captain back and ripe and ready for the next scrap, nodded and went to fetch the Dutchman.

The *Delft*, still lying at anchor, emerged from the dawn half-light. Ned Tyler turned the *Golden Bough*'s bows into the east so as to come up on the Dutch caravel's larboard side, thus trapping her between them and the sandbars that stood a short way offshore at the mouth of a river delta. As they drew nearer, with the *Golden Bough* making little more than two knots in a breeze so faint that he could barely feel it on the back of his neck, Hal could see a scattering of men at her gunwales and atop the mizzen. A few more were up the rigging, ready to scramble out along the yards to release the sails. Clearly Tromp had left only a skeleton crew behind when he set off on his expedition to capture the *Bough*.

They were crouching under the forecastle bulwarks, Hal with his flintlock primed and his sword, only recently cleansed of the blood it had gathered earlier in the morning, in his right hand.

'Aye, well our naked ensign staff should help ease their minds,' Big Daniel replied, just as quietly. 'They'll reckon their skipper won the ship an' struck our colours.'

There were just a few of the *Bough*'s men still on deck, and most of those were doing their best to avoid detection. As for the rest, Hal had ordered them to stay below, as if confined there as Tromp's prisoners, until he gave the word. Tromp himself stood eight paces aft of Hal with his left hand gripping the rail at the foremost end of the deck just above the bowsprit, while his right hand clutched Hal's own speaking trumpet. The morning air was still cool, yet sweat ran in rivulets down the Dutchman's face and splashed in fat drops on the deck, for Aboli was crouched behind him with a ballock knife in hand. The African held the dagger's wickedly sharp blade between Tromp's legs, poised to geld the Dutchman should he deviate by so much as a flicker from the charade that Hal had contrived.

'I reckon Tromp is as keen for this ruse to work as we are,' Hal observed, to which Big Daniel nodded agreement, but tried to suppress a smile.

The remainder of Hal's men, armed with steel and muskets, were poised below decks, eager to pour from the hatches and board the caravel. All the gun ports were closed, but the gun crews were hidden behind them, with their culverins readied to spit fire and iron fury at the *Delft*. Hal was hoping it would take only one salvo to destroy her crew's resolve for that way he could keep the caravel for the most part intact, which would make her a far more valuable prize.

Hal took a deep breath, his nose filling with the scent of the tarred planks by his face, then looked up at Tromp and hissed,

'Now, sir, speak your piece . . . unless you have your mind set on becoming a eunuch.'

The Dutchman hesitated for no longer than a moment, scratching the tuft of beard at his chin, glanced down at the blade poking between his legs then raised the speaking trumpet to his mouth, took a deep breath and yelled,

'Men of the *Delft*! We have won a glorious victory!' Hal knew enough Dutch to be satisfied so far, as Tromp called across the calm water, 'I bring you the English ship the *Golden Bough*, all the treasures in her belly, and all her stores that will soon be in your bellies, too!'

The Dutch sailors' cheers carried across to them and Hal watched Tromp raise his fist to the sky in a gesture of triumph, for he need say no more and his job was done. Aboli looked over his shoulder and gave Hal a great grin. The deception had worked!

Hal waited until they were barely a canvas off the *Delft*'s stern, looming over the much smaller vessel and on the point of colliding with her before he stood, as did the other men beside him.

'To me, men of the *Bough*!' Hal yelled and the hatches opened, spewing armed men onto the deck. Englishmen, Welsh, Scots and Irish all armed with cutlasses and muskets shouted, 'Hal and the *Bough*!' Beside them ran the Amadoda, gripping their lances and boarding axes and whooping with the joy of being unleashed once more. On the gundeck below, the ports were knocked out and the culverins run out loaded and primed.

As his men crowded the main deck, Hal took the speaking trumpet from Tromp who surrendered it with a sad sigh. The threat of Aboli's knife was still close enough to his generative organs to keep his attention focussed.

'Men of the *Delft*,' Hal roared in his basic, working Dutch, 'your captain won no victory. He and his men fought bravely, but there were far fewer of them than us and they are now my prisoners. Give up your ship and I will treat you well and give you food to eat. Refuse and I will send you to the sea bed without a crumb in your bellies.'

The *Bough*'s crew lining the gunwales yelled threats and made crude gestures, but they were all unnecessary. The prospect of a square meal alone was enough for the men of the *Delft*. They threw up their hands and surrendered without so much as a shot fired or blow struck.

The man who came into the cockpit holding a ship's lantern before him grimaced at the stench of fresh faeces. Seeing the corpse, he stopped and cast his light over it, prodded it with the toe end of his boot, then turned back to a tall African whose lean, muscled body glistened by the candle's glow.

'This one's for the crabs,' he said, and by the lamplight Pett saw that although the man was still young he bore the unmistakable air of a leader of men. His face derived much of its character from an eagle-beaked nose that spoke of high birth and he carried himself with the assurance that came both from giving commands upon which other men's lives depended and also knowing that they would always be obeyed.

Pett had positioned himself as far from the door to the cockpit as his chain would allow and had still not been spotted by the two men, whose arrival had told him all he needed to work out the general sequence of events that must have occurred since the expeditionary party had left the *Delft*. Evidently, the Dutch had not succeeded and the price of their failure was the capture of their ship. Here, then, was the victorious captain. He greatly interested Pett, though he was not yet clear in his mind whether he should look on this young commander as a potential client, or a man whom other clients might want dead.

'Even the crabs must eat, Gundwane,' the African said, giving the body a disdainful poke with his cutlass. This man looked every inch the warrior and he was very clearly his captain's most trusted associate. Aboard ship, that would make him the first mate. Pett categorized the African as a potential impediment, to be considered and accounted for should the captain ever need killing. That aside, he had no interest in him, though it did strike him that he had never seen a black first mate before.

'It is a tragedy, sir, that the man died on the very cusp of our salvation,' Pett now spoke up.

He could have died quicker. Much quicker, the Saint sniped in a voice that echoed so loudly around Pett's skull that he could scarce believe others could never detect it. His own voice, however, had been heard, for the white man spun round, lifting the lantern even as instinct made him grip the hilt of the fine sword scabbarded at his hip. 'Who's there?' he demanded, peering into the gloom.

'My name is Pett, sir. I have been chained down here like a slave for these last weeks, so many I have lost count. Yet my prayers have been answered at last. I hardly dared believe my ears when I heard English voices above.' He rattled his leg chain to emphasize his predicament. 'Are you of the ship that cheese-head Captain Tromp meant to capture?'

'I am Sir Henry Courtney, captain of the *Golden Bough,*' the young man said, 'and you'll be glad to know your captivity is over, Mr Pett.'

Courtney gestured at the stinking corpse. 'Of what did this man die?' he asked.

He died of boredom while you took an age to choke the life out of him, the Saint told Pett.

97

'Hunger?' Pett said with a shrug. 'I am not a man of medicine, Captain. Nor did I know the poor man well, though I can attest to what you have yourself no doubt discovered: this is a ship crewed by starving men. They showed no human kindness towards me, seeing me as just another mouth to feed, and throwing me in this floating dungeon. But this one soul who shared my confinement became a true companion. For which reason I would humbly entreat your permission to be allowed to prepare the body for burial myself, rather than have it done by someone who has never laid eyes on the deceased man before now.' He raised a hand. 'If it please you, Captain.'

'I have no objections,' Henry Courtney said, then turned to the black man. 'Ask Captain Tromp where we will find the key to Mr Pett's irons, or failing that have the carpenter bring his tools.'

'Yes, Gundwane,' the African said, disappearing back up the stairwell.

'Very kind of you, Captain, much obliged.' Pett affected a sombre expression to hide the relief he felt at the prospect of wrapping the corpse in its burial shroud. He had no desire to let anyone else see the bruises on the dead man's neck, nor the swollen tongue and eyes that would betray the true cause of his death.

'How did you come to be Captain Tromp's prisoner?' Captain Courtney asked, by now as oblivious to the stink as any man used to life at sea.

Pett sighed, not too theatrically, he hoped. ''Tis a sad and somewhat lengthy tale, Captain, the telling of which will be easier once I have fed my empty belly and sluiced my parched throat.'

'Of course, how thoughtless of me,' Courtney nodded. 'You must join me for dinner, Mr Pett. For now, though, if you will excuse me, I have the rest of the ship's inventory to inspect. Have no fear, one of my men will return to free you at the soonest opportunity.'

'Of course, Captain,' Pett said, still barely believing his luck. Truly the Lord works in mysterious ways, he thought, as the young captain disappeared. Now he was left alone in the darkness, and yet he was not alone at all, for the Saint and all the angels were with him and William Pett felt truly blessed by their presence.

W hen Tromp had ruefully admitted that there was neither gold, nor spice in his holds, Hal had presumed that there was nothing of any value aboard the *Delft*. And at first glance that presumption appeared to be entirely correct. Most of the hold was entirely bereft of cargo and was now being used as quarters for the *Delft*'s petty officers and as a place to treat men whose emaciation had made them too ill or feeble to work. But at its far bow end there were twelve barrels neatly stacked and lashed down with ropes to keep them from moving in the event of rough seas. Using his cutlass Aboli prised off one of the lids to find the barrel stuffed with sweet-smelling wood shavings and dried grass. When Hal caught up with him, he thrust his hand deep into the barrel. After a good rummage his fingers detected several small boxes. Hal pulled out one of them and, upon opening it, found a glass vial inside, no bigger than his thumb.

'I don't think much of Captain Tromp's wine cellar,' he joked, holding the vial up to the ship's lantern and trying to peer through the thick green glass.

'I have heard Hindoo sailors from India talk of Amrit, the Nectar of Immortality. Perhaps it is that,' Aboli ventured, with a grin.

Hal laughed. 'If Tromp had found the elixir of life I doubt he would be sailing this worm-riddled Portuguese tub and picking fights with the likes of us.' He pulled the cork stopper and sniffed the vial's contents. 'Whatever it is, it's sour,' he said.

'I know a good way of testing the man to see if he is indeed immortal,' Aboli said, waving his cutlass, but Hal was in no mood to laugh. He had clung on to the smallest hope that Tromp might have been carrying a more valuable cargo than he had let on. Clearly, however, he had nothing of any worth whatever on board. And yet, there had to have been some reason why these vials had been boxed with such care. The liquid they contained was certainly not a scent for which fashionable women would pay good money. Nor could it be some sort of medical potion, for if it were there would be labels promoting its properties. Hal felt a brief tremor of shock as the thought struck him that he might just have inadvertently inhaled a dose of poison, but a moment's reflection told him that he was entirely unharmed.

The puzzle deepened as Aboli opened the next barrel, from which Hal pulled three pieces of desiccated old wood, getting a splinter in his thumb for his trouble. Each piece was dark as an old ship's timber, though none had the telltale signs of shipworm. 'Do you have any idea at all what these might be?' Hal asked, quite at a loss for a suggestion of his own. Aboli held up his hands and shrugged, admitting that he too was defeated.

'Well, there's only one man who can solve this conundrum,' Hal said. 'Go and fetch Tromp and let's hear what he has to say for himself.'

A few minutes later, Aboli returned to the hold, accompanied by the *Delft*'s former master. Hal held up the pieces of wood and asked, 'What in heaven's name are these?'

Tromp grinned. 'You should not take the name of heaven in

100

vain, Captain. Those are pieces of the true cross.' Hal had personal experience of Christianity's most precious relics. So for a second he was almost prepared to believe that he was holding part of the cross on which Christ himself had died. But if so, why was Tromp smiling? Was he so lacking in faith that he could make a joke of the Saviour's suffering?

Hal kept his counsel for the time being. He said nothing as he put the pieces of wood back where he'd found them and then held up the green glass vial that had been his first discovery.

'Ah,' Tromp nodded cheerfully. 'I see you have found that most sacred of treasures, the ancient bottle that contains the milk of the Virgin Mary. There is another in there that holds the tears the Blessed Mother shed as she watched her son die.'

Now Hal spoke, and his voice was tense with anger. 'By God, sir, I'll ask you not to take the names of Our Lord Jesus Christ and his blessed mother Mary in vain. You may find your blasphemy amusing. Be assured that I do not.'

The Dutchman raised his palms submissively. 'I can see you are a man who is not easily fooled, Captain Courtney,' he said. 'But you are a rarity in that regard, or so I had hoped, for it was my intention to make hundreds of pounds from selling such curiosities.' He scratched his pointed beard. 'Or as I intended to describe them, such holy relics.'

'And the rest of them?' Hal said, pointing at the other ten barrels.

Tromp spread his arms like a spice merchant flaunting his wares. 'I have the teeth, hair, and blood of Christ. I have samples of the linen in which Christ was wrapped as an infant.' He pursed his lips as if trying to recall what was in the other barrels, then smiled. 'I have jars containing saints' fingers and even – and I apologize in advance for my sacrilege – the foreskin of the baby Jesus, cut off during his circumcision.' He swept an arm out toward Hal. 'But now you have all these things, Captain, for my cargo, like my ship, is yours.'

Hal felt his lip curl and Tromp raised a hand again.

'I admit it is an unusual, and some would say unforgivable, cargo,' he said. 'But I was not in any position to worry too much about religious scruples.'

'You do not strike me as a man who worries about scruples of any kind,' said Hal, tartly.

'Ach, you have me again,' Tromp admitted with a disarmingly self-deprecating smile.

'Damn, but this Dutchman is hard to dislike for long!' Hal thought to himself, becoming almost more cross for his weakness in the face of his opponent's charm.

'I believe you English have a saying for life in this corner of the globe, far beyond the reach of civilization and its laws,' Tromp said. 'How do you say it? Ah yes, "All is fair beyond the Line." That is correct, no?'

Hal glanced at Aboli for they had both heard his father say those very words often enough, usually when planning the act of subterfuge, not to mention deceit, with which he planned to take a Dutch ship. Just as Tromp had done with the *Delft* against the *Golden Bough*, Sir Francis Courtney would match his beloved *Lady Edwina*, named after his deceased wife, Hal's mother, against far larger opponents. And, like Tromp, he had not been afraid to use trickery to achieve his ends.

So Hal could not say anything but, 'Yes, that is the saying.' And then he asked, 'So, who would ever buy these counterfeit curiosities?'

Tromp considered how best to answer this. 'I assume, Captain, that you are of the Protestant faith.'

'You assume correctly.'

'Well, so am I. Now, as you know, we Dutch are traders. We

travel the world in search of profit and we have found it in the Spice Islands of the East Indies. The Dutch East India Company has a monopoly on the spice trade—'

'Except when Englishmen take some of that spice for themselves,' Hal said, thinking of the cargoes his father had seized.

'Don't you mean "took", Captain Courtney?' said Tromp with another triumphant grin. 'As you yourself observed, this very morning, our two nations are no longer at war. Any seizure of Dutch spices would be an act of piracy.'

Damn the man again, Hal thought, then said, 'Of what relevance is this to your counterfeit relics?'

'Simply that we Dutch are not great missionaries. The Spanish and Portuguese, however, who have long been our rivals in the East Indies, see the spreading of the Catholic faith as being at least as important as any financial gain. The Jesuits, in particular, have sunk their claws into the people of the Philippines, into China, even into the islands of Japan, whose rulers hide themselves away from the rest of the world. And wherever they go, they take with them relics to use as weapons in their holy war for control of men's immortal souls. Such objects can be effective in kindling the devotion among newcomers to the faith. They appeal to their superstitions and they give them something that they can see and hold as tokens of their new god.'

'Religious relics – true relics that is – can be objects of extraordinary power. I have beheld the true Tabernacle and seen its glory with my own eyes. Can any man who calls himself a priest knowingly peddle false things?'

Tromp shrugged. 'If they bring faith to those who don't have it, then surely the trick is justified in the eyes of God. That is of no concern to me. What I care about is money. I went to native craftsmen in Batavia, the capital of our East Indian territories, and spent almost every penny I had on the manufacture of these relics you see before you. My crew and I starved because I did not have enough cash for decent supplies. But I believe our hunger was worth it.'

Now Tromp's eyes lit up and he became as animated as a market trader. 'Think about it! Think of the huge market for such relics here in Africa. The Portuguese now hold the Captaincy of Mozambique and Sofala. They have trading posts on the coast, and along the major rivers. And wherever there is trade, the Church is not far behind, seeking to convert the natives. The Jesuits will be grateful to anyone who can supply them with sacred objects that will help them in their task. There is a fortune to be made, Captain Courtney. I'm telling you, man, this cargo is as precious as any gold!'

'Not like this,' Hal said, disgusted by the whole enterprise, and with that he took the vial containing the Virgin's milk, dropped it on the floor then set his boot heel upon it.

Tromp flicked a hand as though to dismiss the barrels and their contents. 'You are quite right of course. It is a dishonourable business. It would be unworthy of us to sell goods we knew to be false.' He let that sink in a moment, like the sour milk on the boards by Hal's feet then scratched his bristled cheek. 'But should you take a different view, I would be happy to share my contacts with you.'

Hal ignored the offer. He called out to one of his other crewmen who had come down into the hold, 'Mr Lovell, take Captain Tromp back to his men and make sure they've all had their fair ration of water and biscuit. We at least know how to behave with honour.'

'Aye-aye, Cap'n,' Lovell said, leading the Dutchman away so that Hal and Aboli were left alone in the dark hold.

The big African was tense with barely suppressed anger. 'So your people come to Africa and when they are not making slaves of those born beneath this sky they are tricking them with false relics. With bones and old wool and rancid milk from a cow.'

'They are not *my* people, these slavers and cheats,' Hal said, a knot of shame pulling taut in his stomach. Then he stepped forward and put a hand on the African's muscled shoulder. 'My crew are my people. And you, Aboli, are my brother.'

Aboli glared at him a while, his tattooed face a mask of fury in the dark, but then he could hold the expression no longer, breaking the tension with a great booming laugh.

'You devil, Aboli!' Hal said. 'I thought I was going to have to fight you again, like we used to. Of course, I forgot you're an old woman now!'

Aboli reached out and took hold of Hal's shoulder. 'I would like nothing more, Gundwane, you are a captain now and I think the men will not take you seriously if they see you on your backside sobbing like a little girl.'

And with that Hal laughed too as they turned their backs on the barrels of fake relics and climbed back up to the gundeck to inspect the *Delft*'s demi-culverins.

William Pett took a sip of his Canary wine and swept an arm around the stern cabin, encompassing the tasteful decoration and polished oak furniture, the map table and the captain's cot, now unhooked from the timbers that crossed the cabin roof and placed on its side against the far wall to give Hal's guests more room.

'You have a beautiful ship, Captain Courtney, which must have cost a considerable sum to build and fit to such a fine standard,' he said. 'I hope you will not think it rude of me to inquire, but how did a gentleman as youthful as you come by it? Was it an inheritance, perhaps?'

'No, Mr Pett,' Hal replied. 'My inheritance lies elsewhere. The *Golden Bough* came to me by capture, seized from a deceitful, lying rogue who had come by it, as was his wont, by treachery and theft.'

'I hope that is not the sum of your account, Captain,' Pett said. 'For I confess, you have whetted my appetite for what sounds like a splendid tale.'

'I'm not much of a storyteller,' Hal demurred. 'I do things and leave it to other men to spin their yarns.'

Pett was intrigued. This young pup of a captain had acquired at least one enemy in his time. And when a man had enemies, Pett had hope of new clients. He directed an amiable smile in Hal's direction and persisted, 'Oh, you do yourself scant justice, sir. In my experience, men of the sea such as yourself are always well capable of recounting their adventures to a welcoming audience. Tell me this at least: who was this scoundrel from whom you took the *Golden Bough*? And from whom had he acquired it?'

Hal looked reluctant but then, to Pett's delight, Judith entered the conversation, saying, 'You know, my dearest, although I know very well how your story ends, you have never told me the start of it. I would love to hear it now, if it pleases you to tell it.'

'How can you refuse a request from one so lovely, sir?' Pett added. 'For it will surely be to your benefit to tell her a tale from which, as our presence here attests, you emerge the conquering hero.'

'Go on, sir,' Big Daniel piped up. 'Tell Mr Pett about the Buzzard and how we roasted him!'

Hal sighed, then held up his hands in mock surrender. 'Very well, I will do as I'm asked. Pass me the Canary, if you'd be so kind, Mr Pett. I need some refreshment before I dry out my mouth with talking.'

Hal poured a glass of wine while he composed his thoughts, drained half of it and then said, 'It began at eight bells in the middle watch, in the darkness just before dawn, when I found a ship with my nose.'

107

'With your nose, sir?' Pett exclaimed. 'Was it so dark that you did not know the ship was there until it hit you smack in the face?'

Hal joined in the laughter that went around the table. 'No, sir, the ship did not hit me. But the scent of the spice it was carrying in its holds, a scent as sweet as honey on the wind, struck my senses a blow they could not ignore. I was up at the masthead on the *Lady Edwina*, a fine ship, named after my dear, departed mother, which had begun life in Dutch colours before my father, Sir Francis Courtney, captured her and adapted her to his own purposes.

'I raced to the foot of the mast and informed my father of what I had smelt. We had been at sea for two long months, waiting for just this moment. One of the mighty galleons of the Dutch East India Company was bearing down upon us, bound for the Cape, en route back to Amsterdam. And my father held a Letter of Marque, signed by the Lord Chancellor on behalf of King Charles himself, commissioning him to hunt down Dutch ships just like her, for, as you will recall, Mr Pett, England and Holland were at war in those days and their armed merchantmen were fair game.'

Hal paused for another sip of wine. This time there were no interruptions. He had the full attention of every diner around the table and he was discovering that he rather enjoyed the role of storyteller after all.

'Now, we should not have been alone, out there on the southern waters of the Ocean of the Indies. Captain Cochran, otherwise known as the Buzzard, with his ship the *Gull of Moray*, had sworn to sail alongside my father. But the weeks of waiting had made him impatient and he had left us barely a day earlier and gone off in search of easy pickings.'

'You could smell the *Gull of Moray*, and all,' Big Daniel

commented. 'Once you keep slaves in your holds, like the Buzzard did, ain't nothing ever going to wash that stink away.'

'It is not the slaves who smell,' Aboli said, his right fist clenched so tight around the knife in his hand that the knuckles were almost bursting through his skin. 'The stink comes from the souls of the men who enslave them.'

'Hear, hear,' Hal murmured and got back to his yarn. 'The ship we were about to attack was called the *Standvastigheid*, which means "Resolution". She was far bigger, with many more cannons, of greater size than the *Lady Edwina*, and far more men aboard. We should have stood no more chance against her than Captain Tromp did, sending his pinnaces against the *Bough*. But my father had Dutch colours that he had captured in an earlier engagement and he flew these from the mast to deceive the *Resolution* into thinking that the *Edwina* was a friendly vessel. By this means we were able to approach right under the Dutchman's stern and get a volley away, whereupon my father led the charge up onto the enemy's decks and took the vessel with the sheer force and courage of his attack.'

'You do not tell the whole story of the battle, Gundwane,' Aboli said.

'I've told all that needs to be said,' Hal replied.

'May I ask what has been omitted?' Pett inquired.

'We were betrayed by a cowardly jackal called Sam Bowles,' Aboli said. 'He cut the *Lady Edwina* free from the Dutch ship, leaving all of us who had boarded the enemy stranded on her decks. But now the captain's son showed he was of the same blood as his father, for he sent Sam Bowles and his friends running, turned the *Lady Edwina* around and came back to the fight.'

'He picked those of us who was all out on the ocean in a pinnace up as well,' Big Daniel added. 'Don't forget that, Aboli.'

'The victory was all my father's, not mine,' Hal insisted, though he could tell from the way that Judith was looking at him that she was well pleased by what she had heard.

'You did not say when this battle took place, Captain,' Pett said. 'How long ago was it?'

'It was the fourth day of September in the year of Our Lord 1667,' Hal replied. 'I remember the date for I had only the day before filled in the entry in the ship's log for the very first time.'

'So a little over three years ago,' Pett said, thoughtfully. 'And how old would you have been then?'

'Seventeen years of age, Mr Pett.'

'An admirable performance by one so young. But pray, sir, what does this have to do with this Buzzard gentleman?'

'He's no gentleman, sir, of that I can assure you. But he has a nose for treasure, and the *Resolution* was full of it. There were three hundred tons of hardwood in her hold: teak and balu and other woods the like of which no forest in Christendom has ever grown. That in itself would have been a fine prize, yet it was nothing compared to the other cargo we discovered. For she also carried forty-two tons of spice: barrels of cochineal, pepper, vanilla, saffron, cloves and cardamom – a treasure worth more than its weight in silver. Yet there was silver, too, ten thousand pounds of it in value, and three hundred ingots of pure gold. Yes, well may you sit there, Mr Pett, with your mouth open in wonder . . . And now think on this: there was more.'

'More?' gasped Pett as Hal allowed himself another drink. 'How could that be?'

'Very simple. This Dutchman had a passenger aboard. His name was Petrus van de Velde, he was a fat, blubbery, cowardly mound of poisonous jelly and he was to be the next governor of the Dutch colony at the Cape of Good Hope. My father set the price of his ransom, to be paid by the Dutch East India

Company, at two hundred thousand guilders in gold, or forty thousand pounds sterling.'

'Beggin' your pardon, Cap'n, but you've left out the most precious treasure of the lot,' said Big Daniel with a leering tone in his voice.

'On the contrary, I have listed all the significant contents of the *Resolution*'s manifest,' said Hal, firmly, knowing precisely what Daniel was referring to and having no desire whatever to broach the subject. Daniel realized that he'd overstepped the mark and fell back into embarrassed silence. Hal was about to continue with the story as he wished to tell it, but he had not counted on a woman's unerring intuition.

'I do apologize for interrupting your story, my dear,' she said, 'but since you seem to have forgotten, I was wondering whether Daniel could answer a question for me.'

'I'll do me best, ma'am.'

'Thank you so much. My question is this: was there a Mrs van de Velde?'

Daniel was a man who never quailed in the face of battle and could not be cowed by all the waves and winds that the oceans could throw at him. But as Judith looked at him with an expression of innocent curiosity on her lovely face there was something close to terror in his eyes.

'I . . . ahh . . . I believe as how he might have been a married man, yes, ma'am.'

'Could you describe his wife at all? For example, was she a young woman, or an old one?'

'I'd say she was probably more young than old, ma'am.'

'Well, now that we've got that settled,' Hal cut in, 'I'm sure Mr Pett would . . .'

'No, please, do continue with your questions, madam,' Pett said, with a courteous nod towards Judith.

111

'Thank you, sir,' she replied, with equally decorous manners. 'Now, Daniel, we were discussing Mr van de Velde and his young wife.' A wicked little smile played around the corners of her mouth as she said those last two words. She was teasing Hal, and enjoying it. 'Can you remember her name?'

'Er . . . Kat-something, can't remember exactly . . .'

Hal gave a heavy sigh and then said, 'Katinka . . . Mrs van de Velde's Christian name was Katinka. Now can we please . . .'

'Thank you, dearest,' Judith said fondly. 'I am pleased that your memory hadn't failed you. I just wondered, Daniel, would you say that Katinka van de Velde – what a pretty name that is! – would you say she was a beautiful woman, or an ugly one?'

'Well, ma'am, that's hard to say, ain't it? Like they say, beauty's in the eye of the beholder . . . matter of taste, like . . .'

'She was good looking for a white woman,' Aboli said dismissively. 'And Gundwane was smitten by her, for he was just a boy and had not yet discovered that when a true man is looking for his woman, he will always choose a daughter of Africa. Luckily for him, however, he grew up and made the correct choice . . . once he had come to his senses.'

'Thank you, Aboli, that was very nicely put,' Judith said and then, more seriously, but also more gently she said, 'Tell us about her, my dear . . . Tell me about Katinka.'

Hal poured another glass of wine and downed it in one. 'It is very simple,' he said. 'She had the golden hair and violet eyes of a heavenly angel, and a soul so foul and wicked that the devil himself would tremble in her presence. She was a Jezebel and, yes, she tempted me and I could not resist. But I learned the error of my ways, so help me God. I came to my senses, just as Aboli says, and I would not exchange one second with you, my darling, for a thousand lifetimes with Katinka van de Velde. Now . . . can I get on with my story?'

'By all means,' said Judith, who had now heard precisely the answer she'd been seeking all along.

'In that case, I will make it quick, or none of us will get any rest this night. Now, the Buzzard, as I said, can sniff treasure on the breeze, just as I sniffed that spice. No sooner had we captured the *Resolution* and its treasures than up he popped demanding his share of the prize.'

'But the Buzzard had left you before the prize was taken!' Judith said, sounding outraged at the impertinence.

'That was exactly what my father told him, but the Buzzard wasn't having any of it. He ran straight to the Dutch at Good Hope and led them to the bay where we were repairing the *Resolution* . . .' Hal stopped himself before adding, 'And hiding all the gold and silver.'

'We were hopelessly outnumbered,' he went on. 'My father was obliged to surrender, rather than see all the men who had served him loyally be killed. And then the Buzzard showed himself for the vile, two-faced scoundrel that he was by telling the barefaced lie that condemned my father to torture and death.'

'What did he say?' said Pett, trying to suppress the thrill he felt at the mention of Sir Francis Courtney's evidently agonizing demise.

'You remember, sir, that I told you that England and Holland were at war and that my father had been commissioned by His Majesty the King to harass Dutch shipping, in the prosecution of that war?'

'Indeed I do,' said Pett, 'just as I remember the war itself.'

'Very well, then, my father attacked the *Resolution*, in good faith, as an act of war. What he did not know, however, was that the Dutch fleet under De Ruyter had, some three months previously, sailed up the Thames to the dockyards at Chatham, where the finest ships of the Royal Navy were laid up, burned a dozen or more vessels, towed away two more, including our flagship, the *Royal Charles*, and forced His Majesty the King to sue for a bitter and humiliating peace.

'So when the *Lady Edwina* attacked the *Resolution* the war had actually ended. Of course, we could not have known that. My father gave his word on that, as a gentleman, and the Dutch commander Colonel Schreuder was minded to accept it. He was my family's enemy, Schreuder, and in the end I killed him, but he always fought with honour. Naturally, however, he felt happier having some evidence of my father's explanation, so he asked the Buzzard, whom he knew had sailed alongside us, whether my father was telling the truth. But the Buzzard . . .' Hal suddenly found that it was all but impossible for him to continue. The memory was simply too painful. But Big Daniel stepped into the silence.

'The lying Scots bastard said that he had told Sir Francis that peace had been declared. And he had the brass nerve to say that our Franky – who was as good a man, and as honourable as any that ever set to sea – had told him he was going to ignore the news and go get himself a prize anyway. That was a filthy lie, but the cheese-heads fell for it and it cost the captain his life. We was all taken prisoner, chained up in the slave hold of the *Gull of Moray* with the Buzzard gloatin' over us and taken off to Good Hope where they put us to hard labour like common criminals. I've still got the scars on me back from the whippings I took. I know you have too, Aboli, and you, too, Cap'n, I'll be bound.'

'Yes,' said Hal, his voice thick with emotion. 'I bear the scars too.'

'But we got our own back, mind, didn't we just? You tell the gentleman all about that, now!'

114

'What happened?' Pett asked.

'After my father was executed – the damn Dutch hung, drew and quartered him – we managed to escape and we headed for the bay where the Dutch had first captured us.'

'Why go back to such a benighted place?'

'I had my reasons, among them the knowledge that the Buzzard would very likely be there himself.'

'He had his reasons too, then,' said Pett, who was thinking about the love of treasure that seemed to unite Sir Francis Courtney and the Buzzard, whatever Courtney's loyal son might say, and getting an ever clearer sense of what those reasons might be.

'Yes,' said Hal. 'But matters were more complicated than I had expected. Schreuder had been disgraced, following our escape. He went to his lover, Katinka van de Velde, and, according to the stories I later heard, found her in bed with Slow John, the colony's torturer and executioner.'

'So she really was a Jezebel,' Judith observed.

'She was a fiend in female form,' Hal replied. 'Messalina, Empress of Rome, who prostituted herself for her own pleasure was as chaste as a nun compared to Katinka. But she got her comeuppance. Schreuder flew into a rage and killed her. He fled and managed to talk his way onto the *Golden Bough*, which was lying in the harbour at Good Hope under the command of Captain Christopher Llewellyn . . .'

'Another good man what was done wrong by bad 'uns,' said Will Stanley, who had been sitting silently while Hal's story unfolded. 'Beggin' your pardon, ma'am,' he went on, 'but I was serving on the *Bough* when that cheese-head colonel come aboard . . .'

'Then you can correct me if I get this wrong,' Hal said. 'One of the officers on the *Bough* was Viscount Winterton, whose father had built the ship. He and Schreuder played a game of dice. Schreuder bet all the money he had in the world, but the dice ran for Winterton and he won, whereupon Schreuder called him a cheat and demanded the satisfaction of a duel.'

'That's right, sir,' Stanley agreed. 'So Cap'n Llewellyn says, you ain't having no duel on my ship, wait till we reach shore. But then a storm came, terrible it was, fair tore the ship to pieces and we was forced to pull into this bay . . .'

'. . . Where the *Gull of Moray* was moored,' said Hal. 'The duel was fought and Schreuder killed Winterton. Then the Buzzard tricked Llewellyn out of the *Bough* and thought himself very clever for now he had two boats. But we few men of the *Lady Edwina* who had survived all the Dutch could throw at us had the last laugh because we arrived soon afterwards at the bay and took the *Bough* and most of her surviving crew, leaving the Buzzard raging on the shore . . . And that is how I come to be master of this magnificent vessel to this day, though I will, I swear, return her to her rightful owner, Winterton, at the earliest opportunity.'

'Was that when you killed Colonel Schreuder, Captain Courtney, when you took the *Bough*?'

'No, that was later, during the Ethiopian campaign.'

'And what of the Buzzard. Is he still flapping his wings and dipping his beak into other men's treasure?'

'I can answer that,' said Judith. 'The Buzzard is dead. He died in the flames when the *Gull of Moray* was destroyed by fireships. I know . . . I saw him die and I hope he is burning still, and for all time, in the fires of hell.'

'A well-merited end, I'm sure. But I confess my curiosity was piqued by one small detail of your story. Did the Buzzard find what he was looking for in the bay where you found him?'

116

'I'm sorry, I don't follow your meaning,' said Hal, who followed Pett all too well, but had no intention whatever of providing him with a useful answer.

'It was just that you said that the Buzzard had reasons for being in this bay, as did you, and – correct me if I am wrong – it was the very same bay to which your father sailed after he had taken the treasure-laden ship, the *Resolution*. Is that correct?'

'I was talking about the same bay, yes.'

'Well, my suspicion is that the Buzzard believed, fancifully no doubt, without a shred of good reason, that your father had had time to secrete some of the booty from his captured ship in this very bay.'

'He may have believed that, I suppose. He had certainly ordered deep trenches to be dug across the sands above the high watermark. I suppose he may have been searching for something. But I can promise you this. My father did not bury anything at that bay on that occasion, to my certain knowledge, or on any other occasion that I am aware of. Nor did he ever tell me of anything that he had buried there. So unless someone else buried gold and silver and jewels, and heaven knows what else there, the Buzzard was wasting his time and his men's energy. Besides which, he's dead now.'

'Well, I'm sure we're all agreed that that settles the matter,' said Pett, looking around the table in the manner of a man seeking support for something he's just said. In fact, he was looking at the faces of the men who had been there on that beach with Captain Hal Courtney and he could not help noticing how Daniel and Stanley evaded his eyes, while Aboli fixed him with a blank stare that made such a point of giving away nothing that it gave Pett the conviction the African certainly had something to hide.

And so, as Hal declared dinner over, and started giving his

senior crewmen their instructions for the night, Pett bade his host and hostess a polite goodnight and made his way to the tiny but reasonably clean cabin that had been assigned for his use. There was just room once the door had been closed to sling a hammock. Pett climbed in and lay there, staring blankly at the ceiling. He was thinking about torture and why anyone undertakes it. The obvious answer: to find something out. Question: what could the Dutch – who were not, in his experience, a particularly cruel or bloodthirsty race – possibly want to know so badly that they were prepared to torment a man to death in the hope that he would reveal something to them? It had not been a time of war and so no military secrets or strategies were involved. The man being tortured had recently captured a large ship filled with valuables. Maybe he had managed to hide some or all of those valuables before the Dutch recovered their ship and they wanted to know where they were.

Pett considered that line of reasoning and decided it was sound. He also felt it reasonable to assume that, if the Buzzard had found anything, Courtney would have mentioned it. For either he would have taken his father's treasure back from the Buzzard, in which case he would surely have sailed straight back home to England, or the Buzzard would have held on to it, in which case Courtney would surely have said so, if only to underline the other man's treachery.

So there was treasure, but it had not yet been recovered. The crew, or at least Courtney's most senior and trusted men, knew that the treasure existed. Pett doubted that they knew where it was. No, that wasn't right. There was one of them who might. For some reason Courtney placed particular trust in that black ape Aboli, the man whose stare had so obviously been hiding something.

It was thus, in theory, possible to discover the location of

118

this hidden fortune. This information would be worth a very considerable amount of money. But why let someone else benefit from his discovery? Why not, thought William Pett, go after the treasure himself?

Jahan drove through the streets of Zanzibar with the Buzzard in an open carriage, so that all the world could see the masked man and tremble at his presence. A full company of cavalry preceded the carriage, with another company behind to deter even the most foolhardy troublemaker. Not that anyone would even think of threatening the one-armed monster, for all had heard of his merciless assault on the boy who had dared fling human faeces at him. Many turned their heads away, rather than cast eyes on such an inhuman creature, whom they regarded as an evil *djinn*, a creature of Shaitan who was not truly of this world.

Only an hour earlier Jahan himself had shown the Buzzard engravings of ancient Egyptian temples and burial sites, with pictures of Anubis, the jackal-headed lord of the underworld. 'This is the god of death itself,' he said as the Buzzard tilted his head to give his single working eye a better view. 'See how his snout is almost the same shape as your leather nose. Think of yourself as Anubis, bringer of death, hater of life, the one who takes mortal souls on their journey to the afterlife.

'Speaking of which, I was greatly impressed by the way you avenged yourself for the filth that had been thrown at you. It made me think that we should develop your talent for killing. You must become even more dangerous with one eye and one arm than you ever were with two. You will require training. This morning you will start to receive it.'

Now the Buzzard was being taken to his first session. But he and Jahan were not the only ones making the journey, for a closed coach was following the open carriage. Shutters had been pulled down over all its windows so that its occupants were entirely hidden from view. Nor could the person within look out. It struck the Buzzard that the coach had already been sitting, ready to depart, when he was led out to take his place opposite Jahan. Now, both the conveyances and their escorts passed through the main gates of the city's largest prison and stopped in the middle of a large quadrangle. Jahan and the Buzzard stood by the carriage as the prison governor approached them and abased himself before Jahan. He stood up again and cast a terrified glance towards the Buzzard. Then he clapped his hands and three prison guards, chosen for their exceptional size and ferocity, stepped forward. One carried a heavy iron chain. The other two flanked him, their right hands hovering just above the pommels of the swords that hung at their sides.

The Buzzard could see that there was a padlock attached to one end of the chain. It was also clear to him, for everything that he did carried with it the possibility of his immediate execution for the slightest sign of disobedience, that the cavalrymen would cut him down in an instant if he attempted to resist any of what was about to happen. So he stood stock-still as the chain was padlocked to the brass ring at the front of his leather collar and allowed himself to be led away like an animal through the body of the prison, where the inmates fell silent as he was paraded past them, into a yard surrounded by high walls on all sides. As he darted his head from side to side, trying to get the best possible view of his surroundings, the Buzzard was faced by three blank expanses of dun-coloured mud-brick walls. But there must have been a viewing gallery of some kind in the wall behind him for now the Buzzard heard a familiar sound from there: a playful squeal of pleasure and a cry of, 'I see the Ugly One!' that he recognized at once as the sound of Jahan's favourite concubine, Aleena. She was a Circassian, from the land of Cherkess on the north-east shores of the Black Sea where the women were famed for both their beauty and their skill as lovers. The pick of the Ottoman Sultan's harem in Constantinople were Circassians, as were the finest of those who attended to the pleasures of Jahan's brother the Grand Mogul at the Red Fort in Delhi.

Aleena did not have the prettiest face of all Jahan's girls, nor the most perfectly trim and shapely figure. But there was a wanton fullness to her lips, a lascivious sparkle in her eyes and every inch of her body, every movement that she made, seemed to exist for the sole purpose of pleasure: both giving it to Jahan and receiving it herself. She had been fascinated by the Buzzard when first he entered the harem, escorted by two harem guards whose great height and muscled bodies gave no clue to their eunuch status. While the other concubines had hung back, clinging to one another in fear, she had stepped up close to the strange, masked creature, so close that the Buzzard could smell the delicious scent of patchouli, roses, orange flower and bergamot that she liked to wear, combined with the warm, animal musk of her own, semi-naked body.

'Does it speak, like a normal person, my lord?' she asked Jahan in a husky, deep, yet utterly female, voice.

'No,' her prince replied. 'But it understands what you say.'

Aleena was now standing so close that the Buzzard could feel the gentle press of her body against his. He felt himself becoming aroused, but instead of the strong, blood-filled hardness that had once defined him as a man, now there was just a maddening, throbbing itch from the stump of scar tissue that remained, like a much larger, more intense version of a mosquito bite.

Now the concubine looked up at him and said, 'Is my lord right, do you understand what I am saying, Ugly One?'

The Buzzard did not know what to do. He could not speak on pain of death. And his whole being was consumed by the throbbing, itching, insufferable and yet ecstatic sensation radiating from his crotch. He longed to rub it or scratch it but knew that would not be allowed. He was vaguely aware of Jahan saying, 'You may nod,' but his voice seemed to come from another world away.

The Buzzard nodded and as he did he could not help his hips from squirming from side to side. 'Oh,' said Aleena, thoughtfully, 'it feels pleasure. But how?'

She stood on tiptoe, her head tilted up towards his mask and whispered, 'Stay completely still, Ugly One, if you wish to live. Above all do not move your hand, for if you touch me with so much as a single finger, your death will not be a quick one. Nod that you agree or I will step away this second and never approach you again.'

The Buzzard gave two quick, desperate nods that made Aleena shriek, leap backwards and then giggle. 'Be careful with your beak, Ugly One. My prince would have no time for a one-eyed concubine!'

She approached him again, crouched down on her haunches by his feet and took hold of the hem of his black *djellaba*. 'So, what do you hide under this?' she inquired, slowly lifting up the hem, exposing more and more of his lower legs and then his thighs. 'Ugh!' she exclaimed, her face twisted into an expression of disgust. 'Its skin is red and scaly and so foul-smelling.'

There were squeals of horror from the other harem girls, who were now edging closer as their curiosity overcame their fear.

Behind his mask, the Buzzard's face was burning with humiliation and shame and what made it worse was that the insistent irritation coming from his stump was becoming ever more powerful. His heart was pounding and his breathing was coming in shorter, deeper breaths so that he began to fear he could not draw enough air into his lungs through the meagre hole in his mask. He realized that his lungs didn't hurt, even as his gasps intensified, nor was there any other pain in his body. The only thing he could feel was the itching.

Now there came another little squeal as Aleena lifted his *djellaba* high enough to expose the devastation that the fire had wrought between the Buzzard's legs. 'Look!' she called out to the other girls. 'It is neither man nor woman. But this,' and now she laid her fingers very delicately on the raw skin that sheathed the Buzzard's stump. 'This is like the little pink rosebuds that bring us such delight, is it not? I wonder if it brings delight to Ugly One, also.'

The Buzzard wanted to ram himself into her, but he had nothing left to ram. He wanted to grab her in his arms, but he only had one of those and to use it would lead to his certain death. All the Buzzard could do was to stand on legs that felt as though they might collapse beneath him at any moment, trying to restrain the jerky little thrusts and wriggles of his hips that seemed to be occurring of their own accord while Jahan's favourite plaything examined him and his other *houris* looked on.

He could not see them all through his eye hole and so, with the bird-like movements that were increasingly becoming natural to him, the Buzzard darted his head, focussing on one lovely face, or one plump pair of breasts, or one perfectly tiny waist and curving hips and soft, inviting stomach at a time. He had never in all his days seen women to match them, for these were the prize possessions of a man who could have anything he wanted, selected for the sole purpose of arousing his passions. Had he stumbled upon such a prize collection just a few months earlier, he would have ravished them all, gorging himself in a single, self-indulgent banquet of womankind.

Now though, the Buzzard could do nothing but stand in silence as the tension built and built within him. Aleena looked up at him with something close to professional curiosity and mused aloud, 'I wonder if I could make it feel the pleasure that a real man or woman experiences?' She gave Jahan her most sultry pout and pleaded, 'Please may I play with it, sire?'

The maharajah laughed indulgently and said, 'No, you may not. I want you playing with me. Come here and remind yourself what a real man looks like.' He glanced over to the guards and said, 'Take it away.' And the Buzzard was led, mortified and belittled, back to his chambers. Since then, the Buzzard had not seen Jahan, still less been allowed back into the harem, but now the sound of Aleena's voice reawakened all the sensations that she had aroused in him and he felt himself exposed again, as though his dismemberment was visible for all the world to see and anger mixed with shame at the degradation he had suffered.

'Turn around, Ugly One!' Aleena called out. 'I have something for you!'

The Buzzard did as he was told and looked up to search for the source of the voice. Above him an open gallery ran at first-floor level, too high for any man to reach from down here in the yard. Its function, he presumed, was to provide a vantage point from which guards could look down on the prisoners below. Now though, its only occupants were Jahan and Aleena, whose face was entirely concealed behind a veil, for no true man aside from her master could ever be allowed to see her. Indeed, it was an extraordinary sign of favour that she had been allowed out of the harem at all.

'Look!' she called out. She held out both her hands in front of her and the Buzzard saw that she was holding a long, slender sword that curved at its tip: a scimitar. 'Use it well, Ugly One, and we may meet again.'

Aleena leaned forward so that her hands were beyond the low wall of the gallery and dropped the sword onto the dusty earth in front of him. The Buzzard picked it up and now it was Jahan who addressed him.

'Step back into the centre of the courtyard. Look back at the gate through which you entered. Soon that gate will open again and another man will step through it. He is a murderer. He has been condemned to death. So kill him.'

'Kill him!' Aleena echoed, sounding like a woman who lusted after blood as much as she did for love.

The Buzzard stood on the balls of his feet, legs wide enough apart to give him balance, but not too far to hamper his mobility. For the first time in months he felt strong, capable – filled with a desperate desire to prove himself in front of the beautiful woman up in the gallery, to show her that despite everything he was still a man.

A few seconds later the gate opened a little and unseen hands pushed the condemned prisoner out into the yard. He was small and scrawny, wearing no more than a cloth tied around his waist and between his legs to cover his modesty, and with only a thin covering of wiry grey hair on his head. Yet the eyes that looked across the yard at the Buzzard were not filled with the fear that he had become accustomed to seeing, but with the undiluted malice of a man who was bad to the bone.

The Buzzard could see his quarry sizing him up and searching for his weaknesses. They weren't hard to find. With no left eye or arm and his beak blocking half his field of vision he was desperately vulnerable on one entire side of his body. Sure enough, the old man darted with surprising speed to the Buzzard's left. The Buzzard tried to turn to follow the man's movement, but he was too slow and lost sight of him as he dashed past.

'Behind you!' shrieked Aleena, excitedly.

'Turn round,' Jahan called down.

The Buzzard spun round as nimbly as he could, turning to his left, and caught a fleeting glimpse of the old man dashing past him again. There were more shouts from up in the gallery. But now the Buzzard's own fighting instincts were returning to him. He had turned the wrong way. He should have spun round to the right, leading with his sword-arm and his good eye. And he should have turned with his arm extended, cutting as he went.

He spun again, using the slashing of his arm to give himself momentum and this time he felt the tip of his blade striking something, encountering resistance and then continuing, followed by a cry of pain. The Buzzard came to a standstill and saw the old man standing, hunched over, clutching his right

127

hand. Then something caught his eye, something on the ground. He lowered his masked head and saw two severed fingers lying on the parched earth. As he raised his head again, the old man was backing away, but the pain he was in had knocked the fight out of him.

Unaware of how far he had gone, the man bumped his back against the wall of the yard. Now he was trapped. He looked up at the Buzzard and begged for mercy. For a moment the Buzzard hesitated and then he heard Jahan's voice repeat, 'This one is a murderer. Kill him,' in a flat, unemotional tone of command, followed by Aleena, much more excitedly: 'Kill him, Ugly One!'

The Buzzard did not hesitate. It was an act of butchery, a punch in his guts to make the man bend forward and then a chopping blow straight down onto the back of his exposed neck. The killing felt good. His shaming in front of the women of the harem had made him very angry and the bile had been swilling around inside him for the past few days with nowhere to go. Now it had a focus, but there was no time to take pleasure in that fact for Jahan was already calling to him, 'The gate! Turn towards the gate!'

The Buzzard turned, his head darted as he found his bearings and another man emerged into the yard. He was younger and much more strongly built than the first victim, but he had some kind of impairment of the leg that gave him a shambling, half-hobbled gait. The Buzzard realized now that he had to keep his head moving, so that his eye was always locked on his target, and at the same time his feet had to be in motion too. It wasn't a matter of being in one position, then turning to another, for that involved moments of stillness, and if he were fighting someone with a weapon in his hand then stillness would mean death.

It took a little while for the Buzzard to adapt his tactics, but in the end he cornered the second man and left him lying with his stomach wide open and his guts strewn around him in a red, steaming stew of viscera, blood and sand.

By the time the third hapless wretch set foot in the yard, the Buzzard was into his rhythm and despatched him in a matter of seconds.

'I've had enough,' Aleena said with a tone of spoiled, pampered boredom.

'Good,' Jahan replied, 'we have much better things to do than this.'

They departed without the slightest nod to the Buzzard, making it perfectly plain that he was of utter insignificance to their lives. He was shocked to find that he was hurt by Aleena's indifference, like a schoolboy who has just seen the girl after whom he pines walk off to the woods with the village bully. But then he was snapped out of his reverie by a new, much harsher voice calling down from the gallery.

'Hey, masked man!' The Buzzard looked up to see a massive tree-trunk of a man. He was shaven-headed and bare-chested, with upper arms that were thicker than any normal man's thighs. 'My name is Ali! I am your trainer, and you have work to do. His Highness wants me to turn you into a fighter and so that is what I am going to do. So stay alert, keep moving. And do not stop until I tell you. This is both an order, and my sincere advice. Do you hear me?'

The Buzzard nodded.

'Good,' Ali continued. 'For the men you will meet now are younger and stronger, and you must believe me, masked man. If you do not kill them, they will certainly kill you.'

The trainer was as good as his word. The next two condemned men stretched the Buzzard to the limit as he struggled to manoeuvre them into a spot where he could have them at his mercy. The sixth man carried a stave that the Buzzard had to fight past before he could kill him. The seventh landed several good blows on the Buzzard, who was now shattered and so short of speed and strength that it was only the very real fear of joining the other dead men scattered about the yard that gave him the energy to prevail in the end. One final, weak, exhausted stab finished off his final opponent and then the Buzzard slumped to his knees feeling gorged on death and sick of killing. He was so tired he hardly felt the fingers that prised the sword from his hands. So tired that the first time he knew that he was about to leave this hellish place was when he felt the tug of the chain and was almost dragged up onto his feet and out of the yard.

The Buzzard was shattered, starving and parched. When he got back to his quarters, an African house-slave lifted the spout of the watering can to the mouth hole of his mask and he gulped the cool water down with desperate, helpless eagerness. His *djellaba* was removed and he was led to a hot bath, filled with soothing oils that helped relax his tortured muscles. When he had been dried and given a clean garment to wear he was fed the large bowl of sloppy, mashed up chickpeas, vegetables and minced meat that was his meal for the day.

Later, after the Buzzard had slept for a while, Jahan came to him. 'You did well today,' he said. 'Ali will train you every day from now on. Sometimes you and he will work alone. On other occasions you will be taken to the prison to test what you have learned. There are many men there who can be killed without anyone missing them.'

Jahan stepped up to the Buzzard, placed a hand on his shoulder and looked intently into his eye. 'Aleena is an extraordinary woman, isn't she?' he said, almost as a friend, one man to another.

'Yes,' the Buzzard said, for he was allowed to speak to Jahan in private.

'Sometimes I cannot decide if she is a witch, a whore, or a goddess . . . or maybe she is all three. It was astonishing to witness, the way that she could give pleasure, even to something like you.' He paused and then added, 'She aroused you, didn't she? As much as you can be aroused.'

'Yes,' the Buzzard repeated, and there was a throaty huskiness to his voice now.

'And you would like her to pleasure you properly, I am sure.'

'Oh God yes . . . please . . . yes.'

Jahan gave the Buzzard a rueful smile. 'I thought as much. But you will have to wait a while yet for that trip to paradise, for neither Aleena, nor any of my concubines, will so much as touch you until you have fulfilled the purpose of your existence and killed Captain Henry Courtney.'

'But then . . .?' the Buzzard asked.

Jahan smiled. 'If you kill Courtney, and you make him pay for all the indignities he has forced upon both of us, and upon my people, and upon our cause, then you can have one of the jewels of my harem – perhaps even Aleena if I have tired of her by then – as my gift. You may keep her and do with her whatever you please. Think on that, why don't you, tonight, as you try to bring yourself even some of the pleasure with your fingers that she would surely give you with hers.'

W illiam Pett was a fastidious man: unusually so, some might say. Hal had lent him the use of his olive oil and barilla ashes soap and he had sluiced himself down with buckets of sea water, ridding his skin of the coating of filth, sweat and other excretions that had accumulated upon it during his time locked away in that fetid cockpit on the *Delft*. His concern for bodily hygiene was not, however, the only factor that made him more conspicuous than ever amongst the company that gathered every night at the captain's table.

Unlike the other men around that table, whose faces were weathered by wind and salt water and brown as the *Bough*'s timbers from years beneath the African sun, Pett's face was the ashen white of a high-born European. He had somehow travelled to Bombay and then spent a number of weeks on the *Earl of Cumberland* without acquiring so much as a faint glow of colour in his cheeks, and captivity had only made his pallor even more pronounced. This somewhat deathly aspect was emphasized by his gaunt face and thin, wiry-limbed physique. Hal and his crew were still consuming the last of the fresh food taken aboard before they left, and Judith had passed on tactful words of advice to the ship's cook about the use of spices to add heat and flavoursome seasoning to food that was half rotten.

Two more nights had passed since Hal told his story. In the interim he had sent a skeleton crew of his own sailors to man the *Delft*, under the command of boatswain John Lovell, and the two ships were now sailing in line astern, though their progress was slow as the wind still refused to pick up. The captured Dutch sailors continued to be held in confinement while Hal decided what to do with them, but they were not shackled, they received the same food and drink as the rest of the ship's company and they were given time on deck twice a day to stretch their legs, feel the sun on their backs and breathe some fresh free air. As for Tromp, Hal had thought back to the courtesies his father extended to those he defeated and decided that, even if the Dutch captain's cargo of newly minted relics suggested he did not behave like a gentleman, he would still be treated like one and be invited to dine every night at the captain's table.

Judith's culinary advice had ensured that tonight's main course, a mutton curry served with ship's biscuit, had been tasty enough. The others had wolfed it down, but Pett did not so much eat his portion as move it around his plate. These eccentricities might easily have made him unpopular with his dining companions, but his profession demanded an ability to fit in with other people in almost any situation and he had taken trouble to make himself sufficiently agreeable that his presence at dinner was enjoyed, rather than endured, by those around him.

So Hal was smiling as he passed the wine decanter down the table and said, 'Wet your whistle, Mr Pett. You made me tell you my story two nights ago. Now it is your turn. What twists and turns of fate led you to the particular patch of ocean from which Captain Tromp here . . .' for the Dutchman had, at Hal's suggestion, been invited to eat with them, 'kindly rescued you. And I give you fair warning, Tromp, I will expect your story too, for I fancy your journey has not lacked incident.'

The Dutchman gave a self-deprecating shrug. 'There have been . . . one or two interesting moments,' he said, with a lazy grin.

Pett had by now poured himself half a glass and taken a sip that a sharp eye might observe had consumed almost none of the wine. He cleared his throat and began. 'As you may recall, I sailed from Bombay aboard the *Earl of Cumberland*. I had been in the Indies conducting a number of negotiations with local grandees on behalf of the East India Company, setting up trade agreements and the like. Those discussions had concluded and when I met Captain Goddings at the governor's residence he very kindly agreed to find room for me aboard his ship, the *Earl of Cumberland*, which was bound for London with a cargo of saltpetre aboard.'

There was a hissing sound as Will Stanley and Big Daniel both drew in their breath. 'I don't mind admitting that would scare me half to death, that would. Like turning the ship's hold into one great big magazine, just waiting for a single spark to make it blow,' Stanley said.

'Your fear would be entirely justified, as I shall recount,' Pett said. 'But all was good humour as we set sail. Captain Goddings seemed a cheerful, hearty sort of fellow. He was greatly amused,

I recall, by the nickname given to their ship by his crew, the Sausage.'

There was a very faint smattering of polite laughter before Judith said, 'Forgive me, Mr Pett, but I don't understand the joke in that name.'

'Please do not be in the slightest bit discomfited, madam, for I confess I had not the faintest notion where any humour might lie either. Captain Goddings suggested it pertained to matters of meat and butchery. It seems the people of Cumberland are noted for preparing sausages to a particular recipe. Beyond that, I am at a loss.'

'So tell us about this Sausage, or whatever she was,' Ned Tyler asked, impatience getting the better of him. 'Decent enough ship, then, was she?'

Pett nodded. 'I would say so. Mr Goddings took great pleasure in regaling me with the particulars of her construction. I dare say he was keen to impress upon me what a privilege it was to be aboard such a vessel. In any case, he informed me that more than two hundred trees had gone into her. The pines for her mast and spars came all the way from the colonies but her heart was good English oak from the Forest of Dean. Or was it the New Forest? I confess I do not recall. But I can assure you, Mr Tyler, that all of her, from her masts and rigging to her sails and her great guns, were of the very best quality. For as a plain matter of business, the Company commissions merchant vessels of the very highest calibre, for its profits depend upon the arrival of its cargoes safe and sound.'

'Captain Goddings's name sounds familiar to me,' Hal said. 'I believe that my father knew him. Yes, now I remember. They fought together at the battle of Scheveningen in fifty-three. Father said he was a good man to have on your side in a ship fight.'

135

'Ah, Scheveningen, that was some hot service,' Ned Tyler said, shaking his grey head. 'Too many good men sank to the sea bed that day. Good ships went down with 'em. We should have paid attention to the omens.' He scratched the silver bristles on his cheek as he cast his mind back across the years. 'The wind the night before was fierce as God's wrath. Should have known the Lord was trying to tell us something.'

'Enough of your old tales, Mr Tyler,' Hal said, 'or we shall never get to the end of Mr Pett's story.' He hoisted an eyebrow at Pett. 'You must excuse Mr Tyler. As I am sure you know, we seafaring men are a superstitious lot.'

'And with good cause,' Tyler said. 'Why, I was once coming out of a hostelry in Plymouth when a red-haired beauty came up offering her services to our boatswain before the lad had a chance to get a word in.'

'Or anything else in, hey?' Aboli said with a grin. Then he looked at Judith. 'My apologies.'

'There is no need, Aboli,' Judith smiled. 'I have spent the past year as the lone woman in an army of men. Rest assured, I have heard far, far worse.'

'Now it is I who am at a loss. Forgive, me, Mr Tyler, but what was the significance of the boatswain's encounter with the lady of ill-repute?'

'Ned believes encountering a red-head before coming aboard ship brings bad luck,' Hal explained to him. 'Unless, that is, you speak to the fiery-haired harbinger of doom before she, or he – for the superstition pertains to males too – speaks to you.'

'Ah, I see,' Pett said. 'And what happened to the young man after this encounter?'

'Why he fell off the gangplank and sank like a stone.' Ned shook his head again and clicked his fingers. 'Gone just like that. Poor sod signed up to sail to the Cape and ended up drowning in Plymouth dock.'

'Well I don't put much store in superstitions, Mr Tyler,' Pett said. 'I put my faith in God first, and myself second. And recent events have convinced me that my trust in both is well placed. After all, I am here with you now enjoying this excellent food. Captain Goddings, his ship and all his crew, on the other hand, are merely bones and ashes on the sea bed.'

There was a muttering around the table at those bleak words that conjured up images that were rather too close to home for men who lived with the continual risk of death at the hands of the elements, their enemies and plain bad luck. Ned Tyler was about to say something, but Hal flashed him a warning look that told him to hold his tongue.

'There will be no further interruptions, I can assure you, Mr Pett,' Hal said. 'Now if you please, sir, finish your tale.'

'Of course, Captain. As I was saying, Captain Goddings was sailing back to London with a cargo of saltpetre. As Mr Stanley has already observed, this was a perilous venture and I hope you will all not think me wanting in courage if I say that I would not have boarded the *Earl of Cumberland* had I not wished – as I still do wish, I might add – to return to England, there to report to my masters at the earliest possible opportunity. So there is nothing to be said beyond, "There was a fire aboard ship."'

He cast his eyes over the sombre faces around the table. 'Well may you shake your heads, gentlemen, for even a landlubber such as I knows that fire at sea is the greatest peril of all. Indeed, your story last night, Captain Courtney, ended with just such an event. You, however, knew the cause of the conflagration that killed the, ah, Buzzard, as you called him. I do not know what started the fire on the *Earl of Cumberland*. I can only say

137

that I was enjoying a convivial conversation with Captain Goddings in his quarters, as was our custom after dinner, when sounds of alarm and panic came to our ears. A moment later, in burst a crewman, his eyes wide with fright, crying out in panic, "Fire! Fire!" and then, "Come quick, Captain! For the love of God come quick!"

'Then the captain, courageous man that he was, thinking nothing of his own safety but only of his duty, left the room and marched towards the flames that were now sweeping through his ship, knowing as he did that he was going to his certain doom. At first, I followed him out onto the deck. Men were running hither and yon like flaming torches in the dark. Flames rose high into the night sky, higher than the mainmast itself, hurling innumerable sparks towards the stars and the sound of their crackling was like the rasping breath of Satan himself.'

'So how did you escape, mijnheer?' asked Tromp. 'You who were, by your own words, wanting in courage.'

'By God sir, I'll ask you to withdraw that suggestion,' Pett retorted.

'Perhaps I misunderstood,' Tromp said. 'I thought I heard you say that you did not want to sail on this ship, filled with saltpetre, because you were wanting in courage.' He looked around the table with an air of injured innocence. 'Was I wrong?'

A sudden tension had descended on the cabin and Hal realized that it was up to him to intervene before things went too far. 'You did indeed mistake Mr Pett's meaning, sir. He was asking us not to think him wanting in courage, his point being that it was perfectly reasonable to be nervous about boarding a ship carrying a dangerous cargo. I am sure that, now that I have explained my meaning, you will agree that Mr Pett did not admit to any cowardice, nor can any reasonable man find fault with his sentiments.'

Tromp gave one of his lazy, beguiling smiles. 'Ach! I have indeed failed to comprehend the meaning of your English language. Forgive me for being an ignorant, ah, cheese-head – that is the right word, no, for a Dutchman?'

'Forgive you?' said Mr Pett. 'For a misunderstanding, yes, that I can forgive. But being locked in a stinking hole for no other crime than being a shipwrecked passenger . . . I'm a long way from forgiving that, Captain Tromp. A very long way indeed.'

'As I have tried to say many times, that was simply for your own safety.'

'Gentlemen! Enough! I will not have disputes of this kind at my table. Mr Pett, if you please, be so good as to finish your story, which lacks but one piece of information. How did you, alone of all the men aboard the *Earl of Cumberland*, manage to make your escape?'

Mr Pett said nothing for a moment. He was still fixing his cold, grey eyes on Captain Tromp. But then, as if waking from a dream, or even a trance, he snapped back to life and said, 'Through the two forces in which, as I remarked earlier, I place my trust: the grace of God and my own initiative. I was blessed, as it transpired, by my own inadequacies. There was nothing whatever that I could usefully contribute to the crew's efforts to contain the blaze. On the contrary, had I tried to assist them I should only have been in the way. That being the case, I was faced with a dilemma. Should I stay aboard the vessel, and risk going down with her if she sank? Or should I attempt to escape, knowing that I would be alone in the midst of the trackless wastes of the ocean?

'It was then that I called upon God for guidance and He did not forsake me. I felt His presence and heard His voice as He told me to make good my escape and showed me the means by which I could do so. There, before me, was the captain's bed, very much like your own, Captain Courtney, though somewhat narrower in design.'

The mood lightened as everyone realized why Hal's bed was unusually wide. Pett affected to ignore it and said, 'I knew at once what to do. I used the bed to smash out the stern windows, then threw the bed itself out into the night and threw myself out immediately afterwards. I cannot swim . . .'

The laughter turned to gasps of astonishment. 'But how . . . ?' Big Daniel began.

'I know, Mr Fisher, I ask myself the same thing: how did I manage both to find the floating bed out there in the darkness and make my way to it through the water? I honestly have no idea . . .'

That, at least is the absolute truth, Pett thought to himself, then spoke again. 'All I can say is that I found myself on the bed, adrift on the waters. After a short while I saw a flash of light so bright it was like staring at the sun, so fierce that it felt as though my very eyes were being burned. A second later came the terrible sound of the saltpetre exploding, like the crack of doom. It was deafening. The only thing I could hear was the ringing in my ears, but in time that too passed and then . . . then there was nothing. It was a calm night, with very little wind and the thing that struck me with a terrible force was the silence. The ship and all the men on it had vanished, vanished utterly, leaving not a sight nor a sound behind.'

There was silence, too, around the table as everyone took in the awfulness of what Pett had described. He finally concluded, 'I remained adrift, at the mercy of the elements, until I was spotted by the lookout on the *Delft*, to whose sharp eyes I owe a very great debt of gratitude.'

'Well we all know what happened after that,' said Hal, wanting

140

to nip any chance of further arguments in the bud. 'Now, I'm sure we're all keen to retire for—'

'Excuse me, Captain,' Tromp interrupted.

'Yes?'

'You asked me to tell my story—'

'Well, I'm sure it can wait until tomorrow night.'

'It's only a very short story.'

'Come on, Cap'n, give the man his turn,' Ned Tyler piped up.

'Aye, an' give the rest of us a nice little tot of rum!' added Big Daniel.

'A very little tot,' Hal conceded. 'After all, we are assured that Captain Tromp's is only a very short story. So go ahead, sir, since the table seems to demand it. Say your piece.'

Tromp looked around the table. He cleared his throat, and then he began, 'There was an incident with a girl in Batavia. Her name was Christina. She was an admiral's daughter.'

Now Hal was intrigued and amused, as were the others at the table. The *Bough*'s crewmen made a few suggestive remarks under their breath, which Judith affected not to hear, though a smile was playing around her lips as Hal said, 'Go on.'

Tromp smiled. 'It was the oldest story of them all. We danced, we laughed, we loved . . .' He cocked an eyebrow. 'And then one day she told me that she was with child. Worse, she told her father. I admit I thought he would explode like a powder charge with a short fuse. He liked me well enough as an officer on his ship, but as the man who had put my seed in his precious daughter?'

'So did he explode?' Hal asked.

Tromp shook his head. 'No, worse. The admiral was calm, cold as the North Sea in midwinter. He told me that he detested the very idea of having me in his family, but nevertheless, there was no choice. I must marry the girl within the week.'

141

'So you fled.'

'I did not love Christina and she did not love me. I don't believe so. Not really. So I thought about an idea that had been brewing in my mind for some time. First, I went back to the admiral. I said, "Fine, I will marry your daughter. But it must be a proper wedding, with a church and a feast afterwards, so that people believe it is a true love-match. And for this we will need two weeks at the very least." He did not want to agree, but he could see I had a point. It looked better my way, less shame for him and his family. Then I went to the craftsmen of Batavia and I told them, "Make me these relics, at least six of each kind, in ten days!" Then I went to a ship on which I had served, where I knew all the crew and I said, "I have a plan. Come with me and we will all get rich!"'

'And they believed you?' Hal asked, incredulously.

'Ach! They believed whatever they wanted. Most of them were pressed men. They didn't want to be rotting to death in the East Indies. They wanted to go home. I told them, "I will get you back to Holland with plenty of gold in your pockets and all the girls will come running."'

As he recounted what had happened, Tromp spoke with such enthusiasm that Hal could understand exactly how a group of impoverished, uneducated, mostly illiterate sailors, thousands of miles from their home, could easily be persuaded to join his madcap scheme for self-enrichment.

'This was the crew of the *Delft*?' Hal asked.

'Absolutely!' Tromp replied. 'So, the days go by. I am very nervous. I keep thinking, my God, if these damn natives don't make the relics on time I'm going to be stuck here with Christina and her father – and I should say also her mother, who was even worse – for the rest of my days. But two days before the wedding, the relics were ready. I put them on a cart and drove it to the docks. The *Delft* men were waiting for me. We loaded the crates and set sail. We were free! But . . . and this is maybe something I should have said before.'

Tromp looked around the table and leaned forward, and somehow the others felt compelled to lean in, too, as if being drawn physically into his story. 'The *Delft* was a very special boat. For she was not a navy boat, nor even a Dutch East India Company boat. She belonged to the admiral, Christina's father. She was his little pleasure barge.'

The tension Tromp had created was broken with an outburst of laughter and ironic cheers around the table. 'I salute you, Captain,' said Aboli, once his shoulders had stopped shaking with mirth. 'You take the daughter of a great chief. Now she is no longer a virgin, because of you . . .'

'I cannot be sure of that,' Tromp observed. 'She did not act like a girl who was doing it for the very first time.'

'But you fill her belly with your seed and dishonour her before her father and mother and all her tribe. And then you run away . . . in her father's ship. Why are you not dead? If you had done that to the Monomatapa – the chief of my tribe – he would have sent his fiercest warriors after you. They would have found you and . . .' Aboli sighed with bloodthirsty pleasure, 'they would have killed you very slowly, and painfully, until you were screaming and begging for death.'

'Believe me,' said Tromp. 'That is exactly how Christina's father feels. I can guarantee you that every captain of every Dutch ship that has docked in Batavia since I left has been told to hunt me down. There will be a price on my head, whether it is delivered back to Batavia on top of my living, breathing shoulders, or in a bloodstained sack. So now you have a choice, Captain. If you turn us over to the Dutch we are dead men. But your ship has been at war for months. You

143

have lost men. The only reason you can sail this ship at all is because you have turned African warriors into sailors. But they belong here in Africa. You, however, are currently on a course for the Cape. Beyond that lies the Atlantic, and then you can set a course for England, aye, and Holland, too. I think you want to go home, Captain Courtney. You will need sailors who know the cold waters of the north. So take me and my men . . . take us as your crew . . . and we will take you home.'

Pett heard voices. His head was filled with them. Sometimes they spoke in unison, like a choir, but at others they were as disputatious as a parliament. The urge to kill, however, was more than a matter of a voice in his mind, though the presence of the Saint was certainly part of it. No, the need was something deeper that he felt in his guts, in his heart, in his entire being. It ran in his blood. It seeped into his bones. He was in every sense a man possessed.

He could not tell what brought this feeling on, but he knew it once it had seized him. 'Why so soon?' he asked himself. When he had first taken up his mantle for the Lord, Pett had been known to spend many months or even years preparing a single swing of his reaper's scythe. He had learnt that almost as important as the ability to kill was the ability to bide one's time, to be patient. Yet only a few days had passed since he strangled his fellow prisoner aboard the *Delft*, and Goddings had met his end barely more than a week before that. The intervals between each event seemed to be shortening, as if the more he killed, the less satisfaction he derived from any one individual death. Now he was compelled to do it again and it struck him that if he were able to despatch two people at one time this might sate him more fully and keep the necessity of repeating the act at bay for that little time longer. And there were, of course, two potential victims lying side-by-side just a few paces from Pett's tiny cabin, in the captain's quarters.

To kill both Courtney and the Nazet woman at the same time was, of course, a wildly risky undertaking. For a start, both were proven fighters, well able to defend themselves, and both probably exceeded Pett's abilities in their swordfighting skills. Then there was the matter of covering his tracks. Had the fire not done the job for him, it would have been hard enough for Pett to slip the knife that had killed Goddings in amongst the gear of a known malcontent. This captain and his lady, however, were very evidently loved by the crew of the *Golden Bough*, so that option was not available to him.

Pett didn't care. He had to do this. The Saint had yet to enter the babble of voices currently echoing in his skull, but he felt sure it was only a matter of time. The deep physical yearning could not be denied. And it was possible to commit the act, he was sure of it. He would do it quickly and quietly and then, if no other idea presented itself, he would repeat his trick with the captain's bed – a far more commodious vessel in this case – and make his way to the mainland. He had seen the shores of Africa on the western horizon often over the past few days. He could surely reach them easily enough. He would slip over the side and make his way ashore before anyone even knew that Captain Courtney was dead.

He was a little troubled by the thought of killing a woman, for he had never done so before. He prided himself on being a civilized man, who carried out the Lord's work, and women, in Pett's view, had an essential innocence and fragility that made them improper targets. On the other hand, another voice argued, this woman was not innocent or fragile. She had gone to war of her own free will. She had chosen to march and fight alongside and against men, as if she were one of them. That made her fair game.

She would say that she had been called by God to defend her country and the Tabernacle it contained. But this was his calling and it was just as holy. There were others who killed. He knew that. But none was as good as him and he took pride in his work. When other children had been playing Put Pin or Heads and Points, he had been learning the use of the dagger, the sword, and the steel sling. He had been studying the properties of different poisons. He had been learning the many and fascinating techniques of taking another human life, up close, and with consummate skill. The business of Courtney and Nazet was just another test.

And Pett had never failed one yet.

For his weapon he chose a marlinspike, a foot-long steel tool resembling a giant sewing needle that the sailors used to work with the ship's rope. He had purloined it shortly after coming aboard the *Golden Bough* and had been sharpening it ever since, in whatever private moments he could muster aboard the crowded vessel, until its tip was sharp enough to cut straight through human skin and muscle to the delicate organs beneath.

Pett placed the spike inside the right sleeve of his shirt so that it lay along the inside of his lower arm, cool against his skin, with its tip held in place between two of his cupped fingers, and slipped out of his cabin. His only other tool was a simple ship's nail that he held in his mouth, between two pursed lips. He did not immediately make his way to the captain's quarters, but took the time and trouble to establish the situation aboard ship, making himself aware of anyone or anything that might present a potential threat to his ambitions. Up above, the stars filled the sky with that extraordinary profusion that struck Pett as so typical of the tropics. He stood for a moment on the quarterdeck in the shadow cast by the waxing moon, listening to the hushed voices of the watch. He recognized the deep resonant voice of the African, Aboli, and he could see, over by the mainmast, a group of Amadoda bunched around one of their number who was telling them a story, a tale about a talking lion by the look of it, for his arms were raised before him, fingers hooked like claws.

A board creaked above him and his muscles tensed. He held his breath. Someone was coming. Will Stanley doing his rounds as the officer on watch, he guessed. Pett slipped behind the quarterdeck ladder and froze. He did not need Stanley asking questions as to why he was on deck in the middle of the night, let alone coming close enough to see the nail poking out of his mouth. Bare feet on the ladder were followed by the man himself, but by some stroke of luck Stanley's head turned to larboard as he came down onto the main deck, close enough that Pett could smell the tobacco he was chewing.

Stanley did not see him but walked over to the rail and looked out across the bay, hands clasped behind his back. In a few quick steps Pett could be on him. He could stab the spike deep into his kidney and drag him back into the shadows. He could hide the body in his own cabin.

But what if Stanley were missed and the alarm raised before Pett had dealt with Courtney? What if the boatswain managed to scream before Pett had finished the job of silencing him forever?

Stanley turned and Pett saw his face in profile as the boat-swain looked along the rail towards the bow, his frown visible even in the gloom. Pett did not know what Stanley had seen, or thought he'd seen, and did not care. All that mattered was that Stanley muttered something under his breath and marched away down the deck. Pett let the breath seep out of his mouth, ears still sifting the night sounds for danger.

'*Now, do it now,*' the Saint said and Pett thrilled to hear the sound of that, of all voices, at last. His guide and protector was with him and all would be well.

He moved out from behind the steps and, crouching low, scurried to Captain Courtney's cabin. He raised his right arm so that the marlinspike slid back inside his shirtsleeve and with his freed fingers took the ship's nail from between his lips. Then he slowly inserted it into the lock. His lock picks and his weapons had gone down to the sea bed with the *Earl of Cumberland* but that was merely an inconvenience and the old ship's nail, which he had bent for his purpose, would do the job well enough.

Just then a thought occurred to him. Had not the path been laid out for him since the captain of the *Delft* pulled him from the ocean? Had this young Courtney not been served up like a banquet?

'*You think we do everything for you?*' the Saint asked.

Nevertheless, Pett turned the handle and, as he had known it would, the latch clicked. Tucking the nail into the waistband of his breeches he pushed the door open, slipped inside and closed it behind him, almost laughing at the Lord's designs. It was a source of constant wonder that God could play His part even to the most infinitesimal detail, the mundane minutiae such as a man's neglecting to lock his own door.

And now there was Courtney, deeply asleep. Dreaming of a

golden future, if Pett were to put money on it. Dreaming of heroic deeds and conquest. Of his dynasty perhaps, for there was no doubting that the young captain believed himself to be a man of destiny as his father had been. His woman was asleep next to him, to his left, lying on her side with her face against his neck. The white of her petticoats made a stark contrast against the dark skin of her bare arms and legs, and for a moment Pett allowed himself to watch her. Then he moved closer.

A board beneath his foot creaked and he cursed inwardly, holding still as Judith stirred and made herself comfortable. She did not wake. An inexperienced man might be breathing too fast now, his nerves getting the better of him, but Pett's breathing was deep and natural. He edged closer, moving around the bed until he stood over Henry Courtney who was asleep on his back, his face turned up to the low-beamed ceiling.

Pett flexed the muscles of his stomach and took a deep, silent breath, flooding his blood with energy and releasing the tension that always built before a kill.

Courtney's breathing was deep and even as Pett slid the marlinspike out of his shirtsleeve, held it in his right hand and drew his hand back to strike. As a weapon the spike was perfectly suited to stabbing, but lacked the sharp-edged blade required for cutting. He would therefore have to work with great precision, leaning over the bed and in one movement clasping his left hand over Courtney's mouth while using the right to push rather than stab the blade so that it went into the side of the neck, beside the jawbone and just below the ear, and cutting the right carotid artery in as smooth a motion as possible. There would be a lot of blood, on the body, on the sheets, on Pett himself, and unless he moved with exceptional speed the woman would wake to a nightmare scene. At that point it was simply a matter of stabbing her with as much speed and violence as possible, striking her repeatedly so as to silence her before she could scream for help.

Just then the cabin was washed with a thin silvery light and Pett looked out of the stern windows. A skein of cloud had torn apart to reveal stars and a sliver of moon and their glow illuminated the captain's quarters, and Pett's blood turned cold in his veins. For there on a table at the head of Courtney's bed, caught in the heart of the shaft of light spilling through the glass, was a bible, the gold inlaid cross shining against the black leather cover.

In that moment Pett's mind floundered as he himself had when he'd first jumped from the flaming *Earl of Cumberland* into the sea. Was this a sign from the Saint? Was this the Lord's way of telling him to spare Henry Courtney? Surely not. And yet the Saint had fallen strangely quiet. Normally, it was at this moment above all that his voice was clearest, yet on this occasion he was nowhere to be heard.

Pett felt abandoned, deserted. He stood there, feet stuck to those boards like the crustaceans fastened to the underside of the ship's hull, and felt the perspiration burst from his forehead, rolling in beads down his face.

Give me another sign, Pett's mind demanded. *Anything. Damn you but this is our time! Look at him, helpless as a babe.*

The cloud re-formed and the cabin was cast into darkness again, and yet he could not unsee what he had seen: the cross of Christ illuminated at the very moment he was to kill a man, a sign as loud as a thunderclap in the heavens. But a sign to kill the man, or spare him?

Oh but he was so close! It could be done in a moment. Two quick thrusts and a ripping of flesh and the job would be done. And yet something felt wrong. He had killed many times but this was the first time he had felt doubt, or even felt anything at all other than the inevitable thrill that comes with taking a man's life without being caught in the act. If there were even a chance that the Lord did not want him to kill Henry Courtney then Pett knew he must hold off. But if he did not kill him, how much more insistent would the clamour in his mind become, how much more shrilly would other voices scream for blood, even as the Saint remained silent?

Slowly, his breathing still even, he slid the spike back up his sleeve and backed away from the bed and the young lovers sleeping in it. He was almost at the door, just about to reach for the latch to open it again and let himself out when his right foot landed on a loose floorboard. It creaked. Not loudly, certainly no louder than any of the many other noises of wind in the sails, water against the hull and the constant groans of wood and rope that provided a constant chorus on a ship at sea. But it was a different noise and that was what woke Hal Courtney, who sat up in bed, his eyes wide open, took barely a second to register the scene before him and then, in puzzlement rather than fear, said, 'Pett? What the hell are you doing in my cabin?'

Now Judith was waking and murmuring sleepily, 'What troubles you, Henry?'

The reminder of her presence made Courtney more angry and he snapped, 'How dare you, sir? Bad enough that you enter the captain's quarters in the middle of the night, but to do so when there is a lady present . . . Explain yourself!'

Pett was dumbfounded. For once in his life his gift for dissimulation failed him and he stood in helpless silence for what seemed like an eternity until . . . Oh, glory! The Saint returned and said, '*Tromp. Consider Tromp.*'

Suddenly, Pett's wits returned to him. 'Forgive me, Captain, for this appalling intrusion. It was just that . . . well, I could not sleep, d'you see? There was a matter on my mind and I simply had to speak to you in private, away from the other members of the ship's company . . .'

'In the middle of the night? Are you mad?' Courtney looked at him, frowning. 'You've not been at the rum, have you?'

'No, sir, I assure you that alcohol has played no part in my deliberations, or my actions, it was just that . . .' Pett twisted his face into an expression of profound anguish, 'my soul was so tormented. I have . . . well . . . I have been the victim of a vile slander, sir! And this on top of the most cruel and unjust mistreatment.'

'What slander was that?'

''Twas the Dutchman, Tromp. Oh, I know he pretended to have misunderstood my meaning when he clearly and unambiguously questioned my courage for everyone to hear. But I know the man, both his command of English and his capacity for deceit. How, sir, can one trust the word of a man who boasts of ordering the manufacture of counterfeit religious relics, every one of them a blasphemy spat in the face of the Almighty?'

Both Courtney and the woman were silenced by that, and Pett felt confidence flooding through him as he went on: 'To call a man a coward in front of his peers is offence enough in itself. But this man locked me up like a common criminal in the most vile surroundings. You saw my plight for yourself, Captain. You saw me chained to the ship's timbers, lying in filth and ordure, with only a dead man for company. How can a gentleman of good reputation possibly accept such indignity?'

Courtney rubbed the sleep from his eyes. 'You make very good and fair points, Mr Pett. You have good reason to feel hard done by. But I confess, I do not see why this should require you to enter these quarters in the middle of the night.'

'The reason for that, sir, was that I have a request that can only be made to you in complete privacy, away from all your crew and your prisoners. I request . . . no, I insist, that you consent to my challenging Captain Tromp to a duel, on this ship, at the very earliest opportunity.'

'A duel?' Courtney exclaimed.

'Mr Pett, are you sure?' Judith asked.

'Yes, madam, absolutely. I will not be swayed from this desire. My honour will not allow it.'

'But Mr Pett,' Courtney insisted, 'with the greatest of respect, sir, you are not a military man . . .' He paused for a second to consider that statement and then, as a genuine question, added, 'Are you?'

'No, sir, I am a man of business.'

'Very well, then, you are at home in the marketplace and the counting house, or wherever it is that you transact your business. But however disgraceful his behaviour may have been, Captain Tromp is a naval officer who is very evidently at home in the midst of a battle. Whatever his moral failings – and I agree with you that his behaviour leaves a great deal to be desired – I have seen him fight and he is an opponent I would respect. My point, Mr Pett, is that I fear that if I agree to your request, I may also be agreeing to your demise.'

'That is a very worthy and considerate fear, Captain, but I assure you that you need not trouble yourself on my account. I have absolute faith that my cause is just and, that being the case, that God is on my side.'

'I have defeated whole armies of men who thought that God would ensure their victory, Mr Pett,' Judith said. 'He moves in mysterious ways. We cannot know what He plans for us. I do not mean to doubt your conviction. I merely want to save you from harm.'

'Thank you, madam, but let me ask you this. When you went into battle, knowing that you were fighting for the Tabernacle itself, did you not feel the armies of heaven marching beside you?'

'Yes, I did,' Judith admitted.

'And did that thought strengthen you in your conviction of victory?'

'It did.'

'Then since you had your faith, please allow me mine. If it is God's will that I should perish, so be it. But I would rather die with my honour intact than live with the slur of cowardice against my name. I may be a man of business, but I am still a man and I will fight like one when the time comes.'

'Well spoken, Mr Pett,' said Hal. 'It is my prayer that this matter can be settled without harm coming to you or Captain Tromp. Many a duel is settled to both parties' satisfaction without blood being shed, or not fatally so, at any rate. I very much hope that this will be the case here. I pray that, even now, a way can be found to settle this matter peacefully. But if it cannot, Mr Pett, then, yes, you may have your duel.'

'Are you sure, my love? Must we have more injury, more death?' Judith pleaded.

'I hope not, my love. But this is a matter of honour, and honour must be satisfied.'

Pett worried for a moment that the woman might press her case. But having made her point once, she did not argue further. *She, who has commanded men in their thousands, defers to this one man*, Pett thought, simultaneously admiring Courtney and adding to the pleasure he would derive, when the time was right, from taking such a highly prized life. For now, though, he had found a way, with the aid of the Saint, to escape from an extremely grave predicament. There was nothing to be gained from tarrying any longer and so he uttered a simple, 'Thank you, Captain,' and exited the cabin.

A scant twelve hours had passed since Hal had given his assent to Pett's request for a duel. He did not want to have the matter hanging unresolved over the ship and so the challenge had been made soon after dawn and accepted a short while later. Now the two men stood facing each other, twenty paces apart on the *Bough*'s deck. Pett had his back to the stern, Captain Tromp had his to the bow, and the crew lined the gunwales, thronged the rigging and even straddled the yards on all three masts to get a good view. The eight Dutch prisoners had been brought up from the hold to watch and even the skeleton crew which Hal had put aboard the *Delft*, anchored off the *Bough*'s larboard, hung in her shrouds waiting patiently for the entertainment to begin.

The Amadoda, most of whom were in the rigging for they

were now as sure-footed as any of the men out of Portsmouth or Plymouth, were whooping with joy and chattering noisily.

'You can still stop this, Henry,' Judith said. She stood beside Hal on the poop deck, looking down at the men who were checking their pistols, adjusting the length of the match to ensure the smouldering tip would hit the priming pan when the order was given to give fire.

Hal shook his head. 'It's too late now.' In truth he had been more moved by Judith's objections than he had initially revealed and had sought further counsel from Aboli before he gave the final order for the duel to be held.

'Let them fight it out, Gundwane,' Aboli had said. 'Having them both aboard, and Mr Pett hungering to satisfy his honour, is no good thing for us. Better to cut the ball out and clean the wound than let it fester and poison the flesh around it. This dispute has caused trouble among the crew. Daniel already had to stop two of our men beating one of the Dutch sailors half to death. Let us see an end to the matter.'

'But what if Tromp kills Pett? The men won't like it. Won't that make matters even worse?'

Aboli shrugged. 'Do they care that much? Pett is an Englishman, but he is not one of us who sail on the *Golden Bough*. No one will weep for him. Let them fight. Give the crew a spectacle. Something to gamble on.' He grinned. 'Though of course their captain will not know that they are betting on the outcome.'

Hal considered the matter and concluded that Aboli's point was well made. An unresolved argument might poison the men's spirits, but the chance to witness two men fight, right out in the open, would lift them. And so Mr Pett now faced Mr Tromp.

The Dutchman had tried to settle the matter without recourse to violence. 'It is not right for me to duel against an opponent who cannot win,' he had said, on more than one occasion. But there were only so many times that he could seek to evade the issue without being accused of cowardice himself and so, in the end, he had accepted the challenge, albeit with a heavy heart.

To Tromp's surprise, Pett had given him the choice of weapons. 'In that case, I choose pistols,' he had said.

'I'm surprised by your decision,' Hal had remarked later, when the two men found themselves standing close enough together on the deck to be able to converse without being overheard. 'I have seen you fight with a sword and you handle it well. If you would prefer a pistol, you must be a truly exceptional shot.'

'On the contrary, I would be far more sure of my chances with a sword. And there lies the problem. It would be very difficult indeed for me not to kill that thickhead Pett if we were going sword to sword. But if we fight with pistols, well, they are notoriously unreliable weapons and frequently do not fire at all. Even when they do, they rarely hit their target at anything more than point-blank range. And that is on land. At sea, on a moving deck, well, if Pett does manage to kill me, then God really is on his side and He isn't at all happy about those damn relics.'

Hal had laughed. In truth, for all his scoundrel ways Tromp was much more Hal's kind of man than the cold, pallid, bloodless Pett. Still, whatever his failings, Pett could not be called a coward. Just being willing to take his place on the deck, with his pistol in his hand, proved that there was nothing wrong with his guts.

Captain Tromp's own men stood along the starboard rail amidships, chained to each other by ankle irons, and Tromp called to them now in Dutch, telling them that he would win back their pride by putting a hole in the Englishman's head.

Some cheered him but most did not, for their captain had led them to disaster and they held it against him.

'He's sweating like a ripe cheese now,' an experienced fore-mastman named Ralph Bigg said, pointing at Tromp.

'Aye, he's soggy as a pair of apple dumplings in a Spanish brothel,' another man called, raising a chorus of bawdy laughter and insults aimed at the Dutch.

'But look at Mr Pett,' a good topmastman named Bosely said. 'Not a bead on him. Calm as a millpond he is.'

'Cold, more like,' another man countered. 'Cold as the frost on a witch's tit.'

Both men were dressed in breeches, shirt and nothing else, their feet and heads bare, whereas almost every other man aboard wore some manner of headgear to keep off the sun. Hal swept the broad-brimmed hat from his own head and dabbed his forehead with a kerchief, for it was approaching midday and getting hot. Even Judith was beginning to perspire, though she was born and raised beneath the African sun, and Hal had insisted on erecting an awning to keep her, and the baby she carried, well shaded.

'It's heat, not fear, that has Tromp sweating,' Hal said, though he would not have put money on it. Tromp himself must have been wondering by now why Pett, who was supposedly so much more proficient at business than war, had so confidently given him the choice of weapons and why the Englishman was now standing there examining the dirt under his fingernails as though he had nothing more pressing to do.

'Are you ready, gentlemen?' Big Daniel called from where he hung six feet off the deck in the mainmast shrouds, close to Pett and Tromp, yet away from the line of fire between them.

Both duellists called their assent and now a hush fell across the deck. The wagers had been placed, the catcalls and insults had long since drifted off across the ocean like gun smoke on the breeze, and the stage was set.

'You will not give fire until I give the word *fire*,' Daniel continued. 'Then you may each fire once, as and when you will. Only in the event of a grievous wound to either man, so that he is unable to fire his pistol, or both pistols having been shot, will the duel be over. Do you understand?'

'Let us get on with it,' Captain Tromp replied. Pett simply nodded.

Instinctively Hal stepped in front of Judith. It would have to be an appalling shot, taken at the moment of being shot himself perhaps, for Tromp to hit anyone standing on the poop deck, but Hal would take no chances.

Time seemed to stretch out like the ocean. Somewhere a man farted loudly, which caused a ripple of laughter and only made Big Daniel keep them waiting longer, both men's arms stretched before them, the pistol in Tromp's hand beginning to tremble.

'Fire!' Big Daniel bellowed and there was a delay, then a flash of flame and a wisp of smoke followed by a loud crack from Tromp's pistol and Pett's left shoulder was thrown back though his feet remained planted on the deck. There was a murmur from the crowd and blood bloomed scarlet on Pett's shirt, and Hal thought that both pistols must have gone off at the same time and that Pett must have missed. But then it was clear that Pett had yet to fire, for his arm was still outstretched, the pistol in his hand still cocked, its match smouldering.

Pett hardly felt the wound that was spilling blood down his side to stain his breeches because he was savouring the moment the way a lord might savour his finest wine. He had never missed from this range. He had never failed to kill a man he meant to kill and so he would make them all wait now so that they might see how it was done properly. His attention was so absolutely concentrated on the gun in his hand and the figure of Tromp who was standing with a horrified look on his face – the look of a man who realizes too late that he has been played for a fool and is about to suffer the consequences – that he did not even notice the quiet all around, not just on the deck but also in his head. The voices were silent, all of them.

Then he squeezed the trigger and the dog catch brought the match coal onto the priming pan and there was a flash followed by a report and Tromp flinched as the ball gouged the flesh from the top of his left arm.

'*Jesus Christus!*' he blurted, all teeth and scowl.

Pett looked at his pistol, glaring at it as though it had betrayed him.

'Swords would have been better,' a sailor called Logward shouted, crossly, as an air of anti-climax settled over the deck. Hal, however, was delighted by the outcome, breathing a long sigh of relief that both men had survived. He knew full well that even a scratch could kill if it turned gangrenous, but he would deal with that problem if and when he came to it.

'That's it then!' Big Daniel called. 'It's over.' Both men stood there still, staring at one another. It was clear that neither had received a fatal wound, though it was impossible to say whether each was relieved to be alive, or rather wishing for more powder and shot so that they could try again.

'Are you satisfied then, Mr Pett?' Tromp called, wincing in pain the moment he had asked the question.

Pett handed the pistol back to Big Daniel. 'I am satisfied, Captain Tromp,' he said, but his flat voice and expressionless face were in stark contrast to the storm that raged in his head.

'Aboli, go to my cabin and fetch the French brandy,' Hal said.

'Are we celebrating, Captain?' Will Stanley asked.

'It's to wash out their wounds, Stanley, you mud,' Ned Tyler said.

'I can piss on them to save your brandy,' Aboli called loud enough for the two duellists to hear. His belief that human urine prevented wounds becoming infectious was well known among those who had sailed with him the longest, and some had even had cause to admit, through gritted teeth and a tightly pressed nose, that the treatment appeared to work.

'You keep your great black snake trapped in your breeches,' Tyler shouted, 'or I'll wager Mr Tromp would rather take his chances with the sharks.'

This raised a laugh from the *Bough*'s crew and Hal was pleased to hear it because it suggested that the duel had served its purpose. No one had been killed, but both men were bloodied, and there were several aboard, John Lovell among them judging by the smirk on his face, who had won coin by betting on that exact outcome.

'I am glad that it is over,' Judith said in her rich, low voice, then shook her head. 'You men and your pride.'

Hal's eyes roved over her face, drinking in those honey-coloured eyes with their long, curled lashes, her skin which had the dark translucence of acacia gum, and the full bow of her lips.

'Perhaps pride is a sin as the Papists claim,' he said, 'but I can't condemn Pett for it. I know what it feels like to have everything taken away, to be treated like an animal and come to the edge of despair.' He fell silent as he remembered the days and nights chained like a slave on the *Gull of Moray*, and the long months of servitude in the Cape Colony. 'Sometimes, my love, our pride is all we have left.'

Hal turned and descended the poop deck ladder to join Mr Pett aft of the mainmast. Pett had taken off his shirt in order to examine the wound in his shoulder.

'Just a scratch, Captain,' he said.

Hal nodded. 'You were both lucky,' he said. 'I must admit I am impressed that you managed to keep a steady hand and hit the man after taking the wound. I could expect no more from my own men, but they have been in many fights, while you have never seen action.'

'My father fought in the wars at Cheriton in forty-four and at Naseby,' Pett said. The men nearby murmured at the mention of those bloody battles, for all of them had friends or family who had been killed in the Civil Wars. 'He taught me how to shoot, so I was glad when the Dutchman chose pistols. I fear I would not have lasted long if he'd have gone for swords.'

Hal smiled. 'Then it would seem your luck still holds, Mr Pett,' he said, looking at Tromp who was having his wound examined by Big Daniel. 'More so seeing as I have French brandy for your wound, which is preferable, I'm sure you'll agree, to having Aboli piss on you.'

'I have never tried it, Captain Courtney,' Pett said solemnly. 'It might be beneficial.'

'Good.' Hal nodded curtly. 'Then if you will excuse me I must get these rascals back to work. The wind is returning, Mr Pett,' he said, looking up at the colours stirring atop the mizzen. 'Up anchor, Mr Tyler. Mr Moone, Mr Stanley! Get these lazy sons of Satan to their stations and set all plain sail.' In moments the *Golden Bough* was a hive of industry as the Amadoda raced up the shrouds and scrambled out along the yards. The canvas billowed and the ship seemed to shiver with the thrill of it, as though she too were eager to turn her bows into the south once more and feel the ocean race along her hull.

And as Aboli poured good French brandy into the bloody raw wound on his shoulder, Mr Pett watched Captain Courtney, wondering what plan the Saint had for him and when he would be called upon to execute it.

As for Captain Tromp, Pett could not say how he had missed the Dutchman from that range, yet he knew the Saint had played some part in it.

Two men had been allowed to live when Pett had planned for them to die. Nothing like that had ever happened to him before. There must, he reasoned, be some meaning to such an extraordinary phenomenon. And in due course, he felt sure, he would discover what that reason was.

Two days had passed since the duel and neither Pett nor Tromp seemed troubled by the condition of the flesh wounds they had suffered. With the boil of their enmity lanced, the *Bough* was sailing south on a fresh breeze and in good heart. It seemed to Tromp like an ideal moment to approach Hal as he stood on the poop deck to ask,

'Might I have a word with you, Captain?'

'By all means,' Hal replied. He was the master of his ship, with the sun on his back, the wind on his face and the woman he loved by his side. All was well with the world.

'You may recall that I recently asked you whether you might allow me and my crewmen to join your ship's company. Of course, you have had other things to worry about . . .' Tromp gave a wry smile and cast an eye towards the thin figure standing by the stern rail, looking out across the water. 'Isn't that so, Mr

Pett?' Then he turned back to Hal. 'Have you had time to consider my request?'

Hal laughed. 'No one could deny that you have the devil's own cheek. First you wanted to kill us, now you want to sail with us.'

'I never wanted to kill you,' Tromp protested. 'I just wanted this ship and a square meal.'

Aboli had walked up to join the conversation. 'You can't blame him for that,' he said, grinning from ear to ear.

'Let me join your crew,' Tromp continued. 'I am an experienced captain, but you are the master on this ship and I can see that Mijnheer Aboli is your trusted first mate. Very well, then, take me on as second mate. I know these waters. I have experience of the coast as far north as the Horn and south around the Cape. I have sailed all the way to the Spice Isles, so the waters of the Indies also are familiar to me. I will gladly share the many trade contacts I have cultivated over the years. I have friends, Captain.'

'You must have,' Hal said, 'to have survived this long with so many enemies.'

Tromp looked at Hal with an uncharacteristically thoughtful, almost solemn expression. 'You are a man of destiny, Captain Courtney,' he said, and there was no trace of levity in his voice. 'Anyone can see that for you wear it like a fine cloak. It would be an honour to serve under you.'

Aboli and Ned Tyler, who was standing at the wheel and could hear every word that was spoken, looked towards their captain. Tromp had placed the ball firmly in his court. No one could deny that he had spoken well, nor that he had a good case to make. How would their skipper respond?

Hal was lost in thought, weighing up what Tromp had said. It was Judith who broke the silence. 'Did you not say you were short of crew, Henry?'

'I did.'

'Then would you not welcome such experienced seamen as these?' she asked.

Tromp was staring at Judith, clearly amazed that the woman whose life he had threatened was now pleading on his behalf.

'You are a remarkable creature, my dear,' Hal told Judith, who looked from him to Tromp.

'I have seen so much death,' she said. 'If it is within your power to save this man's life and the lives of his crew, then you must do it.'

'Thank you, madam,' Tromp said, and Judith nodded a silent acknowledgement of his gratitude.

'How do I know you will not try to seize my ship at the first opportunity?' Hal asked. 'It seems to me you are a man who has little respect for authority, and yet you would serve me as a midshipman?'

Tromp smiled and it was reflected in his blue eyes. 'I would owe you my life. Twice over, since you could have fed me to the sharks that dawn after we met. Moreover, I am nothing if not an ambitious man.' His blue eyes fixed on Hal. 'I truly believe that sailing with you is my best hope of advancement.'

Hal considered everything he had heard. In truth even if Tromp broke his word it would be an almost impossible task for the Dutchmen to subdue the *Bough*'s crew and take the ship. On the other hand, the *Bough* was indeed a little short of men these days, and experienced hands would be very welcome.

'What do you think, Mr Pett? Should I let Mr Tromp and his fellows join my crew?'

Pett looked taken aback. 'It is none of my concern, Captain,' he said, a line creasing his brow. 'But you sailors being a super-stitious lot, it cannot be a bad thing having a lucky man aboard.'

'Lucky, Mr Pett? How so?' Hal asked.

'Lucky indeed,' Pett assured him. 'Firstly, he hit me from twenty paces, the two of us standing on a rolling deck. Secondly, my own shot merely grazed him, and I am not accustomed to missing that at which I aim.'

'Those are surprising words, Mr Pett . . . for a man of business,' Hal observed.

'I believe I mentioned that my father gave me instruction in the use of firearms. He was a stern taskmaster and he taught me well. He would not have been pleased to see me fail him.'

'I see.' Hal looked at Pett. There was something about the man that disturbed him, something that wasn't quite right. He knew he was not alone in his unease. He'd heard his crewmen talking about Pett's eerie calm during the duel; the way he had barely flinched when he took Tromp's shot; the cold assurance with which he had aimed at his adversary. On the other hand Tromp had gained huge kudos for the courage with which he had faced Pett, knowing that there was nothing whatever he could do to defend himself. Pett's willingness to take his time and his evident annoyance that he had missed, however, disturbed the men, more than impressed them. Hal did not want the man on his ship for one second longer than was absolutely essential. Tromp, however, was another matter altogether.

'Very well, then, Mr Tromp, my answer to your question is, "Yes",' he said. 'I will take you on as second mate and I would be grateful if you could list the names of all your men and any particular skills that they possess.'

Tromp's face burst into a beaming smile. 'You will not regret your decision, Captain Courtney,' he said.

Hal too smiled, but his words were no joke. 'You'd better hope that I do not. I've placed my faith in you. But be sure that if you ever betray that faith, by God I'll make you regret it.'

169

'I'll be watching you, Dutchman,' Aboli growled.

'Good, then you may learn a thing or two,' Tromp quipped, leaving Aboli wide-eyed and almost speechless at such outrageous impudence.

'Mind your tongue, Mr Tromp,' Hal warned. 'One duel is quite enough to be going on with. I wouldn't want you provoking another.'

'Aye-aye, Captain,' replied Tromp.

To Hal's relief, Mr Tromp proved himself very useful, the two of them poring over charts together, the Dutchman sharing his knowledge of the coast so that between them their combined experience would prove invaluable in the future.

It was, of course, far too soon to tell Tromp about Elephant Lagoon and the treasures there. But he did not have to be told that they were heading south, for a simple glance at the sun told him that and he did know of several safe anchorages between Zanzibar and the Cape where an English frigate might stop to take on fresh water without risk of attack from either Omani Arab warlords or the flotillas of Madagascan pirates which were known to prey on even well-armed vessels.

As for the other men of the *Delft*, they worked hard, if not harder, than anyone and were clearly experienced seamen or 'seasoned Jack Tars' as Ned Tyler had observed with grudging respect one morning when he and Hal had put them through their paces: making them run up the mainmast shrouds, out across to the ends of the yard and down again, only to repeat the activity until they were greasy with sweat and bent double catching their breath.

'They'll do, Mr Tyler,' Hal said, keeping his satisfaction to himself. 'Have our lads accepted them though? That's the thing.'

'Aye, there's the usual banter of course, what with them being cheese-heads, but that's a good sign as you well know, Captain.'

The words were said cheerfully enough, but Hal could sense that there was something else that Tyler wasn't telling him. 'Something's troubling you, Ned, I can see it in you. Care to tell me what it is?'

'Oh, I'm sure it's nothing, Captain . . .'

'I'll be the judge of that. Tell me.'

Tyler gave a long sigh, tamped down the tobacco in the clay pipe he liked to smoke, then puffed away to get it all burning nicely again. Hal let him take his time, knowing that it would be entirely counter-productive to rush the grizzled, weather-beaten helmsman. Finally Tyler said, 'It's Mr Pett. Now I don't mean no disrespect to the gentleman, but I'm afraid that the crew haven't taken to him, like. Haven't taken to him at all.'

Hal had been raised by his father to take good care of his men. 'You're asking them to climb out on the topgallants shrouds when there's a gale blowing, and board an enemy ship when the grapeshot's flying,' Francis Courtney used to say. 'They'll do that grudgingly if they're frightened to disobey you. But if you treat them right, and see to their needs, they'll do it willingly because they want to obey you.'

So now he took Tyler's words seriously. 'Is there anything in particular they don't like?'

'Well, for a start, they don't think he's right in the head. He's polite enough at dinner and can even spin a decent yarn, I'll grant him that. But a lot of the lads say he talks to himself when he doesn't think anyone's listening, like he's having a conversation with someone only he can see. And he talks about God and the angels and suchlike.'

'There's nothing wrong with having a good, Christian faith.'

'Aye, Captain, that's true. But Mr Pett's not like that. There's

171

something . . .' Tyler cast around for the right word. 'I don't know,' he said finally. 'But it's just not right, the way he is. Peculiar, you might say.'

Hal was just opening his mouth to speak but Ned cut him off. 'And then there's that whole duel business, too. The way he stood there and just let Mr Tromp shoot him, like he didn't feel it or nothing. And then, there was a look on his face when he aimed at Mr Tromp, all cold, like he wasn't bothered at all about shooting another man, like he might have been shooting a rat, or something . . . vermin, anyway. And when he didn't kill him . . .'

'He was disappointed, yes, I saw that too,' Hal said. 'And I know what you mean about the crew not liking him. I'd seen signs of something brewing in the men, but until now I hadn't realized what it was.' Hal sighed. 'I'd really been hoping to avoid it . . .'

'What's that, then, Captain?'

'Zanzibar. The whole place is run by Omani Arabs, the very same people whose ships we sunk so cheerfully up and down the Red Sea. I can't see them looking very kindly on the *Golden Bough* if she turns up in their harbour. But then again . . .'

Hal thought for a second and said, 'Ned, be so kind as to tell Mr Aboli, Mr Tromp and Master Fisher that I wish to see them, and you too, of course, in the captain's quarters at midday.'

When the men assembled, with Judith also in attendance, Hal told them, 'It has been brought to my attention that Mr Pett is, quite unintentionally, I'm sure, disturbing the morale of the crew. I will therefore go ashore in Zanzibar with Mr Pett and escort him to His Majesty's Consul there, so that between them they can find the fastest possible means of getting him back to England. This will also be to Mr Pett's advantage, and that of the East India Company, for if he sails north to Suez

172

and then makes an overland trip to Alexandria, whence he can sail back to London, his journey will be far faster than it would be were he to sail around the Cape aboard the *Golden Bough*. As you will gather from his absence here, this is not a proposal over which I plan to give Mr Pett any say. His removal will also put to an end any lingering unpleasantness between himself and Mr Tromp.'

'There is none on my part, I assure you, Captain,' Tromp said.

'And I believe you. Nevertheless, we have done our duty by Mr Pett in rescuing him and providing him with good quarters and regular meals. Now we shall conclude our obligations by helping him back home. I also have various items of mail to send back to Britain. Viscount Winterton, for one, has a right to know what has happened to his ship, and to his poor son, for I fear he may not know of his passing.'

'Are we sailing the *Bough* into Zanzibar?' Aboli asked. 'Surely there will be many there who know of her exploits in the Red Sea, indeed some who have witnessed them and who will recognize a ship that did them great harm.'

'I agree. That is why we will moor the *Bough* at least a full day's sail from Zanzibar City and proceed there aboard the *Delft*. You may have your own command back for the purpose, Mr Tromp. And before you point out that you, too, do not want your ship to be recognized I will say that there is little chance that anyone now in Zanzibar also saw the *Delft* in the waters of the East Indies. We shall change her name. I thought the "Christina" would do nicely. I know it's a name that you regard fondly, after all.'

The men all laughed, knowing that this was the name of the admiral's daughter Tromp had seduced and liking the Dutchman all the better for the fact that he willingly joined in the laughter.

'Damn the woman!' he said. 'I thought I'd left her for good in Batavia!'

'The crew, however, will all be good *Bough* men,' Hal added, 'both because they can keep an eye on you while I am ashore, and because I may have need of them if I am not welcomed with open arms. I shall, of course, go ashore under an assumed name. But Consul Grey will know me at once and he may still harbour a grudge against me.'

'You did betray him, Gundwane,' Aboli observed. 'If any man did that to me, I would not soon forgive him.'

'I did not betray him directly,' Hal countered. 'I bought a Letter of Marque commissioning me to fight with the Arab fleet, and I paid him handsomely for it, too, I might add. Of course, I would never have taken up arms for Mussulmen against a Christian foe. I cannot believe he did not know that, and I am sure that he has not been held responsible for my actions. And even if he has, Consul Grey will always be a man who places money ahead of any other allegiance. If necessary I will soothe his troubles with gold.'

Aboli still looked sceptical, but he remained silent for he never wanted to be seen to question Hal's authority in front of any members of the crew, no matter how senior or well-trusted. The plan was accepted, and the ship's officers left the room, leaving Hal alone with Judith.

'I must ask you something,' she said.

'Of course, my love,' replied Hal. He looked at Judith with a concerned frown across his brow and asked. 'Are you not well?'

She smiled and touched his forearm, reassuringly. 'I am very well. But I am also with child, which means that I now feel sick or exhausted from time to time, and in due course, when the time comes, I will feel great pain.'

'No! I won't allow it!' Hal said.

Judith laughed gently. 'There are some things that are beyond your command, even on your ship,' she said. 'Childbirth is hard, painful. That is why they call it labour. I wish there were another woman on board to help me with it. Perhaps when the time comes we can put ashore somewhere and find a midwife.'

'That may be hard to find in Africa, my darling.'

'Not if I were at home. I would have all the women of my family and servants too. But we shall manage as best we can and there are certain herbs and medicinal preparations that will help me, both removing feelings of sickness and helping to lessen the pain. I'm sure that there will be apothecaries in Zanzibar who will be able to provide them.'

'Of course, I quite understand,' Hal nodded. 'Just let me know what you need and I will find it for you.'

'No, Henry, my love, you will not,' said Judith, though she spoke with such a loving voice that Hal barely noticed that she had flatly contradicted him. 'You have other, more import-ant things to do and besides, you are a man, so you would not know what to get, or understand even if I told you. And you are English, so you cannot discuss this matter with an apothecary whose sole languages are Arabic or Swahili.'

'Perhaps so, but you are the wicked General Nazet, who defeated not one but two great Mussulman armies. Every devout Zanzibari will hate you.'

'They hate the general, that's true,' Judith replied. 'They think she is a monster, a gorgon, the bride of Shaitan, who has come to earth in the form of a human. What they will see when I walk through the market, or step into a cool, dark shop seeking treatment from an apothecary for various female problems is a respectable, polite, modest young woman, with her hair beneath a veil, going about her daily business. Why should anyone look at her and think: "There goes General Nazet"?'

Hal gave her a wry smile. 'Very well. I know when I'm beaten. I don't have any more chance against you than those Arab generals did. We shall go together, you and I, to Zanzibar. And let us just hope that we leave together also.'

T he *Delft*, now bearing the name 'Christina' crudely painted across her stern, entered the harbour of Zanzibar City at dawn. A longboat took Hal, Judith and Aboli ashore – Mr Pett having indicated that he would prefer to remain aboard ship until his meeting with Consul Grey had been arranged. To Judith's delight it transpired that there was an apothecary's shop in one of the old whitewashed buildings that lined the harbour front outside the fortress walls. 'That makes sense,' Hal said. 'He must do a roaring trade with nervous travellers seeking a cure for their seasickness and sailors who just need a cure for the pox.'

Not suffering from either ailment, he saw no need to go in and waited outside while Judith went in to browse among the sacks of herbs, the phials of potions and the various pills and powders that the venerable proprietor, his skin as dry, brown and translucent as ancient parchment, kept on shelves that ran along the full width and most of the height of one wall. There were rows of neatly labelled jars and bottles and a hundred herbal infusions: sassafras root tea to cleanse the blood, jimson-weed for rheumatism, chestnut leaf tea for asthma, mint and cow manure tea for consumption, and many more besides.

Judith explained that she was Egyptian, a member of the Coptic Church en route to a new life in the Indies with her husband, an English merchant, and mentioned that they were looking for lodgings for just a few nights until the ship that was due to take them on the next leg of their journey arrived. The apothecary seemed very interested in her need for a place to stay, so she said that her husband would be happy to pay a very good rate for suitable accommodation.

That she had funds had already been established by the considerable quantity of remedies, soothing teas and tinctures, and cosmetic preparations she had already ordered, for Judith, having found a shop that was a veritable treasure trove, had decided that she might as well stock up for what was going to be a long voyage with few creature comforts.

'I have some rooms that I could make available to you. They are very modest indeed and assuredly far inferior to those to which you are accustomed. Nevertheless for a very modest consideration I could offer them to you.'

'May I see these rooms, please?' Judith asked.

'Of course, of course . . . but please excuse me, I will only be a moment.'

The apothecary disappeared and a moment later Judith could hear the distant sound of a marital dispute as the apothecary tried to persuade his wife that they should vacate their home and spend the next few days staying with their daughter, who evidently lived just a few doors down the road.

Realizing that the resolution of this dispute might be a while in coming, Judith took her purchases outside, removed one or two items that she thought she would need in the next day or two and asked Hal in her sweetest tones – the ones that he had long since realized meant 'this is an order' – whether one of his men could kindly take everything back to the *Delft*.

Judith was just browsing through yet more sacks of vividly coloured seeds, herbs and even petals when the apothecary reappeared, and said, 'Follow me please,' and led her past a scowling elderly lady to a modest apartment, comprising three simply furnished rooms and a flat roof shaded with old sail-cloth. There was a clear view of the waterfront and beyond that the sea. Judith could even pick out the *Delft* – or rather, the *Christina* – bobbing at her mooring. Hal, she knew, would be glad of the ability to keep an eye on his ship. For her part, she could see that the apothecary's wife was a diligent house-keeper for the whole place was spotlessly clean. It also benefited from the combination of fresh sea breezes wafting in from the roof terrace and the heady, herbal scents from the shop downstairs.

'I might be interested,' she told the apothecary, knowing that too great a display of eagerness would be fatal to her chances of securing a decent price. 'How much?'

He promptly named an outrageously excessive sum, to which Judith then replied with the offer of a pittance. They spent an enjoyable few minutes haggling back and forth and then, honour satisfied on both sides, agreed on a sum that both of them would have considered reasonable from the start.

Hal returned with a pair of sailors carrying a chest in which were a number of items of clothing and – for he was well aware that Zanzibar was a place in which one could not afford to be unarmed – the Neptune sword and a fine pair of pistols that had once belonged to his father. Once the chest had been deposited and Judith had begun unpacking, Hal first settled the bill for Judith's purchases and then sat down to write a letter to Consul Grey in which he apologized for any misunderstanding that may have occurred over his activities during the recent, but now thankfully concluded war in Ethiopia; hoped that the consul had not suffered any undue inconveniences as a result of said misunderstandings; requested an audience with the consul, explaining that he was travelling in the company of Mr William Pett of the East India Company, who would be very grateful for the consul's assistance in finding him swift passage back to England; and finally added that he had various items of correspondence that also needed to be sent back to their shared mother country. 'I am sure that the knowledge that we are united as true Englishmen, loyal to our King and Country, will outweigh any minor disputes we may in the past have had,' Hal concluded. There was, however, no mention of Judith. Zanzibar was a place where nothing could stay secret long. There was no sense in doing anything that might indicate that General Nazet, of all people, was present there.

Hal re-read his work and decided that it would do the job admirably. He sent one of his most reliable men off to deliver the missive by hand. Then he, Judith and Aboli, with two seamen acting as guards, set off to see the city, the noisy bazaars and the crowded souks.

'The blessings of Allah upon you!' young boys chirruped, trying to grab hold of Hal or Judith in order to lead them to their family's stalls. Aboli would try to scare them off with growls and fierce expressions, but with limited success.

They passed stalls selling ivory and gum Arabic, a substance prized for its sweetness as well as its adhesive properties. There were baskets full of spices and stalls of shimmering silks and carpets from Muscat whose sellers unrolled them, proclaiming the expert craftsmanship of the weave to Judith as the party passed. There were slaves too; men, women, boys and girls, chained in sorry-looking lines and guarded by thugs brandishing cutlasses or clubs. The slavers themselves, or their quartermasters more often than not, stood there hawking their human stock, pointing out the men's strong arms and shoulders, the women's breasts and skilled hands, and sometimes even the private parts of the young girls, which so disgusted Hal and the others that they would deliberately look the other way so as not to encourage the slavers.

At times the streets became so narrow that the flow of people along them slowed to a crawl, like blood clotting in the veins of the town, and here it was cooler because the sunlight rarely found its way in. Those tenants in the top apartments could almost reach out and touch the buildings opposite, and crows and starlings chattered noisily overhead.

At one choke point, where a vendor stood grilling octopus, squid and oysters, this sea's bounty flavoured with mouth-watering spices, a blind man stood upon an old upended crate decrying the iniquity of those who turned their back on Jesus to follow instead the false god and his prophet Mohammed.

'You will live to see the end of days!' the man called, his blind eyes reminding Hal of the whitish pulpy lychee fruits a boy had tried to sell him earlier. 'You will be cast into torment and the eternal abyss for you have betrayed He that created us in His own image!'

There were plenty of Mussulmen passing but none of them

seemed to pay the blind man any attention and neither did he seem afraid for his life, despite disparaging the faith of those who controlled Zanzibar.

'He is like the hadeda bird,' Aboli said. 'He chatters so much that they grow used to him. After a while they do not hear him at all.'

'This island is extraordinary,' Hal said, his eyes taking in the flow of faces going by. There were black faces, white, brown and yellow and every shade in between. The eyes were almond-shaped or bulbous and popping, and the noses were flat, curved or beaked. Hair was woolly or silken, black or golden, in this cauldron of humanity where the blood of European, Bantu and Arab was mingled with that of the inhabitants of so many other lands that were washed by the western portion of the Indian Ocean.

'When my father led an embassy to Venice, on behalf of our former emperor, Iyasu's father, I became used to the crowds of people from different nations crowding the piazzas, or going to and fro on the canals. But even that was nothing like this.' Judith gave a wry, dry laugh. 'But then, Venice was Europe, Zanzibar is Africa. This is a hotter, wilder, more savage continent.'

She took Hal's arm in hers and leant in close. 'Maybe I should have brought my armour,' she joked, and Hal remembered how fine she had looked in her polished mail hauberk beneath a white tunic, mounted on a black Arabian stallion with its golden armour and crest of ostrich feathers. When Hal had first met Judith in her glorious war gear, he had thought she was a man. He had known her only as General Nazet and had never conceived that the famous warrior and leader might be a woman. Looking at her beside him now, and knowing every inch of her supremely female body as he did, Hal wondered how he could ever have been thus deluded.

'You will have to stay close to me, Captain Courtney,' Judith said, her breath against his ear enough to have his loins stirring, urging him to take her back to their lodgings and the soft bed awaiting them.

'Have no fear, my love,' he said, 'I swear I shall protect you. You are quite safe with me.'

She smiled demurely and kissed his cheek though her eyes darted hither and thither as they drank in the sights all around them, and Hal grinned back, enchanted to experience Zanzibar through her eyes, as though he were seeing it himself for the first time.

His thoughts were interrupted by a sudden outburst of jeering and shouting. Just ahead of them a crowd had gathered around a slaver's block. The slaver, a Portuguese man in rusty back- and breast-plates, was struggling to hold on to a rope on the end of which a black boy struggled and fought like a hooked mackerel.

To roars of laughter the slaver leant back and hauled the boy towards him so that the lad sprawled in the dirt. There were Arabs in finely embroidered gowns and headdresses, hard-bitten Portuguese merchants, ship's captains, agents, craftsmen looking for cheap labour and quartermasters looking for slaves with experience as crew aboard merchantmen. There were stall traders too, these having been drawn away from their own businesses by all the excitement.

The man kicked the boy where his ribs showed beneath the skin but the boy did not cry out. Instead he grabbed hold of the slaver's leg, wrapped his thin arms around it and held on for all his worth. Which would not be much, because few would bid for such a wildling.

The other slaves, three Africans and a European, cowered nearby, afraid of their owner's wrath and the tall, armed guard who held on to the rope which bound them all together.

As men's and women's voices joined in a cacophony of harsh shouts and high-pitched screeches, all offering their view on what was happening the slaver drew his pistol and, gripping it by its long barrel, began to beat him with the stock. But the boy had other ideas and he bit into the soft flesh of the man's bare calf so that he bellowed.

'Stop! Leave him!' Judith called out in Arabic, pushing through to the front of the crowd, shrugging off their hands as Hal and Aboli tried to restrain her.

'What is it to you?' the slaver demanded. Hal grimaced. The last thing they needed was to draw this kind of attention.

'Come away,' he growled at Judith, tugging at her arm. She stood firm.

'What it is to me is I do not like my slaves damaged before I buy them.'

'You want to buy this little brat?' he demanded with surprise.

She nodded. 'But I won't pay you more than half a silver rupee.'

The boy looked up, equally astonished, and Hal saw him properly now. He could not have been more than twelve years old. Under the dirt and grime his skin was the same colour as Judith's, the dark gold of fresh acacia gum.

'Done!' the slaver shouted hurriedly. 'Sold to the lovely lady with a good eye for a bargain!' and struck the wooden auction block with the pistol's barrel to confirm the sale.

With a shrug of resignation, Hal slipped a small coin from his purse and flipped it across to the slaver. That worthy placed his foot on the boy's backside and gave him a hearty shove. The boy bolted like a jack rabbit, ducked under Judith's outstretched arms, and kept running, but not for much further.

Aboli reached out a long black arm and grabbed him by the

scruff. When he lifted him the boy's legs kept on oscillating wildly in the air.

'Where do you think you are going?' he asked in not unkindly tones. 'You belong to my lady now, Mossie.'

'Mossie?' Hal asked.

'It means sparrow. And I think it's a perfect name for him,' Judith answered, with a smile. 'However, I don't think you are going very far, are you, my Mossie?' The child stopped churning the air with his thin stick-like legs, and drooped pathetically in Aboli's great fist. Then with an obvious effort he renewed his defiance.

'I will not be a good slave!' Mossie glared at Judith. 'You just wait and see.'

Hal decided that it was time for him to take over negotiations. He crouched on his haunches so that his eyes were on a level with Mossie's. 'I don't have slaves on my ship, and that's where you're going, on my ship. So if you insist on being a slave, I will just have to throw you overboard for the sharks to eat. Is that what you want, Mossie?'

Mossie glared at him sullenly, but his eyes filled with tears, making it clear that was not what he had in mind, at all. Hal winked up at Judith, and she understood that was his signal for her to intervene.

'Mossie, I will pay you a copper penny for every month you work as my bodyguard on board the ship, and I promise no sharks.' He looked at her with sudden increased interest.

Hal felt his devils urging him for a little more fun, so he cut in again. 'I will pay you two copper pennies a month.' He raised on Judith's offer.

Mossie barely glanced in his direction. 'No.' He shook his head.

'Why not?' Hal demanded.

'Because she speaks my language much better than you do, and besides that . . .' He broke off, and looked away with embarrassment.

'And besides what?' Hal insisted.

Mossie hung his head, and examined his bare and filthy feet, and his voice fell to a whisper. 'She smells nicer, and looks much more prettier than you do.'

As they walked back to their lodgings, Judith induced Mossie to recount his story. The son of a fisherman, he was born in a village near Barawa in the south-eastern coast of Somalia. He had been taken in a raid on his village by Arab slavers and sold on to first one and then another Portuguese trader here in Zanzibar, though both men had soon regretted their purchases. It seemed that the performance Hal, Judith and Aboli had witnessed at the slaver's block was not the first of its kind. On the positive side Mossie had been hauled around the town – albeit on the end of a rope or chain – long and often enough to come to know his way around Zanzibar as though he had been born there.

'I can guide you so that you do not gct lost!' he offered proudly.

'That's a very kind offer,' Hal replied.

'Not you!' Mossie assured him. 'I mean the Mem.' This was an abbreviation of Memsahib. It was a high honorific indeed that he had awarded to Judith.

Mossie's happy prattling continued unabated until they got back to the apothecary's shop. The sailor he had sent to visit Consul Grey was standing there with Mr Pett beside him. Evidently they had been waiting some time.

'It seems we are in luck, Captain,' Pett greeted Hal. 'The consul would be delighted to see the two of us. So much so, in fact, that he has invited us to a luncheon.'

'Today?' Hal was amazed at the speed of the consul's response. 'Then we'd better get a move on. Aboli, if you could take care of General Nazet and her new non-slave, I will go with Mr Pett to see the consul. Who knows, we may not need our lodgings after all. With a bit of luck we'll be able to head back to the *Delft* this very evening and then catch the early morning tide.'

From the moment that he discovered that Courtney was on Zanzibar, Grey moved with surprising speed for one so comfortably built. His domestic staff had been drastically reduced by his months of misfortune and relative poverty. But he still had a cook and there were one or two fine pieces of art on his walls and Persian rugs on his walls that could be taken down to the pawn shop, though he persuaded his broker – a man who had become increasingly accustomed to the portly Englishman's visits – that he would be back to collect them within a matter of days. 'My fortunes are about to take a turn, sir, mark well my words.'

With cash in his purse, Grey was able to rehire, at least temporarily, a few of the staff he had been forced to dismiss, and persuade them in their turn to recruit enough family members and friends to give the impression appropriate to the household of a wealthy man. His cook was packed off to the market with instructions to buy the finest available ingredients as well as the choice of dishes prepared by the city's stalls and street vendors. As a result, when Hal Courtney and his companion Mr Pett arrived for their luncheon they were treated to a veritable feast. There was a pilaf of calf meat cooked with potatoes, onions, spices, coconut milk and rice; shark steaks grilled over an open fire with pepper and other spices; a dish called *Pweza wa nazi*, which was octopus boiled in coconut milk, curry, cinnamon, cardamom, garlic and lime juice; and, to finish, hazelnut bread made with eggs and vanilla.

Grey wolfed the food down, though Hal noted with interest that Pett was far more restrained, even frugal in his consumption. This contrast in appetites was suggestive of their temperaments. Grey was relaxed and self-confident, to a fault. When he assured Hal that he bore him no ill-will for his trespasses in the north, Courtney accepted that unlikely assurance without a tremor.

By the time Hal left, Grey had ascertained that he was staying above an apothecary's shop on the waterfront. The exact address was not mentioned, but there were unlikely to be very many establishments answering to that description. Grey also learned that Hal had not entered the harbour aboard the *Golden Bough* and that he intended to depart with the tide, shortly before dawn the following morning.

Courtney left with warmly expressed good wishes between himself and Grey and a rather less fond, but perfectly polite farewell to Pett, whom he left in Grey's company along with the correspondence intended for London.

No sooner had the gates of his house closed behind the departing captain than Grey gave the letters to one of his servants with whispered instructions to set them aside for his later perusal. Beneath his urbane exterior, the consul was seething at Courtney's arrogance and presumption. To come strolling into Zanzibar, without a by your leave, and blithely assume that he could presume upon the offices of a man to whom he had caused very considerable difficulties by an act of base deception beggared belief. That Grey should now be burdened by the tedious concerns of this Pett fellow, as dull and humourless a figure as he had ever had the misfortune to encounter, struck Grey as adding insult to injury.

Still, he had a role to play and, as yet, the curtain had not fallen upon his performance. So he gritted his teeth for one last time, forced his features into a smile of feigned geniality and, having clapped his hands and ordered more coffee to be brought for his distinguished guest, said, 'Please let me assure you, Mr Pett, that it will give me great pleasure to break from my everyday concerns here in Zanzibar and take up the reins once again as His Majesty's Consul. So, pray sir, tell me: how may I be of assistance to you? From what Captain Courtney suggested, your story is one worth hearing.'

Pett ignored the coffee, pausing before he answered Grey's question to collect his thoughts. 'It is true that I have arrived here by a route that I could scarce have imagined when I set sail from Bombay, a passenger on the *Earl of Cumberland*.'

'Ah yes, the *Earl of C.* has docked in Zanzibar on more than one occasion, en route to or from the Indies,' Grey remarked. He stretched a chubby hand towards a silver plate of Turkish sweetmeats that lay on the table next to the coffee and picked up a small silver fork, with which he speared two of the glutinous pink blobs at once and stuffed them into his mouth.

'Please remind me, what's the name of her captain?' Grey asked, his mouth still filled with greyish pink goo. 'Giddings . . . Gadding . . . Something of that ilk, as I recall.'

'Goddings.'

'Ah yes, of course! Jovial fellow, though rather inclined to be too pleased with himself. Very like young Courtney in that regard. How is he?'

'Dead, and his ship with him. The *Earl of Cumberland* caught fire some weeks out of Bombay. She was carrying a cargo of saltpetre. The combination proved fatal and the ship sank with all hands. I alone escaped.'

'My word, how appalling for all those men. And how fortunate for you.'

'I threw myself from the burning vessel into the ocean and counted upon my god to rescue me.'

'Allah is indeed both all-powerful and all-merciful,' Grey murmured.

'That was not the god to which I referred,' Pett said, with a cold, steely calmness that, for the first time, made Grey question his assumptions about his guest's true nature.

'In any event, I was saved,' Pett continued. 'A Dutch vessel rescued me, although this act of charity was immediately followed by one of cruelty, for the vessel's captain, Tromp, then confined me in a filthy and verminous cell.'

'What possible cause did he have to do that?'

'He claimed it was for my own safety. His crew were on the brink of starvation. He said that he feared that I, being a stranger and lacking all ties to his men, might tempt them into an act of cannibalism.'

'It appears, however, that you did not appeal to their palates,' Grey remarked with a little chuckle that Pett conspicuously failed to dignify with even the slightest flicker of a smile.

'I was rescued from this confinement by Captain Courtney who was also gracious enough to allow me to restore my honour by means of a duel with Tromp.'

'Evidently you emerged unscathed from that, too,' Grey remarked. 'You seem to have quite a gift for survival, Mr Pett.'

'I prefer to think that I am well protected. In any case, I now require a passage back to England. For reasons which I hope are obvious, I am without funds at the moment. I have no more than the clothes I stand up in. But on arrival in London I will immediately collect the sum of five hundred guineas, owed to me in recompense of a service I provided for a distinguished gentleman.'

'Five hundred guineas? Come, sir, am I really to believe that you could possibly be owed a sum of such magnitude? What service did you provide to earn so much?'

Pett looked directly at Grey with flat, emotionless eyes and said, 'I killed Captain Goddings.'

Grey leaped to his feet with surprising agility for so bulky a man. 'Get out!' he snarled, pointing at the door. 'I can see that Courtney has foisted you upon me, with your incredible, cock-and-bull tale of explosions, cannibals and murders. Well, sir, I am not amused. Pray leave my house at once before I have you forcibly ejected.'

Pett did not move, nor did a flicker of emotion cross his face. Instead he waited until Grey had finished his tirade and then, very calmly, said, 'I assure you, Consul Grey, that every word I have spoken has been nothing but the truth. I could prove it, but that would require me to kill you with that little fork you so recently utilized, or the silver tray on which your servant placed the coffee and sweetmeats, or even my bare hands, all of which I could very easily do.'

Grey felt the blood drain from his face. There was something scarily calm and undemonstrative about the way Pett spoke. He simply stated his ability to kill as a matter of fact and was entirely convincing precisely because he made no great attempt to convince.

'I could have you seized by Prince Jahan and tried for murder,' Grey blustered, knowing as the words left his mouth how feeble they sounded.

'No, Mr Grey, you could not,' said Pett. 'I have not committed any crime in Zanzibar, nor any land under the dominion of Prince Jahan or his brother the Great Mogul. No body has been produced, nor any weapon. If you were to claim that I had made a confession I would merely laugh and say that I spoke in jest – just as you yourself said, it was naught but a cock-and-bull tale – and who could ever prove otherwise?

'So let us not waste time with empty threats. Instead let me say that there was a reason for my frankness. I believe that I can earn enough money to fund my passage home and that you or your associates will gladly provide sufficient funds, and a great deal more besides. So tell me, Consul, what do you really think of Captain Sir Henry Courtney, and how much would you like to be rid of him?'

Well that was easy enough, Pett thought, as he watched Grey subside back onto his divan. He said nothing, knowing that the consul already had all the information he needed. Now it was just a question of letting Grey talk himself into the proposition that Pett had been working towards from the moment the conversation began.

Once more Grey reached a chubby hand towards the silver plate of Turkish sweetmeats. Still Pett remained silent as Grey ate the sweets, licked a stray dusting of sugar from his plump lips and then began, 'Since you have told me your story, let me say a little about myself . . .'

Pett gave a little wave of the hand, as if to say, 'By all means.'

'I come from humble stock, and I'm proud of it. I was born and raised in Hebden Bridge in the West Riding of Yorkshire. I know I may not look it, or sound it now, but I'm a Yorkshireman and proud of it. My parents ran an inn, catering to travellers on the packhorse route from Halifax to Burnley. Sometimes we'd get travellers from the south, even London, and I got it into my daft young head that I wanted to seek my fortune. So I left home, with nothing but a couple of pennies in my pocket – oh, aye, I can still talk Yorkshire if I please! Less than two years later I was a clerk at the East India Company itself. Now to my parents, to think that their son was a clerk, with every hope of advancement, was more than they had ever dreamed possible. But to me it was just the beginning.

'You see, Mr Pett, I pride myself on my ability to associate with every class of man, from the highest to the lowest. I enjoy the personal acquaintance, I might even dare to say friendship, of sultans and maharajahs. I have entertained lords and ladies, dined with Portuguese merchants whose wealth would astound you. I have even met the King of England himself on one memorable occasion.'

I doubt His Majesty found it quite so memorable, thought Pett, as Grey went on, 'Equally, one cannot survive, let alone prosper on an island like Zanzibar without being able to treat with the meaner sorts too: bawdies, cut-purses, brigands and traders in human flesh. A man of the world may find himself in some dark alley in Stone Town doing business with the kinds of men who would sooner sell their daughters than do an honest day's work, as easily as in the counting house of a respectable man of business . . .'

'The distinction is not always obvious,' Pett observed.

'Indeed not, sir, well said!' Grey exclaimed. 'My point, however, is that one must always be able to conduct oneself in the manner that the circumstances demand. And I would not have reached the position I have today, sir, were I too timid, or gullible or in the slightest respect incompetent.'

'And yet, sir, if you will not mind me saying so, I cannot help but note that your position appears to be less enviable now than it might once have been. I could not help but note, as we were escorted to this particular salon, that there were blank spaces on some of the walls, indicating the sale of the pictures that once hung there. Though your courtyard is very agreeable, the flowerbeds around the fountain have not been properly tended and I could not help but mark that several of the servants, though they were obedient enough, seemed uncertain of their roles and treated you very differently to the manner in which a servant of longstanding tends to the needs of his master. It struck me, therefore, that you might have brought them in for this meal, where once they might have been part of your regular establishment.'

'You are very observant, Mr Pett,' said Grey tartly.

'It is a requirement of my trade.'

'Then you are clearly a craftsman of some skill, for you are right. Like you, sir, I know what it is to suffer unjust and grievous mistreatment. I took Sir Henry Courtney at his word. I believed him to be the gentleman he purports to be.'

'I gather that he obtained information from you by subterfuge.'

'That is correct. He came here claiming to be my friend, yet he took his ship to fight against the One True God, and the very men he had sworn to support.'

Pett steeled himself to let the blasphemy go unpunished – for now at any rate. There were voices in his head crying out for retribution against this vile apostate who had renounced God and Christ in favour of a heathen deity. But Pett had work to do and it required Grey's co-operation, thus he was forced to keep his silence and his mask of self-possession, no matter that he could barely hear Grey's voice for the Saint screaming in his skull.

'I presume that there were those who, quite unfairly, blamed you for the damage Courtney did to their cause,' Pett said.

'Exactly so. Doors have been closed to me, Pett, doors that once welcomed me into the very highest and finest reaches of society. My fortunes have, as you so perceptively appreciated, suffered considerably. I am at as low an ebb as I have ever been. And now, Courtney has the damned effrontery to show his face around here after the way he played me false. If he had come to me in a spirit of sincere apology, wishing to build bridges between us, to make amends after the disdain with which he treated me when last we met, well, I am a very reasonable man, I might have given him a second chance. But to show only the slightest remorse, and make the most trifling apology . . . by God, sir, it is unconscionable!'

'I put it down to youth. Courtney simply did not understand the gravity of the wrong he had done you. He still acts sometimes as if he is playing a game in which his charm and good nature will get him through any scrape. I could clearly see that he was putting his head in a noose, but I kept my counsel.'

'Only because you wanted to be the hangman.'

'I'm quite sure that you understand the need to make one's living, Mr Grey.'

'Indeed I do. It is made all the greater by the fact that there happen to be, present here in Zanzibar, other men who feel just as aggrieved by him, if not more than I do. They would be very pleased indeed if I could rid them of Henry Courtney and will be very generous to anyone who assists me in that task.'

'Then I shall be delighted to be of assistance. And there is one other element to this endeavour that is worthy of consideration. Courtney is not alone in Zanzibar. His woman is with him, and she is with child.'

Grey's eyes widened, as if they'd alighted on an especially appetizing plate of food. 'Is she now? Tell me, are the rumours one hears true? Has Courtney really walked off with General Nazet, the illustrious warrior who beat the mighty Omani general El Grang and put that little shit Iyasu on the throne?' He twirled ringed fingers through the air. 'Or should I say, His Most Christian Majesty, King of Kings, Ruler of Galla and Amhara, Defender of the Faith of Christ and so on, and so forth. Now there's a fine trinket for Courtney to bring home from Ethiopia – a lustrous black pearl who will cause a stir from the most elegant salons of Westminster to the rowdiest of Southwark taverns.'

'She is indeed General Judith Nazet and I know where she can be found. Now, sir, perhaps we can discuss how best to proceed. I will, of course, require a substantial purse and I have various other requirements. Thanks to the sinking of the *Earl of Cumberland* I am not in possession of the usual tools of my trade. I would also suggest that it will be much easier to deal with both Courtney and Nazet if they are separated. This will require a degree of subterfuge. I welcome your advice in that particular matter, too.'

Grey smiled, 'Oh, I know the one thing that can prise an opening between our two treacherous lovebirds. It's something that both of them care about, over which they have both sworn solemn oaths and for which they have both fought. Are you sure you won't join me in drinking a cup or two of *bhang thandai*? It is a cooling infusion, consumed by the Indians. The taste is pleasantly sweet, but cut with a hint of pepper and spice and the *bhang* – a mixture of the leaf and bud of what Levantines call hashish – is delightfully relaxing. We have a great deal of thinking to do, and I find it of great assistance.'

Mr Pett declined Grey's offer, but the consul ordered a jug of *thandai* and the effects appeared to be exactly as he had predicted, for within a couple of hours of conversation, he and Pett had formulated a plan of action and agreed on what would be required to implement it. Zanzibar's position, close to the equator, meant that the sun always set between the hours of six and seven in the evening so that when Pett left the building he stepped into a hazy dusk in which the sun-baked heat of the day had softened into a more mellow warmth.

For his part, Grey dozed a while, awoke feeling clear-headed and greatly refreshed and made his way at once to Prince Jahan's palace. When he explained to the guards at the gate that he had information regarding the whereabouts of Captain Courtney and General Nazet he was admitted much more quickly and received a far warmer welcome than had been the case for some considerable time. Jahan received him alone at first, but then sent for the creature – Grey could no longer think of him as a man – who had once been Angus Cochran. Further arrangements were made. A messenger was despatched to a particular coffee-shop with instructions for the owner from the prince himself and a purse filled with gold coins to show how much the service would be valued. The shop's owner, overwhelmed by the favour shown him by one of such magnificence, was effusive in his assurances that all would be done exactly as His Highness required. Further preparations were made within the palace itself.

Only when he, Jahan and the Buzzard were entirely happy that everything had been done to their joint satisfaction did Consul Grey bid the other two men goodnight and make his way back home. Before he left, however, he made one request of the prince. 'Your highness, I am sure, of course, that all our plans will go perfectly this evening. But it occurs to me that if Courtney's men suspect that something has happened to their captain, they may come to me looking for answers. He will, I'm sure, have vouchsafed his plans to his most trusted lieutenants. It would ease my mind very much if you could let me have a few burly men – a dozen would be more than adequate – to guard my house and keep me from harm.'

Jahan smiled, 'So you, Consul, wish me to protect you from your own countrymen?'

'I had not thought of it in quite that way, your highness, but I suppose that might be one way of considering it.'

'Very well, you shall have your guard. But six men, I think, will suffice perfectly well.'

'Might your highness stretch to ten?' Grey bargained.

'Eight,' Jahan concluded, 'and not a man more. But do not trouble yourself, Grey. I feel sure that you will have no need of any of them.'

'No, your highness, you're right, as always. But I thank you, profoundly, for your limitless generosity.'

So now Grey had Jahan's official protection and this sign of favour meant that his position in society had been re-established. Strolling along streets that were busier than ever now that the worst of the heat had passed, His Majesty's Consul felt more cheerful than he had done in months. His fortunes were about to take a very great step for the better. His financial prospects that had been so precarious at the start of the day looked entirely secure at the end of it. So certain was he of good times to come that he felt no qualms at all about spending a large portion of the remaining money he had raised by the sale of his personal effects on a particularly pretty boy – tall for his age, slender, with adorably big, brown eyes and just the faintest wisps of hair at the far corners of his top lip – whom he took back to his house. As he walked through the gates and into his courtyard he was already calling out for food and drink. He had a long, active night in prospect and was in need of a good meal to give himself strength for the pleasures that lay ahead.

Even so, Grey was a cautious man. There was just a possibility that all might not go to plan, so he commanded the servants he had hired for the day to stay on for the night as well. They were far from being trained soldiers, but should there be any fighting, a few extra bodies between him and the men of the *Golden Bough* would never come amiss.

al was standing on the roof terrace of the house above the apothecary's shop, talking to Aboli and looking out across the town to the harbour, where torches and lanterns illuminated the ships and flickered on the inky black water. The *Delft* was anchored further out in the bay but Hal knew that one of her longboats would be tied up to one of the stone bollards on the quayside, with a full complement of men ready and waiting to take them all back to the ship, or to spring to their rescue in case of alarm. Hal had tried to persuade Judith to go back aboard the *Delft* this very evening, but when she had asked him whether he planned to leave Zanzibar under cover of darkness he admitted that, no, they would not cast off until the new day had dawned.

'Very well,' she said, 'then I would like to spend one more

night ashore. I will sleep much better in a proper bed . . . and other things will be much better too.'

Hal was about to go back inside, where Judith was quietly embroidering a baby blanket, watched over by a fascinated Mossie, and set about those 'other things' when his love appeared at the doors to the terrace and said, 'Mr Pett is here to see you.' Her tone was polite enough, but the roll of her eyes told Hal that she was less than delighted by the Company man's reappearance.

'Good evening, Mr Pett,' Hal called out, watching the familiar, stick-like figure make his way across the tiled floor towards him. 'Was Grey not willing to help you?'

'Not at all, Captain,' Pett replied, giving polite nods of acknowledgement to both Hal and Aboli. 'On the contrary, he assured me that he would do everything he could to secure me passage back to England and was quite happy to accept my credit as an official of the Company. In fact, he even advanced me a sum that was modest, yet perfectly sufficient to allow me to return some of the hospitality you have so kindly shown me. Perhaps you and Mr Aboli would care to join me for dinner, or if that does not suit, perhaps just a glass or two of tea, or coffee or some other similar beverage?'

Before Hal could reply, Pett leaned forward and spoke again, much more quietly. 'While I was at the consul's house, news reached him of very great significance. I am convinced of the need for you to hear it, but I strongly advise you to do so when not in Miss Nazet's presence. I fancy you will wish to give these tidings considerable thought before deciding whether to pass them on.'

'There is nothing I would not tell Miss Nazet,' said Hal.

'Even something that might tempt her to return to Ethiopia, whether you went with her or not?'

Hal frowned. 'There is no such thing. For pity's sake, Mr Pett, please stop speaking in riddles and tell me what you are talking about.'

Pett sighed, looked around to check that they could not be overheard and said, 'The Grail, Captain Courtney. My news concerns the Holy Grail. Now do you see why we must discuss it in private?'

Hal turned his head to look out across the darkness towards the invisible horizon. His mind was far away in the north, beyond the red rock cliffs and hills of the Gulf of Aden in the ancient kingdom of Ethiopia. There had been so much blood, so much death, and all to retrieve the Grail, the very cup into which Christ's wounds had bled, a talisman for which Christians had searched since the crucifixion. Judith had sworn to protect the Grail in the name of the Christian Emperor of Ethiopia, and Hal had himself taken a similar oath as a Nautonnier Knight. Together they had helped retrieve the Grail when it had been stolen from its hiding place, deep in the heart of Ethiopia. But if any further harm now threatened it, Pett might be right, Judith's honour might indeed oblige her to turn her back on her new life and return to Ethiopia. As, indeed, might his own.

Aboli must have been thinking on similar lines for now he said, 'We should go with Pett, Gundwane. There are times when a man should pay heed to his woman. But just as women talk among themselves about things that concern them, so this matter is man's talk.'

Hal nodded, 'Very well then, Mr Pett,' he said. 'You shall say farewell to Aboli and me after our brief, but eventful acquaintance.' He walked back into the house and took Judith's hand. 'My dear, Mr Pett has the means to repay some of the kindness that we have shown him by taking Aboli and me to a coffee-house for a farewell drink. We will be sure to return to you very soon.'

Judith did not need to be told that no respectable unmarried woman would ever accompany men on an expedition of this kind. She simply said, 'Be sure that you do,' and then called out, 'Don't keep Captain Courtney out long, Mr Pett. I shall soon be sharing him with his entire crew. I would like to have his attention now, before all hope of it vanishes.'

'I entirely understand, madam, and can assure you that I am merely desirous of a brief opportunity to express my thanks for the deliverance from captivity that Captain Courtney brought me, and all his kindness thereafter,' Pett replied.

Hal reached for the hook on the wall from which hung the belt and scabbard containing the Neptune sword. As he put it on, Pett said, 'There's no need for that, Captain. I hardly think we shall face any danger over beverages and pastries.'

'I am walking out into a foreign city at night, sir,' Hal replied. 'Who knows what might happen?'

Pett looked at him quizzically, then shrugged and said, 'As you please, Captain. Follow me.'

He led Aboli and Hal out of the house and down the street. They made a number of turnings down side streets, and along narrow alleys until they came to a small square in which stood a coffee-shop, with tables both indoors and out. Pett led them to an empty table on the edge of the outdoor section, with an uninterrupted view across the square and all the Zanzibari citizens making their evening promenade. As they took their seats Pett said, 'Consul Grey assured me that this was a highly respectable establishment, by local standards at any rate, where one can both eat and drink without too much fear of upsetting one's digestion. And I gather, also, that the owner speaks a word or two of English, which will be of assistance to me for I have no Arabic whatever.'

'Don't be concerned. I am hardly fluent, but I can make myself understood,' Hal assured him. He stopped himself, just in time, from revealing how well Aboli spoke Arabic. For now that would be a card he would keep close to his chest and one glance across the table told him Aboli had had the same thought. Instead, he said, 'As for Mr Grey, I must apologize for obliging you to associate with a man of such dubious morality.'

'If you refer to slavery,' Pett replied, 'I can tell you that I regard it as an abomination against God, who created us all equal in His image. I told Consul Grey as much, too, I might add, when he let slip that he had dabbled in the trade.'

Hal shrugged: 'Slavery, among other things . . . Sadly, we Englishmen have no alternative but to treat with him since he is our monarch's sole representative south of Alexandria. But tell me, what news did he have about the Grail?'

'I shall tell you it all,' Pett replied, getting to his feet. 'But first, please allow me to order us some refreshments. Alcohol, of course, is forbidden in Islamic establishments, but Grey furnished me with advice about what I should order for us here. Please, allow me to find this English-speaking proprietor and order a selection of his finest offerings. I will return in but a moment.'

'But, Mr Pett . . .' Hal protested. But before he could finish the sentence, Pett was disappearing into the depths of the coffee-house, leaving Hal staring after him in puzzlement and frustration.

'We should go, Gundwane,' Aboli said. 'I do not trust this man.'

'You may be right, but we cannot leave now,' Hal replied. 'To spurn his hospitality would be discourteous in the extreme and Mr Pett is a man who does not take kindly to anything he perceives as a slight. Tromp can testify to that. No, we shall stay, but only as long as is absolutely necessary.'

A short while later, Pett returned, accompanied by a portly, bearded Arab in a white robe and headdress who was barking out orders to a gaggle of servants. 'This is Mr Azar, the proprietor,' Grey explained. 'When I told him that my guest was a great English mariner he insisted on paying his respects.'

Hal stood to greet Azar, while the servants pulled another table next to the one at which the three men were sitting and loaded both surfaces with cups of coffee and glasses of mint tea, trays of sweet and savoury pastries and placed a hookah pipe in front of his, Pett's and Aboli's places.

Pett saw Hal looking quizzically at the tall, ornately decorated brass object, from which protruded a long thin pipe, angled upwards from the base.

'Do I take it you are unfamiliar with the hookah?' he asked. Without waiting for an answer Pett continued, 'It's a means of smoking tobacco that I came across in India. Very pleasurable, I find . . .'

'My father was always opposed to smoking tobacco,' Hal said. 'He refused to believe that any good could come of filling one's lungs with smoke when they could be ingesting good, sea air.'

'I'm sure your father was a fine man, Captain Courtney. But he is gone and you must decide upon your own views now. Besides, the purpose of this device is precisely to make the taking of tobacco much more beneficial to one's health by mixing it with molasses and various flavours to one's taste – I believe Mr Azar favours crushed mint leaves and lemon rind – and then passing the smoke through a bowl of water so that the impurities are removed. The result, I assure you, is infinitely more agreeable than, say, breathing in the foul vapours one encounters below decks on a ship and I cannot believe that it is any more injurious to the constitution.'

'I once smoked this hookah with Sir Francis,' Aboli said. 'It was good.'

'So why did he tell me it wasn't?' Hal asked.

Aboli smiled. 'As you will find, Gundwane, what a man tells his son and what he does himself are seldom the same thing.'

'Let me make a suggestion,' Pett said. 'If you two gentlemen join me in a pipe, then I will tell you all I know about the current predicament of . . .' he looked around as if to check that no one could overhear what he was saying '. . . the Grail.'

Hal shook his head. 'I regret that my promise to my father still stands. When he releases me from it I will join you. Until that happy day I will allow Aboli to keep you company. But now, sir, I insist . . .'

'Of course . . . Well then, it seems that the blind prophet we encountered in the marketplace yesterday has been telling all who pass by that the Grail has been seized by the followers of the Omani general Ahmed El Grang, the king of the Omani Arabs, who holds sway over the lands bordering the Ethiopian empire.'

'I am well aware who El Grang is. I was at war with his navy,' Hal said.

'Quite so . . . Well, the prophet says that these events fore-shadow the end of the world. That the theft of this holy cup will plunge us all into darkness.'

Hal gave a sceptical grimace. 'Hmm . . . I'm not inclined to place much weight on anything that blind, babbling old stick ever says.'

'Nor was Grey,' Pett replied. 'Still, he was curious to know whether there was any substance to the prophet's words. He made his own inquiries, for as you will know he is very well connected and, as I mentioned earlier, received more news while I was still in his presence. Mr Grey spoke in Arabic to the gentleman who delivered the information, his countenance becoming more grave with every word they exchanged. When we were once again alone he turned to me and said, "So it is true, as I feared. That precious Christian treasure for which Captain Courtney and General Nazet fought so very bravely has, I fear, fallen into El Grang's hands once more." I confess I was surprised to hear such words from one who now professes to be a Mussulman, and said as much to Mr Grey. Quoth he, "I may have converted to the one true faith, Mr Pett . . ." I may say I recoiled to hear an Englishman talk about any faith but Christianity in that way. "But I would have peace between all." Then he smiled at me and added, "Better for business that way."'

'Yes, that sounds like Mr Grey, all right,' Hal said. 'His belief in gold outweighs his faith in any god. But did he tell you any more?'

'Indeed so . . . He said that the Ethiopian boy emperor, or rather the bishop that advises him . . .'

'Fasilides.'

'Yes, that's the name . . . Well, this Fasilides has sent emissaries far and wide searching for General Nazet.'

Hal's eyes widened in alarm. 'You didn't tell him, did you? About her presence here in Zanzibar?'

'My dear, Captain Courtney! I absolutely assure you, Captain, that I was as discreet in your absence as I was when you and I were both at Grey's table. You will forgive me, sir, but I take considerable exception to your lack of faith in my discretion. As I may have told you, I was entrusted by the directors of the Company themselves with extremely sensitive discussions at the highest possible level and . . .'

'I apologize, Mr Pett. Mine was only the concern of a man who fears for the woman he loves. I meant you no insult.'

'No, no . . . very probably not,' Pett huffed. Then he frowned. 'Mr Aboli, sir . . . are you indisposed?'

Hal turned to look at his first mate and frowned anxiously. 'Aboli? What ails you?'

The mighty Amadoda warrior's face had taken on a greyish hue, his eyes were unfocussed and his speech was slurred as he started speaking in the strange clicking manner of the forest people that was his native tongue. Hal had been tutored in the language since he was a small boy but even he struggled to make out what he was saying. The general gist, however, was clear enough. 'He is not well. Something has made him ill. Excuse me for saying so, Mr Pett, but I cannot help but feel that the smoke you swore to be so beneficial may have brought him to this state.'

Pett gave a sigh of concern. 'That is possible. God made us all equal, but plainly we are not all the same. I have seen men from many Indian races enjoy the hookah without ill-effects and Arabs, Persians and other peoples of the Levant swear by its properties. But it is possible that the African is not suited to its properties. Equally he may have succumbed to bad airs, or eaten tainted food of some kind.'

'Well, whatever it was, we cannot sit around here debating the matter. I must get him back to our accommodation where he can be properly looked after. Perhaps the apothecary will have some sort of medicinal herb or tincture that will restore him.'

'Very possibly,' said Pett. 'Here, let me assist you.'

He and Hal got up, stood either side of Aboli and tried to help him to his feet until he stood between them, like a tall tree swaying in a strong wind. 'Come on, Mr Aboli,' Pett said, wedging his left shoulder under Aboli's right armpit as Hal took up his post on the other side. 'We shall endeavour to get you home . . . Pray do not concern yourself with payment for our refreshments, Captain. I will return in due course and settle my account.'

Oh, I will settle my account, and no mistake, thought Pett, as the three of them made their ungainly way across the square to the narrow street that marked the start of their route back to the apothecary's premises. And then he smiled to himself. *That degenerate old blasphemer Grey was right. The addition of hashish and opium to the tobacco mixture had precisely the effect that he predicted.*

Halfway down the street they came to the entrance to a narrow alley. 'Down here,' Pett said, steering Hal and Aboli into the near-darkness that lay between high walls on either side.

'Are you sure this is the way?' Hal asked, grunting as he did so from the effort of supporting Aboli's weight.

'Entirely,' Pett replied, with a curtness that suggested he simply did not have the strength or breath to utter another word. In fact his attention was wholly directed inwards, for now he heard, more clearly than he had done in many a week, the voice of the Saint assuring him, 'Now, do it now! This is both the time and the place that God has ordained for the removal of Henry Courtney from this earth. You have waited long and patiently. But wait no more. Do it!'

A sense of great peace coursed through Pett, like a warm and soothing tonic that invigorated his body, sharpened his senses and concentrated his mind. He felt as though the African, for all his bulk and might, were no more of a burden to him than a child might have been. His hand went to the pocket of

210

his breeches, where the sharpened knife, placed beside his plate by Azar, the coffee-shop owner himself, was waiting. How easy it had been to place himself here, with his right hand entirely free. And how satisfying it had been to negate the advantage Courtney had given himself by deciding, at the last minute, to bring his damn sword. For now the captain's right shoulder was bearing Aboli's weight and his arm was wrapped around the African's back, from where he would find it almost impossible to extricate it, so that the blade that hung at his hip might as well not be there for all that he could use it.

Pett's grip tightened around the handle of the knife. Moving slowly, without any sudden movement or shifting of his weight, Pett eased his hand and the blade it carried out into the open, then let his right arm hang down beside his body.

They were halfway down the alley now, at the point where they would be equally hard to make out by anyone passing along the streets at either end. This was the perfect moment.

'Do it!' screamed the Saint.

And William Pett struck, as he always did, without warning, at a speed that none of his victims could match, bringing his body across Aboli and swinging his right arm in a great arc so that the painstakingly honed point of his blade was swinging with all his strength at a defenceless Henry Courtney.

*L*ook at the eyes, Gundwane! Aboli had always taught him. *If you watch the blade you will always react too late. The blade tells you what your enemy is doing now. But the eyes tell you what he will do next.*

Hour after hour, day after day, year after year, Aboli had drummed his lessons into his pupil until they had become second nature, so much a part of the way Hal thought that

211

he was no longer even aware of what he had to do. He simply did it.

And so Hal had been watching Pett's eyes. All through the great performance of bringing everything to their table, supervised by the owner himself; all through the conversation in which Pett went to such lengths to convince him of the benefits of the hookah pipe; and especially from the moment that Aboli had fallen ill, Hal had been watching.

It had been the way Pett recounted his conversation with Grey that had convinced Hal that the ever-growing suspicion nagging at his mind had been fully justified. He could have believed that Grey would have furnished Pett with a means to get home if he thought it might bring him to the favourable attention of the directors of the East India Company. But the notion that a corrupt, slave-trading Muslim pederast would suddenly establish some kind of friendship – including the recommendation of a favourite coffee-shop – with a puritanical, High Church eccentric like Pett was simply impossible to believe.

Unless, that is, Grey and Pett were not at all what they seemed. Hal was now horribly afraid that he had made a grievous error in assuming that Grey would not be unduly troubled by the deceit that had led to the *Golden Bough* fighting for the Ethiopian cause, not the Arab one as promised. On the contrary, he now felt sure that Grey had been very troubled indeed, and correspondingly eager to seek retribution. As for Pett, the more Hal considered the whole business of the duel with Tromp, from the moment he'd first woken to see Pett standing at the foot of his bed; to the absolute determination with which he had forced Tromp – by any reasonable measure a far more dangerous combatant – to fight him; to the eerie calm with which he had taken a ball to the arm and then fired with such chilling deliberation; and finally, the patent surprise and dissatisfaction that had seized Pett when he realized that his shot was not a fatal one: well, these were not the actions of a placid, peace-loving man who earned his living conducting business conversations on behalf of a commercial enterprise. These were the actions of a killer.

Then Pett took Hal into the dark and he could not see his eyes. Suddenly Hal became very aware that Aboli's body lay between his right arm and his sword. He thought back to the smartness with which Pett had taken up his position, with his sword-arm free. Except that Pett did not wear a sword, so he must have something else at his disposal, a hidden weapon.

With every step they took into the depths of the alley the light dimmed still further. *I can't see!* Hal thought. *And if I can't see . . .*

Then, suddenly, a shutter swung open, somewhere up above them. In the light that spilled from the open window, just long enough for the stinking contents of a bedpan to be sent splattering into the night, Hal glanced across at Pett.

And then he saw.

Hal reacted at once, with a speed unhampered by conscious decision-making, acting entirely on a warrior's instincts as he shoved Aboli in the back, twisting him in the same direction as Pett so that the latter's momentum was increased still further and he was thrown away from his line of attack, towards the far side of the alley. At the same time Hal swept his right leg across Aboli's ankles, tripping him. Like a tall, felled pine Aboli toppled to the ground, landing directly on top of Pett and pinning him to the dusty, filth-encrusted ground. For a second Hal feared that he might have thrown his friend onto Pett's blade, but then, even in the near-darkness, he could see Pett's arms splayed on either side of Aboli's body and the dull, blue gleam of his blade lying just out of reach of his desperate attempt

213

to grasp it. Hal kicked the knife away while Aboli, whose wits were slowly returning to him, grabbed Pett's wrists in his hands and rendered them completely immobile. Now Hal once again heard the clicking sound of the language of the forests and this time the words were clear: 'Kill him, Gundwane.'

Pett was defenceless. There were opponents whom one could treat like honourable men, to whom it was not only charitable but wise to extend mercy, but Hal knew only too clearly that Pett was not one of them. He drew the Neptune sword from its scabbard.

Hal felt, more than saw Pett staring with his cold, unfeeling eyes. He knew that there would be no plea for clemency, just a flat, emotionless, 'Damn you to hell, Henry Courtney. You and all your spawn.'

Then Hal took his sword in both hands, holding it so that it pointed straight down, and with the full force of his back and shoulders drove it into Pett's exposed throat so hard that the tempered Toledo steel not only severed his windpipe but, finding a joint between the vertebrae, sliced right through his spine as well, killing him instantly.

Hal looked around. The alley was as deserted as ever. The window shutters above him had closed tight once again. No one had heard or seen anything and there was every chance the body would lie undiscovered until morning. Aboli was gingerly getting to his feet as if not quite trusting his ability to stand upright unaided. But Hal had no time to waste. He looked at his friend and said, 'Judith!' And then he started running.

'Wake up, my lady. You must wake up!' Judith woke, to Mossie pleading with her trying to keep his voice low, but unable to keep his panic at bay, 'I'm scared! The *djinn* is coming! What are we going to do?'

Judith blinked the sleep from her eyes. For a moment she thought that the boy had been having a nightmare, for there were no *djinns*, no evil spirits – not in this world. And it was that hesitation that did for her. For when the door to the bedroom was kicked open, she was still in bed. Though she could still turn and grab the *kaskara* sword that she had placed beneath her pillows, she was still lying down, beneath a sheet, and by the time she had sprung to her feet there were five armed men in the room, all with their swords drawn, pointing directly at her.

215

And then there was a sixth, and now, as she looked upon the grotesque leather head, made even more nightmarish by shadows thrown by the silvery moonlight glimmering through the window, she understood that Mossie had been speaking nothing but the literal truth, for if ever there was an embodiment of evil on this earth, this was it. A passing thought darted across her mind: Where is Mossie? Where did he go? But she fought to suppress it for his only hope of survival was that none of these invaders should know of his presence.

The masked man spoke in a voice that rasped like a rusty sword being drawn from a bone-dry scabbard. 'Dinnae try to fight, *General* Nazet.' The rank was emphasized with limitless scorn. 'You'll die if you do. Aye, you and the bairn in your belly too.'

She knew he was right. She had become accustomed to defending herself in the way of a man, but now a deeper intuition told her she would have to resist in the way that women had always done, not by fighting, but by enduring. For men had only themselves to worry about. But a mother had always to live for the sake of her child, far more than for herself.

She put the sword down and got out of bed. She was wearing nothing but a nightgown of linen so fine it was almost transparent. 'May I put on my gown?' she asked.

'No, you may not,' the masked man said and loomed over her, tilting his head this way and that, so that he could examine her thoroughly through his one eye hole. There was something disgustingly suggestive about the long beak that stuck out like an angry, pointed phallus and Judith longed for armour to shield her from his hungry gaze, and those of his men. She felt utterly exposed, vulnerable, soft and weak and she, who had

216

led armies, killed men in hand-to-hand combat and trampled over the bodies of her vanquished foes, now felt possessed by an overpowering urge to cry.

No, by God, I will not give them that satisfaction! Judith thought and forced herself to stand tall and stare right back at this malevolent birdman.

'D'ye recognize me yet, eh?' the voice asked her. 'Och, why would you? I'm dead, after all. You saw me die.'

Her mind raced, she pictured a battle at sea and a man on fire as he went down with his ship. *No! That's not possible! But who else . . . ?*

'The Buzzard,' she said, making her voice sound as dull as possible, denying him the pleasure of hearing her astonishment, finding a way to have another small victory, no matter how insignificant.

'Aye, that's right. I survived . . . if you can call this living, the way I am, the way your bastard lover Henry Courtney made me. Oh, I'm going to have my revenge on that bonnie laddie, God damn me if I don't. But not yet . . . no, there's more that has to be done to bring him down as low as I want him to be. And there's another who wants to make your acquaintance. So now you may put on your gown. And when you've done that you can come with me.'

The Buzzard bowed like a footman in an aristocratic household as he said, 'Your carriage awaits, my lady . . .'

She was gone. The apartment was empty. Hal cursed himself for his foolishness and raged at whoever had taken his beloved and then he heard something else in the bedroom: the sound of a child's stifled crying. It was coming from under the bed. Hal lifted the discarded sheet that had acted like a curtain along the side of the bed and there was Mossie, curled up in a ball, sobbing softly.

Hal reached out a hand to him and softly said, 'Don't worry. You can come out. It's safe now.'

The child looked at him blankly. Hal tried again, but with no more success. Then he tried a different tack. 'Please will you help me, Mossie? I really want to know what's happened to Judith and I think you will be able to tell me what happened. So you will help me get her back and I will be very, very pleased.'

That seemed to help, and Mossie emerged from under the bed and spoke, although at first Hal had no more luck than Judith in making sense of his talk of *djinns*. But then Mossie said, 'The *djinn* spoke! It talked to my lady and I think that she knew it, for she replied and I think she said its name, and she called it Bozrrd.'

Hal frowned, not catching what Mossie had said. So he repeated again, 'Bozrrd! Bozrrd!'

Now Hal heard it and he too felt incredulity give way to horror as he tried to come to terms with the possibility that his mortal enemy had risen from the dead. 'Did she say, "Buzzard"?' he asked Mossie, speaking very clearly and half-hoping he would say, 'No.'

Instead the boy nodded his head up and down several times and squealed, 'Yes! Yes! Bozrrd!'

For a moment Hal was lost in thought as all the apparently disconnected events that had happened over the past hour or so suddenly fell into a pattern that made perfect sense. Grey and the Buzzard, traitors both to their country, their king and their god, were both united by one other thing: their mutual hatred of Captain Sir Henry Courtney. Together, though surely with help from some other, third party, they had concocted a plan that was supposed to end with his death and Judith's abduction. Well, he was alive, and there was one man who could surely tell him where Judith had gone.

'Mossie, fetch my pistols,' Hal said, hoping to God that the Buzzard hadn't taken them, as well.

'What are you doing?' Aboli asked him.

'I'm going to call on His Majesty's Consul,' he said. 'You're going to come with me, and so is every other man we've got here in Zanzibar. And he is going to tell me everything I wish to know or I will geld him like a damned eunuch.'

'No.' Aboli shook his head. 'That is not the way. Think, Gundwane. The consul's house is guarded. The moment he knows you are still alive he will bar his door. We would have to fight our way in and the town guard will come like hyenas to the smell of blood.'

Hal seethed with anger but he knew Aboli was right. They could not expect simply to march into the consul's apartments and demand answers. Grey was a powerful and influential man, who always boasted of his connections here in Zanzibar. Hal did not need a war with the local Omani population any more than the *Golden Bough* needed to face the wrath of those big guns on the fortress walls.

'What do you suggest, Aboli?' he asked, tying a red silk sash around his waist into which he thrust the two pistols that Mossie handed to him.

Aboli frowned. 'Maybe it is not a matter of how many men we need, but how few.'

'You mean, achieve by stealth what we cannot do by force?'

'Correct,' said Aboli with a grin.

The two men talked for a few minutes more. Then, bringing Mossie with them, they went down to where the longboat was tied up next to a flight of steps that led down from the quayside. Hal sent Mossie to the stern of the longboat and told him to stay there, no matter what. Then he and Aboli explained their plan of action to the other men of the *Bough*. They waited until the streets of the city had emptied and its people were asleep. Then Hal and Aboli, along with two of the *Bough*'s most doughty fighters, Big Daniel Fisher and Will Stanley, picked up a length of rope and set off into the night.

J udith was taken through the streets of Zanzibar in a carriage whose windows had been covered so that she had no idea where she was going. There came a point, however, when she heard orders being barked, a gate opened and then the echoing of hooves and wheels as the carriage passed beneath an arch, crossed some kind of open courtyard before passing through a second gate and only then coming to a halt.

The door of the carriage was opened and before her stood a portly, middle-aged man with a chin as perfectly hairless as his shaven scalp. In a high, effeminate voice he said, 'Follow me. His Highness wishes to see you, but he will not wish to set eyes on you looking like that.'

He's a eunuch, Judith thought and then, as she was led into a large, marble-floored room, strewn with soft rugs decorated with intricately woven patterns and heady with the scent of roses, amber and musk wafting from the candles that cast a golden glow over the half-naked women draped in poses of idleness and boredom on the cushions and divans with which it was furnished, she realized, *I've been taken to a harem.*

The man led her into a chamber in the middle of which was a pool filled with softly steaming water and strewn with rose petals. Two young women, servants or handmaidens of some kind, she supposed, were waiting for her. 'See that she is prepared for His Highness,' the eunuch commanded, sounding less like a man than a petulant child.

'Your bath has been prepared, my lady,' one of the servant girls said. 'May I take your gown?'

Judith's immediate instinct was to reply, 'No, you may not!' But there was no purpose in picking a fight with underlings who lacked the power to do anything that might help her. Her quarrel was with the man who ruled them and the only way she was going to see him was if she allowed herself to do what the eunuch deemed necessary. So Judith bathed and was then dried and scented oil was rubbed into her skin. One of the servants asked her to sit and then smoky black kohl was painted around her eyes, rouge was dabbed on her lips and her hair was pinned up and draped in strings of pearls like fabulously extravagant versions of the headdress she had worn to greet Hal at Mitsiwa, just a few weeks earlier. The girls placed ornately jewelled pendants in her ears and then asked her to stand so that they could dress her.

'Oh, my lady, you are so beautiful,' one of the servants said, as Judith stood naked before her. 'The prince will be over-whelmed by desire.'

'Aleena will be wild with jealousy!' the other girl giggled. 'You are bound to be his new favourite!'

They dressed her, if it could be said to be dressing, in a short-sleeved bodice that resembled the ones Judith had seen Indian women in streets of Zanzibar wearing beneath their saris. Those tops, however, had been cotton or silk, whereas this one was a barely visible wisp of sheer gauze, dotted with golden sequins and tiny jewels that barely even covered her breasts. Nor was her modesty preserved by a sari, for the only other garment she was given was a pair of loose pantaloons that hung low on her hips and was gathered at each ankle made from the same material and sprinkled with even more sparkling, glittering decorations. Her outfit was completed by a pair of silken Turkish slippers, embroidered with golden thread.

'Come . . . look at how magnificent you are,' said the first servant girl, leading Judith by the hand to a full-length mirror in a richly carved wooden frame that stood on the far side of the chamber. Judith gasped at her own reflection. She had imagined that she had gone to great lengths to look pretty for Hal but this was something quite different and she found herself both shocked but also fascinated by the blatantly erotic way in which she had been transformed. She had become a dancing-girl, a *houri*, a concubine and she did, indeed, look extraordinary. Had it been Hal waiting for her she would have been thrilled. Just the knowledge of the effect that she would have on him, looking like this, would be enough to arouse her before she even stepped into the same room as him. But to look like this for a stranger, a man who had abducted her by force, felt like a form of violation, as if the act of rape that she was now fearing had already begun.

She was still lost in troubled thought when the eunuch reappeared, examined her – his lips pursed in a thoughtful pout – gave a little, 'Huh!' as if surprised by her presentability and then for a second time said, 'Follow me.'

She was led back through the large salon where she could feel the gaze of all the other women on her and sense them sizing her up and deciding where she ranked in their pecking order. The eunuch wafted a limp hand back and forth to hurry her up and took her down a long corridor to a set of double doors which he opened and ushered her through before following her into the room that lay beyond them, closing the doors behind him as he came.

Judith found herself in a smaller, but infinitely more ornate version of the salon where the concubines were all waiting, just in case they should be required to serve at their master's pleasure. Every surface, everywhere was covered in carvings and inlays that were a priceless profusion of gold, marble, onyx, jade, deep black obsidian, pure blue lapis lazuli, shimmering mother-of-pearl and sparkling mirrored glass. As she walked past one mirror and saw the light glinting off the precious stones, sequins and pearls in which she herself was covered she felt as though she too were just one more perfect, decorative object designed to enchant the jaded senses of the man for whom it had all been brought into being.

The eunuch bowed low before a golden divan upon which a man was sitting and said, 'Your highness, here is the woman who was brought to me earlier this evening. I hope she meets with your satisfaction.'

With that, he scurried away, leaving Judith to look at her captor. The prince, as the serving girls had called him, was dressed in finery that was almost as jewelled, though a great deal less revealing than hers. He wore a bright pink silk coat with matching trousers and at the front of his turban a brooch was pinned consisting of the largest diamond Judith had ever seen, set in gold and surrounded by a ring of smaller stones, above which was a plume of egret feathers.

He was, she estimated, in his thirties and had strong, handsome features, just beginning to be softened by the fat being laid down by a life of limitless self-indulgence. As a young man he must have been very attractive indeed. Even now it would not be the greatest torment imaginable for a concubine to give herself to him, aside, of course, from the shame and abasement that the very state of concubinage brought upon a woman.

Then again, the woman kneeling on the divan by the prince's side, with her lips nibbling at his ear and her hand running playfully over his thighs and groin, did not appear to feel ashamed or debased. On the contrary, Judith thought to herself, she seemed to be enjoying her work.

Judith imagined that there must be bodyguards and servants somewhere nearabouts and there was music coming from somewhere off to one side of the room, but there was only one more person visible: the Buzzard. He stood behind the divan, his one arm straight down at his side, his only movement that characteristic, bird-like nodding and darting of the head.

'My dear General Nazet,' the prince said, and Judith noticed that Aleena – for she assumed that this was the favourite that the servant girls had mentioned – stopped what she was doing at the mention of the word 'general' and frowned in her direction, 'how strange to think that our lives and fates have been so closely intertwined for the past two years and yet we are only now meeting for the first time. I am the Maharajah Sadiq Khan Jahan. Your old adversary, Sultan Ahmed El Grang, leader of the Omani Arabs, served me as you served the child who called himself Emperor of Ethiopia.' The prince sighed and shook his head. 'You know, a woman of your beauty is really wasted on the battlefield.'

'No,' said Judith, 'a soldier of my experience is wasted in this glorified whorehouse.'

'Please, beloved, I do not understand,' said Aleena, sitting up straight. 'Why do you call this woman "general"? Why does she say that she is a soldier?'

'Because, my precious, not only is she your match in loveliness, she was El Grang's match as a soldier. She commanded armies while you just command the guardsman who stands to attention between my legs. Now, go! I must talk to the general. I will call for you later if I need you.'

'Do not wait too long,' Aleena purred, 'for every hour without you is an eternity to me.'

She got up off the divan and made her sinuous, bottom-wiggling way out of the room, barely breaking stride as she passed Judith and yet flashing her a wordless glance of raw hostility that was as much a declaration of war between women as any ruler's opening of hostilities against another man's kingdom.

The prince smiled complacently as his plaything departed, then, leaning forward and looking directly at Judith, said, 'I am a civilized man and I pride myself that I act with honour and in accordance with the laws of God. But I confess I find myself in something of a quandary. Were you a man of general's rank, whom I had captured in battle, I would hold you prisoner. If I felt it was safe to do so, I would offer you back to your people for ransom and, in exchange for the required sum, and your solemn word of honour that you would not bear arms against me or my people ever again, I would release you back to your family. Of course, for a commander of your eminence the ransom would be many, many lakhs of silver rupees: so many, in fact, that I doubt the treasury of the Emperor of Ethiopia himself could possibly meet the price. So that would leave me with the less pleasant option of granting you a swift and honourable death. You would not be tortured or mistreated and you would die like a man.

'But you are not a man and that complicates the issue . . . You are regarded, both by your people and mine, with an awe that no man would ever enjoy, as though you are somehow magical, more than human. A young woman, little more than a girl, who nevertheless leads great armies to victory: truly she must be something more than human. Your people – and of course I talk now about the common folk, rather than the higher class of educated individuals – believe that you have come down to them from heaven, like an angel.'

'And yours think I am a she-demon from hell. I am well aware of that,' said Judith. 'But I am neither angel nor demon. I am a woman, plain and simple. So what are you going to do with me?'

The prince gave a contemplative sigh. 'Ah, there's the question . . . I admit I have thought a great deal, over many months, about what I would do if you ever came into my hands. I have changed my mind on more than one occasion, and I may even change it again.'

'And . . . ?'

He shrugged. 'The temptation to sell you into slavery, to whomever will bid the highest sum for you is a very powerful one. To think of one who has been exalted on high, as you have been, brought to the very depths of human existence . . . who among those who have suffered at your hands would not take pleasure at that? But to give you away like that . . . what a waste! And what pleasure would it really bring me?

'Then again, you are a woman of remarkable beauty and, I am told, fecundity, too. Those are valuable commodities and I could gain great favour by offering you as a concubine to my brother the Great Mogul, or even the Sultan in Constantinople. Were either of them to have a son by you, what a man he might be. But why should I let either of those two men gain such

227

advantage? Surely, since I have you, I should just keep you for my own use.'

Judith almost spat rather than spoke her next words. 'I would rather die than be your concubine. And I would kill my own child, too, rather than let it be raised in your court and under your god.'

'Yes, that was what I feared,' the prince said, nodding his head. 'And in any case, I could hardly keep you as a member of my harem, unless it were in solitary confinement. You've already made a mortal enemy of Aleena, and although she is as pretty as a kitten, she is dangerous as a tigress. Then there are my other concubines to consider. These are young women from many lands, but all have come from very modest backgrounds. The life they lead here is paradise compared to the ones they left behind and all they have to do in return is to please and obey me. They do not doubt that is a very fair bargain and they would never rebel in any way. Yet you might plant ideas in their head that would make them unhappy, disobedient and unwilling to please. This would cause me great inconvenience, not least because I would have to kill them all and find replacements.'

'I'm sure I would hate to put you to such trouble,' said Judith with heavy sarcasm. 'But now that you have told me all the various possibilities you have rejected, what fate have you chosen for me?'

'First, you will join me for dinner. I should like to hear your account of your Ethiopian campaigns – the disposition of your forces, the tactics you planned in advance, the fresh decisions you were obliged to make in the heat of battle, and so on. I shall treat you with respect and ask no more of you than your military insight. Is that acceptable?'

'Do not expect me to enjoy your company, Prince Jahan. But yes, I will engage in conversation at least.'

'How gracious you are, madam. At the conclusion of our discussion, you will be led to your quarters, where you will be confined for the next three weeks. You will want for nothing, as befits your rank. Sadly, I will be obliged to put you up for sale at the slave market, but have no fear, I have no intention of letting anyone else buy you.'

'So why pretend to sell me, then, other than as a means of abasing and humiliating me?'

'Come now, the humiliation of the great Nazet is quite something in itself,' the prince said. 'The news that you were put on the block in Zanzibar and traded like any other piece of flesh will reverberate around Africa, India and the Levant. You can imagine what it will do to your people's morale . . . and to mine. But my true purpose goes beyond that. You are really just being shown in a very public place as bait . . .'

'To draw in Sir Henry Courtney, if he is still alive.'

The prince beamed with delight. 'Exactly! Ah, what a pleasure it is to talk with a woman who understands these things. Yes, I would have both in my thrall. And after that, well, again I confess my mind is not yet completely set, but if I had Sir Henry, I would offer you a very simple choice: give yourself to me, or I will kill him.'

'No . . . I would . . .'

'Kill yourself? But consider this: if you kill yourself, then I will also kill him. Give yourself to me, completely, for a full night and not only will he live, but there will be a chance that you are reunited.'

'What chance is that?'

'Simple. I will set Sir Henry to fight against this creature here . . .' The prince idly wafted a hand in the direction of the Buzzard. 'It will be one mortal enemy against another, each armed with a sword, to the death. You will be watching, for whichever one of your suitors stays alive will take you as his prize.'

The sound of a throat being cleared could be heard from behind the leather mask. 'Hush, Buzzard,' the prince commanded, 'do not say a word. You know the terms by which I allow you here, and you know that if you speak you will forfeit your life. But look at the prizes I am offering you: the death of the man you hate and the body of the woman he loved.'

'That . . . thing will never, ever have my body.'

'Yes, yes, you'd rather die first, so you keep saying,' the prince snapped, irritably. 'But I don't believe you. What mother would kill herself and her child? A mother will do anything, endure anything, accept any indignity to preserve the life of her child. Are you really so different? As for you, Buzzard, you did well today. You brought me General Nazet. And I am giving you something in return. Go into the city. Find a place to drink your infidel spirits. Find a woman if any will go near you. Pretend, for this one night, that you are still a man.'

If Zanzibar was an island on whose shores the peoples of half the known world washed up, then the Tres Macacos, or Three Monkeys, was the place where the scum of the known world settled. It was a drinking establishment located off an alley that ran to one side of the dead end of a side street in the heart of the oldest, filthiest quarter of the city. It sold alcohol, which the Omani authorities, heeding the words of the Qu'ran, officially prohibited, but to which a few blind eyes were turned, providing that it was only sold by infidels to infidels. The payment of large bribes to a number of relevant individuals also contributed to the tavern's continuing existence, all the more so since the individuals in question were regular patrons. Like many Zanzibaris, they went to the Macacos not for the raw cane spirit that passed for rum, nor the acrid vinegar that was sold as wine, but for the cock- and dogfighting that took place in a dirty, half rotten arena, rank with the smells of chicken droppings, dog mess and blood that had been erected in a yard at the back of the property.

The tavern's main saloon, meanwhile, played host to a motley assortment of pirates, smugglers, slave-traders, mercenaries, merchants and seamen of every sort, rank and race, attended to by crudely painted, pox-ridden whores. The air was thick with the heady aromas of tobacco smoke, unwashed bodies, stale liquor and the sinus-clearing perfumes with which the ladies doused themselves after every customer. But even in this grubby temple to depravity and decay, the arrival of the Buzzard, accompanied by his personal slave and a pair of guards whose presence was intended both to protect him and discourage any possible thought he might have of escaping Prince Jahan's employment, brought a hush to the room and turned even the most jaded, world-weary, seen-it-all heads. One drunken wit was fool enough to shout out, 'Sorry, birdie, they don't serve no worms 'ere!' A second later, the Buzzard's blade was at his neck and he was stammering a grovelling apology.

The Buzzard strode to the bar. 'Rum,' he rasped. He gave a wave of his hand that brought the slave forward, holding his drinking can. 'Fill that. Right to the top. If you want money, ask Prince Jahan, for I don't carry any.'

The serving wench nodded in dumb terror. She knew, as all Zanzibaris did, that the prince had tamed a *djinn* who was half-man, half-bird. She had also heard about the killing of the boy who had thrown filth at him and the criminals at the city jail whom the monster had slaughtered. If he wanted rum but saw no need to pay for it, she was not going to argue and nor, she knew, would her boss.

232

The Buzzard's slave picked up the full can and then followed his master across the room to one of the very few empty tables in the place. He then inserted the spout into the mask's mouth hole as was his usual practice and the Buzzard greedily gulped down the first alcohol to have passed his lips in months.

Somewhere in the room someone was foolish enough to titter. The Buzzard swatted the spout away with an angry flick of the wrist, got to his feet and surveyed the room, his nose turning before him like the bowsprit of a tacking ship, and bobbing up and down as his eye scanned the room, just as a bowsprit moves with the impact of each new wave. All laughter stopped, as did all conversation. Then the motion of the Buzzard's head ceased. He stopped and stared at a particular table. Heads turned towards it, following his gaze. The Buzzard got up from his place and strode across the tavern floor, with scarred, grizzled, teak-hard ruffians scrabbling to get out of his way as he passed.

The Buzzard reached the table that had attracted his attention. A single man was sitting there, with a bottle of wine and a pewter tankard in front of him. He did not quail at the Buzzard's approach. He simply sat and stared straight back at the painted eyes of the leather mask, with a look of cussed stubbornness on his face that said, 'I'm not going to flinch. So if you want to scare someone you'd better look somewhere else.'

But then the Buzzard did something no one in the room had foreseen. He stopped by the table, pulled out a chair, sat down on it and said, 'Captain Hamish Benbury, as I live and breathe. How are you keeping, you cantankerous old bastard?'

The stillness in the room deepened, the tension tightened still further as Benbury remained as silent and immobile as a tombstone. Then he turned his head, spat on the sawdust-covered floor, looked back up at the Buzzard and said, 'Good day to you, too, Cochran. My mother used to say, "You're a long time dead." Evidently she was wrong.' He took a long drink of his wine and then added, 'I used tae think you couldn't get any uglier. Evidently I was wrong on that too.'

The Buzzard started laughing, only to discover – for this was another new experience – that his lungs and throat couldn't handle it. For a few seconds he was struck by a violent and agonizing coughing fit that made him slam his fist against the table in protest at his discomfort and frustration. He looked around for his slave, who was still at the table where he had been sitting, and gestured furiously for him to come over. The slave got halfway across the room, realized that he had left the rum behind, dashed back for it and then frantically raced towards the Buzzard and stuck the spout in his mouth once again.

The whole manic performance was so absurd that it broke the tension in the room and around the room the usual pattern of conversation, banter and furious insults resumed. After a while, the cockfights began and the saloon thinned out as patrons went outside to see the slaughter. The Buzzard and Captain Benbury were therefore left to talk in peace.

For the next few minutes, the Buzzard ran through the story of his survival, rescue and recruitment by Prince Jahan. He described his role in the best possible light, emphasizing the degree to which his training had restored his ability to fight and giving a leering account of the concubines he had encountered in the prince's harem.

'Is that so?' Benbury said, after the Buzzard had described the experience of coming face-to-face and body-to-body with the prince's favourite bedmate. 'I always heard that the only men

234

let into these sultans' harems, apart from the sultans themselves, were all eunuchs. I must have been misinformed. I mean, you're not a eunuch, are you, Cochran?'

The Buzzard fiercely denied such a preposterous suggestion and said that this was a sign of the prince's special favour. 'Aye, that'll be it,' Benbury said, though he could see the locks on the back of the mask and the ring on the neck, not to mention the way the two guards never took their eyes off the Buzzard and decided that the Earl of Cumbrae's current status was not that of peer of the realm, but somewhere between a prisoner, a slave and a dancing bear.

The Buzzard could sense the other man's scepticism. He'd seen Benbury's eyes looking at the ring and part of him had wanted to shout out, 'Aye! They can lead me like a damn dog. What of it?' But what good would that do? It was better that there should be a tacit agreement not to take the matter any further, for now at any rate. That being the case, it was time to change the subject.

'So, Benbury, ye've heard my tale,' the Buzzard said. 'Now you tell me what brings you and your *Pelican*, for I presume you are still her master, tae this festering hole?'

'I am indeed still proud tae call myself captain of the *Pelican*, Cochran,' Benbury replied. 'And, d'you know it occurs tae me now that my business here may be of interest tae you and profit tae us both.'

The Buzzard leaned forward and tilted his head so that his one beady eye could focus directly on the man opposite him. 'How so?'

'Well, I am engaged in a form of speculation. D'ye ken a Portuguese gentleman by the name of Balthazar Lobo?'

'I cannae say that I do.'

'He is a most unusual gentleman. I'm sure I dinnae have tae

tell you that for many a long year the Portuguese have had ports all along the Swahili Coast, barred tae all white men but them, from whence they've traded gold mined in native kingdoms deep in the interior.'

'I know all about that, Benbury. Aye, and I've watched many a Portuguese ship sail by me, fat with the gold in her belly and damned the lack of a war against Portugal that would have given me reason tae take her.'

'Very well, then, for all these years, the Portuguese have stayed in their ports and barely ventured inland. Och, they've set up a few trading posts here and there and missionaries have gone out looking for heathen souls tae convert, but they've left the actual mining of the gold tae the native folk. But yon Balthazar Lobo decided that he didnae fancy waiting for the gold tae be brought to the coast. No, he was going right inland, tae a place called the Kingdom of Manyika tae mine the damn ore for himself.'

'I cannae imagine the local chiefs were happy wi' that.'

'Well, I dare say Lobo's paid a good price for his diggings. But he started up a mine and by God there was gold in its rocks and now the man's as rich as Croesus.'

'Are you in his pay now, Benbury? Is that your business?'

'Nay, he's not paid me . . . not yet. But it's my hope that he will. See, Senhor Lobo has a wee problem. He cannae find a woman tae give him a bairn.'

'Maybe the problem isn't the women.'

'Aye, you're probably right there, Cochran. But suppose a man could find a woman, ensure that she was with child and then sell her tae Lobo before her condition was apparent? Lobo would think the baby was his and he'd be truly thankful, would he not, tae the man who had brought him the mother of this wee miracle?'

'Aye, that he would, and I dare say there'd be profit in his gratitude.'

'Now, I've been trying tae find the perfect wench tae sell tae Lobo. I came here to see whether there was one tae be had in Zanzibar. But as I was listening tae your tale of yon sultan's harem I was thinking to myself, I wonder what happens when yon sultan tires of a lassie? I'm thinking he sells her tae another man. And if that be the case, then maybe you, Cochran, could use your influence over the mighty Prince Jahan tae sell one of his lassies tae me I'd make it well worth your trouble.'

And then a smile spread across the Buzzard's hidden face, a grin almost as wide and leering as the one painted on his mask. For here, in the unprepossessing shape of Hamish Benbury, he saw the answer to all his problems, an end to his tribulations and the chance of a new life, freed from the prince and revenged upon Courtney.

'I can do much, much better than that, Benbury. I can get you a bitch that's got Lobo's puppy planted in her belly. And she'll nae cost you a penny . . . save the half share of her sale price to Lobo that you'll give tae me.'

'And why would I do that?'

'Because this is a woman that's worth a king's ransom, and by God she'll make Lobo feel like a king tae own her.'

Then the Buzzard started talking. As he talked he drained his pot of rum, and then another, with a second bottle of wine for Benbury too. When their talking was done and their drink consumed they shook hands on their agreement, and the Buzzard walked away from the Tres Macacos with his slave and his guard beside him feeling a great deal better than when he had arrived, better indeed than at any time since the sinking of the *Gull of Moray*. So much so, in fact, that he looked up into the night sky and said a brief word to his Creator.

'Thank you very much, you old bastard. It was about time you did me a favour.'

The three men moved like wraiths across the rooftops of the town. Barefoot and silent as shadows, Hal, Big Daniel and Will Stanley leapt a small gap onto the flat roof of the house behind Consul Grey's. Getting this far had not been easy. Some of the roofs they'd crossed had been covered in tiles that either clinked under hand or foot, or were treacherously loose so that now and then one would slide off with a heart-stopping grating noise. It had only been the men's long experience up in the shrouds and yards on a rolling ship which had prevented one of them falling to their death. Yet they had got this far at least, to a vantage point perhaps five feet higher than the roof of Grey's property.

In contrast to the front of the property with its grand arched mahogany door, intricately carved with Islamic motifs, the rear of Grey's house was much less richly adorned. But there were windows cut into the wall, and ledges below them. And lower down some of the windows had balconies with simple wooden balustrades. One of these would provide their way in.

'Can you see him?' Daniel whispered.

Hal's eyes, which had always been keen as a hawk's, sifted the dark for Aboli. There were no lamps here away from the streets and the night sky had filled with clouds through which the moon only rarely penetrated to cast the rooftops in fleeting moments of silvery light.

'Not yet,' Hal said. He could see the sentries though: two Africans in white robes standing by the gateway in the middle of the rear wall that would provide entry to the property for tradesmen and servants. The sentries carried blunderbusses, a shrewdly chosen weapon, Hal thought, because it roared like the devil when fired, alerting everyone that there was trouble.

Two more men were slowly pacing the roof opposite them from one side to another. None of these guards had been there when Hal and Pett had come to lunch. But then, Grey was always a man who took care to look after his own skin. He would have made sure that if anything went wrong with the night's dirty work, he would remain well protected.

'There!' Hal hissed. Big Daniel and Stanley crawled up beside him.

'Jesus and Mary but he's a bold sort,' Big Daniel hissed, because there was Aboli on the roof opposite, bent low, knife in hand, moving as fast and smooth as a bird's shadow and coming up on one of the guards from behind.

Hal held his breath, certain the guard would turn around. That he would fire that blunderbuss. But Aboli was already on him like a leopard on an antelope. He clamped his left hand over the man's mouth and nose and thrust the knife into his neck below the ear and Hal saw the blade protrude from the other side. Then Aboli slashed outwards through the throat and as the sentry's legs buckled he lowered him to the floor without a sound.

Aboli was already moving again. But the other sentry was turning now, having come to the eastern edge of the roof, and Stanley cursed under his breath.

'He won't make it,' Big Daniel muttered.

Up came the blunderbuss but the guard was not fast enough and Aboli punched the knife up under his ribs into the heart then hauled the blade out and slashed it across the man's neck before he could scream. Then Aboli was somehow holding the blunderbuss as the guard stood choking on his own blood, already dead before his legs knew it. Aboli swept behind him and laid the man down, then strode over to the edge of the roof and shrugged off the length of rope he'd had coiled like a sash across his body.

Daniel sighed. 'God knows I love him like a brother, but he's deadlier than the damned pox.'

They stood now as Aboli came to the edge of the roof and, keeping hold of one end, hurled the rope coils up to Hal who caught them before they could fly over his head. Aboli tied his end of the rope around his waist before edging out over the side and hanging full length by his hands for a moment before dropping down to a narrow ledge outside a top-floor window, where the servants' quarters would be. If anyone within heard him now, or saw a shadow at the window, Aboli would surely be done for, they'd never get into the house, and Hal might never learn where Judith had been taken.

'God be with him now,' Big Daniel said.

'Something to tie that rope to would be more useful,' Stanley said and Hal feared his friend was right, for there was just the ledge and the window, through which a warm yellow glow seeped out into the night.

But no sooner had the words been spoken than Aboli dropped off the ledge, landed silently on one of the small balconies a further ten feet below, then took the rope from his waist and tied it to the wooden balustrade. No light came from the tall, shuttered windows behind him.

'Now it's our turn,' Big Daniel said, tying his end of the rope around his own waist and striding backward until the line was taut as a yardarm brace. There was nothing on that flat roof to tie off on and so Big Daniel himself would be the anchor, using all his enormous size and strength to take Hal and Stanley's weight as they climbed across.

'Are you sure you are strong enough?' Stanley asked, half grinning.

'You'll soon know if I'm not,' the coxswain replied.

'And so will you, Danny, if that knot's not up to scratch,' Hal said, steeling himself for what they must now do. 'I'll go first,' he said as Aboli waved his arm, gesturing at them to come across. Hal wrapped his arms and legs around the rope, for a moment hanging there like a deer strung up after the kill, Big Daniel heaving back, those great arms and oak-strong legs straining to keep the rope taut.

'Off you go then, Captain,' he growled and Hal began hauling himself out into the night, the Neptune sword hanging beneath him, the two pistols snug in the sash around his waist. There was no talking now, only concentration, muscle and sinew. Keeping his legs crossed over the rope and using them as a grapnel only, he pulled himself out along the line, high above the street below. He'd spent half his life up a mast and was entirely unafraid of falling, but if one of the remaining guards came around the back of the house, or if someone happened

242

to look out of a rear window, then all Hal's skill at climbing would not be enough to save him.

Suspended in the darkness as he was, Hal could see very little around him. But he could hear the sound of his own heartbeat in his ears, the barking of dogs in Zanzibar's streets, the chirruping of crickets and away in the distance the soft sighing of the sea. He waited for a shout of alarm or crash of gunfire. But none came and then he had reached the far end of the rope, alive and undetected.

Hal swung a leg onto the balcony and hauled himself up, scrambling over the railing to stand face-to-face with Aboli. The two men nodded at one another in recognition of their night's work so far, then looked back across the divide to watch Will Stanley come across. Just then the cloud broke and the rooftops of Zanzibar were bathed in the moon's cold luminescence. So too was Stanley, who froze for a heartbeat. Then he was moving fast, pulling himself along the rope hand over hand, the corded muscle of his arms glistening in the moon glow. But the sudden speed jerked the rope and Hal heard Big Daniel curse as he lost his footing and was hauled, skidding, to the edge of the roof. Stanley dropped sharply but clung on and Big Daniel, a great hulking shape in the half-light, leant back and pulled the rope straight as a spar again and his crewmate was already moving.

By the time Stanley had climbed up onto the balcony, Aboli was standing by the windows, holding the dagger he had used so skilfully on the guards. Now he punched its hilt through one of the small diamonds in the leaded glass and thrust in his hand to draw the iron catch from the casement. The window swung open and Aboli sprang into the room, his knife back in a fighting grip, ready to deal with anyone who was inside.

The room, however, was empty, but for some pieces of

243

furniture covered in dustsheets. Hal and Stanley joined Aboli and they moved towards the door. Hal lifted the latch as slowly and quietly as he could then opened it a fraction and peered through the crack. He saw precisely what he'd been hoping for, the colonnade that ran around three sides of the building at first-floor level, looking down onto the courtyard at the centre, with rooms opening onto it. But on the fourth side, directly opposite the room where Hal and the others now stood, the rooms were much larger and there was no colonnade, for they occupied the full depth of the building and faced the courtyard with windows whose decorative iron mullions were picked out in patterns as delicate as lace. These were the finest chambers in the house and so it was reasonable to assume that Grey had reserved them for his own personal use. Indeed, Hal could see the flicker of candlelight coming from behind the windows, suggesting that Grey was still up. *Damn!* Hal thought. *If he's got company that could complicate things.*

Hal gestured to the other two men and they followed him out onto the colonnade. He knew that there were two more guards outside, by the main entrance, but a quick scan of the colonnade and down into the courtyard showed no sign of any armed men beyond that.

The trio made their way around the courtyard, the soft splashing of the fountain in the pool beneath them masking the scurrying of their feet across the tiled floor, until they came to an arch shaped like an onion, within which was set a wooden door. Hal drew his sword and held it at the ready in his right hand as he raised the latch with his left. Then he shoved the door hard with his shoulder and as it flew open he sprang into the chamber, closely followed by Aboli and Stanley.

Hal heard a high-pitched cry of alarm and there, standing before him, barely a pace away, naked but for the fuzzy hair that sprouted across his soft, heaving chest and ran over his rotund belly to his groin, was Consul Grey.

'Sir Henry,' Grey stammered, his flaccid manhood shrivelling into his pubic hair like a startled weevil retreating back into the ship's biscuit from which it had just emerged. On the bed behind him was a naked African boy, his coffee-coloured body glistening with oil, the whites of his eyes glowing in the lamp-light. In his small hand he held a riding crop, which Grey snatched off him and raised at the intruders in a pathetic show of defiance.

'Consul Grey,' Hal returned his greeting, pointing the Neptune blade at his betrayer.

'Someone is coming, Gundwane,' Aboli said. They heard feet scuffing up the stone steps and knew that Grey's earlier shriek had alerted someone.

There was a double rap on the door and a voice called out. 'Consul! Is everything all right? Consul?'

Grey looked from Aboli, to Hal, to the tip of the sword that hovered just inches from his belly button and thence to the door, his face frozen with fear and indecision.

'Help me!' he blurted. The door flew open and two robed men swept into the bedchamber, swords drawn.

Aboli launched himself at one of them, hooking an arm around the man's neck and dragging him backwards, whilst Hal threw up his sword to parry a slash aimed at his face. The blades sang and before the guard could strike again Stanley swept in behind him punching his knife into the man's kidney before hacking open his throat in a spray of gore. The guard collapsed, his robes turning crimson and the tear in his throat pulsing blood across the floorboards. Then Stanley turned back to the bed and glared at the boy who clambered back under the silken coverlet and pulled it up over his head.

245

Over by the door Aboli finished strangling the other guard whose swollen tongue poked out between his lips. 'Go with Allah,' Aboli said in a low voice, laying the corpse down gently.

And Consul Grey wet himself. His urine stream spattered onto the floor and spilled down his leg and he was too terrified even to realize what he had done.

'Where is Judith? Where did they take her?' Hal asked him, putting his sword's point against the consul's bulging belly. Aboli shut the bedchamber door and stood with his back against it.

Grey made no attempt to deny all knowledge of Judith's abduction. He must have known it was too late for all that now. Neither, however, did he seem about to divulge all. Beads of sweat rolled down his face and his fleshy jowls trembled. But he did not talk.

Hal lashed the sword hilt across his face and Grey stumbled but his big legs did not give way. He stood tall again, a bruise already blooming on his left cheek.

'Where did they take Judith?' Hal asked again.

This time Hal used his fist, hammering into Grey's right temple.

Grey reeled and when he regained his balance his eyes were wide with fear.

'You want to kill me, Hal, don't you?' he said. 'Come, my boy, there must be some accommodation to be made.'

'I will not ask again, sir,' Hal said. 'Tell me now what the Buzzard and his men have done with Judith.'

'This is taking too long,' Aboli said.

'To hell with you, Courtney,' Grey snarled, finding his courage at last. Or else perhaps he had given up any hope of surviving this night.

Hal raised the sword hilt to strike the man again.

246

'Wait, Gundwane,' Aboli said. Hal lowered the sword and looked at his companion. 'I can make him tell you what you want to know.'

Hal hesitated, but Aboli pressed him. 'Captain, we shall be here all night unless you let me persuade him to talk.'

Hal wanted nothing more than to thrust the point of the Neptune sword into the consul's heart, but that would not save Judith and so he tried to smother the rage that burned inside him. 'He's all yours, Aboli.'

Aboli went over to the chair by the bed upon which the consul's shirt and breeches lay neatly folded. He cut a strip from the shirt and forced it into Grey's mouth, thrusting with his thumb until it was all in and the consul was retching. He pulled the chair into the middle of the room and sat the man in it before tearing more strips from the cotton bed sheets. These he rolled into thin ropes, using them to tie the consul's legs to the chair's legs. Hal knew what Aboli had in mind. He took Grey's own belt and used it to bind his wrists together behind the chair's back.

Grey stared at Hal with eyes that were swollen in their sockets. The whole left side of his face was turning the deep purple of port wine now and his fat legs were trembling against the seat of the chair.

Crouching behind the seated consul so that he was almost out of sight, Aboli went to work with his knife. Grey screamed but the sound was nothing but a strangled gurgle because of the gag filling his mouth, and Aboli grunted as he forced the blade to break through bone. When it was done, Aboli held up his hand and Hal saw the tip of one of the consul's fat fingers nestled between the African's index finger and thumb. Then Aboli stood and walked around the chair to show the consul the lump of his own fingernail, flesh and bone.

247

'Tell the captain what he wishes to know, Mr Grey,' Aboli said. 'Or would you rather play at being dumb and blind? Maybe I should slice off your tongue and put out your eyes. Then you would not be playing.'

Grey nodded, frantically indicating that he would talk. Aboli placed the severed finger on the floor in plain sight then pulled the gag from Grey's mouth. The consul looked on the verge of passing out. Hal took a jug of wine from the dresser and thrust it to his lips. Grey drank and spluttered and the wine poured down his hairy corpulent belly.

'Where did the Buzzard take Judith?' Hal asked and this time Grey nodded as though he wanted nothing more than to tell Hal everything.

'The truth, Captain Courtney . . .' Grey stared pointedly at the wine jug, seeking to numb the pain and so Hal poured another wash down his throat. 'The truth,' Grey went on, breathing heavily, 'is that you will never see that black bitch again. Prince Jahan has her and will sell her at the monthly slave market, here in Zanzibar. That's where all the prime bucks and prettiest fancies are auctioned.' He glared at Hal, his face now pallid and slick with sweat and then said, 'Once she's been sold you'll never find her. Buyers come from all over the Levant, North Africa and even the Indies, so she could end up any place from Constantinople to Calcutta. The next Courtney will be born and die a slave. And its mother will have the rest of her benighted life in which to rue the day she defied the will of Prince Jahan and the armies of the One True God.'

Suddenly Grey threw his weight back and the chair toppled before Hal or Aboli could make a grab for it. Chair and man thumped on the boards and Grey turned his face to the floor and started shouting for all his worth.

Then Hal heard a scurrying sound, a man's shout of, 'Oi!'

and the thump of a body landing on the wooden floor. He turned to see Stanley lying flat out on the floor and a flash of bare skin as Grey's boy scampered out of the door, as fast as his legs would carry him.

'I tried to catch the little bastard, but he was as slippery as a wet eel,' Stanley said.

There was a muffled shout from somewhere. Orders were being given.

'More of them are coming,' Aboli said, his ear to the door.

'Then it's time we left,' Hal said. He paused by the door, while Aboli and Stanley dashed out onto the colonnade.

Grey was still bound to the chair. Still crying into the boards and jerking like a caught fish to make as much noise as possible.

'Tell Judith to have faith,' Hal snarled at him. 'For I will find her and set her free.'

He left the room and sprinted after the other two. There was a hubbub of voices coming from down in the courtyard and then a single voice shouting out in alarm. A few seconds later a shot was fired and there was a sudden burst of marble chips from one of the columns just ahead of Hal, followed by more shouts and the sound of running feet. He had almost caught up with Aboli and Stanley as they disappeared into the room through which they'd entered the building. Hal slammed the door behind him, whipped the dustsheet off a large chest of drawers and called out, 'Quick! Help me block the door.'

With frantic haste the three men shoved the chest across the door and then ran to the window, closing it behind them as they went out onto the balcony. Hal looked across the gap between the buildings to see Daniel, evidently alerted by the commotion coming from Consul Grey's house, standing by the edge of the far roof, with the rope already held tight and his legs and back braced to take the strain. 'You first, Stanley,' Hal commanded.

Within seconds the boatswain was on the rope and halfway across the gap.

There was a hammering from the colonnade as the pursuers tried to force their way into the room and then a sudden hail of wood fragments and shot against the windows as someone blew a hole in the door.

'You next, Aboli,' Hal said.

'But Gundwane . . .'

'Go! That's an order. I still have these . . .'

Hal gestured at the pistols that were shoved into his sash. Reluctantly, Aboli nodded then grabbed the rope and began making his way across. Hal stood on the balcony with his back to the wall beside the window, watching Aboli's progress in front of him while listening to the sound of their pursuers behind. He took hold of one of the pistols.

Aboli was most of the way across when Hal heard a splintering of wood followed by a shout of triumph. He counted to three and then spun round so that he was framed by the window, kicked it open and took aim with his pistol. His target was a man, clambering over the top of the chest, no more than ten or twelve feet away. Hal forced himself to stay completely calm amidst the mayhem, steadied his arm and then fired. The man screamed in pain and then flopped headfirst over the chest. Hal shoved the empty pistol back into his sash and grabbed the next one. This one he fired into the hole in the door through which he could see a press of jabbering, gesticulating men. He fired again and there was another howl that seemed to go on endlessly.

Wherever I hit him, it hurt, thought Hal, turning to the balustrade and grabbing the rope. He'd bought himself a few precious seconds while the consul's men recovered from the loss of two of their number. But then came the voice of a man who evidently knew what he was doing, taking command and putting some fight back into his men, and Hal knew that his respite was over. He was hanging upside down, pulling himself along the line when he heard another splintering of wood and the first musket fire as they broke into the empty room. He leaned his head back and looked at the far wall. He was about two-thirds of the way across.

'If you'd like to hurry it up, Captain,' Big Daniel called out.

'They're on the roof now, sir!' Will Stanley shouted. 'By God they've got their dead mates' guns!'

Hal heard firing, two shots, and felt the gust of disrupted air as a bullet missed him by an inch before slamming into the wall.

Then there was another shout of delight from the balcony and suddenly Hal was dropping and swinging and smashing against the wall.

They've cut the bloody rope!

He felt himself slide down the wall and knew that Daniel would be struggling to keep a hold of the rope now that he had to take all the strain. Then his downward motion suddenly stopped with a jerk.

'Don't you worry, Captain!' Daniel called down. 'We've got you. Just take your time.'

The hell I will! Hal thought and scurried up the rope with the speed of a man to whom climbing a rope was as natural as climbing the stairs. There were more shouts from down in the street, and more shots, but then he was tumbling over the parapet and onto the roof. 'Well done, Danny,' he said. 'Damned well done.'

'We're not home and dry yet, Captain,' Big Daniel said.

251

Hal grinned. 'Let's get to that boat, then.' And with that they ran, heedless of stealth now but compelled by the need to get back to the *Delft* before Consul Grey roused the city garrison that was manned by Omani Arab soldiers. They fled west towards the sea, scrambling over tiled roofs and leaping across gaps, the shouts of their pursuers becoming fainter until at last, when they were sure they had slipped the noose, the four men descended a stone stairway down to a moonlit thoroughfare two streets back from the harbour front. They stood at the bottom of the steps, hands, on knees, heads bent over, their chests heaving.

And then they ran again.

They sprinted along the harbour front, the sea on their left white-flecked in the half-light, towards the landing steps where the longboat was waiting. But that meant they were running towards the fort that guarded the harbour and the garrison that was certainly mobilizing, the commander's strings pulled by Consul Grey.

They were a cable's length from the fort's white walls when a great iron-studded door creaked open and a platoon of Omani soldiers rushed out, brandishing their weapons. Their officer spotted Hal and some of his men stopped to give fire, their long arms spitting gouts of flame into the night. Hal heard the balls ripping the air around them as he ducked his head and ran the harder.

'Keep going!' Hal called. 'Don't stop!' So they ran straight at the mob of white-robed soldiers who were pouring out of the gates of the fort.

'God and the king!' Hal roared, his Neptune sword in his right hand, the flintlock in his left. 'God and the king!'

And suddenly another dozen voices were heard as the crew of the longboat came racing up the steps from their mooring, bursting out onto the quayside and firing their pistols into the confused mass of garrison soldiers. This sudden, completely unexpected intervention threw the Arabs into disarray as the volley of pistol fire tore into them and those still on their feet turned to meet this unexpected threat.

'God and the king and the *Golden Bough*!' Big Daniel roared, leading the charge, taking a man's head off his shoulders with a sweep of his cutlass. Then the other *Bough*'s men joined the fray, hacking and stabbing like furies.

'The *Bough*!' Hal bellowed, scything his sword at a soldier's face. As the man before him fell he looked around. Now he saw that the advantage of surprise had been lost, sheer weight of numbers was telling against his men.

'Looks like we've outstayed our welcome, lads,' Hal yelled. 'Man the longboats, Master Daniel!'

The ring and scrape of steel blades and the grunts and screams of men fighting for their lives filled the Zanzibar night. Hal saw one sailor he'd known all his life killed by a curved dagger which slashed open his throat and another clubbed to the ground with his skull staved in by the butt of a musket. He saw Will Stanley lop off an Arab's arm and he saw Aboli killing three Arabs in the time it takes a school boy to count to that number.

But more Arabs were pouring out of the fort.

'To the boats!' Hal shouted above the din, and they ran.

Hal was climbing aboard the second boat when he heard the Omani officer shout the command to fire. There was a thunderous fusillade and the lad beside Hal was thrown forward into the water.

'Get us out to the *Delft*, if you please, gentlemen,' Hal called, his back straight and head up as musket and pistol balls whipped into the sea around them.

The enemy fire became more erratic and wild as the range opened, until they clambered on board the waiting *Delft*.

'Take her out, Mr Tromp,' Hal snapped as he clambered up through the larboard port. 'Steer for the channel, if you please. At the earliest opportunity we shall let her run before the wind.'

'The channel it is, sir,' Tromp acknowledged, as he put the whipstaff over. The canvas crackled as loud as the distant gunfire on the walls of the fort as it filled to the stiff night breeze.

'You know the ship best, Mr Tromp, so set the sails as you see fit. But fast, mind. We'd better not linger with those guns staring down at us.'

Tromp barked a series of commands and the *Delft* responded like a thoroughbred racehorse, thrilling to the beam reach on her larboard tack, her sails gleaming white against the night sky as she bore away.

She was flying now so the gunners on the fortress walls had to keep altering their aim and elevation of their guns, by which time the *Delft* was out of range and turning her bows to the south to run downwind.

'Nicely done, Mr Tromp,' said Hal, as they left the island of Zanzibar behind them. 'Now take us back to the *Bough*. If you please.'

The storm came out of the north-east, from India and the high Himalayas, like the vengeance of God. Young Sam Awdy up in the mizzen was the first to see it coming. He had yelled down to the quarterdeck that the sky three leagues off the *Golden Bough*'s stern was changing. A great towering shelf of cloud darkened the sky and no sooner had Hal turned his telescope on the ominous mass than the ocean below it began to seethe, white spume whipping off the racing furrows.

'There's no outrunning her, Mr Tyler,' Hal called, then looked at Tromp. 'Better to reef too early than reef too late, eh, Mr Tromp?'

The Dutchman smiled to hear this age-old sailors' wisdom. 'Reef too late and you never reef again, Captain,' he agreed.

'Let's not give her too much canvas to play with, Mr Tyler!'

Hal said. 'Bring the bows around and we shall introduce ourselves like proper gentlemen.'

Mr Tyler gave the order and men scrambled up the shrouds and along the yards to put some reefs in the sails as the helmsman leant against the whipstaff to bring the *Bough* round to face what was coming.

Hal went back to the stern rail to face the colossal mass of cloud and rain sweeping across the sky and was relieved to see that John Lovell, following in line astern, was also taking canvas off the *Delft*, and was bringing her into the wind, matching the *Bough*'s movements like a dancer with her partner.

Now Hal turned back to his own ship. 'Mr Stanley, secure the hatches. Master Daniel, kindly ensure all the guns are lashed down nice and tight.' The last thing they needed was a culverin rolling around the gundeck, crushing men or punching a hole through the hull.

'She's coming for us, lads!' Hal called. 'And she's got teeth by the looks of her.'

Hal looked over his ship. To an untrained eye it was a scene of chaos, but to a seaman it was a beautiful sight, as the crew rushed to their stations and went about their work, every man, be he an Amadoda tribesman, a Limburger from southern Holland or a Devonshire man, tending to the needs of the ship, giving himself, his crewmates and the *Golden Bough* the best chance of coming through this test unbeaten.

'Captain, do you suppose this is judgement?' Robert Moone asked. 'That we are facing the final summons for what we've got down there.' He gestured towards the main deck but Hal knew he was talking about what lay in the hold beneath it, where the barrels of bogus bones and pieces of the True Cross, the scraps of saints' skin and an assortment of Holy Grails now sat.

'If we are to be judged, Mr Moone, it will not be for the cargo in our hold but for the intent in our hearts. For our actions.'

Moone frowned. 'If you say so, Captain.'

'Have we not once already rescued the one true Cup of Christ from the infidel, Mr Moone?' Hal asked. 'Our cargo is a means to an end, nothing more.'

He had not liked bringing the *Delft*'s strange cargo aboard the *Golden Bough* and truth be told he'd been uncomfortable ever since, knowing it was down there in his hold. But the last thing he needed was a crew fearing divine judgement. Sailors were superstitious enough as it was without them believing they had invited their own doom by seeking to profit from the sale of false relics. Hal switched his full attention to the storm swooping towards them.

'Well, Mr Moone, have you no work to do?' Hal asked, and the man begged his pardon and went to make sure the longboats were secure.

There was no time for the crew to go below and put on their tar-daubed canvas jackets. Not that any sailor worth his salt would be thinking about his own comfort now, for they all knew that a squall moving as fast as this one could be a ship-killer. The mass of cloud roiled threateningly, spreading across the heavens, tumbling towards them like an avalanche.

'Hurry it up, Mr Tyler, if you please.' Hal felt the nerves in his stomach tightening. 'No dawdling now. We don't have long.'

Hal turned away and looked back at the sky. 'I'm ready for you,' he challenged it.

Then his eyes switched to the top of the mainmast, and he yelled, 'Get down, Awdy!' The lad was still clinging to the crow's nest. 'Damn the bone-headed fool!' Being up there in a battle was the safest place to be. In a storm such as this it was suicide.

'The storm will take him,' Aboli said, peering up. The wind was on Hal's face now as Ned Tyler brought the bows round to face into the teeth of the storm.

'Brace yourselves!' Hal bellowed, standing tall and defiant, gripping the windward rail as the storm enveloped the *Golden Bough*, lashing her with freezing, skin-flaying rain, and laying her over so that the sea poured over the lee rail, sweeping men off their feet and rolling waist deep across the deck. Men clung to the shrouds as though to life itself.

'Aboli! Help Ned!' Hal shouted. Obediently Aboli struggled over to the helm to lend his strength to the whipstaff. Just then the *Bough*'s buoyancy took over, rolling and rocking her right over in the opposite direction. Men slid back across the deck, crashing into the lee rail unless they had managed to grab a handhold. Hal was plunged underwater for a terrifying, lung-bursting moment. Then the lead-weighted keel levered the ship upright again, and he heard a keening cry even above the wind's roar. The boy Awdy had been flung from the crow's nest like a pebble from a slingshot. He hit the surface of the sea and in the same instant was gone as if he had never existed, swallowed by the raging ocean.

As yet Hal had heard no screams or wild shouts from between decks, which told him that the great culverins were still lashed down securely and the *Bough*'s timbers were holding. But then Hal caught the rhythmic creak of the pumps, as the teams below worked to expel the sea that was flooding the bilges.

Now came the waves, great walls of water driving up from the north, and when they struck Hal knew that no matter how thorough his preparations had been he would be lucky not to lose a mast or have the spars snapped like kindling.

'Father, be with us now,' he yelled, blinking salt water from his eyes, and calling upon his own father as much as the Lord

258

God in heaven. The next wave coming for them seemed as tall as the mainmast, its crest rolling over itself along its length, breaking into cascading white foam. The Amadoda, none of whom had ever experienced anything remotely like this, were beside themselves with terror, shrieking and chanting invocations to their forest gods.

'She can take it!' Hal shouted reassurances to his crew. 'She's seen worse than this in her life. She can see this bastard off!' But the world turned darker still and that wall of water bore down on them. He braced for the impact. The wave crashed down upon them.

In the darkness and the turbulence of wild waters, he thought he heard a familiar and beloved voice calling to him. 'Hold hard, my darling. We need you. Both me and our baby need you. Please don't leave us now. Please don't leave us ever.'

He called back to her, 'I shall survive. I will survive. Wait for me, Judith, my love! Wait for me!'

For another twelve hours the tempest raged over them. When at last it abated it left the *Golden Bough* battered but still afloat. They had lost only Sam Awdy, and the men were light-headed and grateful to God and Hal to have survived.

Only Hal was despondent. The storm had driven his two-boat flotilla far to the south, away from Zanzibar, and every mile carried him further away from Judith.

'The wind has abated, Gundwane.' Aboli tried to cheer him. 'We can make our way back north again and we will surely reach Zanzibar before . . .' Aboli was about to say 'Judith is sold' but managed to stop himself in time. 'Before the day of the market,' he concluded.

'That we will be near Zanzibar I have no doubt,' Hal replied. 'But in Zanzibar? Jahan and all his men will be expecting us. Every harbour and customs official, every market trader, every porter

. . . the whole population will have been told to watch for me – or for anyone suspicious who might want to rescue Judith Nazet.'

'But you don't want to rescue Judith Nazet,' Tromp pointed out, as if that were a statement of the obvious, rather than the absurd.

'What do you mean I don't want to rescue her? Of course I bloody well want to rescue her!' Hal snapped.

'No, sir, you do not. You want to buy her. That way you can take her away without anyone getting hurt. She will be your property . . . although,' he added with a characteristic smirk, 'if you don't mind me saying, that woman will never be anyone's property.'

'Buy her . . . ?' Hal mused. 'Yes . . . yes . . . I can see what you're getting at. That's a good idea, Mr Tromp. But my original objection remains. We will be wanted men – certainly Aboli and I will be. How can we possibly bid for Judith if the moment either one of us opens our mouth we will be seized and most likely taken into slavery ourselves?'

'What if it is not you who bids? What if it is one who is known in Zanzibar, whose presence will not cause any comment?'

Hal looked at Tromp appraisingly. 'You sound as though you know who such a man might be.'

'Yes. I know a man and we are not very far – two days' sail at most – from where I expect him to be. But Captain, I must warn you that if you think me a rogue, this man is far worse. He is a pirate. He would sell his own mother in that very same slave market if he thought he would profit from the trade, and if you should ever cross him he would cut your throat without a second thought.'

Silence fell as Hal considered Tromp's warning. 'Let me ask you this, then,' he spoke at last. 'This man of yours, if we make a deal and I keep my side of the bargain, will he keep his?'

'If you are a man of your word then, yes, he will certainly be the same. But you should rather stick your head into a shark's jaws than give him any reason to think you have betrayed him.'

'Then in that case, Mr Tromp, I will be sure to keep my word and, if you would be so good, pray tell me where I can find him.'

C aptain Jebediah Rivers, master of the sixteen-gun brigantine the *Achilles*, leaned against the rough-skinned trunk of the palm, enjoying the shade provided by its fronds as they rattled and rustled in the warm breeze. The ocean was blinding to look at, glittering and dazzling under the fierce African sun, and the surf rolled in almost reaching the bare feet of the men who had gathered on the beach, many still rum-soaked from the night before.

But the shouting was beginning to irritate Jeb Rivers. John McCawley was stirring up trouble like a whore in a church meeting. Not that there was anything godly about Ilha Metundo, Rivers thought to himself with a sour grin. Still, the man had high aspirations. He wanted to be Captain John McCawley. Rivers had known it for some time but now McCawley was showing his hand.

'When was the last time we took a decent prize, hey?'

McCawley hectored Jeb. 'I never signed up to this crew so as I could break my back lugging timber and stone like a god-damned slave!' This got a few *ayes* from the men at his back, some of them already with hands on their sword hilts and pistol stocks. This encouraged John McCawley. 'We went on the account 'cause we were promised liberty, equality, and brother-hood. I dare any man here to tell me where these three things are right now. I for one don't have any liberty, equality nor no bloody brotherhood either.'

He did not look directly at Rivers then but neither did he need to, for every man present appreciated precisely where that challenge was aimed. 'We all know how this works. No prey, no pay. Well we ain't going to get our hands on no prize stuck here like bleeding landlubbers.' He pointed behind him at the shimmering blue ocean. 'We should be out there hunting. Instead we toil like common labourers.'

'You mean drink yourselves witless and drown in darling whores, Mr McCawley,' Quartermaster George Dowling corrected him, then stopped up his right nostril with his thumb and blew a shining ribbon of snot out of the left one into the sand at his feet. Dowling was a fierce fighter and powerful as a bull buffalo. However, McCawley was himself a savage in a brawl and his blood was up now.

'Why am I not surprised, George Dowling? I would have wagered my last brass farthing – though the devil knows I ain't even got that – on you taking his side in this,' McCawley spat at the quartermaster. 'You're meant to be representing us, *Mister* bloody Dowling. Not him!'

Dowling, who always led the attack when boarding a ship, swept the cap off his head and used it to fan his bald pate as though his only concern was trying to stay cool. 'If there's a vote, I'll stand by it, whichever way it goes,' he shrugged.

McCawley nodded, relieved to hear that, for as quartermaster Dowling acted as trustee for the whole crew, serving as a sort of civil magistrate aboard ship, so that having him onside, or at least not against the idea of a vote, was a bolster to McCawley's cause.

The whole of Rivers's crew had turned out by the looks of it: one hundred and five men, plus another sixty that comprised the crews of the three captured dhows that, along with the *Achilles*, made up the small predatory fleet. Those vessels lay at anchor in the lee of a headland on Ilha Metundo, hidden from the sight of passing shipping out in the open sea. The island swept south-west where it thinned to a tail of land which was only visible at low tide: this sweep of coralline, ship-disembowelling shallows emerging again after several cable lengths to become Ilha Quifuqui. Together these two islands were slung across the turquoise sea like a hammock, and Captain Rivers doubted there could be a finer base for a man in his line of business.

'Spit it out then, McCawley. Brain's boiling in me skull like stew in a pot,' a white-haired old sea dog by the name of Arthur Crumwell called out. There were murmurs of 'aye' and 'go on, tell us' from the crowd of onlookers.

McCawley grimaced and nodded to assure them all that he was coming to the crux of the matter. Many of the women and children who lived on the island with their menfolk had also gathered to be a part of it all and learn whether McCawley's challenge would see him sleeping in the captain's cabin on the *Achilles*'s tomorrow morning.

'We accept that he who is captain has absolute power when fighting, chasing or being chased,' McCawley said. 'Not a man of us has issue with that. But in all other matters the captain is ruled by the majority wishes of the crew.'

'Aye, we've played our part,' Crumwell nodded. 'None can say as we ain't. We got the holes to prove it, and all!' He lifted his arms to exhibit scars under each, one from a pistol ball, the other probably from a cutlass.

Captain Rivers thumbed tobacco into his pipe and looked out to sea while his underlings prattled on. He pretended to be absorbed by the petrels and gulls which speckled the sky, and the parrots and lovebirds which squawked noisily amongst the mangrove trees like some strange echo of the men on the beach.

'It is us as decides if a prize is worth risking our necks for,' McCawley went on. 'It is us as will be strung up and made to dance the hempen jig if one of the king's admirals brings his frigates here to prise us from our nest.' McCawley turned a glare on his captain now, his scarred face twisted with defiance. 'It is us as decides who our captain will be.' He drew a long deep breath, and then spat it out as viciously as a poisonous cobra. 'I call a vote, and put myself forward as the next captain of this crew.'

'Good!' Rivers nodded as he knocked the tobacco ash from his pipe against the stem of the palm tree. 'You took long enough to come to the point.' Then he pointed the stem of his pipe at McCawley. 'So you want my ship?' These were the first words he had uttered since he had come from his hut beyond the tree line to hear the men's grievances.

'The *Achilles* be *our* ship,' McCawley protested, although without conviction. His eyes grew shifty now, losing their grip on Rivers's own.

'The *Achilles* is mine,' Rivers contradicted him with enough steel in his rebuttal to force even the most ardent of McCawley's supporters to lower their eyes. For they all knew Black Jeb Rivers had earned that nickname by his proficiency with gun and sword during the Civil War. Some said that he'd killed more

265

men than the pox and some even claimed that he'd come back from the dead, on the night when a thousand newly made corpses littered the field at Edgehill.

However, McCawley had gone too far to drop his anchor and halt what he had started. He knew it, too, judging by the incessant twitching of his right eye, and his right hand that was flexing, opening and closing as though preparing to grip the cutlass hilt in his belt. Rivers almost admired the man. No one else had ever dared challenge him to become leader of the crew. And yet with McCawley as their captain they would all be drowned, shot or hung before the year was out.

'We'll vote right here,' McCawley said, 'and Quartermaster Dowling will see that it is done fair and honest.'

Dowling nodded and Rivers saw McCawley's major accomplices were murmuring to the men around them, warning them against voting the wrong way.

'Your time is over, old man,' McCawley told Rivers.

The man was half right. Rivers would give him that. At forty-six he was not a young man. His thinning hair, tied back in a long pigtail beneath his broad-brimmed hat, was silver now and his bones complained in the mornings when he climbed out of his bunk. But was his time over? No, McCawley was wrong about that.

Rivers touched his hat's rim, which was the pre-arranged signal, and the loyalists in his crew went to work. Bendall tried to haul his cutlass from his belt but the dagger in his heart robbed him of strength and he fell to his knees in the sand. It was butchery, and when Rivers picked out Laney amongst the slaughtered he saw the man standing there staring right at him, the grim red smile cut across his throat spilling blood down his naked torso.

Then Rivers was moving and the men cleared a path for him,

scuttling away from John McCawley too, the way woodlice flee when someone puts fire to the log in which they were hiding. McCawley saw him coming, and yet to his credit he drew his pistol, and cocked the hammer.

'Damn you to hell and back!' he yelled and he fired. Rivers felt the ball shred the air by his left ear; but so many had tried to kill him and much good it had done them. And now McCawley hurled his pistol into the sand and lifted his cutlass even as Rivers pulled his own blade from its scabbard. It was a broad-bladed, basket-hilted sword. Not an entirely practical weapon when boarding enemy ships; however, ashore it was a limb-lopping man-killer.

McCawley aimed a blow at Rivers's head. Rivers blocked his blade with a dead hit. Then he slammed the basket hilt of his own sword into McCawley's face. The man staggered backwards but Rivers followed up in the instant and led with the point. McCawley froze as the blade went full length into his armpit. Then slowly his fingers opened and the cutlass fell into the sand at his feet. Rivers leaned close to him and locked his free arm around McCawley's neck like a lover. Then he worked the blade back and forth, enlarging the wound, splitting his heart so that the blood pumped out in a thick crimson stream.

When McCawley's legs buckled under him, he plucked out the long blade and stepped back.

'Anyone else?' Rivers asked in a conversational tone.

His own supporters closed up around him. However, he knew which men McCawley had bought off, the ones who had been busy in the last week coercing others with threats and bribes, and those men were nothing more than meat for the crabs now.

'Captain!' one of his own men called, and for a heartbeat Rivers thought that perhaps the day's killing wasn't over after all.

'Captain! Ships!' the man called again, pointing out to sea.

Rivers pushed his way through the crowd and shaded his eyes to get a better look at the approaching sails.

'That leading frigate is a beauty!' Dowling spoke in awe. 'Fast, light and powerful. Proud as can be. And that's a pretty little caravel following in her wake.'

The frigate was not moving as fast as she could have been, for she only had half her canvas spread to the wind. Evidently her captain had enough sense to be cautious, being this close to the island. He would be taking his soundings and watching his speed, his deep-keeled vessel being almost amongst the shoals and reefs. But *why* was he this close to the island? Rivers asked himself; most passing ships gave it a wide berth, sticking to the deeper parts of the channel or even holding not less than a half league's distance from the mainland.

'Be this yet another ambitious fellow come to snuff out the Pirate Rivers and his cutthroat crew?' Dowling pondered his own question, as he shot his captain a wry look.

'Catch her in our net and we shall be rich as kings.' Someone else voiced his opinion, and Rivers could almost feel the hackles rise all around him as his men steeled themselves to the hunt like the predators they were.

'She has twice our guns,' Dowling said. 'Even with the dhows she'll be a tough nut to crack.' And yet the quartermaster's eyes glinted hungrily at the sight of her. 'We'll lose men. Boats too, like as not.'

Rivers nodded because this was all true. But his crew wanted a prize and so he would give them one. 'They will fly past and need never know that we are here.' He gave a false opinion to stir them up. 'Or . . .'

He left the alternative unstated. He knew that the frigate's captain would soon spot Ilha Quifuqui due south of him and turn his bows west in order to skirt that island, which would give Rivers time to set his trap. 'We'll send the dhows through the channel to cut her off south of Quifuqui. Meantime, we'll give her gunners something to think about. While she flirts with the *Achilles*, the dhow crews will creep up and board her, bow and stern.'

Dowling nodded. It had worked before and, God willing, it would work again today.

Rivers was about to give the order for the crews to get to their stations, when something else gave him pause. 'She's changing course, Mr Dowling,' he said, frowning now not because of the sun's brightness but because something did not feel right. For the frigate was swinging her bows round, not into the west to skirt the southern tip of Ilha Quifuqui, but rather into the east. Towards them.

'Bugger me but she's seen us!' Dowling lamented.

Rivers shook his head. 'She knew we were here,' he said, somehow certain of it.

'Maybe King Charlie has sent his bastards to string us up,' a man suggested.

'They'll never have enough bloody rope!' a woman shouted.

But there was no doubt now. That handsome, powerful ship was coming for them and even if she held a cable length offshore to avoid the sandbars she could bring her broadside to bear on the *Achilles* and the dhows at their moorings.

'We'd best flee, Captain,' Dowling said. 'Through the gap and away we go. But we'll have to go now, and not waste a single minute.'

There was an urgency in the quartermaster's voice verging on panic, for although the frigate was still a long way off it would take time to get everyone on the island aboard their respective vessels.

But Rivers did not move from the spot. He gave no orders

269

other than telling a young lad to run up to his hut and fetch his telescope, though he would not likely need the thing by the time the boy returned. There was something about that ship. For all the sandbars that lay between her position and his own base in the lee of the outcrop, the frigate still came on, as though her captain knew the deep channels.

Or maybe it was not her captain, but someone at her bow rail; someone standing near the leadsman and yelling his commands back to the helmsman by the whipstaff.

Then Rivers saw the signal. He, not one of the younger men or the boys with their fresh eyes, but he with his eyes that had been stung with a lifetime of cannon and musket smoke and seen so much horror that it was a wonder they had not given up their sight. There were two ensigns flapping at the frigate's masthead. One of them bore the Dutch Republic's colours of orange, white and blue, the other was the Union flag. Why would her captain fly both ensigns? The English might be at peace with the Dutch, for now at least anyway, but Rivers had never seen a ship flying the colours of both countries at the same time. Nor would he ever expect to see such a thing again.

Then came the thunder; three peals of it from three of the frigate's great brass culverins, their smoke blooms whipped away on the breeze.

'Well I never,' Dowling muttered as he broke into a smile. That had not been a broadside, but a salute. A moment later he was yelling after those of the crew who were already hurrying across the beach towards the *Achilles* and the dhows, telling them it was all well, that there would be no fighting today.

'Good day, mijnheer,' Rivers muttered to himself as he stared across at the frigate. For that three-gun salute was the pre-arranged greeting from Captain Michiel Tromp, with whom he had done a certain amount of business in the past.

'Wonder what that cheese-head's doing here, then,' Dowling asked nobody in particular. 'But he's been busy by the looks of him.'

Rivers shook his head. 'That ain't *his* ship, lad. He's a greedy whoreson and no mean sailor, but even Tromp's not fool enough to go after a prize like that with this damned truce between His Majesty and the cheese-heads.' He frowned, not entirely convinced by his own argument. 'In any event, how would he go about it?' He dipped his head at the frigate whose bows were now pointing almost directly at those gathered on the beach. 'A beauty like that would pound any ship Tromp will ever skipper to kindling.'

'So . . . mayhaps . . .' John Blighton was frowning '. . . mayhaps Tromp's gone turncoat, bringing some English captain down on us an' now they've come to burn our bloody boats and smoke us out like bloody bilge rats.'

'Calm down, boy,' Rivers shook his head. 'Tromp would not do that.' Although he felt his jaw tighten at the thought of such betrayal. 'He knows that if he did I would hang him with his own gut rope.' He turned to his quartermaster. 'Mr Dowling, you know what to do.'

The man nodded and marched off down the beach.

271

Not for the first time, Hal had put his trust in the hands of a man who, until recently, had been his enemy. And once again Tromp proved worthy of that trust, impressing Hal with his seamanship and guiding them through the sandbars and reefs from memory alone. It was high tide and the dangers were for the most part hidden, but Tromp had the memory of a fox returning to its lair. Guiding Mr Tyler at the helm, he took them in whilst Hal and John Lovell kept an eye on the wind in their sails, constantly glancing up to where the Amadoda hung high up at the mast tops ready to take in what little canvas the *Bough* still showed to the wind.

The rest of the crew held their breath, and held their tongues also, their ears straining for the ominous scrape of the *Bough*'s keel on a coral reef. Likewise the soles of their feet on the deck were still as spiders on their silken strings, ready to sense the slightest vibrations that would alert them to the grounding of the hull.

But there was no rumble of thunder from the bowels of the ship. Nor any tremor in the timbers, which had Hal and the officers exchanging relieved looks and nodding to each other in appreciation of that feat of seamanship. These were dangerous waters and it was little wonder that Rivers and his crew had made their base here in the lee of this spur of the island which protruded into the shoals.

'Ten fathoms, Captain!' one of the sailors called, hauling the lead back up from the depths and making ready to swing it again.

'By the mark, seven, Captain!'

'That's as far as we go, Captain,' Tromp said, coming up to Hal and wiping nervous sweat from his forehead. 'It's the long-boats from here on in.'

'Thank you, Mr Tromp,' Hal said, then turned and gave his orders. 'Get those topsails furled, lads!' The Amadoda raced out along the yards, as nimble as squirrels in an oak tree.

'Mr Tyler, drop the anchor. We are as close as we want to be.' Some two cable lengths of clear, turquoise water lay between them and the white strand, and beyond the beach, no higher than seven feet above sea level, stood a screen of lush vegetation. The settlement, such as it was, must be beyond that.

Hal could not but help admire the choice of such a lair. 'A passing ship might see that brigantine,' he admitted, 'but were she not at her anchorage, this Ilha Metundo would appear as deserted as any of the other islands in the Quirimbas.'

As the *Delft*, too, furled her sails, the *Golden Bough* slowed, her momentum lost so that she began to rock on the easy swell. The anchor splashed into the warm water and the chain sang as it spooled out. The ship swung gently round before snubbing up on the end of the line and those of her crew that were not employed went over to the larboard rail to get a good look at those folk gathered on the beach ogling the *Bough*.

'That's their little armada, eh?' Hal said, eyeing the handsome brigantine sitting at anchor beside three large dhows and several smaller craft in the sheltered bay.

'The *Achilles*,' Tromp said. 'She might not look the kind of ship to have sea captains shaking in their boots, but she has taken more than her share of prizes.'

'I'll take your word for it, Mr Tromp,' Hal said. 'I'll wager she's fast.'

'*Ja*, as an arrow,' Tromp agreed. 'And her gunners service those demi-culverins and sakers as well as any crew afloat.'

The *Achilles*'s guns were not the eight-foot-long ship-killers of the *Golden Bough* but neither did they need to be. More often than not they would be loaded with grapeshot rather than round shot. 'It's in the boarding that Captain Rivers earns his gold,' Tromp said. 'His men are devils, Captain Courtney. *Ja*, most crews would sooner jump overboard than fight them.'

Hal considered the pirate captain whom they had come to meet. He knew the name Rivers. Other captains, friends of his father, had mentioned the man. He was a renegade, a Civil War survivor who had fled England and now stalked the Indian Ocean from the Cape of Good Hope to the East African shore north of Madagascar, preying upon merchantmen and slavers as the monsoon winds allowed, regardless of the flags under which they sailed.

'He's a killer, Sir Henry,' Tromp warned him.

'So I have heard,' Hal nodded thoughtfully. He was now more dubious than ever about the wisdom of dealing with a cutthroat, an enemy of the English crown no less.

'But I have an understanding with the man,' Tromp assured him.

'Aye, you're pirates, both,' Hal said, giving him a flinty eye.

Tromp shrugged it off like water off an oiled sea coat. 'That thing that two men have in common often becomes the grease that helps turn the wheels of trade.' Then, seeing Hal's discomfort, Tromp smiled. 'Nevertheless, I can see that to you, an honourable English baronet, the idea of dealing with such a man is, what can I say? Distasteful.'

Hal sighed, watching the pirates thronging the beach. He was half tempted to yell at Ned Tyler to weigh anchor, spread the canvas to the wind and take the *Bough* back out into the good, deep, honest water.

'I cannot help but wonder what my father would think of it,' he agreed.

'Leave this business to me, Captain.' Tromp was trying not to smile. 'I will deal with Captain Rivers and you will keep your hands clean of the whole thing.'

Hal shot him a sceptical look and Tromp raised a placating hand.

'Nearly clean, anyway,' the Dutchman corrected.

Hal looked back to the beach. *We are here now*, he thought, *so let's get on with it.* But he would do it his way.

'Mr Lovell, prepare the pinnaces!' he called. Tromp could place his faith in this Pirate Rivers, but Hal would not trust him one bit. He would not row ashore, into this nest of pirates, in a damned longboat. No, he would go in a pinnace, upon whose gunnels were mounted swivel-guns and in whose thwarts men armed with muskets and lit matches stood ready.

'Is that him, Mr Tromp?' Hal asked, though he knew he needn't have wasted his breath. There was no doubt in Hal's mind that the tall man with the long greying hair tied back was Rivers. He wore canvas petticoats and a cotton shirt, like almost every other man there, but it was his face and bearing, even from that distance, that betrayed him.

'*Ja*, that is him.'

'He will not be pleased with you for bringing a ship like this into his lair. Not only have you shown me the way through the reefs, but at this range I could pummel his *Achilles* to splinters should I so choose.'

'He might not be pleased with me,' Tromp admitted, 'but a vial of the Virgin's tears will make up for it.' His eyes sparkled. 'Such a treasure will sell for a hundred pounds, or gold and silver rupees enough to fill one of your boots.'

Hal gave a sceptical grunt then looked towards his coxswain. 'Master Daniel, I want forty good men and muskets. And bring up the barrels we took from the *Delft*. Every one, if you please, for I will be glad to see the back of them.'

'Captain!' Big Daniel affirmed, then set about choosing the shore party and ordering the Amadoda down to the hold to fetch the reputed relics.

'Mr Tyler, have the gun crews stand by and keep my telescope to hand. At the first sign of trouble I want you to sink that brigantine and open the gates of hell for those pirates.'

Ned Tyler gave a gap-toothed grin. 'If any of them rogues and rascals so much as looks at you funny, just fire your pistol and the next thing you'll see is bits of that ship pouring from the sky like bloody rain, Captain.'

'Very good,' Hal acknowledged, and with that he turned and strode across the deck past the busy men to his cabin in order to dress in clothes befitting a baronet, a captain of a frigate as fine as the *Golden Bough*, and a man loyal to the crown of England. And if, by God, this Pirate Rivers played them false then he would pay for it with his life.

* * *

'So, Tromp, why come ye here, then, eh?' Rivers gestured at a lad who hurried over with his master's broad-brimmed hat on which lay a white-feathered plume. 'And in such a fine-looking ship, by God.' He put the broad hat on so that he no longer had to squint against the sun and its reflection off the sea behind Hal and his party.

Most of the *Bough*'s men stood with the waves lapping their ankles, but four remained on the half-beached pinnaces, manning swivel-guns filled with grapeshot. Aboli stood at Hal's right shoulder gripping a wicked-looking boarding axe and it was not lost on his captain that the African would look very much at home amongst these rogues and renegades of every colour and creed.

'She'll be for me, is she, Captain?' Rivers asked.

'Ha!' Tromp laughed. 'Even were she mine I would never part with her.' As Hal held back, biding his time, the Dutchman strode forward to shake hands with the pirate. 'And captain no more,' he added without any discernible scrap of embarrassment. 'I am now second mate of the *Golden Bough*.' He turned to Hal. 'May I introduce our captain, Sir Henry Courtney?'

Rivers turned his blue eyes on Hal, measuring his worth before offering his hand. Hal was reluctant to shake it, for fear that he would dishonour himself and his blood by doing so. He felt Tromp beside him tense, heard his men behind him blowing on their slow match to keep the coals red hot in case the whole thing should go sour.

'Gundwane,' Aboli murmured under his breath.

Hal stepped forward and took the pirate captain's hand. 'You are infamous, Captain Rivers,' he said.

The pirate was completely undisturbed by the slight. 'In my business a bad reputation is worth its weight in ivory, gold, slaves, you name it. A merchantman that does not recognize

277

my ship or my ensign might foolishly decide to make a fight of it.'

He glanced at Tromp. 'It is rare but it happens. A captain suddenly values his honour above the lives of his men. That is usually the last mistake he ever makes.' He frowned. 'But I have heard your name too, Captain. You must be Franky Courtney's pup. Why's he not captaining that magnificent ship of yours? Got one even bigger, has he?'

'My father was killed,' Hal said. 'The Dutch settlers at Good Hope falsely accused him of piracy then tortured and murdered him.'

Rivers pointed the stem of his pipe at Tromp. 'The Dutch killed your father and yet here you are in league with one of them?'

'Tromp was never involved in my father's death.'

'Too busy causing mischief elsewhere, I dare say. Isn't that right, Mijnheer Tromp?'

The Dutchman shrugged and smiled. 'Ach, you know me too well, Rivers.'

'That I do . . . so why don't you tell me what brings you here, before I get to worrying that you might be up to mischief now and take those ships of yours for myself?'

'Do not even think of attempting so rash a manoeuvre, Rivers. My ships' guns are all loaded, and their crews are standing by them with lit matches in their hands.'

'You are young, Captain Courtney,' Rivers said, without the slightest sign of concern. 'For a boy like you to have a ship like that, well, it's very impressive. And now I come to think of it, I've heard the Arabs moaning about the havoc you wreaked on them in the Red Sea during the Ethiopian War. What was it they named you? El Tazar, meaning Barracuda, wasn't it?'

'I fail to see what that has to do with our current situation.'

'Nothing at all. Just that even a fish like the barracuda, with all those sharp teeth in its mouth, gets caught in a net from time to time. Trapped you might say. Just as you are now?'

'What do you mean?' Hal exclaimed, as the boom of one of the *Bough*'s culverins carried across the water.

Hal turned with a start to look at his ship and the smoke plume drifting off from a gun port amidship. Ned Tyler had fired a warning shot and now the reason for it was obvious. A small fleet of dugouts had come round the headland that sheltered the bay and now they were coming up on the *Golden Bough*'s larboard, their crews paddling furiously. Hal counted four canoes, each carrying five or six men, as well as one of the large, heavy, flat-bottomed canoes that the Spanish called a *piragua* crowded with perhaps twenty-five more sailors.

'They are coming in under our guns,' Aboli murmured, 'so Mr Tyler cannot fire on them.'

Hal cursed. Those canoes had come from nowhere and the men in them were armed with muskets whose long barrels were all trained up at the rail of the *Bough*, ready to pour a deadly fire upon her crew. He turned back round to see that Rivers had stuck a massive, basket-hilted sword in the sand so that it stood upright in front of him still quivering slightly. What the pirate said next struck Hal like a kick in the stomach.

'My quartermaster, Mr Dowling, and his men carry grenades, Sir Henry, and will happily lob them into your ship.'

Either cast-iron balls or glass bottles filled with black powder and lit by a fuse, these exploding bombs would shock, blind and burn the *Bough*'s crew, and Hal shared a look of alarm with Aboli.

'And when your men are running about the deck like hens with a fox in the coop, my lads will disable your rudder.'

At this many of Rivers's men whooped for joy, exulting in

the prospect of winning themselves such a prize without most of them even having put to sea.

Hal was damned if he'd let Rivers threaten him like that without reply.

'You forget the guns on Mister Tromp's former command, the *Delft*,' he said. 'Not to mention the murderers on my two pinnaces that are trained directly upon you, Captain Rivers. So let us agree that we can both do one another a great deal of harm. And now that we have done that, perhaps you would like to know why I am here.'

Rivers looked at Hal for a second as the silence stretched out across the bay. Then he laughed. 'By God, you must be Franky's boy. He was a cold-blooded rascal just like you. And don't look at me all superior-like, Master Courtney. You may call yourself "Sir" and I'm sure your pa carried fancy letters signed by King Charlie himself, telling him he could blast away at any Dutchman or Portugoose that took his fancy. But the truth is, he took ships for the money and the treasure and the hell of it. He was a pirate, same as me.'

'My father was a man of honour, sir, a Nautonnier Knight of the Temple of the Order of—'

'Blah-blah-blah!' Rivers cut him short. 'Your father was a damn fine sailor and an even better taker of other men's ships. And now I look at her, I'll wager you took that ship off another man. Deny it, if you can . . .'

'I took it off a man who deserved to lose it.'

'Ha! Don't they all?' Rivers looked at Hal. 'Provocative young pup aren't you, boy? I'll bet you've made many a man twice your age angry enough to want you dead.'

'And yet here I am still alive.'

'Aye, there you are.' Captain Rivers drew on his pipe. 'Now . . . I have had a long and trying day and I would very much

280

like to lie down in my hammock and rest awhile in the shade, as any sensible man should when the sun is as hot as this. So why don't you tell your lads to go back to your ship and I'll order my lads back to the shore? No damage done, no one hurt. And as for you, Franky's boy, does this order that you Courtneys belong to forbid the taking of strong drink?'

'I am a knight, not a Mussulman. So yes, I will take a drink with you,' Hal conceded, trying to force back a smile.

'Very well then, come back here at sundown. Alone. We will talk then. You will tell me what it is that you want . . . for if you did not want something you would surely not be here. And I will tell you whether you are going to get it, or not.'

With that Rivers pulled his sword from the sand, thrust it back into the scabbard at his left hip and, turning his back on Hal, strode up the beach.

Torches had been stuck in the sand and their flames flickered and danced in the warm breeze. Hal's two flintlocks were loaded and primed and his sword was snug in its scabbard. If Captain Rivers had treachery in mind then Hal would go down fighting like the devil himself.

As requested, he had come alone, much to Aboli and his other officers' dismay. But in the short time Hal had known Captain Rivers he had learnt enough to be certain that the pirate would have things his own way or not at all. And so here they were, the two of them sitting at a small table on the beach, with a bottle of Madeira wine and a couple of crystal glasses between them, all once the property of the Portuguese captain whose ship had foundered on the reef to the south of the island. Above them stretched the infinite vault of heaven in all its magnificence. Stars glutted the night sky, blazing like jewels, and Hal wondered if Judith was looking up at those same constellations, or was she trapped in some dark, airless dungeon with no sight of the sky by day or night?

'So Tromp tried to take your ship, eh?' the pirate captain said, filling Hal's glass with rum.

'Tried and failed,' Hal agreed.

Aboli, Tromp and Big Daniel were with the longboat down at the water's edge. The pinnaces were back with the *Bough* and Hal was confident that should Rivers's canoes appear again, Mr Tyler could blast them out of the water before they had a chance to get in under his guns. As for Rivers's men, Hal could see none though he knew they must be out there in the dark.

'However, Tromp has proven himself useful to me since then,' Hal said.

He glanced around. The only signs of life were the small crabs scuttling across the sand and the occasional peal of laughter from folk enjoying themselves somewhere beyond the vegetation behind them.

'As you are aware, sir, my enemies have taken someone from me.' The words were almost too painful to speak. 'Someone dear to my heart. I *will* get her back, Captain, and I will kill those who took her. But I cannot do it by myself.'

Over the next few minutes, Hal told the story of Judith's capture and abduction. He explained that she would be coming up for sale at the next big slave market day in Zanzibar and that the only sure way to get her back was to buy her, but that he could not be the buyer.

Rivers listened thoughtfully to what he had to say and then asked, 'How can you be so certain that she will be on the block when you say?'

'My men and I extracted the information from Consul Grey.'

'The same man who betrayed you in the first place?'

'The very one.'

'Why should you believe him now, then? Has it not occurred to you that this talk of an auction may simply be a lure to draw you into a trap?'

'Of course, but then I ask myself: what difference does it make? I may only have a very small chance of recovering the woman I love if I attend the market, but I have no chance at all if I do not.'

'And where do I come into this?'

'I want you to bid for her on my behalf. Clearly I cannot be seen to be bidding and nor can anyone known to associate with me. But there is no connection between you and me – or none that anyone outside this island knows. I gather you are known to the traders at the market.'

'I am.'

'And that Zanzibar is one place at least where you are not wanted for your crimes.'

'I have been careful not to offend its rulers, and as long as that remains the case, I am free to go there. As you have discovered, Courtney, Zanzibar is a law unto itself. The world's laws do not apply there. Think of it as a grand bazaar. You can buy anything there and almost anyone. Well, you know that already. You're going to buy your own woman.'

'Or you are, for me.'

'And what possible reason could I have for doing that, knowing that it will do me no good to be linked with you? I don't mind risking my skin, Courtney. I wouldn't be here if I did. But I like to do it on favourable terms.'

Hal looked at Rivers, who was sitting back wreathed in his own pipe smoke. He knew there was nothing to be gained by pleading or appearing too desperate. He had to remain calm, no matter how savagely every second he was away from Judith tore at his heart.

'Has Tromp ever spoken to you about the trade in religious relics?' he asked.

Rivers nodded. 'At great length, yes. He says the Papists'll pay a fortune for any old piece of tat that they can claim belonged to Jesus or the Virgin. And for once I'm inclined to believe him. I've seen all the pilgrims, lining up to see the relics of St James at Compostela. Could just be old chicken bones for all they know. There's money to be made out of fools like that. Pity Tromp never made it. I might have taken a share.'

'You still can,' Hal said. 'When Tromp attempted the capture of my *Golden Bough*, he and his men were starving. You see, he couldn't afford to victual his ship properly before he left Batavia, the reason being that he had squandered – or, as he would see it, invested – all his resources on the manufacture of religious relics. So when I took the *Delft* I found barrels in her hold stuffed full of relics. There were vials of the Virgin's tears, fragments of the True Cross, even a number of foreskins said to have been taken from Our Saviour at the time of his circumcision. I could not bring myself to trade such fraudulent geegaws, but I don't doubt their value to one who would. And so I am prepared to let you have the entire cargo if you will bid for me in Zanzibar.'

'Are you suggesting I lack morals?'

'With respect, Captain Rivers, your entire existence suggests that.'

'With respect, Captain Courtney, you are talking through your arse. You are right that I would happily tout these relics to the Jesuits, to pilgrims, to the damn Pope himself if he'd buy them, for I regard the Catholic faith as the work of the Antichrist and would do it down in any way I could. I fought for Parliament in the War and I did so because I hated the Stuarts not just as tyrants but as Papists, too. So I will have those relics of yours

284

and I will sell them and reap my rewards with a clear conscience. But the relics are not enough.'

'Tromp assures me that they will be worth many hundreds, even thousands of pounds.'

'I don't doubt it. But my neck is worth still more.'

'So what will it take to make your neck feel that it is getting its due reward?'

Rivers sucked on his pipe as he contemplated the question. He leaned back and looked up at the sky as he breathed a stream of tobacco smoke into the night air. Then he turned back to Hal and said, 'I'll take those relics. And I'll take the ship they came on, too.'

'But the *Delft* is worth five hundred guineas!'

'The *Delft* is stolen, is she not? You as good as told me so yourself. Tromp spent all his money on relics. If he could not even afford food, he was certainly not in any position to buy that fine caravel.'

'How Tromp came by the boat is his business, not mine.'

'Until you come to sell it. For were anyone to discover that you were selling a vessel belonging to the Dutch Navy, seized while England and Holland were at peace, well, you'd be hanged for piracy, would you not?'

Rivers's point was well taken, but still Hal balked at giving in to all his demands. But then, as if reading his mind, Rivers said, 'Calm down, lad. I can see you don't like it, a knight like you having to bargain with an old pirate like me. But consider this: you do not want the relics and you have no use for the ship. But you want your woman very much indeed. So if you trade two things you don't want for one that you do, is that really such bad business?'

'Perhaps not,' Hal conceded.

'In any case, I am only considering your proposition at all

285

because I lost someone once.' Rivers emptied the last of the Madeira into his glass and drank the wine down, lost in his own thoughts. 'What is her name, this woman of yours?' he finally asked.

'Judith.' The sound of her name was torture to Hal's own ears, the taste of it agony to his very soul.

'Good woman, is she?'

'The finest that ever lived.'

'Best thing a man can have, a good woman to love him,' Rivers said.

By God, thought Hal, the leathery old bastard has a heart after all. But that rare moment of sentiment was soon gone because the next thing Rivers said was, 'How did you plan on paying for her? She'll cost a pretty penny, if she's as fine as you say.'

'You know the answer already.'

'How so?'

'You recounted my success in the Ethiopian War. I captured many an Arab dhow, with all manner of cargo aboard. As you said, I am Sir Francis Courtney's son and heir. And while we may argue whether he was a criminal pirate or an honourable privateer, there is no dispute as to his success in his ventures.'

'Then that is all I need to know. So my answer is yes, Captain Courtney. I will come with you to Zanzibar. And when I get there I'll buy your woman for you.'

The slave market's sale of its most prized and highly priced specimens was the talk of Zanzibar, for, as the city's people proudly told themselves, there was nowhere else in all Africa – possibly in the world – where so much human flesh of such high quality was auctioned. On the afternoon before the great event, Judith was taken down to the barracoon, where slaves were penned in a roofed enclosure like cattle before being put on sale. She had become oddly accustomed to the harem costumes that she had been given to wear while a prisoner of Prince Jahan, but now she was stripped of all clothes, bar a tiny apron that flapped in front of her pudendum, offering a bare pretence of modesty. Her hands were tied behind her back, a halter attached to a rope was slipped over her head and she was led into a ring for examination by a crowd of traders who were inspecting the stock in advance of the sale.

Judith was forced to stand, stock-still and mute, as rough hands felt her breasts, like women testing vegetables on the market place. She was bent double with her legs wide apart and her bottom pointing towards the traders so that they could see her most private parts. The men even prised her lips apart and examined her teeth as they would a horse's.

All the while she remembered a conversation she and Hal had had with Aboli one night on the *Bough*. The talk had turned to the two men's experiences as prisoners and effective slaves of the Dutch in the Cape Colony. 'You know your problem, Gundwane? You always wanted to fight. But the first thing a slave should learn is that there is nothing to be gained by fighting back. The masters will whip you at best. At worst they will put you in a cage, or a box, or a hole in the ground and leave you in the baking sun, or the monsoon rain until you either die or learn your lesson. So do not give them that pleasure. Say nothing. Endure their cruelty, their insults, their treatment of human beings as less than animals. Endure so that you live and your children live. And pray that one day you will be free.'

So Judith endured and kept silent. She looked out for Hal in the crowd, not knowing whether she really wanted him to be there, just to know that he was coming for her, or whether it would simply be too much to take, for both of them, to see her degraded in this way. But it was hard, so bitter hard, and what made it worse was that though the men who examined her talked freely about what they were seeing, as if she were just another dumb animal, she understood too many of them all too well.

As a girl, Judith had accompanied her father on diplomatic missions not just to Venice, but to many of the other great courts of Europe also. Being young, with a natural gift for languages, she had picked up smatterings or in some cases a considerable degree of fluency in several European tongues as well as the Amharic and Arabic that were part of her birthright. Now, though, her comprehension was a curse, for she knew when a Dutchman told his friend, 'Did you know that this cow is carrying a calf? *Ja*, and a white man's brat, too.'

One Portuguese merchant asked another, 'Why is the sultan selling a black jewel like that? If she were mine I'd keep her tied to my bed!'

'I heard a rumour that it's some kind of revenge,' came the reply. 'You can tell she's high-born, look at her pretty hands, not a callus on them anywhere. The word is, her identity's going to be revealed when she's put on the block. They say her name alone will put ten thousand silver rupees on the price.'

'Who is she then, the Queen of Sheba?'

'I don't care what her name is, I'd give her one any day of the week.'

And then, on one of the times when she was bent double and utterly exposed, there came an Arab voice saying, 'She has not been cut, look at her lips and her bud still intact. So she still feels pleasure.' And another replying, 'It is shameful and impure when they scream and moan, but women like that are desperate for a man. The more often they are taken, the happier they are.'

'So will you bid for her?'

'Why spend money? A woman like that will give herself to you for nothing!'

She spent a terrified, restless, often tearful night. In the morning she was given a bowl of millet porridge then a bucket of water was thrown over her and a bored, fat, middle-aged African woman slapped fat on her skin to make it shine in a way that suddenly made Judith feel almost grateful for the gentle care the girls had taken to ready her for the prince.

The hours dragged by. Slowly the holding pen where she was being kept, directly behind the sale-block itself, was emptied as one slave after another was led away to be sold. She could hear the Omani auctioneer's voice speaking in Arabic as he described each new piece of merchandise and urged customers to up their bids. Then an African, himself a slave of the auctioneer, came up to her, grabbed the rope that was hanging between her breasts and led her towards the block. Suddenly she realized that the auctioneer was talking about her, saying, 'And now, respected gentlemen, I have a jewel beyond price to offer you, the property of the Sultan Sadiq Khan Jahan himself, whom he captured when she was foolish and proud enough to believe that she could spy in secret on Zanzibar. This woman is General Judith Nazet!'

A gasp went up from the crowd of bidders and spectators, followed by an excited buzz of chatter so that the auctioneer had to shout to make himself heard as he went on, 'She is the pride of the infidel people of Ethiopia, the scourge of the faithful, the killer of those who love God . . . but our great prince has humbled her and now, in his infinite generosity, he offers her to any man who will have her.'

A huge cheer broke out and the auctioneer had to wait for it to subside before he went on. 'But there is more. This woman is not just a vengeful she-demon. She is a whore, a slut who has opened her legs to a man and taken his seed inside her. Now she is bearing a child, who is sold with her . . . the child of the English sea captain Henry Courtney, whom men called El Tazar, for, like a barracuda, he killed without mercy as he struck at the ships of the faithful. Gentlemen, the next item in the auction is General Judith Nazet!'

And thus, to the sound of cheers, catcalls, obscene suggestions being shouted in a myriad tongues, Judith was taken from the pen and led out onto the block to be sold.

Hal wiped the sweat from his forehead and did his best to bring his racing heart under control. There was a covered stand along one side of the market, two rows of benches, raised high enough for the wealthiest buyers to watch the proceedings in some degree of comfort. Halfway along that stand a special box had been built for the sultan and a few chosen guests to sit, screened from the public view. Hal meanwhile, had hidden himself among the common folk and riff-raff, a crowd of several hundred people, crammed into an unshaded, outdoor enclosure in the full glare of the noonday sun, all shouting, jostling and barging as they did their best to get a better view of the slaves when they came up for sale. Facing the unruly mob, the actual slave block looked like a short flight of four steps, viewed side-on. The slave who was being sold was led up to the top step, to give the buyers the best possible view. The auctioneer stood on the second step, occasionally moving up to the third if he needed to see a bidder at the very back of the crowd. At the bottom were two of the auctioneer's largest, most heavily muscled slaves, trusties who both carried long, heavy clubs with which to beat anyone on the block who was foolish enough to jump off and try to escape.

Hal was about two-thirds of the way back from the front. He had not shaved since he'd left Zanzibar on the night that Judith was taken and had also let his hair hang lank and loose about his face. At the same time he was dressed in the most splendid finery he possessed, the intention being to suggest a man of squalid behaviour and morals who nevertheless had the cash to spend on expensive tailoring. Someone like a slave-trader, in other words.

To his great fury, Aboli had been left behind on Rivers's ship the *Achilles*, along with Big Daniel and enough bloody-minded *Golden Bough* men to prevent the pirate and his crew doing a runner and leaving Hal stranded, should anything go wrong.

'I'm sorry, old friend,' Hal had said, 'but you are too recognizable and our association is too well known. If you are spotted then my presence will immediately be inferred. Mister Tromp will be my companion on this occasion. It will be safer that way.'

Of course, Hal knew, as did Aboli, that it would have been far safer still if he had not gone ashore, but left Rivers to buy Judith and bring her back to his ship. But he could not bear to think of her facing the ordeal of being sold into slavery without the comfort of his presence, nor did he trust Rivers not to pull some kind of trick. He was a thief by profession, after all. It would be foolish not to assume that if he could steal Judith he would.

And then, after one poor wretch after another had been sold, the auctioneer was calling out the last and finest item for sale that day, and naming Judith, describing her in ways that defamed and maligned her, even citing Hal as the father of the child . . . and there she was, atop the block, a rope around her neck and hands tied behind her back so that she had no way of covering herself or protecting her modesty from the leering eyes of the men who saw her as nothing more than an object to be traded and then used.

Hal was filled with a rage more powerful than any he had ever known. His blood was pounding in his temples, his vision seemed to blur as the red mist descended and his breathing became heavy and hoarse. He was close to the berserker, fighting madness that had on very rare occasions come over him in the

292

heat of battle and was just on the verge of charging the stage single-handed, when he felt a strong hand grip his right arm, just above the elbow.

'Don't!' Tromp hissed at him, and then again, 'Don't! I know what you are feeling. I know you want to fight them all. But you must be patient. Let Rivers do what must be done. If you draw attention to yourself now, all will be lost.'

Hal barely heard a word of what Tromp said. But the physical restraint and the sound of his voice were enough to hold him back until the fury had subsided just a little.

So Hal held his body and voice in check. He told himself not to panic when the bidding began and the price raced upwards without so much as a nod at the auctioneer from Rivers, for the pirate had said he would bide his time before making his play. But with his eyes Hal stared straight at Judith and in his mind he screamed out, *I am here, my darling. Don't worry. All will be well. I am here!*

There were street urchins at the slave auction as there were everywhere in Zanzibar: trying to sell filthy pieces of fruit to hungry spectators, or picking those same men's pockets, or simply indulging their curiosity, for only a public beheading rivalled a great slave auction as an attraction for any born-and-bred Zanzibari.

One of the urchins, however, made no attempt to extract any money from anyone, either through commerce or theft. Nor was he engrossed by the sale, though he did cast occasional, sad-eyed looks in the direction of Judith Nazet. Instead he devoted his full attention to one man. For he had his orders and they were clear. 'Whatever he does and wherever he goes, follow him. And do not take your eyes off him until he, or you, or both of you cast off from the harbour and sail away from this island.'

And one look into the eyes of the man who had given him his orders was enough to convince the urchin – even if he had not been so inclined to begin with – to follow his orders to the letter.

G rey had persuaded Prince Jahan that he should be the one who searched for Courtney in the crowd. 'It is true that the Buzzard knows Courtney even better than I,' he said. 'But the sight of that masked monster will be enough to distract the crowd, cause men to talk and perhaps even draw attention to our true purpose. I am known to be a man who is always interested in the finest human flesh. I have traded for many years and no one will be surprised to see me. I certainly know Courtney well enough to recognize him. And even if I do not it does not matter. For I plan to spot our target without even looking into the crowd.'

So now he was seated in the front row of the covered stand, with the captain of the sultan's guard by his side, watching the Nazet woman as the bids for her went higher and higher. Grey was half-tempted to put in an offer himself, for by Allah she was a fine-looking woman and almost enough to tempt a man to abandon the pleasures that young boys could bring. But he was not looking at her as either a buyer or a would-be lover. He had a very specific purpose in mind and for that he had to keep his eyes fixed firmly on her pretty face.

J udith refused to let herself be brought low by men who were little better than animals. She was of noble blood and held a general's rank. She would maintain her dignity and her spirit,

294

no matter how hard these beasts tried to strip them from her. But, oh, how badly she needed to see Hal and know that he had come to be with her and rescue her from this torment. For he would come, she knew that. No matter how great the danger, he would be there. But where?

He will be disguised, she told herself. *So look for those things that cannot be hidden. The deep, sea-green of his eyes; the proud curve of his nose; the way he cannot help but carry himself like a young king. Look for the things you love in your man.*

And then she saw him. Out there in the crowd, two eyes that had caught hers and held them and she knew right away, because she felt it in the very depths of her being that they could only belong to the man she loved. So she looked back, and she smiled, just a very little, because she could not hide the joy she felt in her heart.

A nd that was when Consul Grey smiled too, and followed Judith Nazet's eyes across the crowded enclosure and saw a tall, swarthy, unkempt man dressed in an inappropriately smart coat, the clothes of a nobleman on the body of a savage. Then he saw the man's profile and the look in his eyes as he stared back at Judith and he turned to the captain of the guard and, making every effort to seem as though he were engaged in nothing more than casual conversation, said, 'There is your man. That is Captain Courtney. Now tell your men to go and get him.'

T he Buzzard, standing at the back of the prince's enclosure with the slave who now accompanied him everywhere, hiding in the shadows so that the public should not be alarmed by his presence, had also spotted Hal Courtney in the crowd. But then, he and Hamish Benbury had been well aware of Courtney's whereabouts, and deduced the plan he had in mind within hours of the *Achilles* sailing into Zanzibar on yesterday evening's tide.

Benbury and the Buzzard had been deep in conversation with the proprietor of the Tres Macacos late the previous night when Rivers had walked in and ordered a bottle of rum. The three captains, all of whom knew one another, for they were all cut from the same cloth, got into conversation and as Rivers moved on to a second bottle and then a third, they established that he had come to Zanzibar to buy a slave. And not just any slave, but the sultan's prize fancy.

But Rivers was a pirate rather than a slave-trader, just as a man might be a carpenter rather than a printer. If he was suddenly moving from one occupation to another, there had to be a reason for it and when Benbury sent two of his most trusted men to sit on the dockside, in view of the *Achilles*, and mark who appeared on deck, that reason became apparent.

So now, as the auction reached its climax and Rivers finally entered the bidding, the Buzzard stepped a few paces forward, so that he was briefly visible to anyone watching Prince Jahan's private box, gave a single nod of his masked head and retreated back into the shadows. Then, without saying a word, he slipped through the door at the back of the box and down the steps that led back down to the ground, with his slave following him as surely as his own shadow just a few paces behind. The guards who were posted at the foot of the steps made way to let him pass between them, for they knew that he was the prince's creature and obeyed their master in every way. So they thought nothing of it as the Buzzard turned to his right and walked past the enclosure where the public were standing and into the private area behind the block itself.

Rivers had read the auction perfectly. There was only one other bidder left against him now and the price had reached the dizzying heights of three lakhs of silver, a sum far, far greater than any ever paid for a single slave. Courtney would have to sell his ship, give up all his family's wealth and mortgage his balls to raise the money, but that wasn't Rivers's problem.

He was just about to make what he felt sure would be the winning bid when he felt both his arms being grabbed from either side, and the prick of a knife, cutting through his coat and into the skin at the small of his back. 'Begging your pardon, Captain,' a voice growled in his ears. 'But Captain Benbury sends you his compliments and says that if you walk away, right now, and go back to your ship, all nice and peaceful like, we won't be obliged to kill you.'

'Well, you can tell your damn captain . . .' Rivers began. Then he stopped and thought and considered the fact that the *Delft* was already in his possession and he would much rather be alive to enjoy the added firepower it would bring to his private fleet and so he concluded, 'Tell him I wish him a good day and I'd be obliged if you'd let me pass, for I believe my presence is required aboard ship.'

Grey was watching the auction with one eye, while at the same time casting discreet little glances in Courtney's direction. The captain of the guard had secreted a group of his men dressed in civilian clothes to one side of the enclosure. It said much for their disguises that he was unable to spot them making their way towards Courtney, even though he knew that they were doing so. And if he, being aware of their plans, could not distinguish the men in the crowd, how could their prey possibly do so?

Hal's entire attention was concentrated on the auction block. The tension created by the bidding process was unbearable. As the price rose higher and higher he stopped worrying about whether he could afford it. He would be impoverished, that much was obvious. He might well be in debt for years to come, perhaps even the rest of his life. But if he had Judith and his son – for surely she was bearing him a boy – by his side, that would be riches enough.

He turned to Tromp, just for a brief moment of moral support, but the Dutchman wasn't there. Hal thought nothing of it. The movement of men in the public enclosure was much like water against a shore – a continual pattern of ebbing and flowing and eddying and it was all too easy for two men to become separated in the confusion.

He turned back to look at the auction. It took him a second to register that the bidding had stopped. The auctioneer was calling out to 'the English gentleman' asking him if he wished to raise his bid. *That's Rivers*, Hal thought. *What the hell is he up to?*

And then something hit him in the stomach, driving the breath from his body and causing him to double up in pain. Then he was hit again on the back of the head.

And that was the last Hal Courtney knew of the slave auction.

The men who had shoved their way into the enclosure when the entrance gate had first been opened had known that they faced a goodly wait before proceedings began, followed by a lengthy sale. Many had therefore brought canteens of water, assorted items of food to keep hunger at bay and even the odd tot of rum. One group of half-a-dozen tars, who established a little camp in front of the covered enclosure, had arrived with a regular feast of ship's provisions, freshly bought produce and even two wooden casks containing small beer, or watered-down ale, which was traditionally drunk as a means of making water palatable and less risky to one's health. One of the casks was soon drunk dry. The other, however, rolled under the first row of seats in the pavilion. What with all the people milling around, it would have taken a very sharp eye indeed to see the black line of gunpowder that ran from the open bunghole at the top of the cask just a few feet to where the tars were standing, eating, drinking and even smoking pipes of tobacco as they followed the proceedings on the auction block.

But one of the sailors was not watching the block at all. He had his eye on the prince's enclosure. And when the Buzzard came to the front and nodded his head he puffed on his pipe to get a nice glow, stuck a piece of paper into its bowl and waited until it caught fire, then applied that flame to the line of powder.

The flame ran along the line and into the cask and ignited the pitch-covered rags that had been bundled into it. Then they went up too and seconds later the cry went up from the stands, 'Fire! Help! Fire!'

The sale had not been concluded, but the auctioneer wasn't waiting for the final bid. He grabbed Judith, almost threw her down from the block and then he and his trusties dragged her back into the pen from which she'd been led not so many minutes earlier.

The man in the mask was waiting for them. 'I'm taking her,' he said.

The auctioneer hesitated. His trusties were wide-eyed at the sight of that mask with its evil eyes and jagged teeth. 'But my money,' he protested. 'I was assured that I would be paid a commission, even though there would be no sale.'

'Go to the palace in the morning. You'll get your money. But I'm taking her,' the Buzzard said. Then he grabbed the rope to which Judith was tethered and said, 'I can drag you by this or you can run like a human being, but I'm getting you out of here, come what may.'

Judith could hear the panic coming from the auction enclosure. 'Are you taking me back to the palace?' she asked.

The Buzzard nodded. She followed him through the barracoon, moving further away from the chaos caused by the fire to a gate at the far end of the complex. The prince's carriage was waiting there, the one with the blanked-out windows. 'Get in,' the Buzzard said. 'You'll be safer if no one can see you.'

Judith did as she was told, seeing the sense in his words. Even before the fire, she'd been able to sense the strange tension in the air. There were so many men, so much pent-up lust, and greed and raw male energy. She'd spent enough time around armies to know that those ingredients exploded all too easily into violence.

Dear God, please bring Hal safely out of harm's way, she prayed. And then she consoled herself with a simple thought. *If he is safe, and I am still in the prince's palace then we may not be together, but at least there is still hope.*

Only when she was sitting in the carriage did she stop to wonder why she still had her hands bound behind her back and the rope and halter round her neck. She had never been treated like that when she was the prince's prisoner. So why was the Buzzard leaving her bound and helpless now?

The Buzzard saw Judith into the back of the carriage and pushed his own slave in there too. Then he walked around to the front and held up his arm towards the driver. 'Can you help me up please?' he asked, nodding his beak at the empty space on the seat next to the driver.

The carriage driver reached down to pull the Buzzard up.

The Buzzard took the other man's hand in his and then, without the slightest warning, pulled with all his strength, catching the driver off-guard and off-balance and pulling him right off his seat and down onto the ground.

Even as the driver was falling, the Buzzard had let go of him. Then he pulled out his sword and brought it in a backhanded arc that sliced right across the driver's throat.

As the other man lay on the ground, asphyxiating in a pool of his own blood, the Buzzard pulled himself up onto the seat of the carriage, grabbed the reins in his three-fingered hand and screamed at the horses to go. The animals heard the anger and urgency in his voice and all but bolted, sending the carriage racing away down the street.

Grey had only been a few paces from the spot where the fire started. He was one of the first to sound the alarm and then the first to make good his escape. The captain of the guard's first priority was to organize the prince's safe evacuation. But once he knew that his master was safely aboard a carriage, heading back to the palace, he returned to the auction site to supervise matters there.

Grey found him a few minutes later. Having established, for form's sake, that the prince was unharmed, Grey asked the question that was his real concern. 'Have you got Courtney?' he asked.

The captain shook his head. 'No. My men spotted him standing just where you said. They went to the place. But then the fire broke out. By the time they reached where Courtney had been standing, he had disappeared.'

'So he must have escaped with everyone else who was leaving the enclosure.'

The guards' captain shook his head. 'No. My men have been

looking. They have been watching the crowd . . . while they were still in the enclosure, as they were leaving, in the streets afterwards. They cannot find El Tazar anywhere.'

'Then I will have to find him,' said Consul Grey, and thought, but did not add aloud, *For my future prosperity depends upon it.*

T he carriage rattled to a halt, the door was flung open and the Buzzard was standing there. 'Get out,' he growled.

Judith frowned. The Buzzard was blocking most of her view of the outside world, but what she could see bore no relation to the palace.

'Where am I?' she asked.

The Buzzard did not reply. Instead he just said, 'Get her.'

He stepped aside to reveal two other men, one white, the other African, standing there. They made a move to get into the carriage. Judith scuttled away from them, opened the opposite door and threw herself out . . .

Straight into the arms of another man. He caught her and held her as if she were no more of a burden than a baby. She screamed in alarm, but he simply threw her over one of his shoulders and holding her fast started running across an area of large paving stones, down a wooden pontoon that Judith could see was floating on the water. Then the man was jumping through the air and landing on the small planked area, like a miniature deck at the stern of a longboat. The moment his feet hit the boat the man was shouting, 'Pull, you bastards, pull!'

G rey went back to his house; summoned his servants; gave them each a list of names, belonging to everyone from respectable carpet sellers to downright criminals; told them where the names on their lists were likely to be found and then sent them out across Zanzibar City. Then he too took to the streets, although the men whom he sought were the highest in the city, rather than the dregs whom his servants sought.

The wealthy merchants and Omani aristocrats to whom Grey spoke had little to offer him in his search for Captain Courtney. But when the servants returned to the house, one or two of them had worthwhile information. This led him to some new names and from them to a particular quarter of the city. And then Consul Grey discovered what had happened to Courtney, and what was going to happen to him very shortly. He thought for a moment of intervening himself, but realized that would be a futile and possibly even fatal gesture. In order to achieve the result he required, Grey needed help.

And that being the case, he might as well go to the man who could offer the most help available. And with that thought in mind, Grey set off for Prince Jahan's palace.

Hal came to and opened his eyes. He could see nothing. He tried to talk but could not speak. Then he felt the bandana tied tight around his head and tasted the gag in his mouth. He was sitting on a floor with his back against a wall. His hands were tied and his ankles were bound. He was, in short, entirely helpless.

He could hear, though, and he could smell and those two senses were more than enough to tell him that he was in a place that stank of dogs and their filth and that there was a dog, a large one by the sound of it, growling in the very near vicinity.

Hal felt a shot of raw fear grip his body. If the dog attacked him there would be nothing he could do. He heard shouting somewhere close by and then the more distant sound of barking. That set off the dog and the sound of its raucous growls was followed by the shouts of a man trying to keep it quiet, the crack of a whip and a series of resentful canine yelps.

All was quiet for a moment or two and in the relative silence Hal's thoughts turned from his immediate surroundings to the men who had put him here. Rivers must have betrayed him. What other explanation could there be? And then his final memory before he was knocked out came to him: turning round and finding Tromp had disappeared.

I've been such a bloody fool! Why didn't I see it? Tromp led me to Rivers, of course the two of them were bound to conspire against me!

As the queasy sense of betrayal soured his guts Hal heard the muffled sound of a man's voice on the far side of a wall, or door, accompanied by a rising crescendo of shouts and cheers. Hal could not make out exactly what the man was saying, except that it was evidently some kind of introductory speech. For a moment he thought he might still be at the slave auction: that he was the next on the block. But the sound had a different character to that of the auction: it came from fewer people in a more confined space. Then the clamour suddenly rose again – Hal realized that a door must have opened – the dog started barking and growling again, its frenzy even greater than before and completely unaffected by the more desperate shouts of its owner, or handler, and the repeated cracks of his whip. There was a sudden slamming of wood and the turning of a key and suddenly the dog was gone from the space where Hal was sitting but he could hear the barking and snarling redoubled on the far side of the wall and door and the cheering becoming even louder.

A dogfight! Hal thought. *But what the hell am I doing here?*

Before he could work out the answer to that question, Hal felt arms grabbing him and dragging him upright. He made a

306

pointless attempt to shout out in protest, then threw himself backwards and struck the wall but the men holding him maintained their grasp as he bucked and writhed, using all their strength to subdue him.

Hal ceased his struggle. There was nothing he could do now: better by far to save his strength for whenever he could use it better. Once again he felt fear, the kind that comes from not knowing what lies in store and then imagining the worst. But he would not let these men see his weakness and so he fought to quell the panic before it could consume him. He slowed his breathing. He shut out all distractions, letting his mind focus like an eye peering through a telescope. He thought of the ocean and of his ship. And then he thought of his father, who had been subjected to the most vile and inhumane suffering, yet had somehow borne every pain and degradation while retaining his dignity and his honour, right up to the moment of his death. In that appalling memory lay the example that Hal knew he had to follow now. He would never give in, not while his heart still beat in his chest like a ship's ensign in the wind.

He felt someone grasp his hands and cut his bonds. As his right hand dropped to his side, his left was hauled out to the front, an iron ring was clamped around his wrist, and suddenly his arm was heavy because of the chain to which that ring was attached.

Again the first ripples of fear played against the furthest reaches of Hal's mind like water lapping a sandy beach. 'I am a Courtney,' he said aloud, for himself rather than to the men in that place. There came no reply. The men around him did not understand what he had said, or more likely they did not care.

The noise outside reached a climactic cacophony of human and animal noise and then was released and, after a last round of applause and whistles, settled down to a low hum of masculine conversation. The dogfight was over.

Hal felt a jerk on his chain and he was led forward a few paces, then his head was pushed down, hard, so that he almost bent double – that must be the door the dog went through – and suddenly his sightless world flooded with the roar of the crowd. He caught the scent of fresh blood in the air and gave an involuntary shiver, trying not to imagine the slaughter that had just been played out for the people's amusement. Then he heard something else much closer to him. There was a man struggling nearby, and his muffled roars of protest mingled with the curses of the guards attempting to overpower him.

'Your excellencies, gentlemen!' The thin, high voice of a master of ceremonies speaking in Arabic cut through the low roar of the crowd like the cry from a muezzin over a crowded marketplace. 'Prepare to be amazed! Glut your eyes on a contest such as we have never brought you before. There can be no running. There can be no hiding. There can be only blood!'

Hal heard a voice saying, 'Here, take this,' and a sword's hilt was pressed into the palm of his right hand. He took it and held it, hearing Aboli's voice in his head, talking as he had done when Hal had been his student.

Do not wrap your hand tight around the hilt like a club, Gundwane, for that makes the sword a heavy, dead weapon. Your grip must be easy so that the control comes from your fingers. That way the sword can become a fluid extension of your hand.

He lifted the sword now, pivoting it in his hand, releasing and squeezing the grip into his palm so that the blade lifted and fell as he tested its weight. It was a cutlass; simple, crude and brutal. It was quite heavy too, and so he decided on a three-quarter grip, his thumb cradling the ridged handle rather than lining along the back edge as it would were he holding a lighter blade.

Good, Gundwane, he heard Aboli say. *Now you can easily change the direction of your attack. With such a grip the sword is alive.*

He brought the cutlass up to his face, putting the cool brass hilt against his cheek so that he got a feel for the large, fluted shell hand guard. At the end of the pommel he felt the peen block which secured it to the tang, noting that it was a pyramid shape and sharp. Then he made some practice cuts through the air, half comforted to at least have a good blade in his hand, though half terrified too, to think that the man on the other end of that chain, who he could not even see, was likely doing the very same thing.

'Today, many of you may have seen the infidel slut Nazet put up for sale in the market.' That got a cheer. 'Sadly, a fire, doubtless started by the enemies of Zanzibar, prevented that sale from being completed. Now Nazet has disappeared, vanished into thin air.'

No! Hal screamed into his gag. *She can't have disappeared. They can't have taken her from me again, when we'd been so close, gazing into one another's eyes. I can't lose her again!*

'But we will provide you with something even better than the selling of Nazet. Behold, the killing of El Tazar! For it is he that you see before you, he who is fighting for his life . . . and who will keep fighting, against first one man and then another until at last he is dead!'

The announcer waited for more cheers to subside, then he resumed his speech. 'If either of you attempts to remove your blindfold or gag, you will be shot where you stand and fed to the beasts.' The master of ceremonies' voice was warning them. 'Prepare!'

309

Hal took up his fighting stance, feet shoulder-width apart with the leading foot forward and the trailing foot at right angles to it. His knees were bent so that the centre of gravity was kept midway between his heels.

The spectators had fallen silent. With his left hand Hal grabbed a fistful of the chain then took up the strain, the links chinking as the encumbrance pulled taut again.

He heard the shout of, 'Fight!' and the crowd bellowed with bestial excitement.

Suddenly the chain went slack. Hal knew his opponent was coming for him, so he moved to his right, raising the cutlass to protect his face, as the other man's blade struck it, ringing out the first chime of the contest. Then the man was gone again and the chain drew tight.

Hal's ears sifted through the noise which seemed to swirl all around him, but he could hear nothing to help him, neither footfalls nor his opponent's breathing, so that he could only guess where the other man was. He stepped forward so that the chain slackened, then without warning he stepped back and hauled the chain back, twisting his body to put his weight into it, and he felt the stubborn weight of the other man resisting. Then he strode forward slashing his sword left and right, high and low, as the crowd cheered and laughed and hooted.

But he hit nothing, could never know if he had even come close, or if the other man's blade had narrowly missed him, and he let the chain play out again, breathing hard through his nose because of the gag crammed in his mouth.

Where are you? Come, friend, let us end this.

He sensed a movement on his right and swept the cutlass up to block a cut that would have taken off his head, then having found each other, their swords sang, blade against blade, both men striking and parrying as instinct and hard-won experience took over.

The steel kissed and Hal rolled his blade over his opponent's, passing forward to thrust the cutlass's guard into his enemy's face. The blow threw the man's head back and Hal felt a savage joy. The blades rang again and he heard a muffled grunt so he extended and lunged at the sound, driving his attack forward, and this time he felt the blade slice into flesh before his opponent beat his sword away.

His opponent was hurt now, he had to be, and Hal knew he must press the advantage. He had to strike again before the man could recover and so he followed the line of the chain, scything his blade left and right. Now, as the exertion caused his heart to pound and his muscles to feel the strain of combat, Hal discovered a new handicap to add to all the others. The gag made it all but impossible to breathe through his mouth and his burning lungs could not drag in enough precious air through his nostrils alone. As his body struggled for air, Hal's mind was flooded with the horror of his blindness. It screamed at him to retreat from the sharp steel that sought his own flesh, to make himself small, to hide. But there was nowhere to hide and so he attacked, the cutlass an extension of his hand, as Aboli had taught him years ago, so that the blade became a living creature thirsting for blood.

But it found steel this time, not flesh, the jarring impact sending hot pain through the marrow of his arm, then the other man heaved on the chain and Hal staggered forward, unbalanced. The man brushed past his right shoulder and was suddenly behind him and the chain was wrapped round Hal's neck, strangling him.

Then he was falling. He hit the ground writhing like a caught eel but could not break free. He could not breathe. He felt the

311

man's face close. Too close. An elbow in his back. The man's legs trying to wrap around his own, trying to bind him as he hauled back on the chain. The man was too strong. Hal bucked and kicked, his heels hammering the ground. An immense pressure swelled in his face. His skull was going to explode. His eyes were going to burst.

There was no arena now. No baying crowd. There was just silence but for the pounding of his heart in his ears. A beat that was slowing.

I am dying.

No, Henry. You will not die here. I forbid it.

Father?

Get up, Henry. Kill this man and get to your feet. Do it now. My son.

Did he still hold the sword? Yes. But his strength was ebbing. He must strike now. And hard. He released his grip and reversed it, bringing his hand over the hilt and taking hold again with his finger knuckles on top the way he would grip a hammer. Screaming into the gag he brought the sword up hard and fast, hilt first over his head, and the pommel cracked into the man's skull.

Somehow the man held on still, pulling the chain into Hal's neck, but now his strength was failing and Hal managed to get two fingers, then three, between the iron links and his own skin. Enough to draw a breath, and with that breath, new life flooded his veins. He brought the cutlass up again, and again he struck his enemy's skull with its iron hilt and now his whole left hand was between the chain and his neck. He threw it off and scrambled away from the man's flailing limbs, rising to his feet, stumbling, still dizzy from lack of breath.

Knowing he must finish it he followed the chain back, hacking at the ground like a demented butcher, the crowd cheering wildly, louder with each successive strike as he closed in on the other man. Then he heard a rattle of chain and knew it meant that the man had somehow got to his own feet, so Hal swept his sword high and it rang against his enemy's blade. He struck again. And again, beating the weapon down, filled with blood-lust and joy as he felt the other man's strength flooding away.

The next swing hit nothing but the one after that struck flesh and bone, and Hal hauled the sword back from the falling weight, sensing that he had struck a mortal blow.

The noise around him subsided, confirming that the fight was over and that he had won, and so tucking the blood-smeared cutlass beneath his left arm he tore at the blindfold, pulling it back over his head.

And then he had dropped the sword and was clawing at the gag in his mouth because his stomach threatened to purge itself as his eyes took in the scene before him.

It was Tromp.

The Dutchman was on his knees, his face sheeted in blood from the two terrible puncture wounds in his forehead made by the little peen block on the pommel of Hal's cutlass. He was cut in the shoulder too, and his nose was broken, smashed across his face. But the worst of his wounds was the fleshy gash in his chest through which Hal could see the white gleam of his ribs. This foot-long cut was not yet full of blood. It would be soon enough.

Hal felt overwhelmed by a tidal wave of mixed emotions: horror and guilt at the harm he had done to a man who had become his friend mixed with terrible shame at the suspicions he had so unfairly harboured against a man who had not betrayed him, but had remained loyal. And this was how that loyalty had been rewarded. Hal staggered over and fell to his knees in front of Tromp, who was feebly tugging at his own blindfold. He did not have the strength or dexterity to remove it and Hal was torn as to what do. He was so ashamed of what he had done that he thought he must let Tromp die with the blindfold on, never knowing who it was that had killed him. For he was a dead man. The Dutchman's remaining heartbeats could be counted on two hands. Surely.

Let him die now, Hal pleaded silently, looking up at the sky which was filling with cloud.

His eyes scanned the arena as if they might find an answer there, but they met nothing but a sea of hostile, unfamiliar faces. There were four other men in the ring with him: all armed and all looking directly at him, as if daring him to take them on. And then Hal saw the eyes of a child, filled with tears. They seemed familiar but his mind was so overwhelmed by all that had happened that he could not place them and besides, what could a child be doing in a place like this? Hal tried to concentrate on what he knew to be true, and real, and what he had to do. And so, his hands shaking, he reached out and took hold of the blood-soaked silk over Tromp's eyes and lifted it from his eyes.

'I'm sorry,' Hal murmured. 'Christ, I'm so sorry . . . my friend.'

Tromp's eyes seemed to sharpen a touch, seemed to focus on Hal. Then they dulled as though a skein of ice had formed over them. He pitched forward and Hal caught him. He untied the knot behind the Dutchman's head and removed the gag. It did not seem right to let him die unable to speak, unable to damn Hal for killing him.

But there were no words. Hal lowered his friend to the ground and looked up through his own tears to see the four armed men standing around him.

'Take him back to the kennel,' the master of ceremonies spoke. Two men pulled Hal to his feet and as he stood at his full height once again he looked into the crowd and shouted out in desperate defiance: 'Here I am! I'm still alive! What now, damn you? What now, you mad bastards?!'

The crowd responded with catcalls, obscene gestures and threw half-chewed meat bones and stale bread rolls in his direction. But then their shouts of contempt gave way to alarm. People were running for the exits. Even the men guarding Hal were looking around in panic. And then he saw the reason why as a company of armed soldiers, at least thirty-strong, entered the yard where the fighting ring stood and forced their way through the crowd, clubbing and even stabbing anyone who got in their way. Hal's guards turned tail and fled and he was about to follow them, but as he looked around for a way out he saw that it was too late. He was entirely surrounded by troops. Then a man whose plumed helmet and resplendent uniform marked him out as their commander stepped into the filthy, blood- and excrement-stained ring and said, 'Captain Courtney, please come with me. His Highness the Maharajah Sadiq Khan Jahan wishes to make your acquaintance.'

H al had only been in his cell for a few hours when he received a visit from Prince Jahan. Hal had been steeling himself for brutal interrogation, but Jahan's opening question took him completely by surprise.

'Your countryman,' the prince began, 'the one that is called the Buzzard: did he always have the morals of a pig, even when he was a man?'

Hal made an exhausted attempt at a laugh. 'He was born a treacherous, thieving rogue. It's in his blood.'

'Yes, I thought as much. He has stolen Judith Nazet. This angers me because she was my property . . .'

'She is nobody's property. She is a free woman.'

'Very clearly, Sir Henry, she is not,' Jahan pointed out. 'She is currently the Buzzard's prisoner, on a ship sailing south. It is my fault. I should have known better. I saw him betray his god for money. A man who will do that has no honour, no shame. If he were a Mussulman and it was known that he had betrayed the prophet, blessings be upon him and Allah, the all-knowing, the all-merciful, in such a fashion, then if he were to die a thousand times it would not be enough. But you are different. You fought for your god.'

'For my god, for freedom and for the woman I love.'

Jahan gave a rueful sigh and a nod of the head. 'Ah, I cannot blame you for that, El Tazar. She is a queen among women. She was here, in my harem, and her beauty outshone even my finest concubines. No, fear not, I did not defile her, though I was sorely tempted as any man alive would be.'

'So why not? You could have raped her. What stopped you?'

'That is a good question. For of course you are right. Within these walls, and even outside them I may do exactly as I wish. So, what precisely was I thinking . . .?' The prince paused for a moment's thought and then said, 'She and I spoke. I told her that I was waiting until you were captured. I said that I would force her to give herself to me because if she did not, both she and you would die. She was not concerned for herself, of course, for she is as brave as any man. But she would not want you to suffer for her.'

Hal's voice was heavy with contempt: 'Is that how you like to seduce women, by threats of violence if they deny you?'

Jahan's attitude, which had been one of lordly amiability, suddenly turned as cold as frost. 'You are either very brave or a very foolish man to make such a suggestion, for I could have you killed for it.'

'You will have me killed anyway, I have no doubt, if that is what you want,' Hal said.

'Yes,' the prince agreed. 'But whatever you may think, I am not

317

a man who glories in the power of life and death, as some do. Nor do I take pleasure from hurting women or forcing them to my will. For example, the women of my harem belong to me. They exist to please me, that is their function and they must perform it. But I do not hit them, nor threaten them and you may be sure that the others are always jealous of the one who is my chosen one and wish that they, not she, were enjoying my favours. So it would give me no pleasure to force myself on Judith Nazet, and though I am angered by the defeats she has inflicted on the armies that I sent against her, I do not hate her for them. I respect her. Though she is a woman she fought like a true warrior. If she had been killed in battle, I would have rejoiced. But I came to the conclusion that if I were to take her with threats or violence I would be the one who was most degraded.'

'That's a fine speech, I'm sure. But still you put her on the slaver's block.'

'That was a matter of necessity – a means of forcing you back to Zanzibar. I wanted to get you here, in front of me, where I could see this barracuda who treated my ships like so many helpless sardines. I wanted you to fight the one-armed monster I had created. I thought it would entertain me.' The prince looked almost sorry for himself, as though he sought Hal's sympathy as he said, 'It is hard, you know, for a man in my position to find something new to entertain himself.'

'And then your monster betrayed you.'

'Yes, he did. So now you can do me a great service by killing him.'

'I have to find him first.'

'I can help you with that,' Jahan said. 'The Buzzard is in league with another Englishman called Benbury.'

'I know him, he's the master of a ship called the *Pelican*,' Hal said. 'But he's not English. He is Scottish.'

318

'And that is not the same thing?'

'No, not at all.'

'Huh,' said the prince at the surprise of learning something new. 'In any case, one of this Benbury's crew was seized when we raided the tavern where you were found. He was persuaded to tell us all he knew about his master's plans.'

'I heard screaming during the night,' Hal said.

'Persuasion often has that effect. It seems that Captain Benbury and the Buzzard hope to sell your woman to a Portuguese called Lobo. I know of this man. He has a gold mine. I can get you there.'

'How?'

'You will leave in three days' time. You will be taken on a journey that will bring you no pleasure, but it is also the only possible way to get you close to Lobo. If you try to attack him, you will fail. If you pay a social call, he will turn you away, or simply kill you. But there is one way you can get into his mine, though you may wish that you had not. For he works men until they die. And so he always needs new men . . .'

Hal shrugged his shoulders as if he could not care less. 'I know what forced labour is like. I have the whip-marks to prove it. I can survive.'

'Maybe so,' said Jahan, 'but first you have to get there. And that will be no easy matter, for the man who will take you would happily kill you first.'

'It sounds to me as though you want me to die more than the Buzzard,' Hal said.

'Puh!' Prince Jahan looked like a man who had ordered a series of apparently delicious dishes only to find that each tasted worse than the last. 'I want you all gone, all you Englishmen, Scotsmen . . . you are all equally unwelcome in my sight. You will be put aboard a ship within the hour. As to which of you dies, and when, that is no longer for me to decide. Let the will of Allah be your judge . . .'

O n the afternoon after the slave market, Mossie sat in the captain's cabin of the *Golden Bough* as she lay at anchor off the Zanzibar coast, far enough from the city to avoid prying eyes. His shoulders were slumped and his head downcast as he told a story that was interrupted by more than one burst of tears. 'I should have done something. Lady Judith has been taken away, Captain Henry is in chains and Mister Tromp is dead. But I didn't know what to do!'

'Do not blame yourself, little Sparrow,' Aboli comforted him. 'You did exactly what I asked. You followed as close as you could to the captain until he left the island. So it is thanks to you that we know what happened, thanks to you that I could send men to the harbour to find out which ship took Captain Courtney away. Now we know that he was on the *Madre de Deus*, bound for Quelimane. We know that he is with slaves bound for the gold mines. We would not know any of this without you, Mossie, do you understand?'

The boy nodded his head, feeling a little better thanks to hearing Aboli's words.

'Good,' the first mate continued. 'Now, Mossie, listen to me as I tell you how we will rescue Captain Courtney.'

The boy nodded eagerly, as if he were listening to an exciting bedtime story.

'First, we will follow the ship on which our captain is held prisoner. If we catch it at sea, we will attack and take the captain back,' Aboli said.

'Will you kill the bad men who took the captain?'

'Yes, we will look at them like this . . .' Aboli contorted his scarred face into a terrifyingly warlike expression that had Mossie shrieking in fear and excitement.

'Then we will stick our swords and our spears into them like this,' he lunged his arm forward, 'and this, and this!'

'But what if you can't get to their ship in time?'

'Ah, then, I will go ashore with my Amadoda brothers. The mines where the captain is going, and Lady Judith too, maybe, are close to our homeland, the Kingdom of the Monomatapa. So we will know the country around us like we know our own hands. And we will get the captain and his lady and bring them back to the coast, where you and Mister Tyler and Mister Fisher and all the crew of the *Bough* will be waiting for us.'

'So you will bring Lady Judith and Captain Henry back to us, all safe and well?' Mossie asked.

'Yes.'

'Do you promise?'

Aboli looked at Mossie with a deep solemnity in his eyes and said, 'I have known the captain since he was a little baby. He is like my own son to me and I will never let him come to harm. So yes, little Sparrow, I promise. I will bring the captain and Lady Judith back to you.'

'You must eat,' the girl said, pointing at the plate of goat's cheese and fruit bought at a market in Zanzibar that she had put on the table over an hour previously. Judith had not touched it, though she was faint with hunger, for it seemed like an act of surrender to accept food given by men who had stolen her. The girl looked at her plaintively. 'Think of the little one. Even if you can't face it, you must keep your strength up.'

Judith picked up a piece of cheese and bit into it and the girl gave her a strained smile, half glancing back at the cabin's door as though she feared what, or who might come through it.

It was dusk and the *Pelican* had dropped anchor, meaning that the Buzzard would be along soon to check on them: to check on Judith.

When they'd taken her aboard in Zanzibar, they'd shoved

Judith into a locked, lightless hold in the bowels of the ship. They gave her a wooden bucket for a latrine and a ragged pair of trousers and a rough canvas smock that had belonged to a cabin-boy – 'Died of malaria, the little tyke,' a sailor had informed her – then left her entirely alone aside from occasional deliveries of food and water. Hal had taught her how to tell the time from the ringing of a ship's bell. So she knew that two days and nights had passed and it was just after ten in the morning, or four bells in the forenoon watch, when a sailor came to the hold, instructed her to follow him and led her to a cabin in the ship's forecastle. It was cramped and damp but it was far preferable to the hold and Judith had female company there also, for a little while after she had been installed a young woman had been all but thrown into the cabin with her.

'I will prepare your meals and empty your night soil,' the girl had stammered, trembling with fear because the Buzzard had been at her shoulder. 'Whatever I can do to make you more comfortable, such as can be done aboard a ship, I will do.'

'Thank you,' Judith said and then addressed the Buzzard. 'Where are you taking me?'

The solitary eye stared out from its hole and the smiling façade with its white teeth leered, and Judith had looked around the gloomy cabin for anything which she might use as a weapon, just for the satisfaction of lashing out at the foul mask and the even more repellent human being who lurked behind it. She could almost smell the violence coming off him and, unarmed and vulnerable as she was, she realized that she feared him as she had never feared a man before. Judith hated that fear and despised herself for feeling it and yet she could not help herself flinching a little and shielding her unborn child with her hands, as if she feared the Buzzard would take his knife, open her belly and pull the child from her womb.

'Hold your tongue, woman,' he rasped in a voice as rough as old rope. 'Be glad I have given you the wench. There are plenty aboard who would have her, plain as she is.' And then he had left them, locking the door behind him.

A while passed before the girl spoke again. 'They told me you're with child. I had a babe of my own, not so long ago.' There were tears springing in her eyes with those words, and that was all she said.

Now Judith ate and invited the girl to join her. Once she started she did not stop until the plate was empty, though she let the girl take her share too. Her name was Ann Missen and she had been aboard an East Indiaman bound for Bombay when the topmastman had spied the *Pelican* seemingly adrift off the southern tip of Madagascar, her mainsail in tatters on the yard as though she had come through a canvas-ripping squall. Assuming the caravel was a merchantman in trouble, the Indiaman's captain had laid his ship alongside and assured Captain Benbury that he was at the man's service and would do whatever he could to assist, namely by giving Benbury the spare sail in his hold. That was when men had poured from the *Pelican*'s hatches and stormed aboard the Indiaman with pistols and steel and slaughter. Ann's husband, a company clerk out to take up a prestigious post in the Bombay office, fought bravely, killing a man with his pistol before he was hacked to pieces before his young wife's eyes.

'I never knew he had such courage in him,' Ann had said, recounting the tale and Judith had suspected she was still numb from the shock of it, that she had not yet accepted that her husband was gone from her for ever. Judith had not dared ask the girl about her own child, preferring to hope that it had died before the couple had left England for their new life.

Now as they leaned back in their chairs, their stomachs feeling as full as if they'd had a five-course feast, Ann said, 'Tell me more about your life.'

Ever since the Buzzard had sneeringly addressed Judith as General Nazet on one of his visits to the cabin, Ann had developed an insatiable appetite for stories about Judith's past: her childhood in the hills of Ethiopia, her travels around Europe and then her military campaigns. 'What I don't yet comprehend is how you got to be this general. I mean, why did all those men let a woman lead them?'

'Perhaps because I was not really raised to be a woman,' Judith said. 'I was my father's only child and so, since he had no son, he taught me everything that he would have taught a boy. I learned to ride and fight with swords and guns. When I had bedtime stories, they were not about princesses and handsome princes, but about the great military leaders like Alexander, Julius Caesar and Hannibal, the greatest of all African generals.'

'Until you,' Ann said, for Judith had become her heroine.

Judith laughed. 'I was no Hannibal! But I did learn about how battles are fought and won, and because my father was a tribal chief, I rode with the men of the tribe and they came to accept me as my father's heir, as if I were his son. So when the call came for troops to go north to fight for the emperor against the Arab invaders it was I who led my people, for my father was too old and sick to command them. Before we even reached the main army, we encountered some of El Grang's forces and defeated them. News spread of the victory, so when we arrived at the army's main encampment all the soldiers were cheering us as we rode in and the women who followed the army were throwing flowers. So the soldiers adopted me. I became their leader, but also their mascot, almost their good luck charm and suddenly I found myself at the head of the entire army, for they would follow nobody else.'

'I bet all the old men who were generals really hated you for that,' Ann said. But before Judith could reply a key turned in the lock, the cabin door opened and the Buzzard came in, bringing with him the stench of unwashed bodies and fouler things from the sailors' quarters adjacent in the forecastle.

'There's a storm coming,' the Buzzard said as the door swung shut behind him. He glanced at the empty plates on the table then stood staring at Judith as he did each evening when he came to check on her. Ann edged away from him, like a hand recoiling from a flame, but the man was not interested in her.

'Where are you taking me?' Judith repeated, as she did whenever the Buzzard appeared in their midst.

'Nowhere you will enjoy,' he replied, that eye fixed on her, assessing her the way a man appraises a slave at the block before deciding whether or not to bid.

'Hal Courtney will kill you,' Judith said. 'He will find you and he will gut you like the feeble creature you are.'

The man moved, though not towards Judith. He grabbed Ann by the throat and threw her back, pinning her against the cabin's damp bulkhead. She tried to scream but the sound was pitiful and then the man drove a gloved fist into her stomach and stepped back so that she crumpled to the floor.

The masked man came over to Judith who protected her belly but otherwise faced up to him, her chin raised, inviting him to strike her face.

He was so close that it was all she could do not to close her eyes for fear that his wicked beak might peck them out.

'See what happens to the girl when you disobey me,' the Buzzard's voice rasped through the mask's mouth slit. Behind him Ann lay in the dark corner, curled in on herself and gasping for breath. 'I have an interest in keeping you bright-eyed and

326

hale as a prize hog. But her . . .' he jerked his head back. 'She is nothing. Mine to do with as I please.'

'You are a coward,' Judith spat.

The Buzzard turned and walked over to the girl, who whimpered, one arm raised in a feeble defence. He bent and knocked the arm aside then slapped her across the face with enough force to drive her head back against the timbers. He straightened and turned back to Judith.

'You see what's happening here?'

Judith would have given anything to fly at him now and tear at his flesh with her bare hands. No, not anything. Not the child.

She nodded.

'Good. When the storm hits us you will be safe enough if you sit on the floor and hold on to the leg of the cot,' he said, nodding towards Judith's bed. Ann had no bed, just a few blankets on the bare boards. 'Or you could hold on to each other,' he said, tilting his head on one side while he thought about that. In three strides he reached the cabin door and opened it, then stopped at the threshold.

'Don't waste your strength praying for your gallant young hero to rescue you and have his vengeance on the rest of us,' he said. 'Courtney is dead. He was taken to his execution like a bullock to the slaughterhouse.'

And with that he was gone.

The *Madre de Deus* was hell afloat. A Portuguese three-masted merchantman, she plied the seas on the endless circuit by which gimcrack trade goods were exchanged for African human beings who were then transported in her holds to the slave markets of the New World, or the East Indies, or the Ottoman Empire. It mattered not to her owner and captain João Barros whom he carried, where they went, or who bought them in the end. So long as he was paid that was all he cared about.

The Maharajah Sadiq Khan Jahan had not paid him to carry this Englishman who claimed to be Courtney, the famed 'Tazar', to Quelimane. He had simply sent an official along with the soldiers who escorted the Englishman to the docks who said to Barros in Arabic, 'His Highness has been informed that you have a shipment bound for Quelimane.'

'That is correct,' Barros replied, in the same tongue as he rubbed the vivid pink scar line that ran from the corner of his mouth up into his hairline. It was a nervous habit he could not break himself of.

'They have been bought by Senhor Lobo, to work in his mines.'

'Again, correct.'

'Very well, please add this one to the shipment,' the official said as Hal was pushed forward to stand next to him, opposite Barros. 'He is an Englishman. If he survives the journey, His Highness wishes him to be presented as a gift to Senhor Lobo.'

'A fine gift,' Barros remarked. 'Not only is he a white man but he looks strong and healthy. Good teeth. Senhor Lobo will breed from him, I dare say.'

'Very possibly,' the official agreed and then went on, 'His Highness recognizes, however, that voyages at sea are fraught with danger and will not hold it against you if this journey should prove fatal to this individual.'

'You are saying that I am free to do with him as I will?'

'Exactly so. His Highness has decreed that the fate of this man shall be in the hands of Allah, the all-knowing and merciful.'

'What an interesting decree,' Barros said. 'I will be sure to consider it at all times.'

And so, for the second time in his short life, Hal Courtney found himself in the heat, the confinement, the darkness and the overpowering stench of a slave deck, shackled to a ringbolt and soaked in other men's liquid excrement.

Hal estimated that they were six days out of Zanzibar when one of Barros's crew – a man who'd swiftly made himself known to the terrified, half-starved, seasick and dying slaves by the eagerness with which he laid into them with the cat o' nine tails that never seemed to leave his right hand – came down to the hold with two other sailors and, by the light of a horn lantern, poked and prodded the slaves with his whip's knot-end.

'What is that bastard looking for now?' Hal asked himself, squinting against the sudden, uncomfortable brightness from the ship's lantern.

The Portuguese sailors had buried their noses in the crooks of their elbows and one was cursing the stench. The man with the cat thrust it between the shoulder blades of an emaciated African who sat slumped over so that his forehead was almost touching the slime-smeared boards. When the slave did not respond, the man bent and hauled his head back at which the African groaned and opened his eyes. The slaver let go, mumbled a curse and moved on.

'That one looks strong,' one of the whip man's companions said in Portuguese, pointing his cutlass at another African.

'And I have one here,' the other sailor said, 'a proud young cock too by the looks of him,' and Hal knew enough Portuguese to wish he had not sat so straight-backed nor glared at the slavers with such defiance. The man looked at him more closely and added, 'Wait! I think he is white.'

'All the better. Bring them up,' the whip man said.

Hal and the African followed the Portuguese sailors up the ladder that had been widened to allow pairs of slaves to go up and down it without their ankle chains having to be removed.

'Ah, the Englishman,' Captain Barros said, then turned to the taller, more muscular of the other two slaves. 'And this other one also looks strong. Good. An excellent choice. Black against white. There is a certain . . . art to it.'

Barros stood with his officers and his cabin boy by the mainmast, all of them, even the boy, wearing broad hats to keep the sun off. The boy looked so like Barros, even down to the arrogant tilt of his head, that Hal was certain he was the captain's son.

'Get a move on, Fernandes, you timber-toed old goat!' Barros yelled at a grey-haired crump-back who was clumping across the deck on a peg leg. 'I swear you would be no slower if we took off the other leg too.'

'I will tell the surgeon to bring his saw,' a long-faced officer put in, 'and we can place wagers on that also while we're about it.' This raised a laugh from the others, especially the boy.

The crump-back was carrying the six-stringed instrument the Portuguese and the Spanish called a *viola da mano*, meaning 'violin of the hand' for it was played with the fingers rather than a bow. Now he thrust it in the air angrily. 'I am coming as fast as I can, Barros, you mean bastard!' he growled, arriving at the mainmast with a muttered tirade of foul curses.

Captain Barros gave Hal a tired look and, apparently ignoring the fact that he was talking to a man who looked like an unshaven, unkempt beggar and was stained with his own and other men's excrement, said, 'I only allow him to speak like that to me because he was a friend of my father, and because he is a halfway decent musician.' Barros nodded at the instrument in the old man's grasp with its long, ornately carved neck and its strings in six paired courses. 'He might as well be married to that *viola da mano* of his. It belonged to his grandfather, I believe.'

'Great-grandfather, though it was already old then,' Fernandes corrected.

The captain wafted that away. 'The point is that I doubt our young Englishman has ever seen such an instrument, have you?'

'Only in paintings,' Hal said, caught up in the pretence that they were gentlemen conversing in an elegant salon, rather than a captain and a captive on a slaver's deck.

331

Barros nodded. 'Yes it is a shame that the *viola da mano* has long since fallen out of fashion. And yet we still enjoy it now and then, eh, gentlemen?' The five officers nodded and grinned. 'Now then, you English are a civilized race. The mark of any civilization is its love of music, don't you think?' He turned to the man with the cat 'o' nine tails and gestured at Hal's ankle irons. The man took a key from his belt and bent to undo the fetters.

'And will you look at this one's eyes?' Barros said, turning to the muscular, black slave. 'See the way it looks at me. It would like to tear my head from my shoulders.'

'This will be a close contest,' another officer said, frowning as he examined the slaves in front of him.

In Hal's experience most slaves maintained a docility, did their best to look unthreatening in order to simply survive. They kept their eyes downcast and their thoughts to themselves. But this one eyeballed the captain, his well-muscled body naked but for a loincloth, tensed as though ready to fight for his life. Could Hal win such a fight against such a proud, fierce adversary? It appeared that he was about to find out.

And yet fighting was not what Captain João Barros had in mind.

The men nearby were ushered away so that Hal and the muscular slave were left standing in an open patch of deck, a few paces wide and equally deep. Both of them were breathing heavily, not from exertion or fear but simply because they were sucking in the fresh sea air like starving men after all their days below deck.

'You will dance for us,' Barros told them. 'You will dance to Fernandes's music and you will not stop dancing until the old man stops playing. Well, you may stop if you grow weary, but it is only fair to warn you that he who stops first will suffer the consequences.'

332

The man beside Hal showed no sign of understanding a word, until Barros sent for one of his black sailors who hurried down from the foremast shrouds and translated the captain's speech into a language the slave seemed to comprehend.

'What consequences?' Hal asked.

Barros nodded in the direction of an officer who stood resting one bare foot upon a great coil of rope. 'The first one to stop appreciating Fernandes's playing will be dropped over the side on the end of that rope,' he said. Then he turned to his men: 'Those of you who lose money on the outcome of the dance may win it back again on the outcome of the fishing.' He grinned as he turned back to Hal and spread his arms. 'Am I not a fair man?' he asked. 'That is why my crew loves me.'

Behind him the others were already making their wagers, babbling at the ship's quartermaster who was struggling to keep his book up to date.

Hal looked up at the *Madre de Deus*'s mainsail. Captain Barros did the same.

'Ah,' Barros said. 'You are hoping we can keep up this speed. Eight knots, wouldn't you say?'

Hal was thinking of the shoals of tiger sharks that would be following the ship, scavenging on the offal and latrine waste that was flung overboard.

'We have calculated that the sharks swim at an average speed of two knots,' Captain Barros said, 'but they can swim much, much faster in short bursts.' He turned to his officers. 'What do you say?'

'We've recorded them going above eight knots, Captain, but they don't keep it up for long,' the quartermaster said.

Barros nodded and turned back to Hal. 'Of course none of this need concern you; just so long as you keep dancing.' With that he spun on his heel and swept an arm towards the old crump-back, inviting him to begin. '"Jamaica" if you please, Fernandes. But keep it sprightly. The English do so love a jolly jig.'

Fernandes began to pluck the cat-gut strings with his long yellowed fingernails.

The African looked at Hal and Hal looked at the African.

'Well? Get on with it!' Captain Barros said and the man with the cat lashed it across each of them as an incentive.

And so Hal danced.

'I take it that you ken we cannae dock in Quelimane, or any of the ports along the coast.' Benbury looked at the Buzzard, as they both leaned against the *Pelican*'s quarterdeck rail, and he watched the beak rise and fall as he nodded. 'The damned Portuguese control the lot o' them and they'll no' let anyone trade except themselves and the Arabs. Putting a slave ashore counts as trade.'

'Putting a stolen slave ashore counts as a capital offence,' the Buzzard's rasping voice interjected. 'What did you have in mind?'

'Well, my second mate, Pereira, knows where the mines are and swears blind he can find them if he has a sextant tae reckon the way. Once you get there, he can translate for you too, for I gather this Lobo laddie has no other tongues but Portuguese and some language the local savages babble. I'll be putting you ashore by a river delta I know where there's no white men tae be found. Mind, the going's a wee bit swampy thereabouts, but you can take a boat in a good fair way, I'd imagine. And you'll be closer tae the mines than if I took you tae Quelimane.'

'I'm going on this journey am I?'

'One of us has to do so,' Benbury pointed out. 'And I'm the one sailing the ship.'

'It will not improve Judith Nazet's maidenly beauty, marching halfway across Africa,' the Buzzard objected.

'Och, dinnae fash yersel' . . . She's no some delicate white lassie. She's a blackie, same as the rest o' them. She'll feel perfectly at home.'

Hal started slow, as did Fernandes, despite his captain's orders to keep the tune spirited. The old grey-beard's fingers caressed the strings of his instrument, knuckles and sinews warming to their task, reminding themselves of the joy of coaxing music from that smooth-curved figure-eight–shaped body of cypress and cedar. He eased into the tune in his own time, like a lady lowering herself into a hot bath, plucking the strings so that they sang their sweet, soft song.

Hal also let himself merge with the melody, his muscles gathering their strength, his mind striving to forget the humiliation of what he was being forced to do. The only thing that mattered was Judith. All he had to do was survive.

Heel and toe, heel and toe, his hands clasped behind his back as his feet marked out the steps, laying claim to that small piece of the *Madre de Deus*'s deck. Again and again his bare soles landed softly on the planks, beginning to pick up speed as Fernandes let the music gather itself, like a captain hoisting his sails to the wind.

Hal supposed he had the advantage of at least being familiar with the tune, whereas he doubted the African had ever laid eyes on any instrument resembling the *viola da mano*. And yet it soon became clear that music was in the other man's very blood for he moved with a poise and grace which Hal could only marvel at, as the first droplets of moisture rolled down his temples, his bones creaking in their joints after days of captivity.

'Jamaica' had flowed into a tune Hal did not recognize but he was dancing a jig now, pure and simple. The kind of dance sailors could do after a hard day's toil, in their sleep, or even on the end of a hempen rope. Hal held his torso rigid, one hand on his hip, the other arm hoisted behind him almost like a fencer's. His feet were lively and brisk, tapping out their beat in triple rhythm, the muscles of his legs bunching like corded rope so that Hal knew that for all his dishevelment his audience must be impressed to see such a broad-shouldered, well-built man as he dancing with such lightness of foot. And yet he still felt clumsy when he looked across at the African, who seemed to have picked up the steps as naturally as a bird taking to the wing. Moreover, the black man was not even sweating, whereas Hal's eyes were stinging with it, the liquid running in rivulets down his back, each drop tapping out its own beat on the deck.

The Portuguese officers were enjoying themselves. Some of them were laughing and clapping along with the music or slapping their thighs to the off-beat. Others were pointing at Hal or the African, explaining why their man was going to win and why their friend's wager was as good as lost. Captain Barros had a shark's grin on his face and other sailors had gathered at the rails to watch, no doubt putting up their own stakes on the outcome.

Hal was lost to the music now, entranced by the rhythm of his feet on the deck. That rhythm was still gathering pace, too, as old Fernandes belied his years, his fingers doing their own dance up and down the instrument's neck.

'The Negro is lithe as a cobra,' one of the officers called in Portuguese.

'Perhaps he is dancing for his gods,' another said. 'He is calling up a storm to gather him up and take him back to his nine wives.'

'Nine wives? Christ, I'd rather jump overboard than have eight more like my one,' the quartermaster said.

The sun had risen high above the African mainland now. It blazed across the ocean off the *Madre de Deus*'s starboard, its ferocious heat like that from a furnace across the deck. Hal's breathing was ragged. His legs were growing heavy and he was gasping for water, like a caught fish gasping for air. The newly scrubbed deck around his feet was dark with his sweat and he did not dare look up at the African for fear of seeing the man still looking strong and resilient, for that might break his own will to keep going. Yet he could still hear the African's feet thumping on the deck, heavier now at least, thank God, and he could see the blur of the man in his peripheral vision.

And so he danced on.

Then, despite the pain that radiated from all the little bones in his feet, up through his big leg bones and the powerful muscles of his thighs, to his hips and into his neck so that his head felt like a great lead weight, he pitied the African. Because Hal was dancing for the woman who owned his soul and for the child who had yet to take its first salt-tanged breath. A life at sea had forged Hal's body into a hard, unyielding tool. Every muscle and tendon was honed to excel at any physical task.

Even so, that tool was dulling now. He was dancing at half speed, unable to keep pace or maintain any sort of rhythm that bore a relationship to the sound coming from the *viola da mano*. His body was faltering. Above him he could hear gulls laughing at him and he grimaced through the pain. *What must he look like?* he wondered, through the haze of pain and thirst. *Like an old man staggering across the scorching hot Saharan sand,* he thought. And yet even with his body beginning to fail him, Hal knew that his heart would never fail. His jig might be nothing more than a grotesque parody of itself, but only death itself could stop his feet clumping on that deck.

It was a wonder that old Fernandes was still going, for he must have been exhausted too, but that was none of Hal's concern. His arms hung uselessly by his sides and he could barely lift his chin from his chest.

'Keep going, you dogs!' someone growled, and the cat's nine tails lashed the African's back and shoulders and Hal tasted the man's blood on his lips.

'Looks like the sharks will be getting some dark meat for their dinner,' one of the officers said.

'It ain't over yet,' another man interjected. 'Your Englishman is not looking so bloody lively.'

The spectators were calling and shouting but Hal was too tired to make out most of what they said. His long lank hair hung dripping in front of his face. He was barely aware of anything, even what his own legs were doing and whether or not they were still moving. He heard the whip crack again and thought it might have scoured his own flesh this time. Then he stumbled and fell to one knee and his mind screamed in defiance, demanding that he get up. So he did, but as he rose he glanced to his left and saw that the African was down on all fours, his head sagging and his belly sucking in and out as he heaved for breath.

Hal heard a cheer and realized it was for him. He straightened his spine and lifted his head. He put his right hand on his hip and hoisted his left arm until the hand was above his head.

Heel and toe. Step right, step left, step right, hop right. When he rose off the weight-bearing leg to change stance, the other leg almost buckled when his foot landed, yet somehow he was dancing again.

'That'll do *me!*' the quartermaster called, to a chorus of cheers and curses.

'Yes, that is quite enough. You have won, Englishman.' Captain Barros swept his hat off his head and held it high to signal the end of the contest. 'Your countrymen would be proud.'

'Get to your damned feet, shark bait!' the whip man bellowed, lashing the African who was trying but failing to rise. 'Get up, I said!' The cat bit again and then without any conscious thought of what he was doing, or why, Hal saw himself fly at the whip man and felt his stumbling momentum checked by the impact of flesh and bone. Then the two of them fell and Hal's hands were around the man's throat.

'Coward!' Hal spat. Full of rage and hunger to kill these heinous fiends who thought nothing of treating men like the meanest of beasts, feeling fellowship with the African now, rather than rivalry, he brought his forehead down on the man's nose, bursting it.

'Get him off me!' the whip man was screaming, and Hal felt himself being lifted into the air. He kicked and flailed, broke free but fell to the deck and then they were on him again.

'Hold him still!' Barros bellowed as the officers hauled Hal up, one of them wrapping Hal's hair around his fist and yanking his head back so that Captain Barros's face came into view just inches from Hal's own.

'You insolent English dog!' Barros spat, backhanding Hal across his face. 'You would get yourself killed over a filthy Negro?' He struck again, the knuckles splitting Hal's lip.

'I would kill *you* for him,' Hal said, rage driving out any sense of his own best interests, still less those of Judith and their child from his mind. Blood spilled from his lip into his beard and he licked the torn flesh, relishing the moisture in his parched mouth.

He knew what was coming and tensed the corded muscle of his stomach just as Barros drove his fist into it. The blow knocked the wind from him but not enough to prevent him calling Barros a milk-livered son of a Spanish whore.

Barros did not reply. Instead, he went over to the side and pulled one of the unused belaying pins from the rail on the inside of the bulwarks. Brandishing the solid wood shaft like a club, he cracked it against Hal's temple.

White-hot light seared through Hal's vision and in his blindness he heard Barros say, 'You are a friend to the animals, Englishman, I wonder if that affinity stretches to the fish.' He turned to his men. 'Fetch another rope. We shall have ourselves another wager, gentlemen.'

They held Hal and the African down while they tied the long ropes round their chests. Hal surrendered to the inevitable, preserving his stamina for when he would need it, but the African was still fighting, terror overcoming his exhaustion, as he and Hal were manhandled aft and lowered over the stern larboard rail. Down they went, the sailors of the *Madre de Deus* on the other ends of the ropes, and Hal cursing as the flesh of his forearms and lower legs was shredded against the barnacles on the ship's hull. And when he splashed into the ocean he

341

yelled because of the burning pain of the salt water in his wounds.

The men of the *Madre de Deus* let the ropes play out and Hal and the African were swept off into the ship's wake, spluttering and thrashing to keep their heads above water. Hal arched his body and kicked furiously but the rope was long and as more of it was let out he drifted back beyond the worst of the rough, hull-ploughed, bubbling ocean, so that by hauling himself along the rope he could hold his mouth clear of the water.

He looked across and was relieved to see that the African had not drowned either but was gripping the rope with grim determination, the muscles of his arms bunched and swollen with the strain.

'Hold on!' he called, making a show of grabbing with his hands, hoping the African could discern his meaning, even if his actual words were incomprehensible. 'Just hold on. They'll pull us up soon!' Which was what Hal was telling himself, for surely Captain Barros was not such an idiot that he would rather see them die than earn himself the money they would bring in at the slave block.

The ship's officers had removed their broad hats now for fear of them being blown over the side. Hal could see them gathered at the stern rail and beyond them he saw the *Madre de Deus*'s sails, and two dozen sailors clambering up the shrouds.

He's slowing the ship, Hal thought, fully aware of what it would mean if the ship lost two or three knots. But sure enough he could see her topmastmen strung out across the mizzen and mainmast, dark shapes against the blue sky. They were busy furling the topgallants and royals and when it was done there was a discernible drop in his own speed through the water. This at least made it easier to keep his head above the surface and when he looked across at the African he grimaced, an expression that Hal interpreted as relief.

He thinks we are saved, Hal thought. *The fool dares to hope we will come through this trial with a few cuts and bruised pride.* The thought of his own blood in the water made Hal look behind him for the first time. Craning his neck as he clung on to the rope, he strained to see beyond the furrow of his own wake.

That's when he saw the following fins.

He could hear the *Madre de Deus*'s crew cheering now. They lined the merchantman's rails and clung to the shrouds whooping with excitement.

'God help us,' Hal muttered. The shoal of tiger sharks was a cable's length behind them. He was certainly no stranger to the predators that roamed the warm waters of the Indian Ocean: black-tip sharks, hammerhead sharks, the great white sharks that were known to swallow men whole, and the ever-present blunt-nosed tiger sharks which terrified all sailors because they were so voracious and insatiable. Hal had seen some that were twenty-five feet long from nose-tip to tail-tip. He had heard of tiger sharks attacking longboats, even biting off pieces of the hull and swallowing them.

He had seen one bite through the tough shell of an enormous sea turtle. What such a predator would do to his own body did not bear thinking about and yet he could think of nothing else, knowing that the creatures had the scent of his blood in their noses.

The African screamed with terror, for he too had seen the company they were keeping. But Hal had no advice for the man. There was nothing to be done now but hope and, if it came to it, fight.

The *Madre de Deus* was down to perhaps four knots through

343

the water, which told Hal that Barros had struck some canvas from the foremast too. Or perhaps the wind had dropped. Either way it made Hal's blood far colder than the water around him and he hoped that the Portuguese had had their fun and would haul them back up before the sharks attacked.

But the merchantman's crew had not finished with them yet. Wagers had been made. There was money to be won and lost.

Hal did not even see the shark that attacked him. He felt the impact though, its great wedge-shaped head driving into his right thigh and spinning him over so that for a heartbeat he was on his back looking up at the sky through two feet of ocean. Then he righted himself, took a deep breath and let go his grip on the rope. The slack played out until the noose of it dug in beneath his arms, the knot holding, and now he expelled the air from his lungs and twisted until his face was beneath the water, his eyes searching the blue haze for the shark that had struck him.

He saw it. It had fallen back some thirty feet, its head moving from side to side as it swam beneath his wake.

They would pull him back aboard now. Surely. He had been the first to receive a shark's crude enquiry. Barros's men must have seen it and now they would haul him back up to the cheers of those who had won the wager.

But they did not pull him up, and then to Hal's horror he saw another shark coming out of the gloom off his right hip, its tail thrashing as it put in a great burst of effort to catch up with him. Hal screamed underwater, twisting his torso over again and kicking his feet with every scrap of strength he could muster, and his left heel scuffed the shark's snout, sending it careening off to the side, its yellow-white underside a flash in the blue gloom.

He saw another shark to his right and knew from its stocky

shape and broad, flat snout that it was a bull shark. It thrashed its tail to keep up with him, then darted in close so that when Hal went under again he was looking into the creature's evil little eye. Then the bull shark was gone and Hal arched his body, breaking the surface to take a gasping breath before putting his head under again.

When the next shark came it opened its jaws and Hal saw its razor-sharp serrated teeth and even in his terror he thought of Judith because he expected to die then, torn apart for the amusement of madmen. Yet he would not be taken that easily. He screamed and he rolled, kicking for all his worth and somehow those wicked-looking teeth missed him and the creature fell back, its energy spent.

This terror lasted the better part of an hour, Hal fending the sharks off, kicking their blunt snouts and eyes, or somehow writhing clear of their jaws just in time, and he had been aware of the African doing the same, the two of them fighting for their lives. But when he saw a terrible thrashing off his right shoulder he knew with dread certainty that the African had been bitten. The man did not cry out. Perhaps he was too exhausted. Perhaps he had been unable to fight any longer and had given up. The first Hal knew of it was when he came up, gasping for breath, and heard a collective groan from the men at the *Madre de Deus*'s stern rail. Captain Barros was yelling furiously at his own crewmen on the end of the other rope for letting the African be taken. What did the fool expect?

Hal's only thought was of himself. Sharks for miles around would be drawn to the fresh kill. The African's blood and torn flesh in the water would send them into a feeding frenzy and he would be next. If he did not drown in the meantime, for he was bone-weary and feared he could not fight much longer. It was all he could do to keep his head above the churned water of the ship's wake, and though terror was his strength, even that would fail him soon.

Then he realized that he was getting closer to the *Madre de Deus*'s hull. They were pulling him in. Up and up he went, hoisted like the day's catch to the shrieking of gulls, and when they hauled him over the larboard rail he collapsed onto the deck.

He was vaguely aware of them clamping irons on to his numbing legs but did not fight them. Could not have even if his life depended on it. He was utterly spent.

'Congratulations, Englishman, you are too much trouble even for the sharks to want to eat you,' Barros said.

Hal had no strength to reply. But he was alive.

J udith longed to see the sky. For too long now she had been trapped in a world of water, mud, mist and beds of reeds that pressed in from every side, stifling any trace of a breeze in the humid air and cutting them off from the light of the sun, though the heat of it weighed on them like molten lead.

There were ten of them making the journey: Pereira, the Portuguese second mate from the *Pelican*, and three other Portuguese sailors, all of them armed with muskets as well as their cutlasses; two African crewmen who had been designated as porters and were weighed down with supplies; Judith and Ann, and finally the masked man himself and the slave who tended to him. Judith tried to imagine what it was like for him to be trapped inside that leather carapace, for the padlocks that closed it and the ring at his neck made it plain that, for all his monstrous appearance and his command of this expedition, the masked man's confinement was not of his choosing. And despite the strength of his sword-arm and the unrelenting harshness of his demeanour, he was utterly dependent on his servant for food and drink.

One evening, as they sat around the smouldering, smoking excuse for a fire that was the best that could be managed in that world of dampness, she had asked the Buzzard why, having defied Jahan, he had not removed the mask that the prince had placed upon him. 'It must be unbearable in this heat. The air is so heavy. How can you even breathe?'

'Oh aye, I could take this off, but then what would happen? With this mask I can terrify any savage from here to the Cape. Without it I'm just a faceless cripple.'

'I pity you,' Judith said, with an absence of sentiment that made the words all the more telling.

The Buzzard leaned forward and drenched every word in venom as he said. 'Do not pity me, lassie. Keep your pity for yourself.'

They had made their way from the *Pelican* in the ship's pinnace, sailing a network of tributaries that threaded through a coastal fringe of lush vegetation that lay between land and sea. The waterways were more intricate and convoluted in their twists, turns and intersections than any maze the human mind could devise, but the Buzzard and Pereira, a grey-bearded veteran who carried himself with the dignity of officer rank, navigated as best they could. They used strips of canvas tied to the branches of the mangrove trees that lined the river banks to mark their passage, so that if they saw the strips again, as they often did, they knew that they must have turned back upon themselves. Sometimes they argued over which way to go. At other times they pointed to one passage or another, nodding with remembrance and giving their orders to the man at the tiller.

Where the streams slowed and widened into pools, they saw the great, bloated bodies of hippopotami. At the Buzzard's orders the sailors primed their muskets and lit their match cord before giving the fearsome creatures a wide berth. Judith knew them well, for she had often encountered them on the waterways of southern Ethiopia. However, Ann had never seen them before and she could not understand why the masked man took such precautions and the Africans looked so fearful.

'Look at them,' she giggled. 'Just lying there with their heads bobbing up and down, half in and half out of the water. All that you can see is their eyes and noses poking out of the river. It's so funny the silly way their ears twitch. And look! One of them has got a bird standing on his head!'

'You would not laugh if one of those creatures ever attacked you,' Judith said. 'An angry bull, or a cow with a young calf, would think nothing of charging this boat. On land, few men can outrun them, and with those great jaws they can cut you in half with a single bite.'

Just then one of the hippos yawned, revealing huge lower teeth that were as curved and pointed as a headman's axe and the smile disappeared from Ann's face.

And yet the greatest risk to life came not from mighty, charging beasts, but from the hordes of insects that plagued them, particularly at night, stinging and biting so that any exposed skin was soon left covered in swollen, red bites.

At least they had eaten well. Fish, oysters and crab were abundant. The porters hunted water birds with bows and arrows and collected sweet mangrove honey. From the tall white mangrove trees growing nearest the sea Judith pulled the thick, leathery, olive-green leaves, crushing them and adding them to her evening meal for the relief of her stomach cramps. She gathered the unripe fruit and smeared their pulp on the insect bites that covered her body, particularly her lower legs, and she used the sharpened twigs as tooth-picks.

On the second day in the estuary one of the sailors shot a fat, grey-skinned creature that looked like a seal with a dolphin's tail and a gentle face, with eyes as sad and sweet as a dog's and a mouth upturned in a permanent smile. 'It's called a dugong,' the Buzzard told them, in an uncharacteristically sociable moment. 'They eat sea grass. I dare say you'll find it makes good enough eating.'

It had taken five men to drag the wounded creature, which bore an expression of docile puzzlement, into the pinnace, where they beat it to death with a club. They butchered it and salted the flesh, which, just as the Buzzard had promised, kept them well fed for several days, the sailors arguing at every meal over whether it tasted more like beef or pork.

By the time the last of the dugong meat had been consumed, however, they had long since left the boat, for the water was no longer deep enough to be navigable and they were forced to continue on foot, crossing the tidal mudflats and more often than not wading up to their knees through brackish mud and water. From the small, sturdy, black mangroves in the deeper reaches of the mudflats the men cut branches that they burned to smoke and thus preserve the fish they caught.

Troops of white-throated monkeys chattered at their passing. Snakes and other reptiles slithered from their path, plopping into the water around them. Bats whirred overhead at night, while by day they frequently heard the flapping and honking of the herons, ducks and geese that had been disturbed by their passing. Now and then, a mangrove kingfisher streaked by in an arrow-like blur of bright colour.

But as the days went by no clue was offered as to where they were going or what the Buzzard's intentions were. All that Judith knew was that every plunging, strength-sapping step took her further from Hal. But at least she had gained something from the grim, sweaty trek through the mudflats. One of the Portuguese sailors had cut a straight branch from a tree for use as a fishing spear. Using his cutlass he had hacked the stick to a sharp point, when one mislaid chop cut too deep and the tip had broken off. As he trudged off to find another branch, swearing as he went, Judith had pulled the sharp little stake from the mud and tucked it away in her skirt.

It wasn't much of a weapon. It would not defend her against the Buzzard's sword or the sailors' muskets. But it was something of her own. And it gave her a tiny ray of hope.

The *Madre de Deus* dropped her anchor in the bay off Quelimane and all the slaves were herded onto the deck where they waited in fear and uncertainty for their turn to be rowed ashore. They went twelve at a time, not in the merchantman's own longboats, but in tenders rowed out from the shore.

Hal glanced over his shoulder at the *Madre de Deus* sitting serene on the shimmering water out in the bay. *If I ever lay eyes on her again I will send her to the sea bed*, he promised himself, fixing the merchantman in his mind. *And though Barros may beg me for quarter, I'll hoist the bastard to the yardarm and let the gulls pick his bones clean and white.*

When they reached the shore, Hal and the others in his party were ordered to stand in line while they were formed into a coffle: a line of slaves with chains around their necks and hands and linked by more chains, from the neck of one man to the hands of the poor soul behind him. Two of the men in the middle of the line were not harnessed together with the same chains as everyone else, however, but by a heavy wooden beam, perhaps two paces long, which had yokes, also made of wood, at either end. The yokes were positioned on the shoulders of the two men: to the back of one and the front of the other. In this way a rigid distance was maintained between the unfortunate individuals who had been chosen as beasts of burden. As a result they were obliged to march at exactly the same pace, and that obligation was then extended to the other men ahead of and behind them.

Barros had come ashore by the first boat and as the coffle was assembled he looked on, conversing with a man in a large straw hat who reminded Hal somewhat of Consul Grey, for he was round and ripe and, though he was mounted on a mule, he was dripping with sweat.

'As you can see, Senhor Capelo,' Barros told him, 'we have bought nothing but the finest stock in the market at Zanzibar. These are all fine specimens and I am certain that Senhor Lobo will be satisfied by their strength and endurance as workers.'

'One of them is white,' Capelo said, looking at Hal with a disapproving air. 'Whites never last very long.'

'You have no need to worry about this one,' Barros assured him. 'See for yourself. He is a fine specimen. Long-limbed and strong as an ox.'

Capelo gave a sceptical grunt, but accepted Barros's invitation nonetheless. He climbed down off his mule, walked across to Hal and examined him, feeling his thigh and bicep muscles, examining the whites of his eyes and his tongue and prodding his stomach. 'Very well, I shall take your word for it,' Capelo said. 'But if he fails to give satisfaction I will want an extra black to replace him and I'll expect it free of charge.'

'Of course, of course,' said Barros. 'You have the money for these men, though, yes?'

'Of course.' Capelo walked across to the mule, opened a saddle bag and pulled out a canvas sack that was heavy with coin. 'It is all there, the agreed amount. You may count it if you wish.'

'No need,' Barros said, with an ingratiating smile. 'I know that neither you nor Senhor Lobo would ever cheat me. So now, I will bid you farewell. I wish you a safe journey back to the mines.'

Barros departed. Capelo climbed back onto his mule, barked orders to the guards and then set off down the road. A second later, Hal felt the familiar sting of a whip on his shoulders, letting him know that he was expected to get moving too, and so the coffle began its long journey to the heart of Africa.

It took a while for the dozen chained men to get the hang of keeping their dressing as regularly as guardsmen on parade. Some stumbled and fell, bringing others down too, and more than once Hal felt himself dragged to the ground without any means of breaking his fall, for his hands were rendered useless by the chain that linked them. Their guards were Africans but they showed no mercy or sympathy towards their brothers in chains, lashing out with their wooden batons and long leather whips at anyone who did not move quickly enough to satisfy them.

They marched out of the port, through a grove of trees and into the buzzing hive that was Portuguese Quelimane. A newly built cathedral towered over clusters of primitive log huts and whitewashed mud dwellings. In the centre of the village stood the mud-brick ruins of an old fort and beside them the foundations of a new one under construction.

Slaves laboured and sweated in the heat. A team of them

hauled an enormous brass culverin up a ramp into the new fort, the wheels of its carriage creaking in complaint and the men's every step encouraged by the crack of the driver's whip. Oxen lowed as they dragged in heavy loads of cut timber. Men yelled and cursed and argued or suddenly burst out laughing.

A little further on stood a well-built gallows, the wood still new and clean. By contrast the corpse still hanging from the gibbet, turning slowly on the rope, was reeking rotten and seemed to be dressed in a black cloak, but which turned out to be merely a coating of flies that swarmed over it.

Men sat on the edge of the road smoking pipes and mending fishing nets. Their wives waded into the slow-moving black river to do their laundry. Their children played nearby: fighting with wooden swords or kicking a ball or throwing pebbles at a barking dog which was tied to a stake. A blacksmith was at work forging a new anchor, the sound of his hammer ringing on the anvil like the bell of a country church. An old woman hawked baskets of allegedly fresh fish. A pretty bare-chested black girl declared that her mangoes were the sweetest in Africa.

But none of the Quelimane population showed the faintest interest in the pitiful column of slaves and their guards who wended their way past them. It was a sight so common as to be passing mundane. With that reminder of just how far he had been brought down, Hal kept putting one foot after another, matching his strides exactly to those of the man in front of him as they left the outskirts of Quelimane and headed out into the bush.

J udith was nearing total exhaustion. Every muscle in her body throbbed and ached. Her vision swam and her head pounded as if her brain were shrinking in her skull, drying out like a fish carcass on the rack. And yet she kept pace with the rest of the slaves, refusing to let the masked man have the satisfaction of knowing how far gone she was.

The swamps and mudflats of the coast had long since given way to the savannah woodland of the interior. When first she had walked again on solid, dry land her feet, soaked in water for so many days, had been as soft as bread in a bowl of milk. They blistered and bled. But by now they had healed into hard calluses, leaving her with one less agony to endure. Often towards the end of another long day's march she was at the point of collapse, but always she was able to carry on. She could not give in while she carried such a precious burden in her womb.

Keep going! the child inside her seemed to say. *Don't give in to them. We can get through this. If I can fight then so can you.*

Ann also was nearing total exhaustion. Despite her own sorry condition Judith had to help the other girl, encouraging her when she slumped to her knees, drained of all will to go on. It was Judith who urged her on with soft words of reassurance, or at other times tongue-whipped her to her feet; anything to get Ann moving again when it seemed she would rather lie down and wait for death to give her surcease.

The masked man halted the caravan every three hours by his watch, allowing them half an hour's rest. Ann sat in the dust beside her now, hugging her knees, her face buried in her ragged skirts.

'Tonight,' Judith leaned closer to her and whispered. 'We'll do it tonight.'

Slowly and pathetically, Ann lifted her head. She blinked her teary eyes and sniffed. 'Do you mean it this time?'

They had talked about escape many times before, but they had never got further than merely talking.

'This time I mean it,' Judith assured her, afraid to say more because the *Pelican*'s sailors were sitting nearby, sharing a bottle of rag water and listening to the bawdy story one of their number was reciting.

'How?' There was a spark in Ann's sad eyes now, an ember of hope.

Judith glanced over at the sailors, then at the Buzzard who was already lying in his blankets, his hands behind his head, his sword placed carefully beside him. Because of the mask it was impossible to see whether he was awake or asleep. Then, as though he had caught her thoughts on the night breeze, like a predator scenting prey, the Buzzard sat up and turned his head towards her. The fiercely frowning single eye, the absurd, yet frightening beak and that sharp-toothed satyr smile made Ann whimper.

'Do not look at him,' Judith said in a low voice. She could see that Ann was trembling and so she took the girl's hand in hers and placed it on her own belly. 'Pretend we are talking about the child,' she said. Ann was still staring at the masked man. 'Ann,' Judith hissed and the girl swung her head round, then looked down at Judith's stomach, understanding at last, forcing an upward curl in the tight line of her lips.

Then Judith told her how they were going to escape.

It was after midnight and the moon was high. Judith and Ann moved quietly to the entrance of the lean-to shelter, careful not to wake any of the men who lay snoring in their blankets around a dying fire, fast asleep despite the night chorus of crickets and cicada beetles. The man on watch was Pereira, the grey-beard who had helped guide the pinnace through the mangroves and ever since continued to act as the navigator leading them to their destination. For all his age, he was alert enough and he turned as soon as they left their lean-to shelter.

'Ann needs to relieve herself,' Judith explained. 'She is too afraid to go alone.'

Pereira muttered a reply. 'Go there,' he pointed at a patch of open ground at the edge of the camp. Judith shook her head.

'Not in front of the men,' she said.

Pereira pondered his response for a minute. 'Stay here,' he ordered in his heavily accented English, and then walked past them back towards the fire.

They waited, Judith desperately hoping Pereira would not wake the Buzzard. But to her relief Pereira ignored the disfig-ured, sleeping figure; instead he crouched to shake one of his

Pelican crewmates by the shoulder. The sailor sat up and Judith could see his sleepy scowl in the firelight. Then with a resigned shrug he pushed back his blanket and rose to his feet. He lit the end of his slow match from the fire and came over to the two women. In one hand he gripped his musket, while with the other he signed for them to follow him.

'Are you sure you can't wait until morning?' Judith asked Ann. That was the code they had agreed upon earlier. Judith was giving Ann one last chance to back out.

'No, I need to go right now,' Ann replied, hardening the line of her mouth.

Judith nodded. She had expected Ann to renege. *Good for you, young lady*, she thought.

Their chaperon led them to a spot less than thirty paces from the camp where he stopped on the edge of a patch of long grass that swayed in the chill breeze. Even in the depths of night there was enough starlight that they did not need a torch, and Judith looked back to the camp, relieved to see that the thorn bush screen was so thick that even the fire beyond could not be seen. The thin grey smoke and occasional firefly spark drifting up to the sky was the only giveaway that men were camped out there on the savannah.

'Can you go there?' the sailor asked, pointing into the patch of grass.

Ann managed to look coy, glancing from him to Judith, and then back to their warder. She nodded, and made a gesture that he should turn his back while she went about her business. He obeyed her without quibble, and then went one better. As Ann hitched up her skirt and squatted, the young sailor lay his musket down on the ground beside him. Then he clamped his burning slow match between his teeth, unbuttoned his breeches and tugged his manhood out of the fly and began to relieve himself with a noisy gushing that covered Ann's ladylike dribble.

Judith waited until she heard the patter of his urine stream reach its zenith, then she ran her hand down the opening of the neckline of her dress until it closed around the sharpened branch of mangrove. She moved up behind the young sailor as silently as a stalking leopard, and waited until he turned back again towards her.

She launched herself at him and with all her weight behind it drove the sharpened end of the stake into the base of his throat. Then she used her impetus to hook her right leg behind his and carry him over backwards. She landed on top of him and with all the strength of both her arms drove the point of the stake deeper and worked it from side to side to inflict as much damage as possible. He gurgled and choked, but she had so damaged his throat and vocal cords that the sounds he was able to emit were muffled and inhuman, more the sounds of wild animals than those of a human being.

Within a very few minutes even these lapsed into complete silence. Judith pushed herself away from the corpse and sat panting as she regained control of herself. She had killed men before; scores of them on the battlefield. It took little time for her to recover.

'Quick!' she hissed at Ann. 'The musket!' Ann scrambled through the grass, and gathered up the dead man's weapon. Judith unbuckled his belt and pulled the leather shot pouch and powder flask from it. She also took his flint and steel, then snatched the dropped match cord from where it lay smouldering in the grass, and snuffed out the flame. She considered taking his cutlass too, but decided against it, for it was a heavy thing and neither of them needed anything that would slow them down. The musket and shot would have to suffice.

'Water?' she hissed.

Ann nodded, patting the flask at her hip. Judith also had her own flask, which she had rationed in readiness for this moment. She had watched their captors foraging and had learned a great deal about which plants and fruit were edible.

She looked up at the stars to orientate herself and then they ran. They fled southwards, as Judith was counting on the masked man to assume they would trek eastwards, back towards the coast the way they had come. Her intention was to turn east towards the sea only when they had put a goodly distance between themselves and the pursuit.

In the excitement of the escape their fatigue was half forgotten. They ran like driven wild animals.

The pinnace dropped Aboli and eight of his fellow Amadoda on a deserted beach just north of Quelimane. They took no supplies with them for they had no need. The land over which they were about to travel might seem barren and inhospitable to a white man, but to them it was as bountiful as a crowded marketplace. Nor were they weighed down by powder and shot, for they took no weapons but the spears, shields and throwing clubs with which they had been raised.

There was only one item from his new world that Aboli, on reflection, took back to the world in which he'd grown: a grappling iron on the end of a coil of rope. For a sailor on the *Golden Bough* it served as a means to grab on to and get aboard an enemy ship. Where he was going, Aboli reasoned, he might well need to get over a wall or inside an enemy's building in order to rescue Judith or Hal and so the iron came with him.

Big Daniel Fisher commanded the pinnace as it took his African crewmates to the shore. He was not, by nature or upbringing, a man who believed in indulging his emotions. But before he saw the Amadoda off, Daniel hugged Aboli, then took half a step back, slapped him on the shoulder and, with a catch in his voice, said, 'God bless you and your lads. Now go and get our captain back, aye, and his lady too.'

Aboli said nothing, just nodded, and the next thing Daniel knew the Amadoda had settled into the loping run that they would maintain all day, and half the night if they had to, and disappeared out of sight between the palm trees that lined the shore.

That first night, after killing the Portuguese sailor, Judith and Ann had flown like birds, full of fear and the desperate need to escape. But the next day was hard. The sun's heat pressed down on them like six feet of earth. The savage thrill of the murder ebbed away and fatigue flooded in once more, threatening to overwhelm them. They wasted no strength on talk, each lost in her own thoughts, drifting through the sea of tall grass like wreckage in the wake of a storm, until at last Judith admitted that they must rest.

On the second night they huddled together amongst the low-hanging, leafy branches of a khat tree, huffing into their hands and shivering with cold, when a sudden screaming yell came out of the dark. The scream finished with four sharp yaps, and suddenly Ann was clutching Judith's arms, her eyes round and full of terror.

'Jackal,' Judith said, but she saw that the girl was none the wiser. 'It is like a dog but no danger to us,' she explained. 'They eat rodents and birds and fruit. Even insects.' She chose not to mention that jackals would also prey on young antelope. Nevertheless, Ann shuffled closer still and every time the jackal called she started, her nails digging into the flesh of Judith's arm.

Judith had been torn over whether or not to light a small fire, not to keep warm, but rather to have the flame from which to light the match cord should they need to fire the musket. In the end she decided the risk of their pursuers seeing a fire or smelling its smoke on the night air was too great. And so they shivered, praying for dawn and the first pink blush of the sun over the eastern horizon.

Judith had not trusted Ann to stay awake and keep watch, for even as terrified as the girl was, she was down to the dregs of her strength. So Judith tore small pieces bark from the khat tree and chewed them, while the English girl looked on with amazement.

'I never saw anyone eating a tree,' Ann said, trying to muster a weary smile.

'In my country this tree is famous,' Judith replied. 'Indeed it is famous throughout the Horn of Africa.' She pulled off a leaf and offered it. 'Here, try it. But chew it well.'

Ann took the leaf, sniffed it, and put it in her mouth. She chewed slowly, as if half expecting it to poison her. Judith smiled. 'The men in my country can always be seen chewing the khat leaves, as goats chew the cud.'

'I can't imagine why,' Ann said, her lips turned down at the corners. 'It doesn't taste very nice. It's sour.'

Judith nodded. 'But it will make you feel better, stronger. Just wait and see.'

364

They did not have to wait long. After just a few more leaves Ann's chattering reminded Judith of the parakeets that roosted in the tall trees in the centre of the mountain village where she was born. The girl talked about her brave husband and how much she had loved him, of how they had met and of the plans they had made together that would now never come to pass.

Then like a small child wanting her favourite bedtime stories to be repeated again and again, Ann insisted on hearing all about Hal, though Judith had told her a score of times before and it made her very soul ache to think of him. She spoke of how she and Hal had met, when she had been the general leading the Christian army of Ethiopia against an army of Mussulmen. Ann's expression was, as always, a mix of awe and disbelief at Judith's telling of it, and Judith could understand that reaction, for looking at herself now, even she found it hard to believe she had once been the guardian of the Holy Grail and saviour of the emperor's throne.

'I can't believe I know a lady like you,' Ann said. 'And here we are, in the middle of the wilderness, and we're like sisters, aren't we, in a funny sort o' way, even though we're not even the same colour. So we'll stick together and help each other and that's how we'll get through it all, until we are safe again. No matter what.'

'No matter what,' Judith agreed.

For a while Judith let Ann talk, though she allowed her no more khat leaves because, as much as they had lifted the girl's mood, Ann needed her rest for the days to come. Judith craved sleep too but she knew she was stronger than Ann both in body and in spirit. She had, after all, two spirits driving her on. The child, even unborn, was already a warrior in its way, Judith knew, and she was certain it was lending her its own new strength now: a strength which transcended the frailties of her own body.

Moreover, the masked man was not the only predator to be feared out there on the savannah. If Judith slept at all that night she did so with one eye open.

The next day they set off again towards the breaking dawn. Stiffly at first, though relishing the rising sun's warmth on flesh that yet held the night's cold in it. They drank sparingly, barely wetting their throats before thrusting the stoppers back into the flasks. Judith admired Ann's restraint. Unlike her, this young English girl was not used to hardship, yet she seemed invigorated this morning. It was as if she had overturned some obstacle in her mind that had previously thwarted her. This was not quite Christ the Saviour rising from the dead and rolling aside the stone blocking the entrance to his tomb, but it was a miracle in its way, for Ann was renewed. Seeing her thus gave Judith hope that they could after all reach the coast. From there they would gain passage aboard some vessel bound for who knew where, just so long as it was away from the masked man.

'We'll find an English captain. A Company man perhaps,' Ann enthused, seemingly oblivious to her shoes which were torn and flapping, the mound of the little toe of her left foot poking from the split seam and bloody. 'I will tell him my story and he will see us safely delivered to Calcutta, or even all the way home to England.' She looked at Judith. 'The child will be safe there.' Her grimy face lit up. 'You can both come and live with me! I have family near Bristol. It's beautiful there. Peaceful. Civilized,' she added, making the comparison by looking around her. Clearly she was in awe of their surroundings, the sweeping panoramas and the huge landscapes, and Judith could only imagine how different this land was to England.

To the south a herd of several hundred buffalo darkened the savannah, grazing peacefully in the long grass. Their bellows, low grunts and croaks carried across the open space and Judith considered following the beasts, for she knew they would lead her to water later in the day. But she decided it was better to keep moving east while it was still light, and soon the buffalo were far behind them.

'It's safe in Westbury,' Ann said, picking up on the earlier thread. 'There's a church, the Holy Trinity, and the vicar lets me climb all the way to the top of the bell tower. From there you can see for miles around. It has a fine peal of six bells. Six! You should hear them, Judith! Oh but you would love the sound. It's quite beautiful.' Judith did not discourage the girl. It was clear that thoughts of home gave Ann strength, and so Judith allowed her to construct this fantasy. And yet she could not bring herself to indulge Ann completely. Even were they to make it safely to the coast and find a ship with a sympathetic captain, the thought of one day setting foot in the country of her beloved's birth, without Hal himself, was unbearable.

What a fool I have been, Judith thought. *Insisting on going to Zanzibar when I could have been safe aboard the* Bough. *What would it have mattered if Hal had bought the wrong medicines?* No matter how sick she had been, she would have been better off than she was now.

But it was too late to worry about that. She had fallen into her enemies' trap and the child inside her would never know its father. That was the price she had paid for her folly, and it sickened her.

'Look,' Ann said, diverting Judith from her sombre contemplation. The girl was pointing to a small shifting black mass amongst the yellow grass in the middle distance off to the north-east. 'What *is* that?' she asked. 'Looks like birds. But surely they're too big.' She was shielding her eyes against the sun as she tried to make it out.

'Vultures,' Judith said, as suddenly the black congregation

fragmented, several of the birds flapping and hopping, lumbering away to reveal a sight that stopped Judith's heart. Lions. Ann saw them too for she froze as Judith had done, the two of them slaves to instinct and fear which gripped their limbs and dried their mouths and raised the hairs on the backs of their necks.

One of the beasts turned and growled at a couple of birds which had the audacity to sidle in close enough to peck at the carcass, and they hopped away though not for long. Judith counted five in the pride, but knew there could easily be more lying unseen in the long grass.

'They are too busy to concern themselves with us,' Judith said, hoping she was right. Hoping that the kill – a bushbuck or lesser kudu by the looks – still had plenty of meat left on its bones to keep the lions busy. *Eat well,* she thought, watching the beasts tearing into the flesh, the carcass seeming to convulse, its legs jerking as if it were still alive. *Eat well so that you will be fat and lazy tomorrow,* she told them silently, *and so that we may be on our way.*

They continued south-east to give the pride a wider berth, trekking uphill for a while and panting with the effort of it, barely sweating because they had taken so little water. Their lips were dry and split, and Ann's once pale skin was red, burnt and blistered though she did not complain. They followed an escarpment edge for a while before tending right, away from the edge and into woodland, and at sunset they crossed a small stream from which they filled their flasks, but only after drinking until they were fit to burst.

'We should camp here, Judith. By the stream,' Ann said.

'No.' Judith shook her head. 'See there?' She pointed south to where the stream widened and impala and a dozen or so suni antelope stood lapping up the water, drinking with as much appetite as the women had done. 'Leopard and lion, maybe cheetah too will know that this is where those animals come at dusk. It is not safe for us here.'

Ann smiled in spite of it all. 'We don't have to worry about such things in Westbury-on-Trym,' she said. 'My ma's ginger tom is the fiercest animal round our way,' and even Judith laughed at that.

It was dark when they made camp. Judith decided that this time they would have a fire. If not for the lions she would never have risked a fire in case the masked man was nearby. Besides, both she and Ann had spent almost as much time looking behind them as in front in the last days and neither had seen any sign of men following them.

With the flint and steel she had taken from the dead Portuguese sailor, and using an old weaver bird's nest for tinder, she coaxed some embers into flaming life, but only after digging a hole in the ground so that the flame itself could not be seen. The glow from it probably could though, so she did her best to screen it with some soft woody branches from a shrub which was studded with yellow-gold flowers. Without a blade it had taken much effort to twist and break the branches off but it was worth it. She told herself that the lions and any other beasts would smell the smoke and turn tail. And should they need to use the musket, the fire would mean that they could light the match quickly.

'It's strange how even a small fire like that can lift the spirits,' Ann said, a smile on her cracked lips as she stared into the flames. The night chorus of insects and countless other unknown creatures seemed to fill the darkness around them, but the feeble flame was something to cling to, so that Judith was almost certain she had made the right decision.

They ate fruit that Judith had picked from a huge baobab tree. She told Ann that it was called monkey bread, and while

369

they ate, she used strips of tree bark as bandages to bind Ann's bleeding feet. Then, when Ann fell asleep, Judith chewed some more of the khat leaves that she had saved. But even they could not keep her awake.

Dawn was still a long way off when the last of the flames flickered and died.

And then the hyenas came.

The second day of pursuit had ended and the Buzzard's personal slave, Jomo by name, was pouring water into his bone-dry mouth. It was a moment in the day that the Buzzard craved more than any other and yet hated also, for the way in which he sucked at the metal spout, like a baby suckling its mother's teat, only served to emphasize his helplessness. Jomo knew this and was accustomed to his master being even more curt and demanding than at other times as he sought to re-establish his power. It was not, therefore, a good time to approach him with anything resembling a request. Yet the two porters had pestered him until he felt that he had no choice but to speak on their behalf.

'Master,' he began, taking advantage of the fact that the Buzzard could not speak so long as he kept the spout in his mouth hole. 'Forgive me, but I speak for my brothers, too. We

371

wish you to know, oh great one, that we are now very close to the women you seek. If we keep going a little longer we may find them soon enough, even in the dark.'

The Buzzard gave a rough shake of his head to free his mouth. 'May find them, you say?'

'Yes, master.'

'Not "will find them" then?'

'Master, it is impossible to be certain about the future. That is the will of God. But it is likely.'

'Is it likely that it will be easier to find them in the morning?'

'Yes, master.'

'Then that is what we will do. So get me my food and stop babbling at me like a black baboon.'

Jomo went away to make the master's soft porridge, though he seasoned it with a helping of his own piss and snot.

A few hours later, however, he had grabbed the Buzzard's shoulder and was shaking it hard to wake him. The beak turned and the grinning, frowning, terrible visage stared at him.

Before it could speak, Jomo said, 'Master! Master! We have to go now . . . the women!'

'What the hell do you mean?' the Buzzard asked.

'Listen, master . . . listen to the night!'

So the Buzzard fell silent. And he listened. And a moment later he was jumping to his feet and shouting, 'Get up! Get up you scurvy scum!' and then he picked up his sword and ran off into the night as though his very life were at stake.

As indeed it was.

Judith woke to a depraved whooping and lowing. Two hyenas, the biggest she had ever seen, were running back and forth

372

through the long grass in front of where she and Ann lay, their feral excitement filling Judith with terror.

Ann woke, saw the hyenas and screamed, 'Go away!' She crawled back deeper into the bushes, trying to escape. 'Go away you devils!'

Far from scaring the hyenas off, her fear only agitated them more, making them giggle and whoop.

Stiff, shivering with cold and fear, Judith crawled over and peered into the fire pit. The ashes were still warm so she took a stick and stirred them but there were no glowing embers to be seen.

'Shoot them!' Ann pleaded. 'Shoot one and the other will run away!'

But without a flame to light the match cord the musket was useless. And anyway, Judith thought she knew what that ungodly whooping meant and if she were right . . .

On her knees she took up the little leather pouch containing the flint and steel, fumbling at the drawstring, her hands numb from the cold night. Out they fell onto the dirt. She picked them up. The stench of the creatures filled her nose.

'Hurry!' Ann said.

She made a little pile of tinder from what was left of the bird's nest. Struck the flint against the steel and a few sparks flew into the air. But they were not enough to light the tinder, nowhere near.

'Please, Judith. Hurry!'

Most hyenas were timid around humans. They were cowardly creatures, Judith knew, particularly those with striped pelts. But these two with their grey-red coats and dark brown spots were bold bristling beasts. One of them darted in close to Ann, swinging its large head up and down and laughing.

Ann screamed and the creature cackled and whooped and backed off.

373

'Oh God!' Ann cried. 'Oh God help us . . . please!'

The night was suddenly filled with a savage, insane cacophony. Judith did not look up. She did not need to. She knew the first two were calling the rest of their clan, inciting them to come and join the slaughter, and now the beasts were all around them, whirling in the dark, eyes and teeth flashing.

Her hands shook uncontrollably as she struck sparks into the tinder.

'We're going to die,' she heard Ann whimper.

But then, at last, the first spark landed and a tiny flame fluttered into life. She picked the ball of tinder up and cupped her hands round it, blowing softly to breathe strength into the delicate fire within.

'Judith!'

A flame burst from the old grass and the hyenas backed away from her, whooping and chattering, suddenly wary of the fire, and Judith glanced but could not see Ann now for the two dozen or more hunched animals skipping and whirling around her. There was a small pile of sticks beside the ashes but it would take too long to get another fire going. Nor would the kindling burn for long. But she *did* have the musket.

Lord help us, Judith prayed, placing the end of the slow match into the flame and leaving it there while she grabbed hold of the musket, shot pouch and powder flask.

'Away, you devils!' she yelled, lifting the musket and opening the priming pan. She pulled the flask's stopper with her teeth, poured a measure of black powder into the pan, then slid the pan cover back and blew off the excess powder. Then she dropped the musket's butt onto the ground and poured the main powder charge down the muzzle.

'I'm coming, Ann!' she called, crouching and pulling up some grass which she pressed into her mouth and began to chew. She would be aiming low and without a wad to tamp the bullet down it might roll harmlessly out of the barrel. Then she took a ball, thumbed it down the muzzle and spat the grass down after it.

'Don't let them eat me!' Ann begged as Judith drew the wooden scouring stick from its place in the musket's stock and reversed it, striking it against her own chest to shorten it to a handful. She rammed the wad and ball down and saw that the kindling had burnt out but that the slow match had caught and she snatched it up, blowing on the tip so that the cord, which was impregnated with saltpetre, glowed red like a little evil eye in the darkness.

Leave her! the unborn child in Judith's belly said. *We may only get one chance to fire the musket. Do not waste it on the girl. Save it! We will need it. See, the beasts are coming for us too!*

And they were. Whilst most of the hyenas swarmed round Ann, six or seven of the beasts had turned their attentions on Judith again. Stiff-haired, their tails held high and forward over their backs, they ran in close, snapping their bone-crushing jaws at her, rousing one another to go for the kill.

She fitted the match cord into the clamp and pulled the trigger, relieved to see the glowing tip come down onto the pan cover, meaning she had judged the length correctly so that it would hit the powder when she uncovered the pan and opened fire.

'Away!' she shrieked. 'Away!' She stamped a foot and thrust the musket's barrel at the nearest hyena which grunted and cackled and gave ground even as others tried to come at her from behind. Judith twisted, swinging the musket to fend them off, though she did not fire. Not yet.

She waded in amongst the stinking maelstrom of screeching scavengers, heading for Ann, her eyes sifting the chaos for the largest hyena. If she killed that one maybe the others would flee. And there it was, its dorsal mane bristling as it bounded up to Ann who was crouching in the bush, an arm raised defensively as she tried to get to her feet.

But if you miss? Then what? the child in her belly asked. *What will happen to us then?*

'Kill it!' Ann screamed. 'Kill it, Judith, just kill it!'

Judith put the musket to her shoulder and took aim. She knew the beasts were behind her. They were everywhere, buffeting her with their muzzles now, too many to count. She could feel their breath on her, hotter than the night air, but she did not take her eyes off the big hyena. The beast was moving unpredictably, bobbing its big head and darting in and out. It was a difficult shot, too risky.

'Here, you devil!' Judith yelled in Amharic, her mother tongue, blowing on the match clamped in the serpent's jaws. 'Come and see what I have for you!' She could see Ann now, see the tears running down the girl's sun-ravaged cheeks, her eyes blazing with terror. Then she felt something beneath her foot and looked down to see Ann's water flask. She picked it up and hurled it with all her strength and it struck the hyena on the rump.

The creature giggled and turned, swinging its big head towards Judith.

That was all she needed. In a heartbeat she knew she would never get a better chance and her finger curled around the musket's trigger. Even now, the tide could be turned. They might just survive.

Then Ann made the worst decision of her life. She ran.

The beast followed her.

'No!' Judith screamed and pulled the trigger. The musket roared, spitting flame in the darkness, and the hyenas squealed at the thunder of it, dispersing in all directions. Yet Judith felt nothing but despair. The hyena's sudden movement had made it a moving target and she had missed it. She saw the ravening hyena lunge at Ann and knew it had bitten her near her left hip, though Ann's scream was lost amidst the savage howls and demented laughter as the rest of the pack coalesced around the girl. Their shock at the musket's roar forgotten now in the excitement, the beasts followed their matriarch's lead, darting in, biting, pulling back lowing and whooping, then wheeling to go for the girl again.

Judith reversed the musket and, gripping it by the barrel, brandished it like a club, bringing the heavy stock down onto a hyena's back with a crack. The beast screeched in pain, retreating from her, but the others had the scent of blood in their noses now and were only interested in Ann. One animal broke from the pack and to her horror Judith saw that its muzzle was wet with fresh blood.

Leave her, the unborn child inside her pleaded. *There is nothing we can do for her now. But if we stay they will tear us apart.*

'Help me!' Ann screamed.

The entire hyena clan was around Ann now like a seething, cacophonous black sea as Ann's body was pulled this way and that. Judith had experienced enough horrors for any lifetime on the battlefields of Ethiopia, but none compared to this: a woman being dismembered before her very eyes. She felt a sudden, overwhelming shock of nausea, bent double and vomited into the grass. A hyena at the fringes of the mass must have smelt the disgorged contents of her stomach for it turned and loped over and Judith backed away, raising her makeshift club, but the beast was not interested in her as it began to gulp down her steaming vomitus.

Then a sword hacked into the hyena's skull and it collapsed, shaking and frothing, its long teeth bared in a grimace of death. Judith spun and the masked man was there.

'Help her!' she said.

Sword in hand, the man stepped out in front of her, putting himself between Judith and the hyenas, and then the other men were there too, the Portuguese sailors and the two tribesmen, looming out of the darkness, taking up defensive positions around her. 'Help her, damn you!' Judith screamed. 'For God's sake, somebody help her!'

The masked man said nothing. He stood there, head tilted on one side, the single eye behind its hole fixed on the vile scene before them.

'Give me your sword and I will help her!' Judith said.

That leering face turned to her. 'Shut your mouth and watch,' it snarled, as one of the sailors snatched the musket from her hands.

A hyena jumped and clamped its jaws on Ann's upper arm. She stumbled under its weight, her face bright in the starlit gloom, her eyes seeming to fix on Judith's own one last time before she was pulled down into the growling maelstrom and lost from sight.

'Please!' Judith said, but even as she said it she knew there was no helping Ann now. The hyenas were eating her alive. She could hear their jaws snapping shut, hear them gulping down gobbets of flesh.

Even so, she watched, her eyes glutting themselves on the horror of it, until at last the masked man signalled at his men that they should be on their way.

'Lucky for you one of the Negroes got a whiff of your fire on the air,' the grey-beard officer said. 'Otherwise those devils would be feasting on you and your babe by now.'

Judith said nothing. She had no words. She put both hands on her belly, fingers pressing into her own flesh that they might feel a little foot or hand, desperate as she was to touch the child and reassure it that they were safe now.

Yet she knew in her heart that her reassurances were false. For every instinct told her that, however much she had suffered up till now, it was surely nothing compared with the suffering to come.

Hal lost track of the days and could not say how far inland they had walked. At night though, he watched the moon cycle through its first quarter, to full moon, to third quarter, so that he guessed they had been travelling some three weeks, trudging on in silent monotony. Deeper they went, towards the giant granite outcrops and mountains rising majestically out of the bush in the west, into an Eden of golden grassland savannah, miombo forest and flood plain.

Some nights, if the rain was lashing down, they made rudimentary shelters by stringing up canvas from tree branches, and would sit with their eyes stinging and coughing from the trapped smoke, though they would never be without a blaze because all knew that wild beasts smelt fire from miles around and feared it.

'Except for the lion,' Aboli had told Hal once. 'A lion will walk around the campfire to get a good look at what is going on.'

If the days were too hot, however, and there was enough moon and starlight to see by at night, they trekked then with the star-crammed vault of heaven dizzying in its magnificence above them, its unchained enormity like a promise of freedom in another, better world. One dawn found them walking along a spine of high ground overlooking a lake. The waters, whilst low following the dry season, were far from unoccupied, the most abundant and obvious residents being a pod of hippos that wallowed in the shallows. Crocodiles, too, lay basking in the rising sun. They seemed barely conscious, still as logs until some secret sign made a flock of white birds take wing and wheel into the south, at which point the crocodiles slid down the muddy banks into the water.

They rested through the heat in the middle of the day sleeping in the shade of tall borassa palms and it was almost sunset when they came back down to the plain. Capelo seemed on edge, constantly mopping his brow despite being the only man who was not walking on his own two legs. In the distance ahead of them families of warthogs scurried off into cover. Nightjars and bats streaked in the gathering dusk. The column followed the course of a dry riverbed, which funnelled them between two low hills into a valley whose steep sides bristled with spiny gooseberry trees and other thicket and scrub.

Finally Capelo decided to make camp for the night and the slaves, Hal included, were loosened from the chains around their wrists and put to work erecting thick spiny thorn bush fences to protect them from predators, and setting fires that provided further protection and kept them warm. The fat man's mood was still very obviously unsettled and one of the guards asked him, 'What troubles you, senhor?'

'We are being watched,' Capelo said.

'Are you sure, sir?' the guard replied. 'I have seen no one.'

'You do not have to see a man to know he is there. We are being watched.'

Aboli was barely ten paces away from the thorns that surrounded the slavers' encampment. A day had passed since he and his men had struck the coffle's unmistakable trail and they had caught up with it a matter of hours after that. It was tempting to attack now, for it would be a simple matter to overpower Capelo and the guards. But then what?

It was not enough to rescue Hal, he had to free Judith, too. He had already sent two men ahead and they had returned with the news that the mines were only a day's march away. They had also found another trail: eight men and one woman, who had reached Lobo's land this very day.

Within another day, then, Hal and Judith would both be in the same place. That would be the time to go and get them. And until that time, Aboli was keeping his presence secret, and allowing Hal to remain enslaved, however much it pained him to do so.

It was very seldom that Judith and the Buzzard had ever agreed on anything. But, though neither of them said a word, both knew that the other had precisely the same reaction: *this is Balthazar Lobo?*

Here was a man who had carved out his own kingdom in the heart of Africa, who'd discovered hills full of gold and brought armies of slaves to get it for him. Judith was expecting a crude, hard-hearted bully, but she had no doubt that he would

382

be strong, dominant and virile too. Instead Lobo turned out to be a small, scrawny, dried up old stick of a man whose face was dominated by a long, underslung lower jaw that jutted out so far that his lower teeth were further forward than the upper ones. On her travels in Europe Judith had heard stories of the Habsburg dynasty that had dominated Spain, Germany, Austria and the entire Holy Roman Empire at various times. Its members had been infamous for their extraordinarily ugly lower jaws. Perhaps Lobo was some bastard son of the Habsburg line, exiled to Africa to avoid him embarrassing the rest of the clan.

'So,' he said, looking appreciatively at Judith – there was, she noticed, a thin trail of drool trickling down that grotesque chin – 'you're the pretty thing who wants to be my next wife? Well, I dare say you're not looking your best after your long journey. Why don't you go and rest, my dear, eh? Your chamber has been prepared. We've even found a wedding dress for you. It's only been used twice before. You will sleep tonight and then tomorrow you can rest your weary legs, wash off the dirt, eat some proper food – my cooks will prepare whatever takes your fancy. In short, do whatever will best prepare you to look your prettiest tomorrow night. Then you will put on your magnificent gown, present yourself to me and I shall decide what I want to do with you.'

He fixed her with a piercing stare and suddenly Judith felt the full force of Lobo's will and understood how, as a younger man, he had been able to carve out his own corner of the wilderness for himself alone.

'Hmm . . .' He tilted his head to one side as he sized her up. 'Nice plump breasts, rounded stomach, and yet the legs are quite thin. It's almost as though . . . you're not pregnant already are you, girl?'

Judith said nothing.

'Would it matter if she were?' the Buzzard asked. 'Suppose, and I speak on an entirely hypothetical basis, but just suppose that this woman carried the child of a tall, young, strapping white man. Suppose she gave birth to this child when married to you. Why, that would make the child yours. Would it really matter if you had not planted the seed from which it had grown?'

Lobo looked Judith up and down. 'No,' he said. 'I do not suppose that it would. Sleep well, young lady. I want you at your best when next I set eyes on you.'

The Amadoda looked down on the sprawling complex where Balthazar Lobo lived and made his fortune. His house was built in a hollow square, with windowless walls of whitewashed mud, more than twice as tall as a man and topped by battlements on the outside, while the inner part of the house opened on to an inner courtyard that was bright with greenery and flowers. *Surely that is where they have taken Judith*, Aboli thought to himself, pleased that he had possessed the foresight to bring the grappling iron.

He felt a tapping on his shoulder and saw one of his men pointing down to a line of men, led by a fat, white man on a donkey approaching the entrance to the complex. That was Capelo and there, sure enough, the one white man in the middle of the line of slaves was Hal.

'I see you, Gundwane,' Aboli said and the words carried extra weight, for 'I see you' was the formal greeting used by peoples across southern Africa. 'Be patient now, Captain. We will not be long in coming.'

And then Aboli saw something else and he whispered a single word to himself: '*Faro?*'

W hen the sun had risen that day, Capelo had addressed the slaves, telling them where they were going, who their new master would be, and what brutal punishments they could expect if they dared to displease him. Now as the coffle approached the mines Hal, too, noted the small white fort that dominated the area and concluded that Lobo must use it as a residence and as a means of both imposing himself on his slaves and defending himself should they ever rise up against him.

Moving further into the complex, they passed an enclosure, ringed by a sheer-sided ditch at least twelve feet deep and twenty across, like an empty castle moat. There appeared to be two ways of crossing the ditch. One was a rope bridge, with a narrow walkway of planks that led from one side to the other, without even a gate on either end, and the other was a drawbridge that hung from a stone gatehouse on the outside of the ditch and could be lowered back down into the enclosure.

Hal frowned in puzzlement. Whatever was in the enclosure was sufficiently dangerous that it required a ditch to keep it in. Yet a hunting predator like a lion or leopard would be down one side of that ditch and up the other in no time, assuming it didn't just trot across the bridge. Perhaps Lobo kept elephants. Hal knew that they had been used for both ceremonial and military purposes for thousands of years. But if so, they were nowhere to be seen.

Then Hal saw the inhabitant for whom the enclosure had

been built, a huge, two-horned, grey-skinned mass of muscle and fury that trotted to the edge of the ditch, drawn by the scent of unfamiliar human beings, and stood just a few paces away from the coffle's line of march, swinging its great head this way and that, as if eager to avenge itself on anyone or anything for the indignity of its imprisonment.

Capelo turned in the saddle and said, 'Have you ever seen anything like that in your life, Englishman?'

Hal had, many times, but the less he appeared to know, the less of a threat he would be seen to be, so he shook his head in dumb ignorance.

'It is a rhinoceros, though the people here call it "faro", Capelo informed him. 'Senhor Lobo is the only man in the world to have one in captivity. A dozen men died trying to catch it. But Senhor Lobo said that he had to have a rhino, and in this place, his word is the law.'

Lobo nodded towards the beast, which seemed to have armour-plating rather than skin. 'Look at that front horn of his, the big one. It must be twice the length of a cutlass. You should see the damage it can do. I've seen men impaled on it like pieces of meat on a kebab. Take a good look and pray to God you never see it again, for if you do it will be because you have displeased Senhor Lobo.'

Capelo reined in his donkey and let Hal walk level with him before he started moving again so that they were side-by-side as he leaned down and said, 'If a slave is disobedient, if he fails to respect his masters, if he does not work as hard as he should, then he is not just whipped. He's thrown into that enclosure. And he does not come out alive. Do you understand?'

'Yes, master,' Hal said.

'You're not going to be disobedient, or cheeky, or proud, are you?'

'No, master.'

'Lick my boot, Englishman,' Capelo said and stuck out one of his feet, like a bishop presenting his ring finger.

Hal leaned over as best he could, for the collar round his neck inhibited his movement and began licking the dust and filth of the overseer's dirty boot.

Go ahead, humiliate me if it makes you feel bigger, Hal thought. *I've survived far worse than this.*

The sun was starting to drop towards the horizon as they were taken to a stockade of impenetrable thorn bush set up at the foot of a hill. Slaves were pushing wooden carts up and down metal rails which led into tunnels that disappeared into the hillside. The carts coming out of the mine were piled high with ore, which was taken to another area where more slaves with sledgehammers pounded the ore into a powder that could then be sifted under running water to search for specks of pure gold. While the work went on, other slaves were lighting braziers filled with wood and dried grass that would provide both light and warmth as the work continued into the night.

Everywhere there were men, both black and white, armed with whips, guns, clubs and vicious, broad-bladed panga knives watching over slaves, urging and whipping them to work harder, or simply watching to make sure that none dared pocket or swallow any gold for himself.

Inside the stockade stood a row of long wooden huts with thatched roofs. The coffle was brought to a halt in front of one of them. 'This is where you will live,' Capelo informed them. 'It is the last home you will ever know, for you will work here until you die. Soon your shackles will be released. This does not mean that you are free. I shall remind you now, for the last time, that any attempt to escape is punishable by death. Soon

388

you will have food. Eat well, for it is the only meal you will get until this time tomorrow. And in the morning you will be put to work.'

Then the chains were removed from their hands and necks and they were given small wooden bowls containing watery millet porridge in which floated inedible chunks of gristle. Hal had learned in his time at the Cape Colony that a man forced into hard labour should never refuse any food, no matter how repellent, and he wolfed it down, for the less time it took to consume the sooner one forgot how disgusting it was.

There were no beds or even bunks inside, simply two long, low wooden tables, roughly six feet wide that stretched the full length of the hut. As the dozen or so men from the coffle lay down to sleep the arrangements seemed almost spacious. It was only when another fifty slaves appeared, sweaty, rank and exhausted from their labours, and forced their way onto the tables, barging the newcomers out of their way as they did, that Hal realized that the crowding was as bad as on any slave ship. He found himself forced up against the wall of the hut, with just about enough room to sleep on his side, with his back against the man next to him and his face pressed hard against the mud wall. The squeeze was so tight that he could barely move a muscle.

But it did not matter. He was finally in the same place as Judith. For now, the few hundred yards that separated them might as well have been a thousand miles, but he would find a way to bridge that gulf, find Judith and make good their escape. It might take him a few weeks, or even, God forbid, a few years. But he would do it.

And having placed that thought in the forefront of his mind, Hal closed his eyes. For if there was another lesson that the

Cape had taught him it was that sleep, as much as food, was essential to survival.

T he Buzzard was faced with a most reluctant bride. 'Put on the damn dress, woman, or ...'

'Or what?' Judith asked. 'What will you do with your one hand? Hit me? I will evade you. Have some slave or other hold me down while you whip me? That would only spoil the goods before Senhor Lobo can get his hands on them. Kill me? But how much money can you make from my corpse?'

'Prattle on all you like, you proud bitch, but you're in no position to talk. Lobo's got no use for a woman he can't bed. But he's always got a use for another slave. When that wedding bell rings, you'll be down the aisle or down the mines. And to hell with the money, it would be worth losing every penny just to see you getting your comeuppance at the end of an overseer's whip.'

He sat down on a silk-upholstered chair and snapped his thumb and forefinger for his slave to bring him more wine. 'So,' the Buzzard rasped. 'An hour until you decide which you'd prefer, a long life of luxury as Senhora Lobo, or a nasty, brutish and short one as his slave. Personally, I cannot see why you're having such a hard time making up your mind. If it were me, I'd let the drunken old lecher do what he damn well pleased if it meant I got a soft bed and a full belly. But what do I know, eh?'

T he stockade where the slaves were kept was guarded by two men at its entrance and another two who patrolled the perimeter in opposite directions, crossing one another's paths two times per circuit. As one of the guards walked by the position where the Amadoda were hiding in the moon shadow cast by a giant baobab tree, one of the tribesmen rose silently to his feet. He was holding a knobkerrie, a club cut from a single piece of hardwood with a narrow shaft that was easy to grip at one end and a bulbous round head at the other. He waited until the guard was directly opposite him and then threw the knobkerrie as straight and true as an arrow. It hit the guard on the temple and killed him instantly.

The Amadoda emerged briefly from the shadows, ran across to the fallen man, carried him off the smooth, hard path that the guards' feet had beaten down over the years and slit his throat, just to make sure he was out of the way.

A few minutes later the second guard came by. He seemed puzzled, looking this way and that, evidently wondering what had happened to his comrade. He stopped walking and took a look around, close to the Amadoda's hiding place. Once again the knobkerrie flew out of the shadows, with exactly the same result.

The men standing on either side of the gate knew nothing of the Amadoda's presence until they felt the prick of the stabbing spear blades that were cutting their throats. Their bodies were rolled into the bottom of the thorn bushes and two of the Amadoda took their places, while Aboli led the rest of his men into the stockade and, having watched their captain every inch of the way, went straight to the hut where Hal was sleeping.

Aboli's appearance in the hut caused one or two of the slaves to wake. 'Do not trouble yourselves, my brothers,' Aboli whispered in Swahili, the language that almost all the peoples of that part of Africa understood, even if it was not their mother tongue. 'I seek the white man who arrived here today. Our master, Senhor Lobo, is very curious about this white slave and wishes to meet him. Do you know where I may find him?'

He was directed to the end of the long line of sleeping slaves. More were waking now and starting to talk. Some were angry at being disturbed and voices began to be raised.

'Hush, or you will wake your brothers in the other huts,' said Aboli, grabbing Hal's arm and pulling him out of his squashed position like a very large cork from a very tight bottle.

'What if we do? They are not my brothers,' one man argued. 'And who are you? I do not know you.'

The situation was slowly spiralling out of control. 'All is well, we are going now,' Aboli said, as he and Hal made their way to the door. One of the slaves tried to block their way and stood across the entrance facing the two departing men. He was felled by a knobkerrie in the back of the head, thrown by one of the Amadoda waiting outside the hut.

'Run!' Aboli hissed, in English now as he and Hal hurdled the fallen slave and dashed full pelt for the gate. There was no time for either man to express his gratitude or relief at seeing the other. That would come later. For now they just had to survive. Aboli had a panga that had been taken from one of the guards the Amadoda had killed and he passed it to Hal like a relay baton without either man breaking stride. By the time they reached the gate slaves were spilling out of Hal's hut and shouting, 'We are free! We are free!' to the men in the other huts. Hal cursed under his breath for all hope of surprise had vanished and all they could hope for now was that the sudden slave uprising would act as a distraction.

He heard a shout behind him and the crash of a musket being fired. In the confusion he and Aboli had somehow led their small raiding party right past the barracks where the overseers slept and now there was an ever-growing troop of them on their trail. Someone cried out, 'To the stables! We'll ride them down!' But even if some of their pursuers had gone for the horses instead, that still left an ever-increasing number who were on their heels and getting closer. Another shot rang out and one of the Amadoda screamed in pain and fell to the ground, mortally wounded.

'Don't stop, Gundwane!' Aboli shouted. 'We can do nothing for him.'

Hal didn't reply. He didn't have the breath for it. From behind him there came the sound of a volley of musket fire, the response, presumably, to the slaves running wild inside the stockade. Hal did not care about them. He had enough to worry about putting one foot in front of another. His leg muscles were burning, his chest was heaving, he was close to the end of his tether. And then, up ahead, he saw a tall structure looming up out of the darkness and suddenly his spirits soared. There was still hope!

In Lobo's private fort Judith had given in and agreed to put on the wedding dress, which, to judge by the dirt, mould and even what looked like bloodstains ground into its faded silk fabric, had seen repeated service, but not for quite some time. Though she hated to admit it, the Buzzard's logic was unarguable. As long as she went along with the ruler of this private kingdom there was hope. If she reduced herself to slavery there was none.

But then she heard an explosive crackle that she recognized at once as gunfire: a few individual shots and then, in percussive crashes that steadily increased in volume, the sound of volleys being brought to bear with rising numbers of guns. For a moment it struck her that she was probably the only bride in all Africa who could decode the apparently random sounds of battle with such precision.

But even if brides could not work out what was happening, the Buzzard could. 'Stay here,' he said. 'For your safety's sake. I'm going to see what's happening.'

Again she was obliged to see the force in his argument. Whoever won, a woman in a low-cut silk gown would be ravished with a ruthless voracity that would make the hyenas that had eaten Ann seem tame.

Hal pointed up ahead of him and Aboli saw at once what he meant. For there were the stone gateposts that rose on either side of the drawbridge that led into the rhino's enclosure. And there was the windlass that wound the rope that lifted the drawbridge up and down. Hal dashed to it and began hacking at the rope while Aboli and the Amadoda formed a shield wall around him.

Hal knew full well that animal-hide shields would be no defence against musket rounds, but the repeated combination of soaking rain and baking sun seemed to have fused and hardened the fibres of the rope and it was the devil's own job to cut through them. Again and again he brought the blade of the panga down onto the rope. Not twenty yards away the overseers were reloading the muskets that they had already fired.

Biting the end off their cartridges.

Come on!

Pouring powder into the priming pan.

Cut, damn you!

Ramming the rounds into the barrels.

Almost there!

Raising the guns into the firing position.

Yes!

With an almighty crash, almost as loud as gunfire, the

hardwood drawbridge smashed down onto the earth of the enclosure and the Amadoda broke ranks and ran across it into the darkness, towards the waiting rhino.

There was a crackle of individual musket shots behind them, but none of the rounds hit.

They did, however, serve one purpose, which was to rouse the bull rhino.

Hal and Aboli almost ran straight into him as he loomed up out of the darkness.

A rhinoceros has very poor eyesight. Its hearing and sense of smell, however, are both extremely acute. It is therefore at least as dangerous at night as it is by day since its strongest senses work equally well in both circumstances. And irrespective of the hour, a bull rhino is an equally cussed, irascible, ill-natured beast.

It may not have seen Aboli waving his sword, but it certainly heard him yelling at it in the language of the forests, and perhaps it understood those words for the challenge they were, for it tossed its head, answering Aboli's challenge by saluting him with his magnificent horn, which was nearly five feet long, and charging straight at him. Aboli jumped out of its path at the last instant, rolling in the mud and coming onto his feet again as lithe as a panther. The massive beast would have smashed every bone in Hal's body had he not thrown himself aside, sprawling into the mud as the rhino barrelled past, Hal's nostrils full of its musty stink.

The bull tore across the baked mud ground impossibly fast for its size and kept going past the scattering Amadoda and onto the drawbridge where the first of the pursuers had been running into the enclosure. Now, too late, they realized the doom that was bearing down upon them and they turned to try to retreat, but the press of men behind them made it impossible to escape.

The hammering of the rhino's feet against the boards of the drawbridge sounded in the ears of Lobo's men like the crack of doom itself. The bull lowered his horn and speared one young man right through the belly, impaling him. The rhino stopped, as if confused by the weight it was bearing across its head. It snorted and grunted, wheeling round and round its bloody horn protruding three feet out of the young man's back. It thrust its head down, hammering the earth in frustration and swinging this way and that, but try as it might, the bull could not remove the offending object.

One of Lobo's men yelled, 'Now!' and a dozen spears streaked through the gloom, every one of them hitting the beast and every one of them glancing off its armour-like hide, serving only to wake it up and start it moving again, ploughing through the line of flesh, bone and gold, killing and maiming, trampling bodies into the earth, tossing men into the air as a bull will toss dogs at a baiting.

Once again the muskets fired, but they too did nothing to the rhino but spur it on to greater fury and suddenly it was rampaging off towards the guards' huts and the slaves' stockade, scattering and trampling men as it went.

Hal, Aboli and the surviving Amadoda found themselves alone in an empty enclosure, with nothing between them and Lobo's fort. They ran back out across the drawbridge then Hal stopped, grabbing Aboli's arm with one hand and pointing at the fort with the other as he said, 'Look! All those men on the battlements.'

Hal sensed rather than saw the African grin. 'They are looking down at the rhino, watching their friends being trampled.'

'Aye, and feeling pleased that they're not down there. But they have left three sides of the fort completely unguarded.'

They ran round the far side of the fort, still unseen. The slave rebellion, however short-lived it might be, was providing Hal with more distraction than he'd dared hope for. They were within thirty paces of the fort, with just a stretch of open ground between them and an apparently unguarded wall when Aboli said, 'Let me go first, Gundwane. I do not glow like a white shell on the beach, as you do.'

Hal would not hear of it. 'I must be the first, Aboli,' he said, for he could not, he would not, lead other than from the front. He took the rope and grappling hook from Aboli and slung them over his shoulder. Then he tucked the panga into his belt. Hal looked up at the moon and waited for the next skein of cloud to sail across it like a galleon riding the sea.

The cloud came. It had to be now.

He ran across the uneven ground towards the fort then threw himself against the cool, whitewashed mud wall. It was not high to a man used to climbing masts and Hal knew he would almost fly to the top of it, assuming the grappling hook caught and that the sound of it did not bring the guards with their steel and shot.

His ears strained the sounds of the bush for human voices. Nothing. The men on the far wall were blissfully unaware of the danger behind them. Hal stepped out of the shadow, his heart pummelling his ribs, and looked back towards Aboli who nodded. Taking the rope, Hal swung the hook once, twice, three times, then hurled it up and over the wall.

Carefully, slowly, he pulled the hook back, wincing at the soft scrape it made against the ramparts, but then it would come no further, at least one claw having caught hold. And that was all Hal needed. He climbed. No sooner was the rope in his hands than he was atop the wall, crouching low against the parapet, panga ready. Cupping his left hand over his mouth he gave the call of a nightjar, which was the signal for Aboli and the Amadoda to follow him. Hal ran along the wall, bent low, and then looked over his shoulder to see that Aboli and his men were on top of it.

But then a man on the far wall happened to turn away from the carnage down below him, and saw the shadowy figures running along it on the far side of the courtyard and shouted in alarm. A musket cracked, spitting flame into the night as Hal saw some steps leading down into the yard, where one of Lobo's men loomed out of the darkness, his blade flashing as Hal twisted away from it and scythed his panga up, taking the man under his left arm. Then he hammered his right fist into the man's face, dropping him, and turned back toward the collection of tents and mud-brick buildings set against the north wall.

'Gundwane!' Aboli yelled. Hal turned, parrying by instinct a strike from a second attacker that would have opened his side between the ribs. He stepped inside, punching his cutlass's hilt into his attacker's face, sending him reeling, as another sword streaked for his face and he knocked it aside, slashing his own blade across the man's neck even as he strode forward. Aboli made three parries then killed a man with one cut to his neck, then Hal heard the Buzzard rasp his name, pointing his sword at Hal above other men's heads. Yet Lobo's men were in the way, and the Scotsman could no more get to Hal than Hal take the fight to him.

Just then two shots rang out, just behind him and close enough to make his ears ring, and two of Lobo's men, both of them armed with muskets, fell from the roof down to the courtyard floor.

Hal glanced around to see where the shots had come from and shouted with joy. For there stood Judith!

Judith had heard the feet running across the roof above her head and had known with absolute, unshakable certainty that Hal had come for her. She had stepped right out of the dress she had been about to lace up and back into the dead cabin boy's canvas trews, for if she were going to flee for her life across the African savannah she knew which would be of more use to her.

She ran to the door of her room and peered out into the courtyard. Hal was directly in front of her, but with his back turned towards her and Aboli next to him. Around them were the familiar faces of the Amadoda, their expressions lit up with the glee of natural-born warriors who were only truly alive when every next second could bring them death.

One of Lobo's men was lying on the floor right in front of her. He had a sword in his dead hand and two pistols in his belt. Judith took one of the pistols, steadied herself, aimed at a man on the roof about forty feet away and fired. Before he had even hit the ground she was reaching for the other pistol and repeating the process.

In front of her Hal was now staring up at her and joyously shouting her name. Aboli and the Amadoda were moving forward. There were battles going on right across Lobo's entire mining complex, but this particular one was swinging in their favour.

The Buzzard was calculating the odds, as he always did. He could sense the tide turning in Courtney's favour, too. That being the case his first thought, apart from saving his own skin, had to be of Balthazar Lobo. Having made a mortal enemy of Prince Jahan, the Buzzard was in need of powerful friends and if he couldn't win Lobo's favour by providing him with a bride, he would do it by saving his scrawny old neck.

He ran back across the courtyard and into Lobo's bedchamber. The old goat was nowhere to be seen. But then he heard a quavering voice from behind the four-poster bed cry out, 'Who goes there?'

'It is I, the Earl of Cumbrae, come to save you, sir,' the Buzzard replied. Then he walked over to where Lobo was hiding, pulled him to his feet and said, 'Quick, sir! We must leave this building while there is still time!'

Then the Buzzard ran back out into the courtyard, with the raddled old mine-owner hot on his heels, took one look at the ever-growing dominance of Courtney, his savage friends and his black bitch and scurried for the main gate, pulling Balthazar Lobo behind him.

The sight of their master's retreat was the final straw for his men at the fort. As one they turned tail and ran after him.

Hal watched them go then turned to see Judith trying to pull free the dead man's bandolier, on which he carried fresh powder and rounds for his pistols. 'No, my darling, leave that be,' he said. 'We need speed more than weapons. And we must leave at once.'

'Yes,' said Aboli. 'And we must run.'

It took the rest of the night to subdue the slave rebellion Aboli had inadvertently started. Only when dawn had broken could the Buzzard convene a council of war with Lobo and Capelo. 'The men who came after Courtney were part of his ship's crew. They must have followed him when he sailed from Zanzibar. Where did he come ashore?'

'Quelimane,' said Capelo.

'Then there or near there is where the *Golden Bough* will be, waiting for its master. Capelo. Do you know the way to Quelimane?'

'Of course.'

'Then, with your permission, Senhor Lobo, I suggest that we set off at once. Our first aim should be to catch Courtney, his woman and his men before they get aboard their ship. In that case, senhor, I promise you I will bring that woman back to you.'

'So I shall have my wedding night after all!' Lobo enthused.

'Quite so, sir,' the Buzzard agreed. 'But if, by some chance, Courtney should happen to sail away before we catch him, all is not yet lost. I know where he will be going. And if I can catch him at his destination then, senhor, I will bring you Courtney's head, Courtney's woman and Courtney's gold as well.'

A smile lit up Lobo's face. 'His gold? Oh, yes please, I would like that. I would like that very much indeed.'

The Buzzard and Capelo rode mules and marched their men hard, but they were no match for the Amadoda. Like them, Judith had a seemingly limitless well of energy that kept her running, albeit with a shorter stride, but still to the same relentless rhythm. And Hal kept up, day after day, no matter how much harder he found it to do so because he had no choice, and because as long as he had Judith beside him he had wings on his feet.

They reached the beach where Big Daniel Fisher had put them ashore and found the pinnace there, with John Lovell on duty that day, awaiting their return as it had done every day for the past several weeks. Hal and Judith were cheered to the echo when they went back on board the *Golden Bough* and the cheers rose even higher when Hal told the crew, 'I believe I mentioned something about going to get your prize money . . . give us the course for Elephant Lagoon, Mr Tyler!'

When they finally reached Quelimane, the Buzzard spent four days dragging Capelo round the seamen's taverns, trying to find a skipper with a ship for hire. Since the commission involved an immediate departure for a mysterious bay on the southernmost tip of Africa, unmarked on any chart; a journey completed in a time that would require crazy risks to be taken; the likelihood of a battle at the end of it against a seasoned captain who had just proved his worth before their very eyes; and all that just on the promise of a share of that captain's treasure – assuming that it even existed – there were no takers. And then their luck turned. Walking despondently away from yet another failed attempt at persuasion, Capelo saw João Barros stepping off the gangplank of the *Madre de Deus* onto the quayside.

Capelo's blood boiled. Here was the man who was the root cause of all his problems. He had half a mind to have him killed: Quelimane was not a place in which such things were hard to arrange. But instead he decided to make the best of a bad business and, having greeted Barros with effusive bonhomie, persuaded him to dine with him that night.

'You know me, old friend. I am a man who takes care of his stomach. There is not a town in Africa where I do not know where to find the finest food, yes, and know the cook who prepares it, into the bargain. There is a place here, the Blue Elephant. The food is unmatched in all Africa and they have barrels of Alvarelhão from Trás-os-Montes in the Douro . . . oh! To taste it on one's tongue is to be back home again!'

Barros was persuaded and, having sampled both the

food and the wine, agreed that it was just as good as Capelo had said. 'Even if,' he added, nodding his head at the Buzzard, who had sat there not eating or drinking all evening, 'it is a miracle that the very sight of that creature is not enough to sour it.'

'If you've finished your prattling, Captain, perhaps we could start talking business,' Capelo said, suddenly sounding a lot less effusive. 'That white slave you insisted would work as hard as a black has caused serious damage, expense and loss of life to Senhor Lobo. His name is Courtney. He is a captain, also known to some as El Tazar. I believe you know this and I suggest that your best hope of avoiding Senhor Lobo's justifiable retribution for the trouble you caused him is to help us catch this Courtney. In the meantime, however, every minute we waste here takes that English bastard a little further out of our grasp.'

'What did this Courtney do then?' Barros asked.

Lobo did his best to tell the story of Hal's rescue and escape without making the fiasco sound too shaming, though there was no disguising the fact that Courtney and his woman had been stolen from under his nose and the Buzzard's leather beak. By the end of the account, far from seeming concerned, Barros was pouring more wine for himself and slapping his thigh as he roared with laughter.

'And you want me to leap aboard the *Madre* and set out after Courtney and this woman Nazet, is that right? Well, let me tell you, I happen to be heading in that direction anyway. I have forty pairs of magnificent elephant tusks in my hold and a merchant in the Cape who will happily take them back to Holland. But forget your threats of retribution. I do not fear an old man like Lobo who lives a thousand leagues from the sea where I ply my trade. Just give me one reason why I

405

would want to make a detour and risk my neck to help you along the way?'

'May I?' the Buzzard asked Capelo with exaggerated courtesy.

'By all means.'

'Very well then . . . I knew Courtney's father, Franky, knew him very well indeed. Now, he had two qualities. First, he could sniff out a prize as well as any man afloat, and second, he kept every damn penny he ever took off every ship he ever took. That man never shared – not even with his pals, men like me who had a right to their cut – and he never spent a brass farthing either.'

Barros opened his mouth to speak, but the Buzzard held up his three-fingered hand. 'You were, I venture, about to ask me how great the Courtney treasure might be. Well, let me tell you this. The last ship old man Courtney ever took was a Dutch East Indiaman called the *Resolution*.'

'Ah! Yes . . . I remember that,' Barros said. 'It was the talk of the Cape Colony. But the *Resolution* was recaptured, with all her wood and spice still aboard.'

'Och aye, the cheese heads got back their precious ship and their spice and their wood. But there was a lot more on that ship than a few barrels o' cloves and a load of teak, I can tell you. There was fifty thousand Dutch guilders' worth of silver and three hundred, aye, you heard me . . . three hundred ingots of pure gold, any one of which would be enough to set a man up for life, and in fine style too.'

Barros gave a low, low whistle as he contemplated the staggering wealth of the Courtney hoard, totally unaware that the Buzzard – thinking he might keep a little just for himself – had not even mentioned the one hundred thousand guilders, in coins, that also lay waiting there.

'Now do you see why a man would chase after that treasure?'

the Buzzard went on. 'And believe me the booty from the *Resolution*'s not the half of it. Yon Franky had plenty more prizes beside that one, you can take my word for that.'

'That's all very well,' observed Barros, his deal-making instincts now firmly back under control, 'but do you even know where this treasure is?'

'That's a very good and very interesting question. The answer is yes . . . and no. See, I know roughly where it is. I know it has to be within less than half a day's journey from the point where Courtney took it all ashore. I also know where it isn't, because I had the entire beach dug up, in case he's buried it there and there wasn't any sign of it.'

'Where is this beach?' asked Barros.

'Place called Elephant Lagoon . . . but don't even think of trying to double-cross me, Captain, for you won't find it on any chart. But I know where this bay is and I'm absolutely certain that Courtney's bound for it right now. We just let him get there, wait while he gets the treasure for us and then . . .' There was a crash as the Buzzard slammed his fist down on the table. 'We hit him when he's not expecting it, kill him, take back the woman and take the treasure, too.'

'I want half the treasure,' said Barros.

'The hell you do!' snarled the Buzzard.

'Gentlemen, gentlemen, please,' Capelo intervened. 'Each of us depends upon the other. Of course, Captain Barros, you are the one who has the ship. But our masked friend here is the only one who knows where to direct your ship. And that, Captain, means that you will not have to pay for provisions, fresh water and fresh gunpowder and shot, meaning that the money you make from your ivory will be pure profit, even if we do not get a single speck of gold from this treasure. I am the only one here with authority to borrow money, on Senhor

Lobo's account, to pay for the cost of this expedition, in full. So let us stop wasting time on squabbling and agree: we will each receive one third of the value of the treasure, as and when it is recovered.

'On top of that, I will take the woman, who was Senhor Lobo's property and return her to him. You, Captain, will take Courtney's head, for whoever carries that back to Prince Jahan will receive his immense gratitude. And you, Senhor Buzzard, may have Courtney's ship . . . if you can find any men willing to crew it with you as its master.'

'Very well,' said Barros, 'I agree. But from what you say, Courtney has several days' start. And it will be at least two days before I will be ready to sail. How can we possibly catch him?'

'Because,' the Buzzard answered, 'Courtney thinks he's safe. Och, he'll sail swiftly enough, but he'll see no need to take any chances. But we will. For we'll be sailing as though the devil himself were chasing us.'

And so they had set sail. Urged on by the Buzzard, Captain Barros had driven his crew harder than any of them had ever imagined possible. At every hour of night or day, either Barros or the Buzzard was standing beside the helmsman, setting the course, demanding that every last scrap of sail be spread so that not one breath of wind should be wasted. When the weather turned nasty, the Buzzard insisted on keeping far more canvas than would normally be deemed safe and more than once the ship came within a hair's breadth of floundering. But the *Madre de Deus* survived to sail another day . . . and another . . . and both Barros and the Buzzard knew that they must be reeling the *Golden Bough* in, so that the five days' start that she had possessed must have shrunk to much less. But how much narrower the gap had become, none of them could say. Nor could they know how long Courtney would spend in Elephant

Lagoon. All they could do was to keep pushing, keep flogging the ship like an exhausted stallion until they reached their destination. And pray that when they did, they would not find that Courtney had already been and gone.

'**M**y eyes are very good, sir,' Mossie said. 'And my voice is loud. You could hear me all across the ship. Listen . . .' The boy let loose a high-pitched scream that would have drowned out a trumpeting bull elephant, causing Hal, standing right beside him, to wince and cover his ears.

Mossie grinned in triumph. 'So you see, sir, I would be a very good lookout.'

Hal gave a rueful shake of the head. He had to hand it to the lad, he was nothing if not persistent. The *Golden Bough* had barely escaped from Quelimane before Mossie had been on at him, begging to be allowed to be the next lookout boy. Hal had said, no, it was out of the question and then come up with one reason after another why there was no chance of the request being granted: Mossie was too young, too small, couldn't climb rigging, wouldn't be able to tell one kind of ship from another, and couldn't shout down to the quarterdeck. One by one those objections had been challenged and in the almost festive atmosphere that now reigned on the *Bough*, as she sped south towards what the crew all knew would be the greatest payday that any one of them had ever enjoyed, or would be likely to again, the conflict between the most senior and junior of the ship's company had become a constant topic of conversation and speculation. Many a wager had been offered and taken as to whether the captain would give in to this scrap of a lad, and, if so, when.

'I can tell you, lads, it ain't never going to happen,' Big Daniel had assured a group of mainmast hands he'd found in heated debate one afternoon. 'And here's why. There's only one person in this world can make the captain do what he's told, and he knows full well that she'll have his bollocks cut off an' slung overboard for the sharks to eat if she sees her little pet up a mast.'

'Aye,' one of the men agreed, 'the captain's lady's not a woman a man would want to anger. I've seen what she can do with that sword of hers.'

That very thought was now playing on Hal's mind and having run out of other cards to play he decided to deploy his last remaining trump. 'Think about Lady Judith,' he said, knowing that Mossie's devotion to her was as great as hers to him. 'If you fell from the mast, high up there . . .' Hal pointed up to the very top of the mainmast, just to underline his point, 'and fell all the way down here – crash! – against the deck, you would be dead and she would be very unhappy. And you don't want to make Lady Judith unhappy, do you, boy?'

Mossie gave the matter due consideration and then his face split into a huge grin as he hit upon the perfect retort. 'But I will not fall, Captain Courtney, sir! In my village I was the one they sent to climb the cliffs for gull eggs. I could climb to the moon if you gave me a long rope.'

This made Hal laugh. 'Aboli,' he called down to the main deck where the African was assessing the Amadodas' work on the oakum, the tribesmen painstakingly unravelling old tarry ropes into fibre. 'Do you think I should let the boy climb to the mast top?'

'He'd better be right about not falling,' Ned Tyler said. 'I'm not having him making a mess on my nice clean deck.'

'We all had to make our first climb, Captain,' a young topmastman called out as if he were one of the old hands, though he was not a day over eighteen.

Aboli grinned and lifted his big arms up and down. 'The boy is a sparrow, Gundwane!' he called. 'If he falls he will flap his little wings. Besides, you were his age, maybe even younger, when you first climbed the mainmast. Though if I recall, your father was below in his cabin, asleep at the time.'

Hal smiled at the memory. He remembered Aboli hissing at him, 'Don't look down, Gundwane. Resist the urge to look down.' Hal's legs had trembled and his heart had pounded in his chest but he had reached the main top and sat up there feeling like a king as he had swung like a pendulum with the ship's pitch and roll.

'That mast was not as tall as this one, Aboli,' Hal said.

'No it was not,' Aboli admitted, then gestured at Mossie. 'But if he falls I will catch him, just as I would have caught you.'

Hal looked down at Mossie, at those determined eyes, and he realized he respected the boy, admired the courage the lad still had in him after all he had been through, first at the hands of the slavers and then witnessing Judith's abduction by the Buzzard.

412

'And if by some chance I do not catch him, then we will clean up the mess before my lady discovers what is happening,' Aboli said, putting on his most grim expression though his eyes were laughing. Not that Mossie was in the least put off.

'Before my lady discovers what?' a female voice asked, slicing as sharply as the blade of its owner's sword through the hubbub of manly debate.

'Oh, nothing, my darling,' Hal said, making a painfully transparent attempt to deflect Judith's curiosity. But any hope he might have had of getting away with it was dashed as Mossie piped up, 'The captain said I could climb the mainmast . . .'

'I said no such thing!' Hal blustered.

'And if I fall Mr Aboli is going to catch me.'

'Is this true?' said Judith, and eyes more experienced than Hal's in the ways of women might have noticed that she was only just succeeding in suppressing a smile.

'It is certainly true that this cheeky scamp was trying to persuade me to let him climb the mainmast, but it is absolutely not the case that I had said he could. You can rest assured of that.'

'Cap'n's right, m'lady,' Ned Tyler intervened. 'He wasn't letting the boy climb the mast. Not likely!'

'Really?' asked Judith, and now it was her turn to adopt an air of complete innocence. 'Why on earth not? I'm all for boys being given challenges. How will they grow up to be big, strong, brave men if they're never allowed to test themselves?'

'But I thought . . . I mean, you said . . .' Hal searched in vain for the right words to express the outrageous injustice he had just suffered. Judith absolutely had made it clear that she didn't want Mossie being put in harm's way – and she knew it.

Judith, however, knew precisely when she'd pushed things far enough. So now she walked across to her man, took his arm, looked up at him adoringly, for all the crew to see, and then said, 'I know you were doing what you thought I wanted, and I thank you for that. But this is your ship and it is for you, not me, to decide these things. If you feel Mossie is ready to climb the mast, then I will not object.'

'Please, Captain! Please-please-please!' Mossie piped up.

Hal knew when he was beaten, and in truth, he knew that both Aboli and Judith were right. He had done this sort of thing when he was a lad and it had indeed helped prepare him to be a man. So he got right down to business. 'Very well, then, Mossie-my-lad, listen carefully. Once you start the climb, do not look down until you are safe at the top.'

'No, sir,' said Mossie. The grin on his face was as bright as the afternoon sun and his little feet danced a jig on the spot. 'When I am up there with the gulls I will tell them who I am. I will tell them who you are too, Captain sir.'

'I'll tell them myself, boy,' Hal said, 'because I'm coming up there with you.'

'What?' Judith gasped, having been caught completely unawares.

'I'm sure I don't have to tell you the first rule of good leadership, my dear general. Never ask any man – or small boy – to do something you would not do yourself.'

There were plenty of grins and a few stifled chuckles among the crewmen. That was their Hal Courtney, all right.

'Damn, but he reminds me of his dad sometimes,' Ned Tyler said to Big Daniel as they stood together, looking on.

'Aye, bet old Franky's looking down on this and loving it,' the massive boatswain replied.

Hal took off his shirt so that he stood there bare-chested and bare-footed, looking like any other sailor on the *Bough*, his torso, like theirs, sinewy with hard-earned muscle and scarred from many fights. There were other scars too and as Mossie saw them now his eyes grew large and his mouth fell open though he said nothing.

'I too have lived like a slave, Mossie,' Hal told the boy, knowing how terrifying were the whip-marks which latticed his back and flanks.

'You must have been very disobedient, milord,' Mossie said with a grin.

Hal laughed. 'Yes . . . even more than you, lad.' His hair had grown long and he pulled the leather thong from it and re-tied it so that the thick dark pigtail fell between his shoulder blades. 'Shall we?' he said, gesturing towards the mainmast the way he might invite a lady to go for a stroll at sunset.

'Let's see if the captain still has the legs for it!' one of the men shouted.

'Aye, I'll wager a shilling that the boy beats him to the top.'

'Ha! You haven't got a bleeding shilling, Evans,' Will Stanley said.

'Nah! Young Courtney was born in the shrouds. He'll be up there like the king's hand up Nellie Gwyn's skirts,' another man called.

'Win, my darling, win for me,' Judith whispered, under her breath. The sight of her man, in all his youth, his strength and his virility had made her wish that she could drag him away from this race and off to their cabin. But since she had no option but to bide her time, she wanted her man to prove himself, to win and to mark himself unmistakably as the dominant male in the *Golden Bough*'s pack.

'You devils get back to work!' Hal bellowed at his idling crew, though he knew very well that every man aboard would be watching to see how well he climbed.

Aboli appointed himself the starter. 'Are you ready?' he called

415

out, raising his hand in the air. Both the contestants nodded back at him, their bodies tensed in anticipation.

'Go!' Aboli shouted, and Mossie was off so fast it seemed that he was on the mast and climbing as the word was still leaving Aboli's lips.

Hal cursed and set off after his young competitor. It was hot work. The sweat streamed down Hal's face, stinging his eyes and rolling down his back and chest. He tried to keep the mast between him and the sun so that its fire did not blind him as he climbed, but mostly he tried to keep up with the boy.

'He's a natural born topmastman,' Ned Tyler observed, like a trainer observing a yearling's form on the gallops at Newmarket Heath, though he had to shout to be heard over the cheers and cries of encouragement coming from the men all around him.

'Aye, but the captain still climbs like a monkey with a burning bum,' Big Daniel proudly replied.

Their words were lost to Hal for he was now far above the deck, but still chasing the boy in front of him. But then Mossie looked down.

'Eyes up, lad,' Hal said, yet it was too late and the boy froze, arms clinging to the shrouds and his whole body trembling.

'I am stuck, Captain sir!'

'Take a breath. There's nothing to it,' Hal said. 'Up you go.' He could have told Mossie to go down, that he had gone high enough, but he knew that if the boy did not make the masthead now he might lose his nerve forever.

Down below, the men had fallen silent. They had all had to make their first climb and overcome the fear that struck all but a very few first-timers. So now they understood exactly what the boy was going through. The race was over as a contest. But the challenge facing Mossie was greater than ever.

'My legs, Captain. They betray me, sir.'

'They'll do what you tell them, lad. Now get up there.'

'I cannot move,' Mossie said in a crestfallen voice on the verge of tears. His bony little knees were about to give way. Hal could count every rib as the boy's belly sucked in and out like bellows.

'You will climb to the masthead or I will put into the next port we pass and put you up for sale in the slave market,' Hal said. It was a cruel threat. He knew it was. But he had to make the boy fear something more than he feared the height, and sure enough, though he was crying now, Mossie reached up and took hold of the next ratline.

'That's the way. Not far now,' Hal said.

'Yes, sir,' Mossie said. Up he went, his legs still trembling but the pale soles of his feet flexing over the ratlines. Then he was up and over and into the masthead crow's nest.

'We'll make a topmastman of you, boy,' Hal said, climbing over the lip to sit beside him as cheers rang out from down below.

But Mossie was scowling.

'You did well, Mossie,' Hal said, pleased with his own performance too for he knew he had been fast and lithe and already his breathing was slowing, becoming measured again. 'The whole ship saw you climb and you have earned their respect. Listen, they're cheering you.'

'But I . . . I could not move.'

'You looked down,' Hal said. 'I told you not to.'

Mossie seemed ashamed but Hal would not coddle the boy. 'So we've seen you climb. How is your eyesight?' He pointed south at a ship running up the coast on a course parallel to their own, but with far more sail, pushing as hard as her captain could drive her.

There's a man in a hurry, thought Hal. There was something

417

familiar about the outline of the ship, though Hal could not quite place it. *Damn! Are my eyes starting to betray me already?*

'What colours is she flying?' he asked Mossie.

Mossie shook his head. 'No colours, Captain,' Mossie said, knuckling the last residue of tears from his eyes.

'Strange,' Hal muttered. He would have liked to stay up there longer to take another good look at the mystery ship. But their first descent from the top of the mast was often even worse for new sailors than getting there had been. Mossie needed guiding back down to the bottom, and his men needed livening up. The sight of a ship outpacing the *Bough* so comprehensively served only to remind him how casual their progress had become.

'Come on then, boy, let's get back down to deck,' Hal said.

'My legs will not betray me again, Captain,' Mossie said, defiantly.

'I know they won't, boy,' Hal said. 'Now let's get down to that deck.'

The Buzzard was crouched in the shadow of the tall trees that grew on the rocky heads that guarded Elephant Lagoon, looking past the gun emplacements where once the Courtneys had placed culverins to defend their hidden refuge, across an expanse of dark green water that was deep enough for the mightiest warship in any king's navy to drop anchor without the slightest fear of running around. And yet there was not so much as a rowing boat to be seen, either bobbing on the lagoon or pulled up on the beach of shining white sand, where the only inhabitants were not men, but three elephants, quietly walking along the strand, like huge, grey gentlefolk taking a promenade in the park. Barros was not in a mood to be charmed by the sight.

'Damn you! I have worked my men to the point of mutiny and my ship is held together by little more than my prayers . . .

and for what? Nothing! Courtney has been and gone! We will not see a scrap of gold, not the tiniest speck of it.'

'Stop whining, man! Your ship's perfectly sound. You've torn a couple of sails, cracked a spar or two and you've a few loose timbers, but you know as well as I do that's nothing – less than a day's work for the boatyards at the Cape. As for your men, they'll be fine as long as they think there's a spot of good stuff at the end of the voyage.'

'But I don't see any stuff around here, good or bad!' Barros complained, his voice rising in pitch as well as volume.

'You didn't think it would be laid out on the beach for you, did you?' The Buzzard's eye winked at him from beyond its mask hole. 'Come with me.'

'Will it be safe down there?' Barros asked, showing the first sign that he had even noticed the creatures from which this secret world took its name.

'One sniff of your stink and they'll be gone like smoke in the wind.'

They pushed a way through the thick forest that fringed the lagoon until they came to the remains of the huts that had once been slept in and fought over by both the Courtneys and the Buzzard.

Aye, when I was still a man, with all my limbs, and everything else in perfect working order, he thought to himself.

There were the scattered ashes of old campfires dotted here and there, but it was obvious that they all dated back to that earlier time.

'No one's been here in months,' the Buzzard gave his opinion.

'If I were Courtney, I would not allow my men to come ashore,' Barros said. 'I would keep them on the ship and then go with one or two of my most trusted officers – no more than that – and fetch this treasure.'

The Buzzard gave a croaking burst of laughter. 'Young Courtney would not do that. He'd let his men off the ship to fish, hunt for fresh meat and find wood to repair the ship. The boy's as soft as warm butter.'

'A great weakness.' Barros shook his head deprecatingly.

'Aye, it'll be the death of him yet.' The Buzzard laughed. 'And pretty soon, too.'

'So what shall we do?'

'We anchor your *Madre* in the next bay to the south of here, so that Courtney doesn't spot it as he comes in from the north. Leave lookouts watching the lagoon, with their longboat well hidden. When Courtney arrives one of his first moves will be to go and check his bonny little treasure trove, wherever he has stashed it away. When he returns to his ship we will be right there to give him a right royal welcome, relieve him of his treasure and follow that up immediately afterwards with an equally royal funeral.'

They pulled the oars with long strokes, driving the two boats into the swift current of fresh water flowing out of the gorge. Their presence in this secret place disturbed the flocks of water fowl that rose shrieking and honking into the sky.

So far they had not been disappointed with this secret place. No sooner had the *Golden Bough* dropped her anchor than her crew had been greeted by the sight of a small herd of elephants shambling out of the forest onto the beach, taking their lead from an old bull with massive tusks. When they saw human beings aboard the anchored ships, the grey giants stood their ground, raising their great heads, spreading their ears as they trumpeted a challenge at them.

'Oh, what magnificent beasts,' Judith said, watching them from the bows.

'And cleverer than many people I have known,' Aboli said in all seriousness.

'Why don't we shoot a few of them?' Big Daniel suggested eagerly. 'There's a fortune in ivory right there. Good God, but the tusks on that bull must be ten feet long.'

'There is easier plunder waiting for us, Dan,' Hal said with a shake of his head. 'I think we'll leave them in peace.'

Hal had anchored the *Golden Bough* opposite the ruins of the old fort, and ran out all the guns, loaded with grapeshot in case of a surprise attack from savages of any colour; brown, black or white. Then he took Judith aside.

'I am going to ask you to stay here, instead of undergoing a long couple of days in a pinnace. Besides there will be very little leg room on the way back, if you get my meaning. On the other hand, if you wait for my return here you will have fifty men and more to watch over you, and those long sandy beaches on which you and the baby can relax.'

'For the sake of the baby I will do it. But promise you will return as soon as you possibly can; for I will miss you desperately.'

Before they had launched the two longboats and prepared the twelve-strong shore party the great grey pachyderms had lost interest and moved back into the forest, vanishing in an eerie silence.

Now, as the men bent to the long sweeps, Hal, Daniel and Aboli looked up at the cliff tops on either side of them from which troops of baboons barked a challenge.

They had rowed little more than ten miles from where the *Golden Bough* lay at anchor, the sails furled on her yards, until the fresh water stream narrowed abruptly and the cliff faces on either side of them were more sharply defined, as though the Great God Thor had cleaved them out of the rock with his celestial hammer.

'This is the place, Master Daniel,' Hal called to the other boat, and put the rudder across to steer her into the southern bank and moor her to the identical rock which his father had used for the same purpose. Hal sat for a moment in silent homage to the man who had given him birth and had prepared him so meticulously for the hard life on the ocean wave. When he roused himself and looked up, Aboli was watching him. They exchanged glances and Hal nodded at his friend and companion of the years; both men in total accord.

Hal stood up and looped two coils of hempen rope over his shoulders so they crossed over his chest. 'I'll go first, you next,' he told Aboli. 'Daniel, keep four men with you to load the boats with whatever we lower down to you. The rest of you, light your match and keep your eyes wide open.'

Hal jumped onto the narrow ledge below the rock wall and began to climb.

'Go carefully, Gundwane,' Aboli called after him. 'There is no hurry.'

Hal ignored him, for he was suddenly in a dreadful hurry. Had the treasure lain undisturbed all these years or had it been discovered by one of the many who were hunting for it? Was the cave barren or was it glutted with gold?

Even though there was no obvious route up the rock face, he never paused, climbing with speed and fearless agility until he swung himself onto the narrow ledge that was invisible to those in the longboats far below. The stones blocking the cave's narrow entrance were stacked as neatly as he and Aboli had left them so long ago. And his heart started to sing and rejoice, as he removed them one by one, and set them aside.

When the hole was large enough he crawled inside then stood up carefully, for the roof was low and uneven. He waited while his eyes adjusted to the thin shaft of daylight that probed through the opening he had made, but the depths of the cave were shrouded in darkness.

He reached up head-high to the stone ledge on the wall beside him, and his groping fingers came upon the articles that his father had placed there on their last visit. He hugged them to his chest and sank to his knees. On the rock floor of the cave he set out the two tallow candles, and then he struck a shower of sparks from the flint with the steel. The oakum tinder was dry as the Sahara, it flared into flames and Hal lit both candles from it. Then he sat back and with hope and dread equally mingled he raised his eyes and peered into the depths of the cave.

It was all still there. It was untouched. Every keg, barrel, sack and chest was stacked just as he and his father had left it. The silver plate and gold ingots stood in neat piles. The precious metals were bright and unsullied.

He sank back on his knees and remembered the words of his father.

Every one of us owes God a death. When the time comes for me to pay my debt I want this to be my legacy to you, his father had said.

'It is far too much, Father. What do you want me to do with such riches?' Hal spoke aloud, and another voice answered him immediately.

'Just for a start you could pay Viscount Winterton what you still owe him for the *Golden Bough*. Then you could find yourself a few thousand acres of prime land on England's green and glorious shores and a mansion to fill with a lovely woman and a dozen squealing infants.'

Startled, Hal jumped to his feet and turned to find Aboli behind him. He was breathing heavily from the exertions of his climb up the cliff. Hal clasped his shoulder, and the two of them stood in silence for a while, as if in homage to the man who had won this mighty fortune for his son, and paid for it with his life.

They remembered the agony he had suffered at the hands of Slow John, the torturer and executioner who did his terrible work on the orders of van de Velde, the governor of the Dutch colony of the Cape of Good Hope.

'Was it worth it, Aboli?' Hal broke the silence at last.

'Your father believed it was.' Aboli shrugged. 'He gave his life for this, so now it is your duty to accept it, lest his sacrifice be in vain.'

'Thank you,' Hal said softly, but sincerely. 'Without that sound advice I might have spurned my father's legacy and spent the rest of my life suffering for it.'

They spent the next two days swaying this tremendous weight of metal and precious stones down the cliff face and packing it into the two longboats. By the time they had completed the transfer and the loading there was very little free-board remaining on either boat. Hal ordered most of the men ashore with ropes to tow the boats along the bank, while he and Aboli steered them with the tillers. It was slow going and they had to camp the first night on the river bank. Before sunrise the next morning they set off again.

They had another half a league to go to reach the head of the lagoon where the *Golden Bough* was anchored when there was a rumble in the sky ahead of them, like distant thunder. Every one of them paused in their labours and looked up at the sky in surprise. However, though the clouds were dense and dark, there was no other sign of an approaching storm.

'Thunder?' hazarded Daniel.

'No!' Aboli yelled from the leading boat. 'That was not thunder; that was a cannon shot!'

'Like as not, a distress signal from the *Golden Bough*!' Hal cried. 'She must be under attack.'

He was not the Buzzard, damn all of them who thought it. He was and had always been Angus Cochran, Earl of Cumbrae and a Nautonnier Knight of the Temple of the Order of St George and the Holy Grail, just as was Hal Courtney and his father before him.

The only difference between them was that they made a great fuss about honour and dignity and the battle for Christ and the Holy Grail, whereas he had always known that they were meaningless medieval claptrap. They had sought to mock him by calling him the Buzzard, just as Prince Jahan had tried to humiliate and enslave him by locking him into this bloody mask.

But now the mask empowered him. It had brought him back from the edge of fiery death. It had covered his ruined face and converted him into a creature of mystery. It struck terror into the hearts of his enemies. He was strong once more. He was again a warrior fierce and pitiless.

He had set his snare and caught young Hal Courtney in it; with his breeks around his ankles and his arse flapping in the wind.

Cochran might have lost an arm, an eye and most of his cock, but his brain was still in perfect working order, and the sword in his right hand was still deadly.

For the last three days, ever since the arrival of the *Golden Bough* at Elephant Lagoon, the *Madre de Deus* had been ready for immediate action. Now her topmastmen were at their stations, ready to unfurl every scrap of canvas she could carry, and the gun crews were standing by their cannons which were shotted and loaded.

The Buzzard's spies had seen the two pinnaces leave the *Golden Bough* and row up to the top end of the lagoon, where they entered the stream of fresh water, and disappeared around the first bend in the river heading up through the valley towards the inland plateau. Through their telescopes they had even been able to recognize Hal Courtney and his black henchman, Aboli. But they had not seen them return. Of course they might have done so after nightfall, when the lookouts would not have spotted them, but they could not escape from the lagoon without him knowing about it.

Thus before dawn on the fourth day of waiting, the Buzzard decided finally to close the trap on Hal Courtney. With his crew at their battle stations he sailed in through the heads that guarded the entrance to Elephant Lagoon from the Indian Ocean. He stood in the bows of the *Madre de Deus* with his telescope tucked under his arm, and his single eye glaring out through the hole in his leather mask across the waters of the lagoon. He saw that the *Golden Bough* was lying at her anchorage deeper in the lagoon, with her gun ports closed and her masts and yards bare of canvas. Her decks were empty, and there was only a single lookout at the masthead.

One of her pinnaces was beached near the head of the lagoon. Her crew had very obviously been filling the water barrels from the sweet water stream. The second pinnace was on the far side of the lagoon from the *Bough*. Her crew were busy loading bundles of cut firewood into her. But this early in the morning both crews were gathered around the fires on the beaches, swigging coffee and tea and guzzling their breakfast.

It was obvious that Hal Courtney was preparing for the long

voyage home around the Cape of Good Hope and then back up the Atlantic Ocean to the British Isles. But his crews were separated from his ship, and oblivious to the sudden and silent appearance of a three-masted fighting ship in the mouth of the lagoon.

The Buzzard turned and called back to Captain Barros on the poop deck. 'Give them a gun shot to wake these apes out of their trance, please, Captain.' Although distorted by his speaking hole, his voice was clearly understandable to the officers on the poop deck.

Barros snapped an order to the master gunner on the deck below him, and a single cannon shot thundered out across the waters, and echoed off the hills that surrounded this wide body of water.

The British crews looked up in total astonishment as the *Madre de Deus* appeared miraculously before them in full battle array.

'Steer for the *Golden Bough*,' the Buzzard gave his next order. 'She will be easy pickings, for she is isolated from her men.' He cleared his damaged throat, and spat a lump of yellow phlegm over the rail. 'I want Courtney, do you hear. But if he is not aboard, then I want his woman.'

Judith Nazet was in the cabin of the *Golden Bough* that she and Hal shared; she was sitting at the small writing desk below the stern windows. There was a timid knock on the cabin door and Mossie stuck his curly mop of hair around the jamb.

'Good morning to you, my kind mistress. I have coffee for you; no milk and no sugar.'

'Thank you, Mossie, how did you know that is just how I like it?'

'Because that's how you always have it,' he said with a wide white grin. This was an on-going ritual of theirs. He came in and closed the door carefully behind him and stood on tiptoe to set the silver mug on the desk before her.

'Should I blow out the lamps for you, my lovely mistress?' He reached out a hand to the lantern in its bracket on the bulkhead above her head. There were half-a-dozen of these identical lamps hanging from the ceiling above the double bunk, and at other odd points around the cabin.

'No thank you, Mossie. It's a dark, overcast day out there. Leave all the lamps burning until the sun breaks through.' Mossie bobbed his head and tugged at his forelock as he had been taught to do, and backed out of the cabin. Judith smiled to herself. She had truly become fond of the lad. Then she sighed, dipped the nib of her pen into the inkwell and poised it over the open page of her diary.

Then she began to write, '. . . the little brute inside me kicked me awake all last night. I shall be greatly relieved when he pops out and stands on his own two feet . . .'

The cannon shot was so close and clear that it could have been fired in the same cabin as she was. She started so violently that the nib of her pen splattered ink across the page of her diary. Then she jumped to her feet and stared out of the stern windows across the lagoon.

The *Madre de Deus* was ghosting across the lagoon directly towards where she sat. She had never seen this ship before, but the warrior instincts which she had finely developed warned her that it was hostile, and that it posed a deadly threat.

The frigate was flying battle ensigns and all her gun ports were open with the long barrels of her cannon run out.

She wasted not another second, but pulled open the top

drawer of her desk. Her two pairs of matching pistols lay close to hand in their moulded tray. All four of them were loaded and primed. She stuffed one pair into the yellow ribbon around her waist. She cocked the hammers on the second pair, and held them ready to fire. Then she crossed to the door of her cabin and threw it open, and then climbed the companionway to the main deck.

Before she reached the deck the ship shuddered under her feet and there was the crash of another hull coming into violent contact with that of the *Bough*. Simultaneously there came a wild burst of cheering, and the clatter of running footsteps from above. She stepped out onto the deck and looked about her quickly.

Another vessel lay alongside the *Golden Bough*, bound to her by a row of grappling hooks thrown from the strange vessel, and then a man's head rose above the gunnel. She recognized him instantly by the description that Hal had given her, especially by the vivid pink scar that ran from the corner of his mouth up into his hairline.

He was the Portuguese slave ship owner who had once captured Hal, and sold him into slavery. His name was João Barros. She knew his ship was the *Madre de Deus*, and she made the immediate deduction that this must be his ship that lay alongside the *Bough* at this very moment.

Without even a second's hesitation she brought up the pistol in her right hand and fired. The ball struck Barros in the centre of his forehead, and snapped his head back with such force that she heard his vertebrae part with a crack. He was thrown from her sight, but another head replaced Barros.

It was a head without a human face. Instead it wore a leather mask, fashioned into a grotesque parody of humanity. It had a single eye and an eagle beak for a nose. The hole in the mask that served it for a mouth was lined with rows of glaring white false teeth, set into a hideous grin.

'The Buzzard!' she gasped and the shock was so intense that for a heartbeat she was paralysed. Then she dropped the empty pistol in her right hand, and started to raise the pistol in her left hand. The Buzzard moved as fast as a striking adder, his sword blade darted out and sent the pistol spinning from her fingers. It slithered away down the deck. For an instant her whole arm was frozen by the force of the blow. She did not even consider trying to reach for the pistols in her sash. She knew he would cut off her hand at the wrist before she could take a grip. She ducked under his blade, and threw herself backwards down the open companionway. She tumbled down the steps in a tangle of skirts and both the pistols tucked in her sash flew out and clattered down the steps with her. One of them discharged of its own accord in a burst of smoke and flame, but the ball flew wide and gouged a cloud of splinters from the woodwork.

When she reached the bottom of the companionway she glanced up and saw the Buzzard charging down the steps after her, brandishing his sword and shrieking like a maddened banshee, but with his mask frozen in that insane toothy grin. His back was humped and his one shoulder was higher than the other so he moved more like a great ape than a man.

Judith rolled back onto her feet and ran to the door of her cabin which stood wide open. Once she was in she slammed it behind her, but in the next instant he crashed into it with all his weight behind it. It flew open again and threw Judith backwards onto the double bunk.

The Buzzard reared up over her with his sword over his head, but as he chopped down at her face she rolled to one side and the blade hacked through the frame of the bunk.

Judith was thrown in a tangle of skirts over the end of the

bunk and ended up against the far bulkhead. The Buzzard's blade was trapped in the woodwork of the bunk. He tried to lever it free and a torrent of filthy language came from behind his mask.

'You stinking whore, I am going to slit open your foul and rotting womb and pull out your living bastard, and I am going to chop him into little pieces and force them down your throat.' He was still trying to free the blade of his sword.

Judith rolled away down the bulkhead and came to her feet. Desperately she looked about her. She had no weapons and the Buzzard blocked her way to the single door. The only escape route that remained open to her was through the stern windows at the far end of the cabin. If she could climb out through them then she would have a good chance of swimming to the beach.

She pushed herself off the bulkhead and darted towards the stern. The Buzzard saw her coming and he let go the hilt of his sword and aimed a swinging punch at her as she passed him. His fist caught her on the shoulder and knocked her off balance. She piled into her own writing desk below the window. She pulled herself up the bulkhead and stood at bay with her back pressed to the woodwork, facing the Buzzard as he came towards her with his humped-back, leg-dragging gait. He was reaching for her with his single three-fingered hand.

'Please . . .' She was pleading now. 'Please let my baby live.'

Then she felt the heat on the back of her head. She lifted one hand to avoid it and her fingers touched the glass funnel of the oil lamp. There was a sharp hiss as her skin burned and blistered in the heat. Her spirits surged from blank despair to vaulting hope in the pain. She closed both her hands around the glass oil reservoir, and with all her strength tore it from its bracket and hurled it at the masked head in front of her.

The glass shattered and the viscose oil sprayed over the

433

Buzzard's masked head and shoulders. The flames spread and enclosed him in a dancing cone of searing heat. He fell backwards onto the bedstead, clawing feebly at the flames with his one good hand.

The bedclothes caught fire and the flames shot as high as the ceiling. The Buzzard lay in the centre of the inferno like the carcass of a pig on the spit. His mask burned through and the tatters of his real face were so ghastly that Judith fled from the spectacle. She ran from the cabin and up the companionway.

As she burst out onto the open deck and stood weeping with release from fear, and gasping the sweet sea air to purge the smoke from her lungs, a pair of strong arms closed about her and a beloved voice demanded of her, 'What in the name of Almighty God is happening? Why are you weeping so?'

Judith spun around in the circle of Hal's arms, and clung to him. 'My darling! Thank God you are here. He was going to kill us, me and the baby.'

'Who was it?'

'The Buzzard!'

'Cochran? Where is he now? I have to stop him.'

'He is in our cabin, but the ship is on fire. It is the only way I could stop him.' She wasn't making good sense, but Hal knew that they were caught up in dire circumstances. He glanced around quickly to make an assessment of the danger. He saw the strange ship had cut herself free and was making all haste to escape through the heads and get out into the open sea again.

'Let them go!' he decided. 'Where is the fire, you said it is in our cabin?'

Judith nodded vigorously. 'Yes! In our cabin!'

Hal released her, and spun around. 'Aboli! Big Dan! Fire! Fire down below. Man the pumps!'

* * *

It took all the ship's pumps and the entire crew half the morning to bring the flames under control, but when at last Hal was able to lead Judith back to the master cabin the two of them stood in the doorway and stared in at the blackened and still smoking interior and the charred body lying on the bunk amongst the smouldering ashes like the carcass of a piglet left too long on the spit.

'Is that the Buzzard?' Judith asked in a whisper. 'But he seems so small.'

'Fire does that to a man.' Hal placed his arm around her shoulders. 'He burned the first time as Cochran. Then he burned the second time as the Buzzard. Now he will burn through all eternity with Old Nick, the devil, stoking the flames around him.'

She shuddered against him, and he led her from the blackened and burnt-out cabin up onto the open deck. Big Daniel Fisher was waiting for him at the top of the companion way. He knuckled his forehead to Hal.

'Orders if it please you, Captain.'

'Firstly,' Hal replied, 'get the cargo out of the pinnace and safely stowed in the main hold.' Big Danny grinned at the mention of the treasure.

'Aye aye, Captain. And what next?'

'Get the carpenters to clean and repair my burnt out cabin. Tell them to paint it white this time. General Nazet and I are tired of those sky blue coloured bulkheads.'

He went on issuing orders to the coxswain for a little longer, and then he turned back to Judith and took her by the hand. He led her up to the poop deck, the only place where they could be alone. They leaned together on the stern rail with his arm around her shoulders, and they were silent for a while. At last Judith sighed and said softly,

'The Grail is saved. My duty is done. I have had my fill of fighting and killing. Cannot we find some place where I can have our baby; and you and I can live in peace and happiness together for the rest of our lives?'

Hal chuckled. 'You have just accurately described High Weald.'

'High Weald? What a strange name! What is it and where is it?'

'It is my ancestral home in the south of England; the safest and the most beautiful place in the whole wide world.'

'Take me there, my dearest. Please take me there at once; Please! And pretty please!' She turned in the circle of his arms and kissed him, while he hugged her tight.